SPIDER

SPIDER

Book II

The Chesapeake Tugboat Murders

By

Leah Devlin

www.penmorepress.com

Spider by Leah Devlin

ISBN-13: 978-1-94609-12-6-(Paperback)
ISBN-13: 978-1-94609-13-3 (e-book)

BISAC Subject Headings:
FIC014000 Fiction / Historical
FIC008000 Fiction / General
FIC031010 Fiction/ Thrillers / Crime

Cover work by Christine Horner
Editor: Chris Wozney

Address all correspondence to:

Penmore Press LLC
920 N Javelina Pl
Tucson. AZ 85748

Or visit our website at:
www.penmorepress.com

DEDICATION

For Kathleen, a partner in crime

"Will you walk into my parlour?" said the Spider to the Fly,

'Tis the prettiest little parlour that ever did you spy;

The way into my parlour is up a winding stair,

And I've a many curious things to show when you are there."

-Mary Howitt, 1829

CHAPTER ONE
The Glen River on the Upper Chesapeake

"Goddamn spiders!" Alex Allaway leapt at a spider web dangling in the galley. A swish of her broom vanquished the web. "That's all I do, Nina, every morning, clean spider webs off this boat. I hate spiders almost as much as ticks." She frowned at the black dog sleeping under the table. "Water Boy's a tick magnet. They're impossible to find in his coat." Alex circled the galley of the *Vital Spark*, her broom poised for attack.

"You work in a marsh all day," Nina Vega said. "You, of all people, should be used to creepy crawlies."

"Yeah, I guess." Alex relaxed. "I don't mind snakes, eels, or snapping turtles because they hurry away at the sight of humans, but spiders are defiant and territorial. Every morning I sweep them away, and every night they return to torment me."

Nina couldn't help but grin. Nothing had changed. Alex was the same insectophobe she was their senior year at the University of Maryland when she and Alex had shared an apartment on Paint Branch Parkway. At the time, it wasn't spiders that were Alex's annoyance but cockroaches.

"The computer geeks next door never do their dishes! That's why *their* cockroaches come into *our* apartment," Alex had said nightly. Her complaint was punctuated with a biology or chemistry textbook flattening a roach scurrying across the kitchen counter. Nina's appetite was then ruined. Alex's crusade wasn't always against cockroaches. Once it was the squirrel that chewed through their cable line and impelled Alex to camp out between the bicycles on their balcony and shoot it with rubber darts from a plastic gun from the Dollar Store.

Nothing about Alex had changed and that was a good thing. Their friendship would resume just where they left off, when they had packed up their apartment after graduation and departed to their respective graduate programs. Alex had headed to a Maryland fisheries lab, and she northward to the University of Rhode Island's Department of Sociology.

Nina's dissertation at URI had focused on the socioeconomics of the fishermen of southern Rhode Island, but it was time for a change. It was time to expand her research horizons beyond the Ocean State. If she was to earn tenure and eventually achieve the rank of Full Professor, her research and publications needed to encompass many types of maritime fishing communities. This would earn her an international reputation for her scholarship. Her first idea was to move northward to study the Maine lobstermen, but she was from New Mexico and Maine's winters would be more brutal than Rhode Island's. Then her old apartment-mate sprang to mind when Alex's Facebook post displayed photos of a pyrate festival in the village of River Glen on the Chesapeake. Alex's companions at the event were an attractive grandmother, a brawny boyfriend, and a pack of black dogs in skull and cross bone bandanas. Alex, she recalled, was from a family of crabbers. This prompted her to give Alex a long overdue call.

"I know them all … the crabbers, oystermen, herring fishermen, middlemen, distributors, and pickers," Alex had said. "I can introduce you to anyone you need to talk to."

A move to Maryland's eastern shore sounded better and better. Even Ricardo liked the idea. A study of the socioeconomics of the Chesapeake watermen seemed just the ticket. Two tenure track jobs were available in the area, one at the University of Maryland Eastern Shore (UMES) and one at Tolchester College. She didn't make the short list at UMES, but she did get an interview at Tolchester.

Tolchester College was a pretty undergraduate institution on a cliff overlooking the bay. The views out to the white-capped water were stunning and the immaculately groomed grounds burst with flowers in lovely arrangements. Her interview was during the week of MayFest so white and blue balloons, the school's colors, had been tied to the Victorian lampposts that lined the walkways. The college was in solid financial shape, the president and academic dean had explained to her. Enrollments were on an upswing, so much so that the college was expanding their faculty numbers. In addition to two new sociologists joining the faculty in the fall, there would be a psychologist, mathematician, and historian. A fresh new tier of faculty would be her cohort. The college pulsed with energy and promise.

Then more good news. A job offer arrived shortly thereafter. With Alex's connections to the fisheries network in the Chesapeake, Nina would have access to countless people to conduct oral histories and interviews. Tenure at Tolchester College was in the bag. Plus, the River Glen area with its farms, quiet inlets, fresh organic food, and clean air would be the ideal place for Ricardo and her to start a family.

Nina gazed out a porthole to the unfamiliar terrain while Alex navigated the *Vital Spark* through a narrow channel. On Narragansett Bay in Rhode Island where she had shared a house with other sociology grad students, the rocky shoreline was battered by waves. It was a wind-lashed landscape of greys and blues. But here, orange cliffs crowned with lush forests loomed over the old tugboat. Green water lapped against muddy beaches and the August air was heavy and still. This was her new world.

"This looks like a good place to anchor," said Alex from the pilot's wheel. "For its size, the Chesapeake's an amazingly shallow bay." She shut off the motor. The grind of a rusty anchor chain, then a splash, was heard from the bow. "But the water here is deep enough so we won't scrape the keel." Spiders and ticks no longer a concern, Alex declared "Now we initiate you to Chesapeake life! Maryland crabs in Old Bay spices. No one can live on the bay without knowing how to eat crabs." She unscrewed a thermos and filled two plastic mugs. "Cheers, Nina! To your move and new job!"

Nina sipped from her mug. "Delicious. What is it?"

"A Hurricane. Two shots of light rum, two shots of dark rum, one shot of vodka, grenadine, grapefruit juice and pineapple. All shaken, not stirred." Alex pulled nutcrackers and picks from a drawer, and headed out to the deck. She unfurled newspapers across a wooden crate. "This is how we do it." She dumped a pile of steaming crabs onto the newspaper. "No plates, no silverware. Just newspapers, nutcrackers, and crabs. Just toss the exoskeletons overboard, since they're biodegradable."

Leave it to Alex to improvise. There were no chairs in sight. Their seats would be the hard planks of the deck. Nina felt way overdressed. When Alex had invited her to dine, she had expected eat in Alex's cottage so she brought flowers and a bottle of table wine. And inappropriately she had worn the new summer dress that she bought for the Welcome Meeting of the Tolchester faculty. Alex had greeted her in camo cargo shorts and a purple t-shirt that read *Ravens Country.* Nina had forgotten that Alex was the queen of quirky casual. "We'll be taking a cruise up the Glen River and eating on the water," Alex had said, leading her along the dock.

Nina glanced at the planks once again. Oh, what the hell … she was a Chesapeake girl now. She hiked up her dress and dropped amidst the crab pots, Clorox bottles, and mooring lines. Besides, after a few more sips of the potent cocktail her butt would be numb to the unyielding boards.

"You open the crab like this." Alex pried off the carapace. "And don't eat anything in the central cavity or you'll be eating guts, the heart, and parts of the vas deferens."

"Way too much information," Nina laughed. The August heat and alcohol were taking effect.

Alex grinned. "That's the downside of being a biologist, knowing the anatomical parts of the thing you're eating. Oh, definitely don't eat that … the testes and the gills. And only eat the white meat in those lateral chitin compartments and the meat in the legs. There's not really much meat in those rear swimming legs." She flung them over the gunwale.

"Okay. I see."

Alex watched her break open the crab, like a teacher supervising a pupil on an important task. "The ring's really beautiful."

Nina stretched out her left hand, now covered with brown spices. "It belonged to Ricardo's Abuelita and Mamacita."

"Mamacita? That's what he calls his mother? A mamacita's a sexy woman. Is she hot?"

"No. She's hideous and five hundred pounds!"

"Really?"

"No, only three hundred. Ricardo's the only boy in the family. He's spoiled rotten by all the women. The wedding's next year in New Mexico. I'd love it if you'd be a bridesmaid."

Alex's eyes widened, probably in the realization that she would have to wear some frippery and footwear other than sneakers or flip-flops. "Yeah, okay."

Nina pointed up at the cliff. "What's that place?" Her changing the subject was deliberate. At the moment the wedding was a testy topic with Ricardo's family. Her ideal wedding was small and intimate, but Abuelita wanted to invite the relatives from Mexico. All four hundred of them.

An abandoned cottage perched precariously on the cliff's edge. Its porch had plummeted to the beach some time before, as evident by rotting planks in the sand below.

Alex squinted upward. "That's Henry Herssen's place. People build too close to the cliffs. It's a big problem around here. Then the cliffs erode during storms and hurricanes. A lot of people have lost their homes that way. Herssen was an insane man, allegedly. We wouldn't go near that place when we were kids. He up and disappeared years ago. Maybe a decade or more ago. I don't know for sure. People report seeing lights in the place at night. Others say the place is haunted. They're probably tall tales to keep children away from the cliff."

"There are a lot of tall tales surrounding this region. Like the legend of Giles Blood-hand. I just read a history of Kent County. I always like to know the local history before I move to an area."

"That's why you're the professor. Giles Blood-hand Day is the best day of the year. You're going to need a pyrate costume for the celebration, now that you're a local. Thar be pyrates in River Glen and unspeakable treasures."

Nina grinned. "Really?"

"Really. Giles did exist. I'm related to him."

"No way."

"Yeah, I am. Distantly on my father's side of the family. And there's a pyrate graveyard here in River Glen. I can show it to you sometime, if you're game."

"Sure. That sounds fascinating. Does anyone know what happened to Giles' treasure?"

Alex shrugged. "Who knows?"

The roar of a boat approached and they peered over the gunwale. Alex leapt to her feet. "Nina, wrap up the crabs and grab your drink! I need to move the boat or that idiot's going to swamp us!" She dashed to the helm, switched on the engine, and raised the anchor. Water Boy yowled.

"This idiot from Miami thinks she owns the river! If I can't turn this boat ..."

"What?"

"Every summer this asshole in a yacht moors at the Smyth's Marina," Alex called from the wheel. "She has no idea that there's something called a no-wake-zone!"

Nina rolled the crabs in newspaper, hurried to the helm, and pushed her face next to Alex's scowling one at the windshield. A glistening yacht sped toward them.

"Brace yourself, Nina!" Alex wrestled with the wheel, and turned the bow into the channel.

The yacht flew by in a white streak. An ominous row of waves approached.

"Hold on!"

The bow reared upward and slammed on the backside of the first wave. Water splashed over the bow and water cannon, and collided with the windshield. They were blinded. The bow reared upward again ... up-slap, up-slap ... frothy rapids cascaded over the deck.

Water Boy yowled again.

"Shut-up, goofball!" Alex said. "You're only making matters worse."

He dove for Alex's shoe and anxiously chewed her shoelace.

The waves dissipated and water trickled off the deck. Henry Herssen's broken porch floated in the swells.

"Alex, look!" Nina pointed. The surge of waves had carved away the base of the cliff.

"We're outta here!" Alex jammed the throttle forward but too late.

The dirt wall crumbled and burst into an orange cloud. Herssen's house creaked and plunged off the cliff. It was like a glacier had calved into the water. There was no time to turn the bow into the giant wave. It crashed against the stern, lifting the *Vital Spark* skyward. Water rushed across the deck and smashed the crab pots into the gunwales. For minutes debris and water swayed in the afternoon heat. Then all was silent. Planks, dry wall, and window frames floated in the shallows around the tugboat. Something else gripped their attention.

"Do you see that?" Nina whispered, as though phantoms might awake.

"Yeah," Alex whispered back.

They gazed upward. Poking from the cliff were grey bones – countless bones – bones from bodies buried under Henry Herssen's cottage.

Detective Jay Braden's cell phone vibrated on Julia's bedside table. He stretched for it with an irritated groan. Now what? It was 5:48 pm. His day was over and he was just falling into a deep sleep. The plan was that he and Julia would nap, then wander over to the Nauticus restaurant for drinks and dinner on the back deck. Walk the dogs down to the Point, then bed. It was too goddamn hot to do anything else but drink and sleep.

Jay's eyes came into focus. It was a text from Dr. Zera Lim, River Glen's medical examiner. "At Henry Herssen's place upriver. Come ASAP."

"Fuck." He stood stiffly. His sciatica was killing him again.

"Yes, later," Julia mumbled from her pillow.

He smiled wryly. His eyes traveled along his naked companion. A sheet covered her hips and her black-grey hair cascaded across the pillow. How different Julia was from Laura. Laura would have asked him a thousand questions before he departed. *Will you be home soon? Be careful! Watch yourself. Where are you going? When are you coming home?* Laura would be frantic until he returned home safely. She was never suited for a life with a cop. It's probably what made her go crazy.

No, the two women could not be more different.

Julia never asked – never asked if he would be sleeping at his place or hers. If he showed up, fine. If not, also fine. Laura was so needy and dependent on him. Julia was so not. It was impossible to decide if he loved that quality about her, or resented it.

His fling with Julia Hale had started out as a Friday night tumble. Then Friday spilled into Saturday. She had formidable talents in the bedroom arts; as an actress for the Royal Shakespeare Company she had been pursued, and captured, by many dashing actors. Her vast skill-set prompted him to walk his dog Clark to the Point on Wednesday and Thursday evenings – two nights a week wouldn't be too obvious – as an excuse to pass her place. "Just to say hi." The ploy always worked. Invariably she would be on her porch and coyly ask him if he wanted a glass of Royal Lochnagar. One thing would lead to another. Julia had many assets, a curvaceous body, unflappable self-confidence, cagey charm, but her Scottish accent captivated him. She could read him the phone book and he would get a hard-on.

He searched the floor around the bed. "I can't find my pants."

"The kitchen, lad."

The way she said *lad* put a spring in his step. He stepped over the black dogs, his Clark and her Miranda, and headed to the kitchen. She was right. His khakis and boxers were there, where the party had started that afternoon. His shirt and tie were located on the recliner in the living room. He dressed quickly.

"Can I leave Clark with you? It was Zera. Something's up."

"Hmm."

He would take that as a 'yes.'

He dashed to his unmarked car and sped up the cliff road. Henry Herssen's cottage was familiar to the River Glen PD as they had hammered *Danger Keep Out* signs on the trees around the property years before. There had been numerous discussions about placing a hurricane fence around the property and along the cliff side, but the small, understaffed police force had no funds to spare for fencing materials. The signs seemed sufficiently cautionary to keep trespassers off the land. Besides, teenagers preferred to party at the Point. The Herssen place was just too creepy, even for druggies, drunks, and horny teens.

Jay climbed from his car and halted. Herssen's cottage was gone – completely gone – vanished! Zera and the forensics team moved tentatively along the cliff's edge as if the ground might give way at any time. His young assistants Will Wilkins and Lisa Paco were in the overgrown grass and weeds far from the edge, swatting at gnats.

"What is it?" he asked them.

"Alex and a friend Nina Vega were boating and noticed bones protruding from the cliff," Will said. "Alex called me."

Alex Allaway. Julia Hale's granddaughter. Will's on-again-off-again girlfriend. Will was lovesick over her, but Alex clearly had commitment issues. That seemed to be an inherited trait. Alex's dog Water Boy was the father to Clark, Miranda, and Will's dog, Peppy. In River Glen, everyone was somehow related. He was related to the locals by his dog.

"Bones? So no fresh bodies?"

"No, sir. Just old bones."

"Finally something interesting!" Lisa said.

Leave it to Lisa to blurt the inappropriate. Jay frowned in an attempt to set an example of professional decorum though he was in secret agreement. It had been a slow summer. Parking violations, speeding tickets, DWIs around Giles Blood-hand Day, RiverFest, and the 4th of July, and the robbery of wide-screened TVs from the Walmart down the highway. There had been no serious crimes, no murders in River Glen since ... he lost his beloved Laura to those demented Whitby brothers. Two years later, thoughts of that horrible day on Mutter Island made him sick.

Jay shook himself back to the present. "Let's have a look."

"I'll stay here, if you don't mind," Lisa said. "I'm not that fond of heights or the water."

"Alright, but find out anything you can about Henry Herssen and where he ran off to."

"paco@rogerthat," she said.

Will followed him to the cliff's edge. "Sir, I remember Herssen. A loner. He had a small fishing boat and fished alone. Most fishermen fish in pairs or teams but not Herssen. He was always alone. He had a woman for a while, but they kept to themselves. She disappeared. Then years later, so did he." Will was a wealth of local history as he had been born and raised in River Glen.

"How long ago?"

"Maybe twenty, twenty-five years ago? I was just a boy."

"This property's been abandoned that long? That seems impossible. Who's been paying the taxes on it?"

Will shrugged.

"Find out."

"Yes, sir."

The CSI team parted to let Jay through. Zera Lim was on her knees next to a hole in the earth.

"This looks like an archeological dig," he said.

"Exactly." Zera looked worriedly at the sky. "We need to get a tent up before the rain starts."

"So what do we have?"

"Too early to tell. The women in the boat could see more from the water. They reported human bones at different levels. The excavation will take some time since we're going to have to sift through a lot of soil."

The ground seemed firm enough under foot so Jay inched toward the cliff's edge. Bits of the cottage floated in the river, whereas other pieces had washed up on the beach. He returned to the pit and studied its placement inside the weed-bordered foundation. One thing was clear. Under the floorboards of what had been Henry Herssen's bedroom was a mass grave.

CHAPTER TWO
Wednesday

Nina Vega had a tension headache so she searched the boxes in the living room for a bottle of aspirin. Not many possessions had been accumulated while in Rhode Island since the rental house had been furnished; it didn't take long to locate the box with supplies for the medicine cabinet. She shook aspirin into her hand ... her hand with Abuelita's stunning engagement ring ... and swallowed them down with a paper cup from the kitchenette. She peered into the cabinets. They were empty. She reached for her iPad and added new dishes and glasses to the growing list of household items for her new apartment. The dishes would have to have a southwest design. Ricardo would insist on that. She really should be further along with the unpacking, but it was much more fun to explore the countryside. She had found a mattress store and ordered a king-sized bed. Ricardo had insisted on a king. The bed was really more than she could afford, but what the hell ... she had a tenure-track job ... a job for life. The days of scrimping were over, she had reminded herself when handing the clerk her credit card. When Ricardo arrived from New Mexico, they would split expenses. He worked in IT and earned a six-figure salary. The two-bedroom apartment was just a temporary stop until they could find a good neighborhood where they could purchase a single-family home and start having children.

She headed to the bathroom to check her appearance in the medicine cabinet mirror because she hadn't purchased a full-length mirror yet. Her attire was appropriate for a day of setting up her office on campus. Not too dressy, yet not too casual. Capris, a cotton blouse, and comfortable shoes. Her first stop would be the Security Office to obtain a campus parking pass and to sign out her office key, then a stop at Computer Services to pick up her new laptop. The Dean of Academics Gloria Wines had agreed to purchase her a new high-end laptop and statistical software as part of Nina's startup package.

Nina had taken a quick drive through the campus the day before and discovered that her office would be in the Riddel Building, the oldest building on campus. It was also where the Security Office was located. The gray stone building was run-down and badly needed paint around the door and window frames. Its slate roof had cockeyed, loose tiles and the gutters sagged, but all in all, the building had a certain charm. Boxes with her coffee maker, favorite mug ... purchased from the Zion National Park gift shop where she and Ricardo had hiked ... pencils, pens, calculator and her sociology and economics textbooks were already in her trunk. She grabbed her purse and locked the apartment door behind her.

Driftwood Apartments had been recommended by the college president Mary Blodgen. The old woman had explained that most of the young faculty lived there temporarily until they bought homes. This way the new faculty members could meet one other, socialize, and scout out the area before making that very important decision of purchasing a home. It sounded like a reasonable plan so she had opted for the two-bedroom model so Ricardo could have a place to set up his office. Being in software design, he could work from home. Maybe they should get a puppy? Water Boy was friendly, if not a bit neurotic and clingy. Ricardo could walk the dog during the day while she was at the college, then the three of them might take leisurely walks in the evenings. A dog first, then children in strollers, trikes, and bicycles.

The door slammed at the apartment next to hers. A trim, black-haired man, about her age, smiled and headed toward his car. His green SUV was parked next to her Prius. She climbed in and started the ignition. She looked to see if he was pulling out first. He was obviously wondering the same. He smiled again and gestured that she leave first. She nodded and gave him a brief wave of okay.

Tolchester College was only a mile drive from the apartment complex. On nice days, she could walk or ride a bike to work. She glanced in the rear mirror. The SUV was right behind her. She turned onto College Avenue. The SUV turned also. She passed the beautifully groomed hedges and flowerbeds at the Administration Building, the SUV still on her tail. Was he following her? No, it was her imagination running wild. Yet the SUV was still behind her as she passed the athletic fields and the College Union Building. Her heart now pounded. She turned into the Riddel Building parking lot. So did he! Worse, his SUV pulled into the spot right next to hers! He *had* followed her! She checked that her doors were locked. What to do, what to do? She tugged on her collar. The door to the Security Office was only fifty feet or so away. A security guard in a blue uniform was smoking a cigarette under the eaves. Nothing could happen to her with the security guard present, could it? Maybe she should run over to him ... tell him that she had been followed ... by her creepy neighbor no less! The creep left his SUV and tapped on her window. She glanced desperately at the security guard, who watched them from a cloud of cigarette smoke. The creep tapped again. Since the security guard was nearby, it was probably safe to lower her window just an inch.

"Hey, do you work here?" he asked through the crack.

What to say? "Mm ... yes." Ricardo had accused her of being pathologically honest.

"Me too. I'm the new historian. Levon Bakanian. I'll be teaching American History."

She rolled down her window. "Nina Vega, the new sociologist."

"They seemed to have put all the new profs here in Riddel," Levon said. "Where are you coming from?"

"Rhode Island. And you?"

"Charlottesville, Virginia." He looked doubtfully at the building. "Crazy old building. There's a bee hive outside my window. Somehow the bees are getting into my office. I've been killing them all week. Thankfully I'm not allergic. I put in a work request, but Maintenance is slower than slow. All colleges are the same. Hey, I bought a grill last night. Come by some time for a burger or dog." He patted the roof of her car as a farewell and headed into the building. Levon Bakanian was not a creep at all but a handsome man wearing great aftershave. He would unnerve Ricardo to no end.

Nina fumbled in her purse. A form of ID and her car registration would be needed to obtain an office key and a parking pass. Everything was in order so she climbed out of her car.

"That b-bugger B-Bakanian keeps slamming the front door!" the security guard said to her. "He shakes the whole building!" The guard's nametag read Burt Sweeny. His furrowed face was punctuated with dark, downcast eyes. "He frightens the gulls."

"What?"

"There!" Burt Sweeny pointed upward.

She put her left hand over her eyes as a shield from the sun but it was no use. The turrets were barely visible in the morning glare.

"They nest up there," he said.

Agitated seagulls looped around the pinnacles, shrieking, skimming the slate roof, and flapping aloft again. Suddenly a sharp object struck Nina's hand, knocking it from her eyebrows. An agonized cry burst from her throat. A wildfire of pain shot up her hand and arm. Warm fluid splashed against her cheek and spattered her blouse. Her knees buckled. Burt grabbed for her elbow. She stared down. They laid on the pavement, tan and liquid red. She wavered as the world went grey. An ear-piercing caw, the glint of Abuelita's ring at her feet ... blackness.

The place had a strange smell. It wasn't her bedroom in Rhode Island that smelled of salty air and sea. Nor was it her new apartment in River Glen that smelled like carpet cleaner. Nina opened her eyes. A dull throb pulsed in her left hand and an IV line tugged at her right wrist. This was a hospital.

That sullen security guard, whose name she had forgotten, flicked an unlit cigarette between his fingers as he paced. "This is all my fault! Everything I do or touch breaks."

Nina inched herself up in the pillows. "What? What are you talking about?"

"If I hadn't shown you the gulls' nests, you wouldn't have come over to the eaves and looked up. The slate wouldn't have fallen."

"Slate?"

"The slate that ... hurt you." He paused. "I gave it to the surgeon. To show him. He has it. Its edge ... was razor sharp."

"I don't remember. Tell me!"

He stepped apprehensively toward the bed. His nametag was now visible. "You passed out so I carried you to the security van. I went back to get them. But I wasn't fast enough. This is *all* my fault."

A rustle in the corner of the room caused Nina to turn. Alex was in disarray, her sneaker tapping out a chatter of anxiety. Spiders, ticks, cockroaches, and hospitals sent her into a tailspin.

"I-I hope you don't mind," Burt said. "I took your cellphone from your purse, to find an ICE number. I didn't find one so I called the last number you called. I saw that it was local. I called Alex."

Alex sprang from the chair and kissed Nina on the head. "You're coming home with me. No discussion about. I'm taking care of you!"

Nina's view bounced between Alex and Burt. "Went back to get what?"

Burt looked helplessly at Alex, as though she might break the bad news. She didn't. Instead Alex glanced nervously at the ball of gauze that was Nina's left hand.

"Your two fingers," he said. "Your pinkie was there but your ring finger ... it was one of those seagulls. They were so upset. The bird must have thought it was a shiny little fish. It swooped down and ..."

Nina stared aghast at the white gauze.

"The surgeon was able to reattach your pinkie but your other finger ..."

"My ring finger? Abuelita's ring?"

"You're coming home with me!" Alex cried.

"My phone, Alex! Text Ricardo for me!" It would be impossible to type while one hand was bandaged and the other was attached to an IV.

"Okay!"

"Alex, you'll take her home, right?" Burt asked. "The Security Office is so understaffed. I should be getting back to the college now."

"Yes, yes, of course. She's coming to my place."

"Professor Vega, I'm so, so sorry." Burt backed toward the doorway. "This is all my fault."

"No, Mr. Sweeny, it was just horrible luck. Thank you for bringing me here."

"My bad, bad luck ... everything I touch, everything I do ..." He departed.

"Alex, text Ricardo and tell him to call me immediately! Tell him I'm in the hospital. That we need to talk."

"Yes!" Alex typed into Nina's cellphone. "The doctor said that you could be discharged today. We'll swing by your place to pick up your stuff, because you're staying with me."

Nina's phone chimed. It was a text from Ricardo.

I can't talk right now. I'm on my way to Cousin Carmen's birthday party.

Maybe it was the Percocet distorting reality, but everything about River Glen was outright weird. First was the motor yacht that almost capsized the *Vital Spark*, then the skeletons in the cliff. Now this. Nina's hand throbbed so she had taken a pill before she and Alex left the hospital. A punchy drowsiness kicked in immediately. Alex had sent a second text to Ricardo on her behalf.

I lost a finger! They reattached the other. You need to move here sooner than we planned.

Nina hadn't the heart to tell Ricardo that a hungry seagull had absconded with the same ring finger encircled by Abuelita's engagement ring. He simply wouldn't believe it. She could hear his incredulous laughter ... 'Chica, you have too much imagination!' That conversation would have to wait until her thoughts cleared. And weirder yet, Alex knew her next-door-neighbor Levon Bakanian; Nina discovered this when they had swung by Driftwood Apartments to pick up her things.

The moment Alex's pickup truck pulled into the driveway, Levon rushed out outside and inquired of Nina's wellbeing. Word of the freak accident had spread at light speed across campus.

"Nina, can I help you with anything?" he had asked, assisting her from the truck. "Make you a meal, pick up groceries or carry-out for you, help you unpack ... anything?"

When Levon noticed the driver, his eyes widened, and he looked expectantly at Nina for an introduction. Every boyfriend Nina ever brought by the apartment on Paint Branch Parkway had been mesmerized by Alex, despite her mismatched clothes and shoes, and a book on The Crustacea or Coastal Ecology in her hand. After Nina offered an introduction, Alex and Levon looked at one another with the same mystified expression.

"I know your name from somewhere," he said to Alex.

Alex had nodded. "I remember now. I emailed you about Giles Blood-hand, when I was doing some family genealogy."

"Right! Now I remember. Then we talked on the phone about my dissertation. How'd your research go?"

"It went nowhere. I got distracted by a new job. I suppose I should wander the River Glen graveyard and see how far back I can trace the Allaways. What are you doing here?" There was a suspicious edge to Alex's question.

"I just joined the history faculty at Tolchester," he answered. "The best place to find primary research materials is by pouring through local town halls and archives of historical societies. Most small historical societies haven't digitalized their records yet so I needed to be closer to the eastern shore. I don't know how much of my dissertation you read, but I'm primarily interested in Juan Carlos del Castillo, a Spanish pyrate who operated at the mouth of the James River. An oblique reference suggested that he made a foray to the northern Chesapeake so I'm here to track that down. And I wanted to work at a smaller institution in a more rural setting. There's too much politics at large universities."

"Was Juan Carlos contemporaneous with Giles Blood-hand?" Alex asked.

"Not exactly. He appeared almost a decade later."

"So what happened with your Giles Blood-hand research?"

"It was pretty much a dead end. But if you're interested, the new faculty members have to give research lectures.

Right Nina? I'm first in the queue. I'm lecturing on the pyrates of the Chesapeake this weekend. How about you both come to the lecture?"

"Sure. I can be there," Nina said.

Alex shrugged. "Yeah, why not."

After exchanging emails and cell numbers, Levon had departed inside with a wave, and she and Alex loaded some belongings into the truck.

From Driftwood Apartments it was only a short drive to the village of River Glen and the Alternate Reality that Alex called home. The Percocet and blood loss made Nina jittery so she slung her arm over Alex's shoulder while crossing a yard of plastic lawn ornaments, nautical flags, and a rusty Harley motorcycle-turned birdbath. Wind chimes and birdfeeders dangled from a birch tree growing through a VW's engine. Alex's grandmother and her younger boyfriend were drinking cocktails on the porch while Water Boy and two other black dogs chased each other along the water's edge. When she and Alex had set up their apartment the August of their senior year, it was not a mother or father that had helped Alex move in but two old men – her grandfather Randy, and his friend Old Ben. At the time both men were pleasantly stoned.

After seeing this place, Alex now made sense. But Nina was too exhausted to think about anything or anyone, even her querido Ricardo. They entered Old Ben's cottage where Alex now lived.

"I'll sleep on the *Vital Spark*. You take my room," Nina heard Alex mention.

Nina collapsed onto a bed and Alex covered her with a blanket. Wakes, bones, seagulls, and Abuelita's ring swirled amidst opiate-dizzy thoughts. As she fell into a vortex of sleep, the window shade, a pyrate flag rustled quietly in the summer night.

Alex pressed her eye to Old Ben's telescope. Over countless evenings of her youth Old Ben had taught her the constellations with this instrument, but instead of stars, it was directed at floating dock B at the Smyth Family Marina. "I want to know who that bitch is. Every summer she comes here and acts like the Queen of Sheba."

"Forget about it," said Will Wilkins. "Come back to bed."

Alex turned toward the berth of the *Vital Spark*. Will was just how she liked him, butt-naked and sprawled across her mattress. His body was cast red from a candle. "Can't you arrest her for creating that monster wake and eroding the cliff? She clearly hasn't read *The Rules of the Road*. All boaters in Maryland are supposed to take the Boater Safety course."

"It's impossible to enforce with the boats coming from out-of-state."

"I'd like to blow that pompous yacht out of the water. Turn my water cannon on her and ..."

"No Alex."

"*Knot-A-Care*. Only a bimbo from Miami would name her boat that." She returned her attention to the telescope and the marina. "It looks like she's drinking champagne and eating caviar with her two boy toys. Another ménage à trois tonight. I bet she's a drug dealer. How else does one afford a yacht and an endless flow of pretty boys?"

"Gary Smyth told me that she's a model. Her name is Pamela."

"Pamela what?"

"I don't know."

"Why does she come here every summer? There are a hundred other marinas on the Chesapeake where she can be Empress."

"She's looking for Giles' treasure, like the other treasure hunters who flock to River Glen every year."

Alex took a tug from a rum bottle. "Then let's send her on a treasure hunt. Let's start a rumor about the treasure being out on Mutter Island or some godforsaken place like that. Let her go and sift sand with the mosquitos for the summer. Ha ... it would be too funny!"

"That's a terrible idea. Just leave her be. Come back to bed."

"Where's your sense of humor? It would be hysterical."

"Really, really bad idea. She hasn't done anything to you."

"She nearly swamped my precious tug!" Alex peered through the telescope again. "She clearly wants servicing. She and the boy toys have disappeared to her stateroom. It's probably gold-plated."

"This boy toy needs servicing too."

She turned from the telescope. Will's hands were behind his head in the pillow. He grinned. She took another tug of rum and crawled across the mattress. "I want a ménage à trois tonight."

"With who?"

She flung her leg across his hips.   "With you in duplicate."

CHAPTER THREE
Thursday

Like the rolling waves that pounded the *Vital Spark*, it was going to be a day of rolling humiliations and embarrassments. Nina was sure of it. Covering the wad of gauze with a plastic bag, she had managed a one-handed shower, but she needed Alex to snap her bra and zip up her new dress. Ricardo would be able to help her with these annoying inconveniences until the bandages came off. One consolation was that she was able to slide her panties on and off with her good hand so that she was at least able to pee on her own.

Yesterday she had lost her finger. That reality was just sinking in.

How it was her hand going to look? What functions might be impaired? Abuelita's ring was gone and she had missed Ricardo's call last night while knocked out by the Percocets. For pain relief that day she would rely on extra strength aspirin because the narcotic made her too spacey. It was important to be as alert as possible for the Welcome Meeting. She glanced at the time on her phone and calculated the time in Albuquerque. With the two-hour time difference, it was too early to call Ricardo. Hopefully he had packed up his car last night and was already on the road. That's probably what he was calling to say, that he was on his way. His IT work could be conducted from Albuquerque, River Glen or Bora Bora, as long as there was a satellite connection.

The next embarrassing thing was breakfast. Alex kept no sustenance in the cottage except rum, Monster drinks, and Twinkies, so she ate breakfast every morning at her grandmother's house next door. Julia had prepared them a meal of pancakes, bacon, and fruit ... fortunately no haggis or other unspeakable intestinal culinary surprise ... but being left-handed Nina was challenged by a knife and fork in her right hand. Alex offered to cut up pancakes for her, but she opted instead for bacon and a banana that could be managed with one hand. And the breakfast conversation was more Allaway Alternate Reality. The spry grandmother with the amazing voice chatted about a sultan friend whose jeweled spider climbed around his robes during a banquet at an oasis. Nina felt vaguely nauseated by the idea of spiders anywhere near food, but the topic fascinated Alex. For the rest of the meal Alex barraged Julia with spider questions. "What was the species of spider? Was it domestic or imported, and if imported, from which country? What did the sultan feed it?"

The whole story was certainly bunk because Julia could answer none of Alex's questions. And that morning nothing about living spider jewelry was in the least bit interesting to Nina; her hand pulsed with pain and its appearance was no doubt grotesque. Despite feeling bitchy and non-communicative, she mustered a question, albeit mundane. "Alex, what did you do last night?   I hardly remember anything from yesterday."

"I messed around with my telescope on the boat."

It seemed a straightforward enough answer, but Julia guffawed. "Lass, I've never heard it called a telescope before. Is that an American expression?"

Alex gave Julia a self-satisfied smile and squeezed syrup onto her pancakes. Alex had an impressive appetite that morning.

After breakfast Alex drove Nina to Tolchester College on her way to work at the marine station. They rattled along the coastal road in the pickup truck while crab pots, a fluke anchor, lines and assorted trash and debris slid about in the bed. Having survived Alex's weaving between the lanes of the road, Nina climbed out of the truck in front of the Riddel Building. She would get her keys from Security, her laptop from Computer Services, and proceed through the opening meetings. This way some sense of normalcy would be restored. Her Prius was still in the parking lot of the Riddel Building.

"I'm certain that I'll be able to drive myself home with one hand," she told Alex.

"But I want you to stay at my cottage until Ricardo arrives."

"No, no. I really need to set up my apartment and get myself ready for classes next week."

"You sure?"

"Yes."

"Okay, but call me. If you need anything, call me."

"I'm fine. Really. The pyrate lecture by Levon. Don't forget that." Alex was late for everything in college, on the off-chance she remembered the event at all.

"Yeah, I'll be there." Alex waved and drove off.

Nina headed toward her car. "No way!" She whipped the parking ticket from her windshield with her one functioning hand. "Fifty bucks!" She hurried to the Security Office. Burt Sweeny would certainly vouch for her. After all, she was on her way to get her parking pass when the accident happened. She pushed through the door, but unfortunately Burt was nowhere in sight. Instead a glum-faced woman sat behind a counter.

"I'm the person who had the accident yesterday." She held up the gauze club. "The ticket's unfair. I was incapacitated. I shouldn't be fined."

"If you don't pay it, they'll simply take it out of your paycheck," the old grouch said.

"Who can I talk to about this?"

"Only President Blodgen."

"Right. Like I'm going to talk to her about a parking ticket."

God only knew which unpacked box contained her checkbook. She sighed. Fifty bucks was a drop in the bucket compared to the looming surgeon's bill. How much was it to reattach a finger? Whose insurance was she under anyway? URI's? Or Tolchester's? With her shitty luck, both institutions would deny her coverage and she would have to pay out-of-pocket, which would take a decade or more on the pathetic salary Dean Wines had offered her. She had no choice but to take it. Tenure track jobs were in fast decline while administrators padded their huge salaries and hired adjuncts for minimum wage. The good news was that her driver's license and car registration were updated so the grouch gave her a parking pass and key to her office. She quickly hung the plastic parking pass on her rearview mirror before she received a second ticket.

'Stay positive, stay positive. You have a new job and a new office,' Nina told herself. She didn't have to share an office with anyone. In grad school, she shared with five other students, one whom who left condiment wrappers on his desk; this made the office smell of stale mustard and attracted ants. Maybe she would line her windowsill with cacti and put up a poster of the Albuquerque Balloon Festival or Zion National Park. Her own wonderful space! Room 205 Riddel.

She climbed the stairs to the second floor of the building and walked the hallway, searching for 205. The floor appeared to have been once occupied by ROTC offices as yellowed memos from the 1990s about the Rangers and AirBorne divisions were still on the bulletins boards.

Stand up, all victims of oppression ...

The Internationale got louder as she headed to the back of the building. Finally ... 205. Odd. The plaque on the door read Professor Bob Randolph, Entomology. Had the grouch in the Security Office given her the wrong key?

A man with a blond crew-cut stepped from the next office. "You're in the right place." He extended his hand in introduction. "Griffin Blake. My door still says Professor Sheila Myers, Business." He pointed to his door. "I'm the other sociologist that they hired."

"I'm Nina Vega. Nice to meet you."

"I heard about ..." Griffin winced.

Nina's cheeks reddened. "The whole thing's surreal. No doubt my missing finger will be the topic of the day."

"It is," he said honestly. "It seems as though they had a bunch of retirements and put all the new faculty up here together. The psychologist Joanne Trent is there, and the mathematician Boris Yulak is there. And Levon ... he said he was your neighbor at Driftwood Apartments ... is in the corner, sharing his office with the bees."

"Let's have a look." She turned the key to 205 and stepped inside. "What is that?"

Heavy plastic sheeting shaped like a funnel hung from the water-stained ceiling. The spout of the funnel drained into a tall trashcan in the middle of the room. She peered over the rim. Inches of dusty, stagnant water sat in the trashcan.

"I have a rain funnel too. So does Joanne. This wing of the building is called the Rainforest," Griffin said comically. "Apparently the slate roof leaks when it rains. But rain beats the hell out of yellow jackets."

"This water is rancid. It's a breeding ground for mosquitos. Great ... that's all I need on top of my hand ... malaria and zika."

"Yes," he grinned. "I'll let you settle in." He departed to his office.

The trashcan was too heavy to carry to the women's room with one hand. Dumping it in the toilet would have to wait until the bandages were removed, or until Ricardo visited her office. Griffith seemed pleasant enough and would probably do it for her, but he was dressed in a pink dress shirt, a University of Michigan tie, pressed pants and black leather shoes for his first day on the job. Later today she would pick up candles from the chandlery in the village to cover the disgusting odor.

So come brothers and sisters, For the struggle carries on ... the communist anthem continued from a nearby office.

Nina checked the time. There was just enough time to pick up her new laptop from Computer Services. She hurried from the Riddel Building, and across the close to the Science and Technology Building. A new computer with extra RAM to perform complex statistical analysis! There was no reason why she wouldn't be able to get two manuscripts out of her dissertation. Barring another crisis, the new statistics software ordered with her startup money would make it possible to finish her first manuscript within a few weeks. Then she could start the interviews with the Chesapeake watermen and generate data on the local crabbing industry.

At Computer Services a disheveled staff member handed her the computer case. She opened it. "This isn't the laptop I ordered when I submitted my equipment list to Dean Wines."

"Oh."

"This one will never be able to run my stats software."

"Well, I guess we can order you a new one."

"Yes! Great! Please do that. When do you think it will arrive?"

"I'll put your name on the list." He waddled over to a whiteboard. "What's your name again?"

"Nina Vega."

"Oh, okay." He scrawled her name at the bottom of a list of names.

"When will it get here?"

"Uh ... sometime this semester. After Dean Wines signs off on it. Things sit on her desk for awhile."

"Sometime this semester? I need to start my research this week!"

"Oh. Better discuss it with her. In the meantime, use this one."

"At best, this laptop might be able to word process."

"It's all we have available at the moment."

She huffed audibly. What was her choice? "Alright."

"We'll need to set up your passwords. We use three. One to open the computer. One to access the internet. One to access Tolchester's email.

"Whatever."

By the time Nina created three passwords that were easy to remember ... Laptop Pieceof Shit ... the Welcome Meeting had started. There was no time to drop the laptop at her office so she hurried to the auditorium. A table with trays of cookie crumbs and a punch bowl of watery juice had been set up in the foyer. She pushed through the double doors of the auditorium. All of the seats were taken. She spotted Griffin and Levon standing along the back wall. Next to Levon was a bearded man dressed in an olive drab military uniform and beret. The Fidel Castro clone waved to her as if they were old friends.

"Hi Nina." Fidel extended his hand. "Brad Smyth from the English Department. We're neighbors. My office is next to Levon and the bees."

This explained The Internationale. "Hello."

"Sucks about your finger," Brad said.

What to say to that? "Yeah, it sucks." She leaned toward Griffin. "What did I miss?"

"Nothing. They can't get the AV system to work."

The First Line Staff was in a row of chairs on the stage. The white-haired president Mary Blodgen sat erect in a tailored suit with a white and blue Tolchester scarf. Next to her was the Dean of Admissions and Retention Lana Hinkie. Gloria Wine, the Dean of Academics, was in the third chair. At the end the row sat a middle-aged man in a suit, the Director of Business Services and Physical Plant Hank Stupens.

Dean Wines grudgingly put her cell phone away and approached the podium. "Since we can't get the AV equipment to work," she said, glaring at the projection booth, "I can't show you the presentation I prepared on our international courses to Japan, Mexico, and England this past summer. So I'll start by introducing our new faculty. As your name is called, please raise your hand."

The names Griffin Blake, Levon Bakanian, Joanne Trent, and Boris Yulak were all called. At the name Nina Vega, all heads turned. She gave the gawkers a wave with her right hand. The introductions were followed by Dean Wines droning about the mandatory components of the syllabus: office hours, email, attendance policy, etc. Nina could hardly concentrate; her hand still ached.

Next Hank Stupens moved to the podium. President Blodgen gave him a kindly, reassuring nod. He talked quickly about a renovation to the men's bathrooms in the Riddel Building, then abruptly sat down. He was clearly not comfortable with public speaking.

Then Dean Hinkie stepped to the podium. She boasted about the boom in enrollments. "This is the largest incoming freshmen class in Tolchester's history!"

"They lowered admissions standards again," Brad Smyth whispered.

"We'll be teaching chimps," Levon whispered back.

"Did you notice the trailers in the field?" Brad said. "They don't have enough classroom space. Can you imagine paying 50K a year to have your classroom in a trailer?"

"That's probably where they'll assign me to teach," Griffin said. "Sociologists get the short end of every stick. I hope the trailers have AC. Otherwise they will be ovens on hot days."

Finally it was President Blodgen's turn to speak. She rose from her chair and scanned the auditorium. The administrative minutiae dispensed with, it was time for a Presidential Address ... just like those Nina had heard at the start of every semester at URI ... a brilliant inspirational speech by an engaging orator who would energize the faculty for a semester of great teaching. They had certainly saved the best for last. Maybe Blodgen's message would be on a new teaching philosophy, learning in the digital age, innovations in the flipped classroom model of teaching, or blending the STEM disciplines with the humanities and social sciences. There were countless compelling topics in higher education to choose from. President Blodgen had been at Tolchester for eons, she had told Nina at the interview. The old woman was witness to all sorts of cutting-edge trends in higher education.

President Blodgen cleared her throat and adjusted the microphone. "Welcome Tolchester faculty ..." she said with a deliberate pause. "You might have noticed changes to our website."

"Have you seen it?" Levon whispered. "It's a train wreck. You can't find anything. In the faculty and staff listing, the names aren't in alphabetical order. I finally gave up."

"Yup," Griffin said. "I clicked on the Employee Services link. It was dead. I have no idea if I have health insurance right now, or where my retirement contributions are going. Am I even receiving a paycheck this month?"

"On the intranet section for faculty and staff use, there's a new form," the President said. "The work request forms are now found in the Building Maintenance Folder. The form is no longer in the Academic Affairs Folder."

"And it was located in Academic Affairs in the first place why?" Griffin asked.

"And it's a completely new form." Blodgen's voice quavered. "Greatly streamlined. We removed the box where you once had to describe the rationale for the work."

'Rationale?' Nina wanted to shout. 'How about that the roof has razor-sharp slates that slide off and slice off entire fingers! How's that for a rationale?'

Nina had never associated any emotion with her body parts. They were always just there, taken for granted that they would always be there. But her ring finger was irretrievably gone. That fact hit like the unexpected death of a loved one. Irretrievably gone. It felt like the death of her mother ... Mama who always smelled of sugar and sweet things, who always had a dusting of flour in her black hair from the bakery. Her beautiful mother with the glistening dark eyes and warm smile. Nina suddenly felt light-headed. It was the accumulating stressors: the blood loss, surgery, parking ticket, stagnant water in her office, pathetic laptop ... all of it. What she needed was an unrestrained cry in the privacy of her apartment.

"Another piece of wonderful news," the President chirped, "is that a donor has given a generous gift to expand the flower beds around the college. Please have a stroll around our delightful campus to view our lovely gardens."

"How about a donation for a new classroom building so we don't have to teach in trailers?" Brad said under his breath.

Griffin checked the time on his cellphone. It was 11:48 am. "It's twelve o'clock somewhere."

"The song goes that it's five o'clock somewhere," Levon said.

"Twelve o'clock ... five o'clock ... same difference," Griffin said. "I'm heading to the tiki bar at the Nauticus restaurant. The guys in IT said that my office internet won't work until next week. There's some problem with the cables in my wall. Does this campus even have wireless? I guess I'll be working from home until then."

"Mine doesn't work either," Levon said. "Maybe it's a wiring problem with the whole Riddel Building."

"Get used to it, comrades," Brad said. "The campus internet hardly ever works."

"Then who's up for drinks at the tiki bar?" Griffin asked.

"Can't," Brad said, "but another time."

"I'm in," Levon said. "Nina, how about you?"

She mulled it over. If she went back to her apartment, she would cry and wallow in self-pity for the afternoon. Her new colleagues seemed like nice guys. And a giant Hurricane, like the one that Alex had made her, would numb the pain in her hand.

"Why not?"

"Traipsing around islands to bury pyrate treasure is in my blood," Alex told herself. Not only was the blood of the Scottish pyrate Charles Allaway, who was descended from a proud line of cut-throats and highwaymen, coursing through her veins, she was a direct descendent of the notorious Giles Ian Hale, aka Giles Blood-hand, the scourge of the Seven Seas ... well, at least River Glen on the Chesapeake. This meant that Alex's father Colin, whose father was Randy Allaway and mother was Julia Hale, was 100% pyrate. So what that Colin had been a neoclassical architect who restored historical buildings for the city of Philadelphia.

Then he married Alex's mother Carole Lowe, an attorney from a hoity-toity Philadelphia family. During the colonial period Philadelphia was a major pyrate enclave so there was a remote possibility that Carole had pyrate DNA. Colin had died prematurely, before he realized his true calling ... the champion of the River Glen treasure. Alex knew little about her parents since they died together when she was only months old, but she liked to imagine that she was conceived on a boat while Colin and Carole were rollicking from Caribbean rum. So, she was only 50% pyrate. Hey, no one's perfect.

In her outer life, Alex was an unassuming fisheries biologist who worked at a one-roomed marine station and wrote reports on water quality, pollutants, and species distribution for the State of Maryland's fisheries service. It was all a clever ploy to disguise her real identity ... a Chesapeake pyrate who drank rum, spied on invading treasure hunters through spyglasses, and messed around with fellow pyrate Will Wilkins on the evenings he wasn't taking his daughter Carly to soccer, hip hop, or Brownies.

It was her and Will's destiny to be the protectors of the River Glen treasure. They both had the pyrate mark, the cut across the left thumb. The ceremony had been performed on an October night, on a full moon, when they were children. All Allaways and Wilkinses had the mark. This October Carly would be initiated into the clandestine pyrate clan of Allaways, Wilkinses, Smyths, and Collinses, the founding families of River Glen.

It all started when Charles Allaway, Giles Hale, and the scallywags on the pyrate ship *Raven* captured the Spanish treasure galleon *El Espíritu de la Virgen* in 1688. According to Giles Hale's memoirs in Julia's safekeeping, the *Raven's* captain Bartholomew "the Hangman" Dodd was a sadistic bastard, his cat-o-nine-tails cracking the tropical air from dawn to dusk. The mute cabin boy from Dublin died under Dodd's lash. That was the last straw. Dodd had violated the pyrate code, violated the code of the brotherhood. He killed one of their own, a defenseless child no less. It was decided. Mutiny. That night the crew seized Dodd and cast him to tiger sharks that fed on goat and pig entrails tossed overboard by the cook. The pyrates fled northward, bypassing the usual haunts where they boozed and whored away the booty. When they settled on the remote river of the northern Chesapeake, an unfathomable treasure remained intact in the *Raven*'s holds.

Hmm. Where to bury the first bit of 'treasure' that Pamela *Knot-A-Care* will search for, while cursing, sweating, and smacking away the insects? The boy toys would be recruited to assist, who might grumble that Pamela was so not worth being eaten alive by ticks, green flies, and mosquitoes.

"This is too funny!"

Alex's first impulse was to bury the 'treasure' on Mutter Island, but that was a bad idea, a terrible idea. She would never be able to return there. The island was cursed and haunted by the evil spirits of Clyde and Desmond Whitby who murdered Jay Braden's wife Laura, and tried to kill Will and her on that horrible day two years before. That day had only one good outcome; it put an end to the ancient pyrate feud between the Allaways and Whitbys.

No, Miss *Knot-A-Care*'s treasure hunt would be here ... on Turtle Island. The island was aptly named; the dome in the center resembled a turtle's carapace. The unusual topography meant that activities on one side of the island could go undetected by those on the other side. Maybe she could spy on *Knot-A-Care's* dig while she hid in the underbrush at the top of the dome? Except that her laughter would alert the Miami tramp and boy toys to her presence and foil her whole plan. And the *Vital Spark* was big and clunky and easy to spot should the treasure hunters wander to the opposite side of the island. She would go about her work at the marine lab and be nowhere in sight when the dig occurred. Besides, the herring migration report for her boss Mr. Ward was due in Annapolis next week.

"Here ... perfect." Alex thrust the spade into the sand and started to dig. She dumped the 'treasure' in the hole and covered it up. She hurried to another site on the beach and dug another hole. She repeated this a number of times, her backpack lightening of its load. The 'treasures' were metal-based and would cause *Knot-A-Care's* metal detector to go berserk. "Too funny!"

Lastly Alex dragged fallen branches and rolled rotten logs into a clearing to create what might have been a primitive dwelling. Stones were arranged to resemble an old fire pit. She had thought of everything. She dumped charcoals from the chimenea on Julia's porch into the pit and sprinkled them with sand to create the illusion that sand had blown across the fire pit and campsite for eons. She put her fingers to her lips and whistled. Water Boy bounded from the trees. Spade in hand, she admired her handiwork.

"It's perfect, Water Boy, it's just perfect." She patted the black lab's head. "Now we set our plan into motion."

She and Water Boy waded through the shallows and climbed aboard the *Vital Spark*. Just a few more errands ... checking the crab pots, delivering fresh crabs to the Hoffman's Dockside Café and the Nauticus restaurant ... and her day would be over. Then a bubble bath, dinner, rum, and Will for dessert. She was 50% pyrate after all.

Pamela Dodd checked the beverages-calorie app on her tablet. A wine spritzer only had ninety-six calories which meant that she could have a second one. She signaled the bartender. He was generous with the fruit in the spritzers so the second drink could be rationalized as a source of natural fructose. Anything but the enemy ... high fructose corn syrup. She would burn off the carbs on the treadmill, and with the pretty twins later. She peered around the grinning tiki to the marina and floating dock B. The twins were on the sunning beds of her yacht. How to get rid of Josh and Jason without outright offending them? If she was to run the most successful modeling agency in the South, it was important to indulge her self-absorbed, neurotic models. The boys' chatter about *Project Runway* was beyond tedious and prompted her escape to the tiki bar at the Nauticus ... on the pretense of making important business calls. The tiki bar was preferable to Harlow's Pub because it was frequented by gay men so there was no fear of being hit on by the inbred locals. Harlow's was a meat market with sporting events blaring from the row of TVs over the bar. Except for kitschy ukulele music, the tiki bar was quiet; since it was mid-week, it was only her, the bartender, two men at the bar, and three people having lunch.

How to politely get rid of Josh and Jason? Yes, that was it. She typed a message to her personal assistant in South Beach. "Arrange for a job, any job possible to get the twins out of River Glen. And book them airplane tickets leaving from Philadelphia or Baltimore-Washington International to

Miami immediately ... tomorrow morning at the latest. Charge it to my expense account."

She would appeal to the boys' vanity. 'Gorgeous twins are required for this modeling job. You two are the only ones for this job. This could be the break you're looking for.' The boys were dullards. They would fall for it. "And book them first-class," she typed. The opportunity to sip champagne in wide, comfortable seats would coax them back to Florida.

That settled, Pamela clicked on the maps app. A map of the upper Chesapeake appeared on the screen. 'Where you are? Out there somewhere. I can sense it.' A burst of laughter at the only occupied table distracted her.

The handsome dark-haired man and a blond with a crew-cut were sharing steamed crabs while the Hispanic woman with the bandaged-hand picked at hummus and pita bread with her functional hand. The handsome man was clearly not gay as she had noticed him checking out her legs. But the blond guy was because he was checking out the bartender. The woman with the bandage repeatedly checked her cell phone, as though waiting for an urgent message. Pamela had a PhD in Social Psychology and was an expert on social dynamics and body language. After all, her business was bodies, beautiful ones. The blond ordered them another round of Hurricanes. Just for fun, Pamela typed Hurricane into the beverages-calories app. Ouch! Three hundred calories. Two shots of light rum, two more of dark rum, vodka, and grenadine. Thankfully she only had to walk down the hill to her boat, and not be on the road when this trio drove home.

The handsome man's phone vibrated.

"What is it, Levon?" the blond asked.

"The email announcement for my lecture tomorrow night."

"What's the topic?"

"The pyrates of the upper Chesapeake. Particularly the Spaniard Juan Carlos del Castillo, and the Scottish pyrate Giles Hale."

Pamela's ears perked up. Levon? Pyrates of the upper Chesapeake? Levon Bakanian? No ... it couldn't possibly be. She had read all of his scholarly papers. In fact, she read anything and everything related to pyrates, from bogus websites created by thirteen-year-olds, to refereed works in history journals by professors of colonial history.

"When and where?" asked the black-haired woman. "So I can let Alex know where to meet us."

Thank you, woman of the bandaged hand!

"At the auditorium at 7:30," Levon answered.

Pamela opened Google images and typed Levon Bakanian. Unbelievable! It was him. She had envisioned Bakanian as a withered scholar, but instead he was in his mid-thirties and devilishly attractive. He must have been invited to give a lecture in River Glen though she had no recollection of seeing his name on the list of lecturers at the River Glen Historical Society. She checked their calendar of events weekly. Besides fucking, working out, and searching for pyrate treasure, there nothing else to do in the village. She definitely would have remembered if Levon Bakanian was on their roster of speakers. She never missed one of the talks in the summer lecture series. One never knew if a vital clue about the location of Bartholomew Dodd's treasure might be mentioned. Her mission in life was to recover the lost treasure belonging to great, great ... great Granddaddy

Dodd. It was her destiny to restore the treasure to the Dodd family.

What auditorium ... what auditorium? Where else was there an auditorium in River Glen besides the puny one at the historical society? Nowhere. She was sure of it. Every square inch of the town and proximate coastline had been combed over in search of the Dodd treasure. It was an amazing feat of bravery that Great Granddaddy Dodd survived the shark attack in today's Tampa Bay. He was reputedly a giant of a man. It took the combined efforts of Giles Hale, Charles Allaway and the Whitby brothers to drag his livid body across the deck and lift him over the gunwale. Just as they were dropping him overboard, Dodd had grabbed for Giles, hoping to take the slender man with him. Instead, Dodd snatched the dagger from Giles' belt. Giles had cursed furiously from the railing above while Dodd splashed in the water. Dodd was left treading water in the *Raven's* wake as tiger sharks circled under a full moon. Ironically, Giles' dagger had saved Great Granddaddy's life. Dodd lunged out with the blade. It struck the side of a passing shark; Dodd held firm and sliced. Guts spurt from the gash; sharks swarmed and devoured their own brother. Dodd had fought off the other fish and dragged himself on shore. How long he lay prostrate on the beach is unclear, and he would have perished from his wounds and dehydration, had a Calusa woman not found him and nursed him back to health.

Pamela's attention returned to Levon and his friends. There was something humorous about Fidel Castro and a whining dean's description of the fall syllabi. Of course. These were faculty members having one last hurrah before the start of the fall semester. There was only one college nearby and that was Tolchester. It most certainly had an auditorium. Tomorrow she would be attending a lecture there at 7:30. She glanced down to the sunning beds, pulled a fifty from her wallet, and told the bartender to keep the change. She was in too good a mood not to celebrate. The twins suddenly looked delectable. By tomorrow morning they would be gone and by tomorrow evening she would have a new adventure buddy, one with incalculable volumes of pyrate knowledge in his beautiful head ... one Professor Levon Bakanian.

CHAPTER FOUR
Friday Evening

Dr. Levon Bakanian's hands jittered throughout his lecture, despite having given it countless times. One reason was that his new boss President Mary Blodgen and the Dean of Admissions and Retention Lana Hinkie were seated in the front row. From the doorway, as if a sentry, was the lugubrious business manager Hank Stupens. The academic dean Gloria Wines was nowhere to be seen. She reputedly never attended academic events.

And his jitters were also caused by Alex Allaway. At 7:40, when she was still a no-show, he feared that she would not attend. Nina, who was sitting with Griffin, craned her head, looking for Alex. The lights had not fully dimmed so he spotted Alex hurrying through the side door. Her hair was flattened from a motorcycle helmet in her hand. Nina, who had saved Alex a seat, waved. Alex stumbled over the laps of attendees, her helmet clanging into a metal chair. Everyone turned at the commotion. "Shh, shh, sorry!" she whispered.

Everything about Alex Allaway was delightfully distracting and put him on edge. He had noticed her years earlier, in her low-cut wench dress, at the annual Giles Blood-hand Day festival. He had even asked her to dance on a few occasions. His identity was concealed by an eye patch, black wig, and the black hat of his Captain Hook costume. Though she was not particularly graceful, she loved to dance, and danced with boundless energy. Her dancing was fueled by the merlot that Jim Pitcher kept plying her with. Jim Pitcher the vineyard owner, James Collins the village lawyer, and Will Wilkins the cop all had a thing for Alex. Levon made it a point to check out all the locals. As far as he could tell, she was the only female ... and a nubile one at that ... in River Glen under the age of sixty. Then out-of-the-blue, two years ago, she had emailed him at UVA. She was doing family genealogy on the Allaways and the Hales, she wrote. Whenever someone from River Glen contacted him, his radar pinged. Genealogy ... bullshit. They were looking for the lost treasure of the *Raven*. And Alex, being both an Allaway and a Hale, would be privy to documents and diaries from both pyrate lineages. Yes, lovely Alex Allaway was the key to finding the River Glen treasure.

When accepting the job at Tolchester, he had imagined that it might take some time to meet Alex, perhaps run into her a few times in the village, before introducing himself. Then the stars aligned in his favor. What astonishing luck. She appeared in the parking lot of his apartment complex. He had rushed out of his apartment on the pretense of talking to Nina, and pretended that he had no idea who Alex was.

Move aside Jim, James, and Will. There was a new man in town.

Levon slogged through the lecture while focusing obliquely on Alex. She seemed to be enjoying his talk. Most of his Powerpoints pertained to the bloodthirsty Juan Carlos del Castillo. There was a vast literature on Juan Carlos and his ship *Tereza* in the archives in Madrid ... until the Spaniards headed up the Chesapeake. At that point there was no further mention of them.

"How did an entire pyrate ship and its crew literally vanish?" he asked the audience.

The rhetorical question seemed to fascinate Alex. She leaned forward, listening. His erudite jokes, slipped in at all the usual places, seemed to impress her also. She giggled often. So did President Blodgen. But his humor overshot Dean Hinkie who had a permanent scowl on her face.

The last few Powerpoints focused on the Scotsman Giles Hale. After Giles massacred Neville Whitby and his family, Giles, his wife and two children fled to Aberdeen, Scotland. Giles died a few years later, his body riddled with tropical diseases. That was all anyone knew of Giles Blood-hand.

The lecture ended with a brief Q and A session. President Blodgen asked the first question. "Why was the colonial government of Virginia unable to apprehend Juan Carlos and the *Tereza* in the lower Chesapeake?"

Levon fielded her question with ease. "The Virginians were battling Dutch warships. Their resources were stretched too thin. A single pyrate was low on their list of priorities."

Despite the fact that eighty percent of his talk was on Juan Carlos del Castillo, the audience was mostly interested in the local phenom Giles Blood-hand and the lost treasure of the *Raven*. Burt Sweeny's son in a pyrate hat and eye patch raised his hand. "For what period of time were Giles' hands bloody?"

He had to wing that answer. "Maybe one night, until he washed them." The audience chuckled.

Next a teenage girl asked him, "Does the headless spirit of Charles Allaway really haunt the pyrate graveyard, or is it just a rumor?"

Another one to wing. "I'm not a paranormal expert, but maybe you can find that information on a ghost-hunter web." That answer seemed to satisfy her as she bent over her cell phone.

Then Alex raised her hand and Levon's heart jolted.

"More a comment than a question," she said. "I'm wondering why no State archeologists have surveyed or excavated Turtle Island. There appears to have been a small encampment there. Maybe it was where Juan Carlos resided if he made it as far as the northern Chesapeake. Or where Giles hid the Allaway and Hale families on the night of the Whitby family murder."

The audience went dead silent.

Levon's heart jolted for a second time. His thoughts scrambled. What encampment? Could Giles' treasure be ... on an island? Turtle Island? He had never heard of it. Certainly a boat would have to be chartered to get there.

He shrugged nonchalantly. "I'm not aware of any State-sponsored surveys to look for pyrate encampments. Besides, I doubt there would be much there, other than remnants of clothes and cooking utensils. But no treasure. Most scholars agree that the legendary treasure of Giles Blood-hand was all spent in the Caribbean, long before the pyrates headed up the east coast."

Most scholars agree – his canned response at every lecture. Amazing how a professor's word was gospel to the general public, instead of recognized for what it really was – self-serving drivel.

Indistinct murmuring was heard in the auditorium, and President Blodgen stood and offered kind words of thanks for the "enlightening lecture."

Turtle Island, Turtle Island ... where the hell was Turtle Island? During his every visit to River Glen, some hopeless sap was weaving along the shoreline at the Point with a metal detector ... only to find beer caps. It made perfect sense that the pyrates would have hidden the treasure on an island.

He had to get to Turtle Island first!

What an imbecile Alex was to have mentioned that place ... and at a public event! Had it never occurred to her look for the treasure herself? How could she not have put two and two together? With any luck the locals were equally as witless. Hopefully her comment had gone right in one ear and out the other. Still, it might be wise to encourage a friendship with her because she had a boat; plus she was pleasant on the eyes.

Levon was vaguely aware of clapping. Maybe he managed a smile. Who could possibly think straight! President Blodgen congratulated him again and departed with Dean Hinkie and Hank Stupens. It was his original plan to see if Nina, Griffin, and Alex wanted to get a beer at Harlow's, but how could he possibly hold a conversation at a time like this? Only one thing mattered – the encampment at Turtle Island. He had to get to his computer and study a map. Pronto.

Nina, Griffin and Alex strolled up to the podium and offered him additional kudos. Nina and Alex were heading back to Nina's apartment to unpack, Nina mentioned. He passed on drinks at the tiki bar with Griffin. His singular goal was to check out the whereabouts of Turtle Island on Google Earth. Alex, Nina, and Griffin wandered out of the auditorium together. As he pulled his flashdrive from the podium's laptop, there was a movement in his peripheral vision. He recognized the woman immediately. It was the strawberry blonde who had flashed him a provocative smile when she slid off the bar stool at Nauticus. The woman oozed wealth and confidence that came from having not a care in the world.

"Most scholars agree ..." She laughed sarcastically. "I loved that phase. Everyone bought it, except me." Her cobalt blue eyes narrowed. "I believe that you and I have a common interest. That you and I both know is somewhere here in River Glen. Perhaps we should discuss it. Perhaps on my boat, over a glass of champagne. The name's Dodd." She extended her hand with blood-red fingernails. "Dr. Pamela Dodd."

"Freaky good luck." Alex pulled on her motorcycle helmet in Nina's parking lot. For days the method to spread the rumor about *the pyrate camp on Turtle Island* amidst the yachting crowd at the marina had eluded her. Then she spotted the target of her prank in the audience – the rich bitch from the glitzy yacht that nearly capsized the *Vital Spark*. Alex's initial bristling at the sight of the woman was followed by a reversal of emotions – a joyous sense of karma. This was her chance. Though public speaking utterly terrified her, Alex found herself on the edge of her seat in anticipation of the Q and A session.

I'm wondering why no State archeologists have surveyed or excavated Turtle Island. There appears to have been a small encampment there ... blah, blah, blah.

She could barely speak the words without cracking up. Then came another reversal of mood – the pang of guilt. Will would be pissed. The practical jokes that she and Carly pulled on him annoyed him to no end. He had urged her to let it go, to drop the whole thing.

"Your boat didn't capsize. You and Nina were unscathed," he had said in the berth that night. "And the giant wake that caused the mudslide at the cliff revealed that a sociopath was, or is in River Glen, that we need to put behind bars."

As far as Will was concerned, the episode on the river had a silver lining. The detectives had something interesting to investigate after a summer of monotonous calm.

Anyway, her remark at the lecture was merely harmless speculation about an archeological dig. Nothing more. Besides, Will would never find out about it.

After fastening her chin-strap, Alex looked over her shoulder. Nina's silhouette in the doorway waved a sad goodbye. That evening, after they had dragged the king-sized bed to the opposite side of the bedroom and built Ricardo's computer table in the spare bedroom, Nina had asked Alex to remove the bandages. They had rummaged through the cardboard boxes for a pair of scissors and headed to bathroom.

Nina's reflection in the mirror was despondent; at any moment she might burst into tears.

"Are you really supposed to remove the bandages so soon?" Alex had asked.

"Who knows? I don't remember anything from the hospital. The bandages are filthy. I want fresh ones."

"It won't be bad. Really. It won't be so bad."

Nina had reached for a roll of toilet paper and blew her nose. "I don't know why Ricardo hasn't contacted me."

Alex cut through the gray, frayed gauze. Her stomach tightened as she unraveled the bandages. Fishermen and crabbers occasionally had missing fingers, and her own hands bore countless scars from lines and wires on the crab pots. A lost finger was not an uncommon hazard of a waterman. But she had never seen one recently removed. Nina's pinkie finger was covered in a metal brace and was not visible, but what was visible was bad. Alex suppressed a gag. It was very bad. Unspeakably bad. Nina's entire hand was black and blue. Where there was once a ring finger was a hollow-stitched-up concavity.

"How is it?" Nina whispered fearfully, her eyes averted.

Alex swallowed. "Really, not bad."

Nina glanced downward. "Dios mio!" Her knees gave way and she collapsed onto the toilet seat. "Not bad! It's worse than horrible! Cover it up, cover it up now!"

"Okay, okay!" She hurriedly rewrapped the hand with fresh gauze and tape.

"What the hell am I going to do?" Nina cried. "It's dreadful! Wear a glove for the rest of my life? I'll look like Michael Jackson. Students will be terrified of me. Abuelita must be furious about her ring."

"Your hand is what's important, not the ring. You need to let it heal. You'll get used to it over time. Many people lose appendages. Like soldiers, who lose entire arms and legs. Does it hurt?"

Nina sniffled. "All the time."

"I can get you medicinal marijuana. There's a ton of it growing in the village. Do you want some?"

"No. With my horrid luck, I'd get drug tested and lose my job."

They had sat silently in the bathroom, Nina on the toilet seat, she on the edge of the bathtub.

"I think I'll just take a Percocet and go to bed," Nina finally said. "Thanks for your help tonight."

"Sure. No problem. There's a lot of rain in the forecast, but if you want to do something this weekend, let me know."

Alex waved goodnight to Nina and slung her leg over the old Suzuki sportbike that she had bartered for crabs from Gary Smyth at the marina. The windows of Levon Bakanian's apartment were dark. Attractive man. Good sense of humor. His was an interesting, well-presented talk. She pushed the starter and let the motorcycle rumble between her legs while she zipped up her leather jacket and flipped down the face shield. The smells of metal, gasoline, and leather mixed in the humid air. She knocked the bike into first gear; she let out the clutch and eased down the throttle. In second gear, she weaved through the parking lot at Driftwood Apartments. At the entrance to the coastal road, she kicked the bike into third gear and pulled down the throttle. It was Friday night and there was a ritual to perform with her fellow treasurer Will ... the checking of the treasure from the *Raven* ... a vast trove of emeralds from Colombia, rubies from Brazil, pearls from Margarita Island, and Peruvian gold and silver. She knew exactly where it was hidden. She was a River Glen pyrate after all.

CHAPTER FIVE
Saturday

Lisa Paco estimated that Dr. Zera Lim was five feet, ten inches tall. If Lisa was better at math, she would be able to calculate exactly how much surface area of skin Zera had compared to her own frame at five three. Zera's convoluted body, with a nose, ears, fingers and the like, would make such a computation almost impossible. Now, if Zera was a three-dimensional rectangle that was five feet, ten inches tall, and say, one foot wide and four inches deep, Lisa could use that equation length times width times depth. Wait, did that calculate volume or surface area? #pacosucksatmath

"Stop looking at me like that," Zera said. "It's unnerving."

"I was just wondering, if you ever decided to get your entire body tattooed, how much surface area would be available for the tattoo artist."

"Not one tattoo is going into my dermis."

"I wouldn't expect you to tattoo your neck and face."

"No tattoos ever."

"I bet you didn't know that ink doesn't take well to the palms of hands and feet."

"I did know that," Zera sighed.

The last comment had been a test. Of course Zera, the State of Maryland's all-knowing Goddess of Crime-solving, would know that bit of dermal trivia. And at the moment the Crime Goddess was testy because she had been working incessantly for days on the skeletons pulled from Henry Herssen's foundation. A serial killer was on the loose so Jay and Zera were back and forth on their phones all day. Zera had been taking catnaps on the leather sofa in her office, showering in the bathroom by the lockers, and eating fast food from Taco Bell and Subway that her secretary brought in. Cheap, commercial food put Zera in a bad mood. Zera liked the finer things in life and she could afford them since her children had grown up and her husband had left her for a younger woman. Zera seemed to have no interest in replacing him. That's why she and Zera had so much in common. #menareasnooze #deadbodiesarecooler

Lisa had the unbelievable good fortune of being invited to Zera's condo – albeit only once. It was for Jay's fifty-seventh birthday party. A surprise party. Zera kept a sisterly eye on Jay since Laura's murder by Clyde Whitby on Mutter Island. Jay had been lured to Zera's townhouse on the pretext of helping her move a new living room furniture set. Will, Norman from IT, Cloris the secretary, and Zera's forensics team had all awaited Jay's arrival on the back porch that overlooked the bay, prepared to shout "Surprise!" and shower Jay with confetti. There was an impressive spread of snacks – Zera called them hors d'oeuvres – and imported beer and wine, but Lisa was craving Doritos, Tostitos dip, and a Bud Lite. And Lisa had been in no mood to socialize with people she saw 24-7 ... not when there was a once-in-a-lifetime chance to study Zera's condo and discover new facets of the elusive Crime Goddess. She had been baffled by what she saw. There were no paintings or pictures of the bay, crabs, sailboats or Maryland sport teams but only mountains and cliffs. There were the sandstone cliffs of the Canyonlands in Utah, the Grand Tetons, the Swiss Alps, and more. Nothing made sense. Zera had a degree in biochemistry from Princeton, and a medical degree from Penn. Why the fixation with rock faces and craggy mountains? Zera was wiry and athletic in appearance. Was she a fossil-hunter, amateur geologist, a rock-climber? How incredibly incongruous. Fascinating!

"Here, Lisa. Put these on." Zera handed her a disposable gown, mask, and booties to slip over her shoes. "And spit out your gum."

"But?"

"But no. There." Zera pointed resolutely to the trashcan.

Lisa spit reluctantly. "That piece was only five minutes old. It still had tons of flavor."

"I'll buy you some for Christmas."

"Yeah, great, but it's only August." She followed Zera to the sterile examination room. "Ahhchoo!"

"God bless you."

"I don't sneeze if I have gum to chew."

"Oh well."

There were ... three, four, five bodies on the stainless steel examination tables. "Sweet!"

"Lisa ..."

"Yeah, yeah, I know. Jay always tells me to rein in my inappropriate enthusiasm for corpses."

"I agree."

Lisa stepped excitedly toward the tables. "How'd they die? Who are they?"

"Your work's cut out for you, my friend. I have no idea who they are, or how they died, except one. They're all at different stages of decomposition. Only one shows signs of foul play. This one." Zera lifted the sheet from the first body. "A female, roughly twenty years old. Her pelvis and rib cage were crushed. My guess is that she was run over. She's been in the ground for about four years. Before she was killed, she was in good health. They were no surgical incisions, no indications of pregnancies. She had excellent teeth, no cavities, and they were straightened by braces as a teenager."

Lisa tapped that info into her tablet. "I'll check on missing persons from four years ago."

Zera uncovered the next two bodies at the same time. "These two were buried together, side by side, about five or six years ago. Their bodies show no signs of violence. The male is in his mid- to late sixties and had osteoarthritis and dentures. The arthritis in his left hip was quite bad. He probably walked with a limp. The female, about the same age, had very bad osteoporosis and had thoracic kyphosis. She had a knee replacement."

"I know that term, kyphosis. She was a hunchback like Quasimodo. Did you know that Quasimodo was based on a real person, a hunchbacked stone mason who worked at Notre Dame in the 1820s?"

"You're a wealth of knowledge."

"And a goddess of crime-solving."

"Goddess, get this sick one off the streets of River Glen."

"If he's still here."

"Or she."

"But probably a *he* since it would be difficult for a woman to move the bodies, especially that large one." Lisa leaned over the male with the bad hip. "He was very tall."

"Make no assumptions, never assume anything. Maybe it was a pair of murderers? A cult, a secret society, a gang? Who knows? The last two bodies were males in their forties."

"Weird! No pattern. Both males and females. In their twenties, forties, and sixties. And none were wearing clothes?"

"No clothes. Clothes reveal too much about profession, socioeconomic status and the like. Our killer was obviously aware of this." Zera pulled back the sheets from the last two bodies. "These two males were found in the deepest layer of the pit. There's hardly anything left of them since they've been there the longest, just over twenty years. Both men show signs of hard labor as they had very strong arm and leg bones, indicative of lifting or strenuous exercise like weight-lifting. Maybe they were farmers, fishermen, or stone masons like your Quasimodo. This one in particular had damage to his face. Perhaps he'd been beaten up. There." Zera pointed. "Broken zygomatic arches that had healed. Enlarged brow ridges, calcifications of the frontal bone, possibly from being punched repeatedly."

"Maybe he was a Neanderthal," she laughed.

Zera grimaced. "He fought back. He had broken knuckles and fingers."

"But these blows didn't kill him?"

"No. They had healed up long before he died. Maybe he was a boxer."

"What?"

"A boxer. See there? The two central incisors in the maxilla are missing."

Lisa stared at the boxer's skull; sweat formed around her collar. "Ur, I should be going."

"Are you okay?"

"Yes, yes. Just very busy. Gotta run." She stepped away from the table.

"Okay. You be careful," Zera said. "Have your wits about you, in case this killer is still around."

Lisa tore off the disposable gown and mask, crammed them in a trash bin, and dashed out the door of the morgue – still wearing her booties.

Will Wilkins had never seen a crime board that looked like this one. Typically photos of the victim were placed next to photos of possible suspects. Lines, arrows, and question marks were scrawled on the board, suggesting relationships and motives. Instead, this crime board had a column of nameless bodies in progressive states of decomposition, each associated with a different layer of soil, moving back in time from four to six to twenty years ago.

Female 1 age 20? 4 yrs in ground
Female 2 age 65? 6 yrs in grd
Male 1 age 65? 6 yrs in grd
Male 2 age 40? 20-25 yrs in grd
Male 3 age 40? 20-25 yrs in grd

Five nameless victims. Zero suspects.

Worse, the crime board with the strata of soil reminded Will of freshmen geology class at the University of Maryland

... Cenozoic, Mesozoic, Paleozoic, Precambrian. He had taken geology to fulfill science credits and nearly failed it because he spent the entire semester pining away over the girl from his hometown, Alex Allaway.

Nothing had changed ten goddamn years later. Nothing at all. He was still pining. The difference between then and now was that he was in Alex's bed a few nights a week ... on the nights he wasn't taking Carly to hip hop, soccer or Brownies ... but he was clueless about Alex's feelings for him. The sex was enthralling, but one would think that at some point, especially after two years together, they might have a conversation about their feelings for one another. Love? Commitment? Were those words even in her vocabulary? Last Valentine's Day he had given her a dozen long-stemmed roses, chocolates, and a romantic Hallmark card. Her gift to him was a stuffed parrot to wear on his shoulder during Giles Blood-hand Day. Their after-sex routine was a study in frustration. Just as he was rallying the courage to discuss the possibility of co-habitation, she would spring from the bed, reach for her phone, and call for pizza delivery.

"I'll wait for it outside. You relax." She would pull on her clothes and dither on the deck with her lines and crab pots until the love-sick delivery boy hurried down the dock with his beloved's pizza. After searching for crumpled bills from the countless pockets of her cargo shorts to pay the boy, she would return to the cabin, drop the pizza box on the bed, pull off her clothes, and dig into the food. Why she had to eat pizza in the buff was just another inexplicable *Alexism*, and of course he didn't mind, but it distracted him from blurting out his well-rehearsed lines:

"Alex, I'm madly in love with you. I have been since we were in elementary school. If you feel the same way, I think we should live together."

It made sense that he and Carly move into Alex's riverfront cottage. Besides, he couldn't wait to escape his parents' house. His mother Belle was so bossy. No small wonder his father John was always high on Luna's weed. Alex's place had a small beach for Carly to swim, and Peppy could play with Water Boy, Miranda, and Clark. Alex's cottage was tiny, but perhaps an addition could be put on the back. Carly could sleep on the living room sofa until the addition was completed. A ton of money had been saved by living with his parents so a modest addition was entirely in his budget right now. How nice would it be to wake up next to Alex, have breakfast together, walk the dogs, go for a swim, do the normal things that normal couples normally do.

Jay suddenly appeared over him. "Will, how are you doing on the Herssen file?"

"Oh, um, fine, sir." He fumbled for the file folder. "Herssen was a strange bird. Not much on him. No police record. It's hard to find anything on these guys that live off the grid. He was born in Cleveland, Ohio, to a factory worker and a homemaker. In his early twenties Herssen worked on a long-liner on Cape Cod before moving to the Chesapeake. What brought him to the Chesapeake is unknown. Maybe the woman he briefly lived with?"

"Do we know who she was?"

"No clue. I remember Herssen coming into the village occasionally for groceries and supplies, but she never came with him. They lived in the cottage on the cliff. He had a little fishing boat called *Atrax.*"

"Atrax? Peculiar name. What the hell's an atrax?"

He shrugged.

Jay pulled his phone from his pocket and typed onto the screen. "*Atrax robustus*. An Australian funnel-web spider. Nasty beast. Venomous. Did Herssen have any connections to Australia?"

"None that I know about. He had no passport and never left the country, according to Immigration. No credit card, no computer, no cell phone, no nothing. He paid for everything in cash or check apparently."

"Checks from where?"

"The River Glen Bank. He has about 100K in a checking account there. Every year he sends a check to pay his property taxes."

Jay frowned. "He disappeared roughly twenty years ago, yet he still pays taxes. That doesn't sit right. How old is he now?"

He checked the dates on Herssen's birth certificate from a hospital in Cleveland. "Six-eight."

"Roughly the same age as Female 2." Jay stared at the crime board. "Maybe she's the alleged girlfriend?"

"So maybe he kills Males 2 and 3 twenty years ago, which is why he disappeared. Then, finding the abandoned cottage the perfect place to hide bodies, he buried victims Male 1 and Female 2 six years ago, then the young woman, Female 1 four years ago. Maybe he continued to pay taxes on the property to keep people from snooping around?"

"Interesting hypothesis," Jay said. "Let's you and I go back there and snoop around."

"No wonder my foot keeps slipping off the gas pedal!" Lisa had dashed from the morgue in her booties. Zera must have thought her insane.

"Where to go? To headquarters?" No, she needed to compose herself.

"Go home? No, anywhere but there!"

"The Point? Yes, yes! That was a serene place to calm down."

She stuffed another piece of gum in her mouth. Then another. This was more than she could handle! Her head was going to explode at any second – it was – any second! There would be grey matter all over the windshield and rearview mirror. She stuffed a fifth piece into her mouth and chewed frantically. The blue police sedan lurched to a stop in the parking lot at the Point, not far from the bathhouse where Clyde Whitby had murdered Penelope Bannister, Carly Wilkins' mother.

On the beach families lounged on blankets and towels, and children with plastic shovels and buckets wandered the water's edge. If her parents had ever taken her to the beach, she couldn't recall it. No, impossible. It had never happened. In fact she had no recollection of ever seeing her parents together, except in heated exchanges in the apartment.

Breathe, twenty times, breathe. She had read that somewhere. Maybe on an online mindfulness meditation site. Who can breathe at a time like this! A sixth piece of gum was necessary – absolutely necessary! She ripped open the wrapper. Jay would be ballistic if he saw gum foil all over the front seat of the cruiser. She stuffed the shiny wrappers into the pocket of her uniform pants.

"Figure it out, figure it out, you are a virtuosa of crime-solving like Zera Lim." She closed her eyes and leaned her head back against the headrest. Breathe … breathe …

What had happened that day? She must have been about ten. Yes, definitely. It was twenty years ago. It was before her mother Wanda was diagnosed with MS, before she was confined to a wheelchair, when she was still strong from carrying trays at the diner. Lisa had been playing a video game on the living floor of their apartment. That year it would have been the Legend of Zelda: Majora's Mask, or Diablo II. Her parents were going at it in the bedroom … again. That day was bad, very bad. She had turned up the volume on the video game, trying to block out shattering and smashing sounds coming from her parent's bedroom. Wanda finally emerged, her face bloodied. Her father had followed, equally battered. He stomped toward the front door, holding his gym bag and boxing gloves.

"If you come back here, you bastard, and I promise, I'll kill you," Wanda had said.

"Lisa!" he shouted.

She had stared in panic at the TV screen.

"Lisa, I'm fuckin' talking to you!"

Her hands vice-gripped the game controller. As he approached, her eyelids fluttered, her hands shook uncontrollably.

"You touch her and I'll …" Wanda clenched her fists.

Her father had knelt in front of her, smelling like he always did, of grass and sweat. His face with the hooded eyes, broken nose, and caveman brow ridges, moved toward hers. He pressed his tongue through the opening where two front teeth should have been. He hissed like a viper.

That was the last Lisa saw of Owen Paco's monstrous face.

Will glanced at Jay behind the wheel of the unmarked police. Jay seemed to have gotten it right with Julia Hale. Jay and Julia actually spent time together, outside the bedroom. If he could only have such a relationship with Alex then all would be perfect in the universe. River Glen was just a tiny village so one ran into their neighbors often. He had seen Jay and Julia dining on the back porch of Nauticus, buying candles at the chandlery and pastries at the bakery, and together at the dog park. Once, when he had been waiting for Alex – she was late for everything – he saw Jay and Julia dancing on Julia's porch. Julia had reached down to pull Jay out of an Adirondack chair.

"I'm not a dancer," he said.

"Oh, yes, you are. Up."

He stood despite himself.

"Drink, lad." Julia had handed him a glass of scotch.

He took a sip.

"All of it."

He obediently tossed back the drink.

"You are no longer flesh and bone." She unbuttoned the buttons of his dress shirt. "You're ready." She took his hands in hers. "Imagine yourself as hot flowing water and you can tango."

Jay turned the car into Henry Herssen's driveway. On either side of them was tall grass. If there had ever been a mowed yard, it had long disappeared. It was now covered with weeds, bushes and small trees. The entire property had been sifted over by the police, but it was always Jay's way to have a second look on his own.

He and Jay walked to the edge of the cliff and cautiously peered over. Pieces of the cottage had been retrieved by the police boat and were now spread out in the space metal building behind Zera's crime lab. They zigzagged across Herssen's property, through clouds of gnats and mosquitos, until they returned to the driveway and gravel road.

"The woods, Will. You check there." Jay pointed to the forest at the edge of the clearing. "I'll check the other side."

"Are those woods even part of Herssen's property?"

"Don't know, don't care."

"Yes, sir."

Will trudged into the underbrush, looking for anything that resembled a trail. Jay disappeared in the opposite direction. Would it be inappropriate to ask Jay about his success with women? Jay had been married to Laura for thirty years before her death, and seemed to be getting it right with Julia. No, it was the kind of question one might ask one's father. Unfortunately his father was a stoner with one singular interest (besides weed) ... the Baltimore Ravens. His parents' marriage was held together by dumb luck.

He was almost thirty-years old, Will reminded himself, and a decorated police officer for his role in the Allaway murder investigation. Certainly he could figure out the mysteries of Alex on his own, without advice from elders.

Tango lessons?

Yes, tango lessons! "I am fluid, I am water, hot flowing water." It would be an ideal way to spend more time with Alex. It would be *their thing*. Maybe they could have dinner at Nauticus or the Dockside Café before the dancing lessons. Dinner would be the perfect opportunity to have a meaningful conversation with Alex about their future. Why not? Nothing ventured, nothing gained. He pulled his phone from his pocket. He had two left feet, but tango lessons would be fun. "I am fluid, I am water, hot flowing water!" Alex would go for it. Definitely! She loved to dance at the Giles Blood-hand Festival, especially when fueled by Jim Pitcher's merlot.

Will kicked through the leaves and typed his text. *Alex, let's talk soon, tonight. There's really something I need to ...* the earth collapsed under his shoes and he felt himself falling falling falling ... into a black funnel of soil and roots ... and nothing.

Alex, let's talk soon, tonight. There's really something I need to

Alex looked curiously at her cell phone. She texted back: *Need to what?*

No response.

She forced her attention back to the graph on her laptop. She rarely worked Saturdays, but the herring report for Mr. Ward in Annapolis had to be perfect. Her next raise depended on it. She fidgeted in her chair and glanced up at the wall clock. No response from Will after five minutes. She sprang from her chair and crossed the marine station. At the lab bench she cleaned dirt and salt water from the beakers. No response after ten minutes. A hollow dread set in. She returned to her desk and gazed blankly at her Excel spreadsheet.

Will had chickened out. That explained the incomplete message. He was ending their relationship. It had to be that. What else could it be? He was dumping her, but breaking things off by an impersonal text message was the wrong thing to do. At the last second, he had decided to wait and tell her face to face.

'I met a wonderful woman at the gym.' It's probably what he was going to say. 'I found the perfect mother for Carly. We can still be friends. I'll still see you every Friday night to check the treasury, but I can't join you in the berth of the *Vital Spark* afterwards.'

Yes, definitely. That was it. That's why he had stopped mid-sentence. His plan was to let her down gently, in person. He would say something kind, like she wasn't a complete klutz in bed and that the pizza was always delicious. Thank God she hadn't blurted out her true feelings, the words she had rehearsed a gazillion times. 'Will, I'm madly in love with you. I have been since we were in elementary school. If you feel the same way, I think we should live together. You and Carly can move out of your parents' house and live with me. I know my place is puny, but maybe we can build an addition on the back of the cottage for Carly's room. I've saved money in the past two years since I haven't had to pay rent. Maybe we could build a deck and get a hot tub.'

She had even thought to mention his dog Peppy. 'Peppy loves to chase Water Boy and Miranda around the beach. And Clark too, when Jay's visiting Julia.'

Thankfully she had refrained from the mortifying confession of love. She would simply do what Julia always told her to do during hard times. "Keep a stiff upper lip, lass." That would be the strategy. When Will breaks it off, she would say with her stiff upper lip, "Hey, good times. No problem. It was just sex. I wish you the best."

It was fortunate that she didn't give him the crab-shaped key chain engraved with their initials for Valentine's Day that was stashed in her underwear drawer. In retrospect, the green parrot for Giles Blood-hand Day had been an appropriate and neutral gift for a friend with benefits.

Will was too good for her, too kind, too decent. His dumping her was punishment for her killing Clyde Whitby, though she had no choice that day. It was kill or be killed. It came down to that simple equation. Her punishment for killing another human being would be to watch Will and his lovely wife and children flourish in River Glen, while she withered away, a decrepit spinster.

She walked outside to the dock. Through the late afternoon haze she could just see it, the duck blind in the marsh where Clyde Whitby had spied on her. Her heart pounded.

The Whitby brothers had murdered her parents, Clyde had told – boasted – to her while circling the *Vital Spark* on his jet ski. Her entire history distilled to that one single fact at that one single moment.

"You're a dead, fucking Googan!" He showered the tugboat with bullets and motored toward the bow.

She hid behind the water cannon, listening, swiveling the nozzle in the direction of his engine. Her hand on the trigger, a handgrip, quivered. "Please work, please work." She inched her head over the gunwale to check on his whereabouts. His gun was at his shoulder. She ducked; a bullet whizzed by her earlobe. But she had seen just enough and moved the nozzle a few degrees to the right.

"Do your worst!" she screamed savagely.

She squeezed the handgrip ... *a cannonball splintered planks ... a man flailed among sharks ... a severed head jammed onto a pike* ... a jet of water ripped from the cannon, the tug shuddered ... *a spark flickered in the piney dark* ... molten blood coursed through her pyrate veins. A subterranean rage of twenty-six years, transferred from her elders to her, erupted with ferocious vengeance.

She squeezed harder.

It was a direct hit. Time paused. Bone and cartilage bowed and snapped – the crack raised goose bumps on her skin – as his chest imploded. A guttural wail filled the air, a last breath from crushed lungs. He was launched through the air before he hit the water. He floated briefly, before disappearing in a mist of bubbles, pulled to the bottom by the weight of pyrate gold.

She had murdered a man. That was a fact. True, it was in self-defense and she was avenging the death of her parents and grandfather. But as she pulled that handgrip, a perverse thrill overtook her. She was 50% pyrate after all.

Anyone, if pushed hard enough, is capable of murder, Lisa concluded. Even her sweet mother Wanda. Best to be prudent and say nothing about the current case but instead monitor Wanda's behavior for the rest of the evening. Her mother had the capacity to murder her father; she could give as good as get in the brawls. She wasn't the type of woman who had stood there and taken it. She had given it right back. Owen Paco was an abusive asshole and had it coming. But was her mother capable of murdering *four other people*? Had Lisa been raised by a serial killer? Did this explain Lisa's preoccupation with the criminal mind?

"Fresh bread for dinner tonight," Wanda called from the kitchen. "I tried a new recipe. Olive bread."

"Yum." Lisa circled the living room, searching for clues. "Maybe I'll try sour dough tomorrow. Best gift ever."

Wanda was delighted with the bread maker that Lisa had bought for her birthday, along with a box set of DVDs of the new *Miss Marple* series.

"The new season of *Sherlock* starts tonight," Wanda said.

"Can't wait. The actor who plays Moriarty gives me the willies."

"Yes, brilliant casting. I made your favorite. Spaghetti and meatballs."

"Double yum. I smell the extra oregano."

Lisa scanned the shelves and shelves of Wanda's books and DVDs, all mysteries and crime fiction. Wanda had no higher education, but she had completed high school. She was a prolific reader; she had a ghoulish fascination with murder that she had instilled in her daughter. Since childhood, Lisa was determined to be a cop, a detective.

Wanda was highly intelligent and capable of planning a flawless murder, but how was it carried out? Lisa eyed the wheelchair in front of the computer. When not on the computer, searching for online bread recipes or listening to concerts on You Tube, Wanda watched re-runs of crime shows all day long. An opened DVD case revealed that her mother had been watching an old season of *DCI Banks*. The DVD player was still warm. It was their mother-daughter bonding thing to watch the new ones together. It was also their thing to stop the DVD fifteen minutes into the story to discuss various hypotheses as to the identity of the murderer. It was a fifty-fifty split between whose hypothesis was correct on any given night. Yes, Lisa had inherited her great sleuthing mind from Wanda.

How would a woman with MS carry out five murders? The murders were spread out over twenty years, probably to avoid detection. The first two murders, Male 2 and 3, were certainly executed long before Wanda was diagnosed with MS. Lisa suspiciously eyed the wheelchair once again. What if her mother didn't really have MS? What if it was all a ruse? Her mother worked diligently with the light barbells to improve arm strength, and shuffled along the hallway with her walker many times a day to maintain her stamina.

What if Wanda had a psychological disorder – a factitious disorder like the Munchausen syndrome where one feigns an illness to garner sympathy? Lisa ran her finger along the windowsill. There was no evidence that her mother had climbed out the window using the fire ladder, to bypass the squeaky front door. The windowsill was dusty. The Paco family had lived in this apartment for nearly three decades; Lisa knew all the neighbors. One of them would have mentioned to her if Wanda was sneaking out the window during the night.

"Honey, come eat. You must be hungry."

"#crimegoddessisstarving"

Bowls of steamy noodles, tomato sauce, and Parmesan cheese in the kitchen beckoned. She stuck her gum to its usual spot, the corner of the kitchen table, and filled her plate. Four of the bodies showed no signs of physical trauma. Only the young victim, Female 1, exhibited extensive wounds. She had been crushed by a car or other type of large vehicle. This made no sense. Her mother didn't drive. Did her mother have an accomplice? "Rule nothing out," Zera always told her. Since there was no evidence of physical violence on four of the victims, did Wanda kill them by poison? Lisa paused in spinning the noodles around her fork. No ... no way her mother would poison her. They were bonded; they were as close as a mother and daughter could be.

"So what's happening up at the Herssen place?" Wanda asked.

Lisa's fork halted in front of her lips. Why did Wanda ask that? To see how much the police knew?

"It's all everyone's talking about," her mother added. "The man who delivered the groceries today told me all about it."

"Oh. What did he say?" she said casually.

"That they found a number of bodies up there."

"That's correct. We don't know who yet."

She just lied to her beloved mother! Well, maybe it was only a partial lie, since the identity of the other four were still unknown. Worse still, she had withheld information from Jay, Will, and Zera. She *did know* the identity of Male 3, whom Zera called the Boxer. The small bit that she knew of Owen was that he had spent his time either at the boxing gym or the Lame Dog Saloon. Decades later the saloon was still frequented by scumbags. The cops kept a wary eye on that dump.

"Mom, did Dad ever come back here? After that fight?"

Wanda seemed to ponder the question before answering. "No. I never saw him again."

"So you never divorced?"

"I wanted to, but I could never locate him."

"Where do you think he is?"

"Rotting in hell somewhere," Wanda said decisively.

Everything about the shed in the woods caused alarm bells to ring in Jay Braden's head. Rope and duct tape found together was never a good sign. There were the usual tools that one might find in a shed: a saw, hammer, screwdrivers, wrenches, and the like. From what he could tell, there was no evidence of blood on the tools, workbench, or ground. The shed was old and dusty, and filled with seasons of leaves since the door had rusted off its hinges long ago. A ladder was in the leaves next to the shed. Was this even Herssen's property? Was this Herssen's shed? Now on top of everything else, his team would have to check the property lines. Like they didn't have enough goddamn work to do. One body was bad enough but five was overwhelming the understaffed police force of River Glen. The forest was a steam box and his sciatica was flaring up again. His doctor had told him that back surgery was required to relieve the compression on a disc, but who the hell had time for that? Scotch and Julia's stories about sultans, rock stars, and the Burning Man Festival were perfect antidotes for pain relief in the evenings, but pain shot up and down his leg throughout the day.

Another burning zing shot toward his Achilles tendon when he bent under the workbench to retrieve a cardboard box. According to a peeling label, the box once held ten reams of 8"x11" jam-free paper for office copy machines. He knelt with a bombastic groan, and lifted the lid.

"What the –? What are these?"

Cylindrical containers of transparent plastic, about six inches long and three inches in diameter were the only items in the box. Air holes in the lids suggested that they were for storing some type of animal. Mice, chipmunks, insects?

He pulled out his phone and sent Will a text. "Found something. Come have a look." The containers were empty except for one. A spider had climbed into it and died. Wait, impossible. The lid was screwed on. Had someone – Herssen? – been collecting spiders? The spider was long dead; some of its brittle legs had broken off. Still, he hesitated in reaching for the plastic cylinder.

"It's dead," he reassured himself.

This was an imposing spider. Goose bumps popped from his skin. It was not the extraordinary size of a tarantula but easily over an inch in size ... closer to two inches. He was not thrilled about bugs in general. No, it was not only bugs that he hated. He hated invertebrates of all phyla. Sea nettles in the Chesapeake were his least favorite. His skin burned just thinking about them.

"It really is dead. Dead spiders don't bite through plastic. Do they?" Best not to touch it. Zera would scold him if his prints were all over the containers.

Where was Will?

Jay gazed across Herssen's overgrown yard to the opposite forest. Will was a local; he would know what the hell the bug was. They definitely didn't have monster spiders like this in Vermont where he had grown up. He checked his phone. Still no text from Will. Poor cell reception in the woods? Or was Will was chatting with Carly, Alex, or Lisa?

Jay's attention returned to the spider. It was macabrely fascinating, as long as he didn't have to touch it. Those fangs would leave a nasty welt. There was faint writing on one of the containers. He used a stick to move it into view. The letters were faded but they appeared to read B Randolph.

Where was Will? It was getting late. The light sifting through the trees was the orange-yellow of late afternoon.

The sun would be over the mouth of the Glen River by now, directly west. The good news was that within an hour or two he would be on Julia's porch, listening to a story about her life in London as a young actress. Maybe tonight's story would be about a wild party that she had attended with Mick Jagger or Peter O'Toole. Were any of them true? Who cared? They were hilarious, especially after a scotch or two.

He texted Zera. "Send a team back to Herssen's. There's a shed in the woods that needs dusting."

He labored to his feet and flexed his back before crossing Herssen's property. Then it dawned on him. Herssen's boat had been called *Atrax*. *Atrax* was a type of spider. From where? Australia? Yes, he was certain that it was Australia. He pulled his cell phone from his pocket again. He typed B Randolph and *Atrax* into the search engine. An impressive list of citations for scholarly papers in entomology journals appeared. Robert Randolph was an expert on spider venoms, in particular, venoms from *Atrax robustus*, the Australian funnel spider. Interesting ... very interesting. Professor Randolph was a faculty member at Tolchester College.

"What? ... that bastard doesn't even have the cojones to tell me in person? Ricardo is breaking off the engagement, dumping me outright ... in a text? All because of Abuelita's ring? Cabrón!"

Nina paced amidst the unpacked boxes. Abuelita had never liked her. Neither had Mamacita. That was obvious from the start. Las brujas were at the center of the conspiracy against her. They never failed to underscore her humble roots and infinite inadequacies. Her mother had worked in a bakery. Ricardo's parents were wealthy ranchers. Her mother had never finished high school, and had been a single parent raising two daughters. Ricardo's parents had MBAs from the University of Texas, and a long, wonderful marriage (they hated each other). She was descended from Guatemalan peasants; Ricardo was a noble mexicano, descended from conquistadors. During every visit to the ranch, Abuelita reminded her of 'la buena suerte asombrosa' in landing Ricardo.

"Pendejos ... todos!"

Nina sniffled into a tissue – with her one functioning hand! How the hell she was going to afford a two-bedroom apartment on her miserable salary? What was she going to do with a king-sized bed and an ugly computer workstation that she had bought for two hundred bucks? Since she and Alex had built the thing, no way the store would let her return it now. And Alex had tossed the box into the dumpster before leaving on her motorcycle the night before. Like she really had the inclination to climb into a filthy dumpster to retrieve the box, disassemble the computer table, and repack it ... all with one hand! The only consolation in this catastrophic mess was that she had not purchased kitchenware with a southwest design. That's all she saw at the ranch house ... southwest designs. Her new plates would have blue crabs and sailboats. Bowls and cups with the Baltimore Orioles logo, that ridiculously happy bird, would be preferable to a goddamn southwestern pattern.

After moping around and blasting music CDs that Ricardo hated, Nina decided to prepare her office for the start of classes next week. She drove to campus and parked in front of the Riddel Building. Burt Sweeny was at his usual post, smoking a cigarette by the door of the Security Office.

He gave her a bleak nod. Her nod back was equally bleak. She glanced worriedly at the turrets. Perhaps she should ask Dean Wines if she could use start-up funds to purchase a hardhat for entering and exiting the treacherous building. That's all she needed – on top of malaria, zika, and a lost finger – a concussion, or worst, permanent brain damage. The gulls appeared to be dozing on their various perches, yet she still dashed through the front door to avoid any razor-sharp projectiles.

Brad Smyth's anthems of la Revolución were absent from the hallway, but music came from Griffin Blake's office. It was music from her mother's era. In fact her mother had this same CD, Neil Young's *Harvest*, which Ricardo hated and complained about whenever she played it. Griffin stuck his head out his door when she stuck the key in her door. He had covered up Sheila Myers' nameplate with a 8"x11" paper that read Dr. Griffin Blake, Assistant Professor of Sociology. Under his name in rainbow colored letters read PRIDE.

"I put in a work order for a new nameplate, but Brad Smyth told me not to bother," Griffin said. "He said it would take forever."

"I guess I should cover up Bob Randolph's name and add my own. That way students can find me."

"You definitely don't look like a Bob Randolph. Come in and see how I decorated my office."

"Alright." She dropped her backpack on her desk and walked next door.

Griffin had the same plastic funnel taped to his ceiling that drained into the same type of plastic trashcan, though his office lacked the stale water smell that permeated hers. He had obviously been cleaning. Paper towels and lemon cleanser were on his windowsill. It was an old office like hers but meticulously clean and organized. A pine-scented candle burned on his bookshelf.

She turned to a poster of a tropical paradise. "Where's this?"

"The Florida Keys. My father was an executive for General Motors, but he hated corporate life so he divorced my mother, moved to the Keys and opened a coffee shop in Marathon."

She looked at his bookshelf in the center of his office. "This is a great idea."

"I moved it to separate the room into two distinct spaces. That's my personal work space back there." He pointed to the area with a desk and fold-up camping cot.

"And sleep," she jested.

"Yeah, my living arrangements fell through. The woman I was going to rent from is a homophobe. I've been sleeping here and showering at the gym."

"You can stay at my place until you find something else. I have an extra room."

"But your fiancé?"

Nina's vocal chords tightened. "There's no fiancé anymore."

"I'm really sorry ..."

"Don't be." She turned back to Griffin's office arrangement to distract herself. He had positioned two chairs and a table by the window. "So you meet with students there. I really like this."

"Do you want to do the same with your office? I can help you move your desk and bookshelf."

"Would you? That would be great. And can you help me dump the malarial water in the trashcan?"

He grinned. "Of course."

They entered her office.

"Ugh, this place reeks." He grimaced, grabbed the trashcan, and hurried to the men's room. He returned a moment later. "Where do you want your desk?"

She pointed. "There. And the bookshelf there, to divide the room like you did."

They dragged the desk to one wall. Then they positioned the bookshelf to serve as a partition in the middle of the room.

"Hey, there's something taped to the back of your bookshelf."

"Really?" She craned her head around the back.

Yellow tape crackled and fell to the floor when he peeled it off.

"What is it?"

"A document of some sort."

They leaned their heads together. It was the Annual Report of the Finance Committee, written by the two co-chairs of the committee, Drs. Bob Randolph and Sheila Myers, six years ago.

The silence was deafening. Jay couldn't remember where he had heard that phrase, but it circled like a mad dog in his thoughts. Will's non-responsiveness had a horrible familiarity. It felt too much like that day two summers before, when that psychopath Clyde Whitby slaughtered his beloved Laura, shot his own cousin Desmond Whitby at point-blank range, then sprayed the *Vital Spark* with bullets, nearly killing Will and Alex. It was he who had assigned Will to security detail to the Allaway women during Randy Allaway's murder investigation. It was Will who took a bullet in the shoulder, attempting to get a wounded Water Boy into the boat. Will was almost a third fatality that day. And it was Alex, who amid Clyde Whitby's gunfire, had crawled to the water cannon and blasted him across the Chesapeake. His body was never recovered. Pyrate gold in Clyde's wet suit had dragged him to the bottom, Alex had reported during the inquest. People imagine crazy bullshit when under extreme duress. He and Will were police officers who understood that they might point their gun at another human being and end their life. But how does the civilian brain get around the fact that they had killed someone, even in self-defense?

This was no time to dwell on the past. Jay flung open the trunk of the car and pulled his shoulder holster and pistol up his arm. Forensics and another police cruiser would be arriving at any time, but he was not waiting a second longer to find Will. He ran toward the forest.

The silence from Lisa Paco was equally disconcerting. Her usual modus operandi was to report epiphanies about the case by rapid-fire texts or a gum-smacking stream-of-consciousness-running-monologue throughout the day. That day she had gone to the morgue to look at the bodies and to speak with Zera. That was normal enough. But for the rest of the day, she had worked in uncharacteristic silence behind her computer before springing from her chair and announcing that she needed to check on her ill mother. Dead bodies thrilled Lisa; never before was she so uncommunicative.

Jay located the narrow pathway that Will had taken into the forest. He probably should have waited for backup as he might be in the killer's sights at this very moment, though the probability that the perp was in the forest on this exact one hundred degree afternoon was unlikely. The alleged lights at Herssen's place had only been seen at night. Besides, no killer would be so stupid or brazen to hang around while police were combing over the place.

"Will?"

No response. Will had definitely come this way as the underbrush was tamped down.

"Will?!"

Jay followed massive footprints down an embankment. Only a giant like Will wore such a large shoe. Will had definitely been this way. Jay faltered. Up the trail the ground literally disappeared. He moved gingerly forward, gliding his feet, inch by inch, as so not to collapse the soil, just like Julia had instructed him to do while dancing the tango.

"Running water doesn't stomp, lad. Glide your feet like you're ice-skating."

Despite his boyhood in the north, he had hated ice-skating on the town pond. His ankles always buckled. He ended up ass-cold on the ice, pucks and sticks clattering around him, slicing skate blades just missing his fingers as he scrambled to his feet like a wobbly-legged fawn. Instead, he took up ice-fishing, conveniently by the girls doing pirouettes and carving figure eights at the pond's edge.

Jay got down on his hands and knees and peered over the edge. Some mother-fucker had placed a meshwork of branches over a deep pit that had collapsed in on itself. No, it wasn't a pit at all. It was more like a funnel, a very deep, steep-walled funnel. It was impossible to climb out of unless someone was a particularly skilled climber. At the bottom was a wood chair with leather restraints, reminiscent to an electric chair.   Next to the chair, covered with sticks and leaves, was Will Wilkins.

Exhausted, Levon Bakanian turned the key to his apartment.   It had been two days of stress and emotional upheaval.   The first stressor was his talk at Tolchester last night; the second stressor had been slogging around Turtle Island that day in suffocating heat. Nothing was turning out as expected.   His plan when moving to River Glen was that he and Alex Allaway might cruise around the bay in her beat-up tugboat, searching for Giles Blood-hand's treasure.   If he could bed her, all the better.   Instead, a descendant of the sadistic pyrate captain "Hangman" Bartholomew Dodd turned up at his lecture – a hot babe who invited him back to her yacht for champagne.   The evening was full of amazing revelations.

First, Pamela Dodd's library of pyrate literature on the *Knot-A-Care* far eclipsed his own collection – that he had thought, until that moment, substantial. Second, Pamela had incredible recall, reciting passages from scholarly papers – including his works – verbatim, and even the page numbers upon which the quotes were located.   Her IQ was probably double that of Alex's.   While perusing Pamela's bookshelves, his annoyance at Alex lingered.   Her faux pas at his lecture was unforgivable.

More astonishing was Pam's news that Bart Dodd had survived the shark attack in Tampa Bay.   Up to that point in time, Levon had read nothing further about the fate of the pyrate captain.   Historians had presumed Dodd dead.   Pam had led him to a stateroom that served as her personal office and showed him a .pdf on her laptop. The original document was in a safe at her home in South Beach, she had explained.

According to the rare chronicle, Captain Dodd had been nursed back to life by a Calusa woman with whom he later had children. A band of Spanish soldiers and missionaries who passed through the Indian village had recorded Dodd's account of the seizure of the treasure galleon *El Espíritu de la Virgen* by the pyrates of the *Raven*, and the subsequent mutiny led by the power-hungry Giles Hale. Dodd had implored the Spaniards to pursue the *Raven* and retrieve the stolen treasure.

"The ship was heading up the coast, to the Carolinas and colonies beyond. Take me with you," the deposed Captain Dodd had pleaded. "Let me assist in capturing and hanging Giles Hale and the vermin of the *Raven*!"

But the Spaniards departed in the night, leaving Dodd and his parchment behind. What became of Giles Hale and the *Raven*, Dodd would never know.

Pam then suggested that their historical discussion continue in her hot tub on the upper deck. The tub was nothing like the puny one his father had bought after being awarded the Insurance Salesman of the Year for Charlotte, North Carolina. This one had jets everywhere and seats in every position. Another bottle of champagne was uncorked. They stripped off their clothes and chatted about Edward Teach, Sam Bellamy, Juan Carlos del Castillo, and Giles Hale until Pam became restless and climbed onto his lap. Not one to look a gift horse in the mouth, he proceeded to pleasure the insatiable beauty to the best of his abilities in the hot tub and then in her gold-plated stateroom, Alex Allaway drifting from memory with each thrust.

That morning Levon had awoken to a breakfast of Bloody Marys, croissants, fruit cocktail, and more fast, furious sex. His new partner spread an array of electronics, including high frequency metal detectors to detect gold, across the deck and said that they were going treasure hunting on Turtle Island. Sure, why not? It was a glorious Saturday and he had found the perfect woman, in fact every man's dream – a wealthy nymphomaniac who loved anything and everything pyrate.

The *Knot-A-Care* had too deep a draft to navigate the tributaries of the Glen River so Pam lowered a *Zodiac* inflatable into the waters of the marina, filled it with equipment and motored upstream. After Alex Allaway's lame-brained public comment, Levon half-expected Turtle Island to be swarming with treasure hunters swishing metal detectors across the sand, but one circle around the small island revealed that they were the only ones there. The *Zodiac* was driven onto the beach and they looked around. A rise in the center of the island was the perfect vantage point from which to survey the terrain, and they immediately spotted what appeared to be the mysterious encampment. Pam gasped with delight and dashed through the underbrush toward it. She was quick and agile and beat him to the site. By the time he had arrived, perspiring and winded – professors were not the most athletic of individuals – she had circled the area and found the remnants of the fire pit.

"This is Giles Hale's camp!" she squealed. "I can feel it! I bet Giles cooked at this very fire!"

They lugged metal detectors from the *Zodiac* to the encampment. Pam started the treasure hunt at one end of the camp, he at the other. The day heated up fast and by mid-morning they were trudging through pockets of gnats and mosquitos.   The hunt was less fun by the second, especially since he was still in his khakis and a dress shirt from last night's lecture. Plus, Pam's incessant whining gave him a headache. On her reckless sprint from the vantage point to the beach below, she had run through poison ivy.

"The urushiol will blister. It might leave scars all over my legs!"

"The what?"

"The urushiol. The irritant, the oil in the sumac." She rolled her eyes at him like he was an ignoramus. In addition to pyrates, she was an expert on oils and skin products.

Pam's metal detector soon pinged and her mood instantly improved. She stared at the monitor. "Four inches down! Here!"

"I guess I'm digging," he muttered.

"Of course."

He stabbed the spade into the sand under her twitching pointer finger.

"Gently!"

"If it's metal, it's not fragile." The sooner he could get a shower in his quiet air-conditioned apartment, drink a cold beer, the better. He got onto his hands and knees over the hole. His fingers grazed the sandy object.

"What is it? What is it?"

He pulled the artifact from the sand. It was very heavy. "A ship's bell."

"Fascinating! Any name on it?"

He brushed the sand off it.   "The date and the ship's name have been scratched away. I was hoping that it read *El Espíritu de la Virgen* or the *Raven,* and even the name of Juan Carlos' stolen sloop *Tereza.* But no such luck."

"Sly bastards. It could be from any of those ships. I bet that the pyrates were trying to conceal its identity. Why would they bury their ship's bell?" she asked in afterthought.

"Who knows? To smelt and make other objects?"

"That makes sense. Many pyrate ships had blacksmiths onboard to repair their weapons." Pam snatched the bell from his hands, laid it in the sand, and photographed it with her smartphone. "I have a nautical archeologist on retainer. He should be able to identify this for us. I'll email him the photos. There's no time to waste!" She lifted her metal detector and hurried to a new area of beach.

The find had perked up Levon also so he headed to an unexplored patch of sand. His metal detector pinged. He dug. This time a rusty belt buckle set off the alarm.

Around noontime the sound of an approaching outboard engine was heard. Levon recognized the boat's occupants immediately. Burt Sweeny, the Tolchester security guard, and his son, wearing a pyrate hat and eye patch, motored toward the beach.

Pam dropped her metal detector, lifted the spade, and strode toward the water's edge. "Get lost! We were here first!"

"Th-this is public game land," Burt said.

"I said get lost! Go look there!" She pointed upriver. "At the Devil's Spit."

"Th-there's nothing at the Spit," Burt argued. "Just swamp and quick sand. This is public land."

She shook the spade in the air. "You step on this island and your boy gets hurt!"

Burt's dark eyes boiled and his doughy body tensed. He glared at Levon who averted his eyes and stared at his sand-encrusted dress shoes.

"Beat it assholes!" she shrieked.

"D-dad, let's go," the boy whimpered.

Burt yanked the outboard. Their boat made a U-turn and they headed up the narrow creek toward the Devil's Spit.

Levon felt sick. Pam's behavior, threatening a boy, was atrocious. Worse, he had done nothing in Burt or the boy's defense. He was pathetic, a coward. He would never be able to look Burt Sweeny in the eye again. His enthusiasm for treasure hunting with Pamela Dodd evaporated. Yet, for three more hours he had carried on. He had moved to River Glen to look for treasure. Then fuck it, he would look for treasure ... despite the bug bites, lukewarm water bottles, soggy fruit for lunch, his horrid partner ...

By the end of the afternoon they had located: a ship's bell, an old buckle, a statue of the Eiffel Tower that read made in China, and a small wooden treasure chest with metal pieces of eight that had been purchased in *Ye Olde Gift Shoppe of River Glen* for $10.99. To cap off the miserable day, a text from Pam's archeologist friend said that the bronze bell was from a ship of the Revenue Cutter Service, the predecessor to the US Coast Guard. The bell was casted long after the Golden Age of Piracy. There were countless bells like this one on *ebay*; it was completely worthless.

That bit of news shut down Pam's speculations for the rest of the afternoon. She drove the *Zodiac* back to the *Knot-A-Care* and unloaded the equipment in sizzling silence.

"I'm going the find that cunt that sent us on this wild goose chase," she said in a lethal tone.

Fortunately he had never mentioned Alex's name throughout the evening. He had kept his cards close to his chest, discussing only widely read, well-known pyrate literature.

"She didn't send us," he said. "She mentioned the site, but we went on our own volition. This has nothing to do with her."

Pam eyed him suspiciously. "Wrong. She knows exactly where the treasure is."

"Ridiculous," he said perhaps too quickly. "It was just a passing comment at a Q & A session. Nothing more."

"She knows. I'm sure of it."

"How?" The evil in her smile sent a chill up his spine.

"At your lecture, she mentioned a place where Giles Hale hid the Allaway and Hale families on the night of the Whitby family murder.   Never, ever in all of my readings and researches, did I ever hear of Giles doing that."

Levon shuddered. Neither had he.

Plunk ... plunk. Will felt something drop onto his head. Carly always tossed popcorn on his head when he fell asleep during one of her Disney princess movies. He blinked away the dirt. This was definitely not his parents' living room and thankfully Carly was not with him in this dark pit of roots and soil. He spit dirt from his mouth. Another *plunk* on his head. He twisted and attempted to stand, but a sharp pain shot through his ankle. It was his bad leg with his bad knee – the one he had blown out playing football at Maryland. He brushed debris off his head and arms, and struggled onto his one functioning foot. He blinked upward into a circle of sunlight and green canopy. Jay and Zera peered down at him from the edge of the circle.

"Should we help him out?" Jay asked Zera.

Jay grinned and *plunked* another pebble onto Will's head for good measure.

Tired as he was, Levon Bakanian felt compelled to talk to Alex Allaway that evening. Alex had made an innocent comment about Turtle Island, but Pamela Dodd was right. There was no mention anywhere in the literature about Giles Hale taking the Allaway and Hale families to an island while he returned to slaughter the Whitbys. But it made perfect sense. The murderous Neville Whitby jabbing Charles Allaway's severed head onto a pike would have prompted such a cautious action in Giles. Giles' first impulse would have been to protect his family and Allaway's wife and children. After all, Charles Allaway was his best friend. Giles and Charles had grown up in the same rural village in Scotland. Every step of their adventure, starting with their impulsive teenage lark to Edinburgh, the bar fight that landed them in Old Tolbooth Prison, the prison break, and their pyrating forays in the Americas would have created an unbreakable bond between the young men. Giles would have shielded their families from the bloodbath that was to ensue in River Glen when he put Neville, Emmaline, and their two children under the knife. Alex, somewhere, had come upon this information. Levon just needed to know where. Then he would let Pamela know of the document. As far as he was concerned it was another piece of the historical puzzle solved. In the spirit of scholarship, academics willingly shared their historical sources. No harm, no foul. All would soon be settled. Pamela would cease and desist. Alex was a friend of Nina's. Nina was a neighbor and a colleague. He would smooth everything over.

On Monday morning he would go to the Security Office, seek out Burt Sweeny and apologize for his companion's horrible behavior.   He had seen enough of Pamela Dodd. Their professional and physical partnership was over.   Once Pamela was given the source of Giles' information he would distance himself from her once and for all.   And with any luck, she would turn the *Knot-A-Care* down the Chesapeake and head south for the winter with the snowbirds.

Levon knew where Alex lived because he had seen her walk home after a number of Giles Blood-hand festivals. Her home could be seen from the River Glen bridge in the middle of town.   She lived near the Point in a wooded area that consisted of two homes and a dock where she tied up the *Vital Spark*.   Hers was the smaller of the two homes, the cottage. It was dark when he crossed the bridge. He slowed his car on the river road. This he had to watch.

Alex was on the porch of her next-door-neighbor, an older woman.   The two of them were sparing, each flicking an épée. The older woman was tremendously skilled, in fact, from what he could tell, expert. She was instructing Alex on proper technique; she paused to reposition Alex's hand and feet. Alex nodded from behind her fencing mask.   The instruction period over, the two went at each other, leaping around chairs and knocking over cocktail tables. The older woman fenced with great flair, whacking at flags hanging from the eaves and effortlessly fending off Alex's spastic attack. He rolled down his window to listen. Metal clicking, the woman's boisterous baiting laughter, Alex's pants and curses, and cricket song mixed in the summer night. Levon was enchanted.

The combined efforts of Jay, Zera, and a forensic scientist were required to pull Will from the pit because he was six six and weighed two hundred and fifty pounds. Will could only use his arms and one good leg to assist in extracting himself from the hole. His left ankle throbbed. When he was pulled over the edge of the pit, Zera confirmed his worse fears. She pulled up his trouser leg, rolled down his sock, and applied pressure in various spots.

"Yow!"

"It's broken, Will."

He moaned again, though this time at the dreary news. This meant dreaded desk duty. The best part of his job was being out and about with Jay conducting interviews. It was Lisa who loved cyber-sleuthing at headquarters with Norman from IT. An injury during the most interesting case of his career! Five bodies had been buried on Henry Herssen's property and he would be stuck inside, listening to the secretary Cloris complain about her cat's hairballs. If not Cloris, then it would be the state trooper Denny rambling about his wife's orthodontia.

En route to the Emergency Center in Middletown, Delaware, Will realized that his cell phone was missing. It had to be somewhere in the woods, or in the pit. With any luck, someone on Zera's team would find it and return it to him. But now he had no way to contact Alex and finish his text to her. His impulse was to ask Jay if he could borrow his phone, except that Jay always growled at him and Lisa about making personal texts and calls while on the clock. Even if Jay said yes, sending Alex a romance text from his boss' cell phone wasn't the smartest of things. What if Alex thought the text was from Jay? Jay was ruggedly handsome and had a way with women. What if Alex sent an amorous message back to Jay? What a colossal mess that would be. The text would have to wait.

By the time he and Jay hung around the ER and an orthopedic specialist set his ankle, it was early evening. Carly, his sister, and mother were at the family's condo in Rehoboth Beach for the weekend. At this time of night Carly and her cousins would be bouncing under the neon lights of the boardwalk, cotton candy or popcorn in hand. Perhaps they were already on the spinning rides at Funland. Invariably one child would throw up.

Since Carly was away, this evening would be the perfect opportunity to talk to Alex alone. She might help him wrap his cast with a plastic bag so he could shower and wash the dirt from his hair and ears. Then they could eat crab cakes at the Hoffman's Dockside Café since Alex only had energy drinks, rum, and Twinkies in her cottage. Harry Hoffman knew how to make the perfect crab cake. Will's pet peeve in life were crab cakes with too much breading ... so few cooks knew how to make a really decent crab cake. Then he would blurt, "Alex, I'm madly in love with you."   With any luck, Alex would throw her arms around him, press her mouth against his, and their conversation might culminate in the bedroom. Their celebration would be a bit hindered by his cumbersome cast, but that was okay. Alex liked it on top.

"Sir, can you drop me off at Alex's?" Will could barely mask his elation. They passed the sign to River Glen, Population 86, a village of happy eccentrics. He and his beloved lived in the best town in America.

"Works for me. I'll see if Julia's up for dinner."

"Alex can drop me off at headquarters tomorrow to get my car."

Maybe tomorrow, after a day behind his computer at headquarters, he and Alex could go to the Hot Tub City factory outlet. If they were building an addition, they might as well build a deck with a hot tub.

"Spiders, Will.   I don't know how, but this case is all about Bob Randolph and his spiders."

With a hot tub, he and Alex could ...

"Will?"

"Hmm ..."

"Are you with me?"

"What?"

"Spiders."

"Oh, yes, right. Do you think that Herssen and Randolph were raising spiders together?"

Jay frowned. "Don't know, but tomorrow I'm checking out Tolchester College."

Their unmarked cruiser rattled across the bridge and turned down the river road. The front door light at Alex's cottage was on. Julia's porch was also illuminated. Julia was on her porch, smoking a cigarette from her black cigarette holder. Will's eyes jumped back to Alex's doorway. Alex was under the light, talking to a dark-haired man in a festive tropical shirt. The man lifted Alex's hand and pressed it to his lips.

"Um, maybe you should drop me at my parent's place," he told Jay.

Julia Hale placed her binoculars on the windowsill and turned toward the TV. The ten o'clock news glowed in the darkness of her living room. One irksome bit, among many, about the American news was that it broadcasted the weather report in the last two minutes of the program. That meant an insufferable twenty-eight minutes of local politics and other provincial nonsense until the single important piece of information – The Weather. To Americans, the continents of Asia, Africa and South America were as remote as Mars or Jupiter. If the events on those continents did not impact Americans ability to shop or eat, they had no relevance whatsoever. Thank God for the BBC news at eleven o'clock from a station in Philly that reassured her that the rest of the planet beyond North America still existed. Yes, the Brits knew how to do the news, but alas, those Americans …

The meteorologist at the Hurricane Watch Center drew her interest. Tropical Storm Beau amassing near Bermuda had three proposed trajectories: Virginia Beach, the mouth of the Delaware Bay, or Long Island. Sustained surface winds were currently averaging sixty-eight miles per hour, not enough to be upgraded to hurricane status.

A storm following Trajectory Number 2, traveling up the Delaware, would impact the waterfront village of River Glen and swell its shallow river. Her home and Alex's cottage were less than twenty yards from the river's edge and built long before building codes mandated after Hurricane Katrina.

Yes, storms were brewing literally and figuratively. The psychic Luna had portended it. Days ago she had visited Luna to discuss their upcoming road trip out West – the Burning Man festival had become an annual event – when Will's father John dropped by to pull buds off the *Cannabis* plants in Luna's basement. Spread across her crab trap table was an ominous pattern of Tarot cards.

"Changes coming," said Luna breathlessly. She mixed a concoction of rue, copal and osha. "Changes in the wind.

Follow me!" The three of them rushed outside and sprinkled a Mayan anti-evil remedy along the town docks.

So far, so good. Tropical Storm Beau was just that, a tropical storm, but other storms were brewing. Julia turned off the TV and returned to her sentry post at the window. The room was now in darkness. She took a long sip of Royal Lochnagar and lifted the binoculars to her eyes.

Alex's front step was dark and empty. But who was the swarthy stranger who had kissed her granddaughter's hand earlier that evening?

And who was the strawberry blonde, staring back at her at this very minute from behind her binoculars, on the deck of that white motor yacht in the marina?

CHAPTER SIX
Sunday

Lisa Paco slyly slipped another piece of gum from her pocket. If Jay saw her chew a fourth piece of gum on the short ride to Tolchester College, he would know that something was up. He was observant like that. She faced out the passenger side window and chewed slow, very slow, imperceptibly slow. All the while she suppressed the urge to stuff the whole pack in her mouth, and chew frantically until her jaws ached. She wanted to unroll the car window and scream at the top of her lungs. The pent-up tension was that intense. The birds in the cornfield would burst into the sky. Jay would pull the cruiser onto the shoulder and say "Lisa, what the fuck?"

Her mother Wanda had murdered her husband roughly twenty years ago. That fact was plain enough. Lisa had seen the skeleton of Owen Paco on Zera Lim's stainless steel examination table. How creepy was that! But how had Wanda done it? And who were the other four bodies that her mother had cast into the earthen pit? Lisa knew that her mother was smart, but until last night, she was uncomprehending of the depth of her mother's stealth and intelligence. All the while, as they had eaten spaghetti, done dishes, then watched a DVD of *Inspector George Gently*, she watched her mother from the corner of her eye. What a clever disguise, a middle-aged woman with MS who makes bread and watches Frank Sinatra concerts on You Tube all day long. Ingenious actually. And she, Maryland's goddess of crime-solving, second only to Zera Lim, had no clue how Wanda had done it. No clue whatsoever! That was the most frustrating thing of all. She could barely concentrate on Inspector Gently and John Bacchus closing in on the killer. Then her mother held up her needlepoint.

"What do you think, Lisa? I'm making Aunt Helen a pillow for her birthday."

Lisa could hardly focus on the seagull, buoy, and blue crabs stitched into the fabric. "It's beautiful, Mom." She had suppressed saying 'Brilliant touch, Serial Killer, the needle point.'

Could the man at the sewing store be Wanda's accomplice? He was very fond of her mother and always gave her discounts on thread and yarn. He had a black windowless van with which they could transport dead bodies.

Lisa glanced briefly at Jay. He bore a vague resemblance to the silver-haired George Gently, except that Jay's face was beaten up from his days as a cop in Baltimore. He had broken his nose twice, and had a scar across his chin from a brawl with a heroin dealer. If Jay had been in the movies, he would have hung out with Charles Bronson and Clint Eastwood characters, none of the wimps and pretty boys that were in the movies nowadays. Ben Affleck, yeah, right.

Maybe Jay, Will, and Zera were closing in on Wanda at this moment. Maybe they were saying nothing to Lisa because they didn't want to tip their hand and reveal their damning evidence against the mother of one of their colleagues. Since the State of Maryland no longer had a death penalty, Wanda would be served with multiple life sentences for the five murders. In prison there would be no more murder mystery watching, no more bread-making, and no more Frank Sinatra. The prison warden might let her mother continue her needlepoint, unless he was a sick bastard like Warden Norton in the *Shawshank Redemption*. The absence of daily sleuthing and the crooning of Old Blue Eyes would invariably cause her mother to go insane.

What do to? What do to!

"Stop smacking your gum so loudly," Jay said. "You know it bugs the shit out of me."

"Yes, sir."

What to do! This was a moral dilemma, and a moral dilemma of gargantuan proportions. Jay had told her and Will that moral dilemmas, not criminals, were the toughest part of the job. Turn in her own mother?

"Lisa ..."

"Okay, okay!"

No way could she turn in her mother – absolutely impossible! Wanda was the best mother in the world, even if she was a cold-blooded killer. There was no choice here. She would protect her mother at any cost. All she needed was time, time, time ...

Jay handed her an empty Stryofoam cup. "Spit it out."

"I promise I'll stop!"

"Now."

"Please?"

"Now!"

Lisa spit her gum into the cup as they passed the ornate sign for Tolchester College.

Eureka! She would identify some person at Tolchester with a dubious past and pin the crimes on him or her. This would be her plan. In *Inspector Morse*, the killer was always a pompous Oxford dean or chancellor. Maybe the president of Tolchester was a dominatrix with a kinky sex den in the basement of the Administration Building. In *Midsomer Murders*, the murderer was always a creepy groundskeeper whose hobby was taxidermy. No doubt they would discover that the entire English Department was in bed together. And artists were always devious, usually blackmailers or forgers.

Who knows what she might uncover at Tolchester College, to draw suspicion away from Wanda?

This was the single morning of the year that Hank Stupens dreaded the most, the breakfast meeting at President Mary Blodgen's elegant Georgian home on the back corner of the campus. Breakfast with the First Line Staff was an annual event held the Sunday morning before the Monday when classes started. It would be an insufferable hour or two for a number of reasons. First, he was the only male amidst the three old crones. Dean Lana Hinkie was a manipulative bitch, and Dean Gloria Wines was a self-absorbed dolt who posted selfies on Facebook daily, if not of her parakeets. The more he knew of academics, the greater his certainty that PhD stood for Phenomenal Dunces.

Hank was testy for another reason. President Blodgen had postponed his summer vacation. "You're invaluable to me, Hank. Next week, I promise." Even he if could slip away for a day or two, the trout would be fished out of the streams of the Poconos by now. Instead, she had him supervise the placement of "the Learning Lodges," aka the trailers in the field, and a renovation of the men's rooms in the Riddel Building. The bathroom tiles that she had chosen were on back-order which meant waiting around for two weeks ... when he could have been trout fishing! To pass the time, he had fixed the dripping faucets in the chemistry lab and the sink in Blodgen's basement. His brief moments of pleasure all summer were in the weight room of the Athletic Building since no students were around. The singular piece of good news was that he could now bench-press one hundred and eighty-five pounds.

Since it was a Sunday and the campus quiet, Blodgen had allowed them to 'dress down' so Hank didn't have to wear a strangling shirt and tie. The meeting was held in the president's sunroom that had a view to the bay; it was a room he knew all too well, since he or one of his crew cleaned the countless glass panes every spring and fall, and watered her begonias weekly. Blodgen was a botanist in her former life before administration. Lana Hinkie had been a Communications professor and Gloria Wines' specialization was Women's Studies, whatever the hell that was. As usual Gloria had to finger all of the pastries before deciding that she shouldn't be eating carbs at all. He had to agree; her ass was as wide as a horse.

All Lana wanted to talk about was the bodies found on Henry Herssen's property, but President Blodgen reminded them that "We have many important agenda items to cover. Fortunately the murders occurred far away from the college and shouldn't impact our recruitment efforts." Then Blodgen commended Lana – once again – on "the superlative efforts at bringing in so large a freshmen class." Lana inappropriately gloated. The truth of the matter was that she had ground her young admissions team into the dirt.

She wouldn't even reimburse them for gasoline for their travels to the high schools around the mid-Atlantic region. "Budgets are so tight this year. You can do this for the team."

Blodgen's next agenda item was the College Accreditation Board's visit to Tolchester that past spring. The accreditation board had gigged them for a hiring a disproportionate number of adjuncts and paying them the lowest wages on the eastern shore, the lack of minority representation on the faculty, and insufficient space for academic activities.

"The new academic space, the five Learning Lodges will certainly impress the accreditation board members during their next visit," Blodgen said cheerfully.

"They look like trailers in a field to me," Gloria said.

Hank silently agreed. They were in fact just trailers in a field. If a student needed to use the bathroom, they would have to traipse through the heat, rain, or snow to the closest building, Riddel. The consolation was that they would get to pee in bathrooms with new salmon pink tiles.

"Gloria, Gloria, where's your imagination?" Blodgen sighed. "The Learning Lodge ... it has such a lovely ring to it. I thought that up myself. Lana, you will have our student tour guides call them Learning Lodges, won't you?"

"Yes, yes, Mary," Lana said, brown-nosing again.

Blodgen smiled. "The accreditation board will be pleased to know that we had a very successful year replacing our retired faculty with diverse candidates. Though the new math professor, Boris Yulak is a white male, we can claim him as a diversity candidate on the EOP forms since he's Russian and was born in Murmansk. I think Bakanian is an Armenian name so we can list Levon as another international faculty member. Do you think it matters that he was born in North Carolina?   The psychologist, Joanne Trent is an African American and a female, and Nina Vega is Hispanic and a female, so with Joanne and Nina we can tick off two boxes.   Blake Griffin is unfortunately another white male but fortunately a homosexual."

"I thought his name was Griffin Blake," Lana said.

"I'm sure it's Blake Griffin," Blodgen insisted.

Gloria eyed the pastries. "Oh, does it matter?"

"I do want to meet with Nina Vega about her hand, and offer her some type of compensation," Blodgen said.   "I do wish she had filled out a work order about the roof. We put such noble efforts into improving our online forms. Gloria, perhaps you might add another thousand dollars to her startup funds."

"Why does it always have to come out of my budget? Lana's the one with all the money?   These new faculty are eating up my budget with their computer and software requests!"

"They do need to do their research," Blodgen said calmly. "It's our job to support them to the fullest so that they get tenure. The accreditation board was quite adamant that we increase our tenure-line numbers and reduce the number of adjuncts. This has strained my salary budget considerably. Perhaps I might contribute two hundred and fifty dollars from the President's Discretionary Fund."

Blood vessels popped from Gloria's forehead. "Only two hundred and fifty?"

"Okay, Gloria, calm down," said Blodgen in a grandmotherly tone. "I'm sure I can come up with five hundred for Nina."

"Nine-ah," Lana smirked.

"What?" Blodgen said.

Lana tittered. "Nine-ah. Nina can change her name to Nine-ah since she now has nine fingers."

"That's not funny!" Gloria cried.

"Ladies, ladies ..." Blodgen said. The front door bell chimed. "Oh, who could that be?" She glanced at her watch. "Hank, would you like to get that?"

"Of course." He was grateful for a reprieve from the deans' chatter. He walked the polished hallway that his janitorial crew waxed weekly. At the door was that lazy-ass Burt Sweeny, and behind him, a plain-clothed cop and a young female cop in uniform. Since the tragic death of Sweeny's wife, Blodgen didn't have the heart to fire him, even though he did little else but chain-smoke cigarettes and watch seagulls on the turrets.

The cop with the hard face presented his badge. It read Jay Braden of the River Glen PD. The mousy female was Sergeant Lisa Paco. "I'm looking for the academic dean, Gloria Wines," Braden said. "I heard she was here."

Hank glared at Sweeny, who must have divulged that information, and ordered him back to the Security Office. He led the two detectives to the sunroom. President Blodgen and the two deans rose at the interruption, and Braden and Paco flashed their badges once again. Blodgen introduced her staff and offered the officers pastries. Braden passed, but Paco grabbed a scone, one that Gloria had already handled.

Braden turned directly to Gloria. "We're looking for information on Dr. Robert Randolph. You were his immediate supervisor."

"Is he a suspect in the murder investigation at the cliffs?" Lana butt in.

"We're information gathering." Braden's steely-eyed gaze bore into Gloria Wines.

Gloria tightened. "Uh, ur, I barely remember him. I believe he retired the same year that I took this job. Six years ago. Was he in the Science Division, Mary?"

"Yes, he was a biologist."

"An entomologist," Braden said to jog their memories.

Blodgen nodded. "Yes, you're right."

"How long was he employed here?" Braden asked.

Gloria swooped down on a pastry. "I don't know. My only meeting with him was during the exit interview." She bit off a huge piece.

"I remember him very well," Lana interrupted again. "Bob was here for decades. He was very active in the faculty senate and other important committees. He was all over campus. He came to all of the events sponsored by Student Life, despite his bad ankle or knee. He walked with a cane."

"Yes, Lana's right. He was one of our more outstanding faculty members. A lovely man," Blodgen said.

"I'd like to see his research lab," Braden said.

"We're just a small undergraduate teaching institution," Blodgen explained. "We have student teaching labs for physics, chemistry and biology, but they're not for faculty research. Many of our science faculty, who have specific equipment requirements, form affiliations with research labs around the area. At the University of Delaware, Temple, Penn, and so on."

"And Randolph worked with whom?" Braden asked Blodgen and Hinkie. He clearly realized that Gloria knew next to nothing.

Blodgen's face wrinkled in thought. "Do you remember, Lana?"

"No, but we attended one of his lectures together. It was on spiders. Don't you remember?"

"Yes, yes, now I remember! It was a most interesting lecture. We don't have enough lectures on the sciences on campus, biology in particular. All everyone wants to hear about is our pyrate history."

Paco looked up from her iPad. "Bob Randolph's publications were with Dr. David Towers at the University of Maryland Eastern Shore."

"UMES was a former agricultural college," Blodgen said. "That makes sense that they would have entomologists on their staff."

Braden turned to him. "You are again?"

"Hank Stupens, the Director of Business Services."

"Then you have a master key and can show me Randolph's office?"

"It's been renovated since Randolph left and it's now occupied by another faculty member," Hank said.

"I'd still like to see it."

Hank looked questioningly at Blodgen.

"Yes, of course," Blodgen answered. "Please show him the office, Hank."

"It's one in the Rainforest," he said hesitantly.

"Rainforest?" the cop said.

"The Rainforest is the thorn in my side, Mr. Braden," Blodgen said with an ironic chuckle. "The Riddel Building is very old and has a leaky roof. Rain drips in with every big storm. I keep looking for a donor to fix the roof, but most donors only want to support our athletic teams."

The walk across the college campus flooded Jay with bittersweet memories. His perfect romance started his freshman year at the University of Vermont. His roommate had been the amiable, if not dim-witted, baseball player Troy Blackwell. Troy's sister, a sophomore and art major at Middlebury College, made a surprise appearance at their dorm one Friday afternoon in late September. Jay had answered the door.

"Just dropped by to check on my little brother, my bad boy, Troy," said the smiling girl in the hallway. Her "little brother" was six four and had a fastball clocked at ninety-three miles per hour.

He stared, she stared, he stared, she stared ...

"Are you going to let me in?" she finally asked.

"Sir, we'll need to talk to David Towers next," Lisa Paco murmured to him.

"Um, yes."

Jay wasn't sure why but President Blodgen and the two deans had decided to go with them to the Riddel Building. A brooding Hank Stupens led the group across the campus. Stupens obviously spent a lot of time at the gym. Lisa Paco's eyes moved guardedly between her iPad and his broad back. Surly macho men unnerved Paco for some reason.

The President's house was on the far side of the campus so they walked toward the college center on a series of crisscrossing sidewalks. The mosquitos were out in force and Jay smacked one off his ear. The mosquitos off Lake Champlain during Troy's scrimmage with the University of Maine had been out in force that Saturday afternoon. Jay had begged and pleaded with that kid from New York City to take his hours in the university cafeteria where he worked. No way he could leave lovely Laura Blackwell to watch the ballgame alone.   Thankfully the New Yorker needed the money and filled in for him that afternoon.   More amazing luck – UV beat UM so Troy and his teammates spent the evening at the beer-sticky bar of the frat house, singing "Take me out to the ballgame" and doing shots of anything and everything. Troy's abandonment of Laura for his frat brothers meant that she was unattended to once again. Jay wasn't much of a dancer but if Laura wanted to dance, then hey, he was more than willing to give it a go. He and Laura danced for the entire party. Before Troy was unable to stand, he and Laura slung Troy's arms over their shoulders and they carried him back to the dorm, but not before Troy puked twice in the bushes.

Hank Stupens veered off the sidewalk and headed toward a trashcan. Some students had used the trashcan as a basketball hoop. Either they had horrible hand-eye coordination or were drunk, possibly both, because beer cans littered the grass around the trashcan.

"Not members of your basketball team, I hope," Jay said.

Stupens shot him disgusted look, dropped the empties in the trashcan, wiped his hands on his Dockers, and wordlessly walked on.

President Blodgen guffawed. "Amusing, Mr. Braden! No, we're not even Division II."

Why wouldn't Blodgen be happy? She was making 350K a year and had a free house on campus with a beautiful view to the bay. She probably drove a college-leased vehicle to boot.

There was no life in the Tolchester dormitory building at that early hour on a Sunday morning, but the cooks were busy in the cafeteria because the humid air smelled like institutional food.   Jay remembered that oily smell all too well.

That night at the UV dorm, he and Laura had tucked Troy into bed, but not before Laura put a trashcan next to her brother's bed.

"Done this before, Jay," she said.

Laura was wildly spontaneous and unorganized in all things – it was part of her charm – and had decided to take a road-trip to see her brother without bringing pajamas so Jay gave her a pair of clean sweatpants and t-shirt to sleep in. He had insisted that she take his bed so he slept on the floor with Troy's blanket and pillow because Troy was too plastered to miss them.

The next morning he took Laura to breakfast at a diner. She couldn't hang around UV, she had explained; she had to get back to Middlebury for play try-outs that afternoon.

"No way I'm good enough to get the part of Lady Macbeth, but how cool would it be to play one of the witches?"

"You'll definitely get a part." Laura was perfect after all.

Laura looked demurely over her coffee mug. "Jay ..."

"What?"

"... my roommate has a homie and goes home most weekends ... if you ever want to visit me ..."

Jay vaguely listened to Dean Hinkie's remarks about a mud-wrestling event on Student Welcome Day. Blodgen and Hinkie giggled like schoolgirls. Wines was clearly the odd-girl-out in that conversation and too engrossed by her smartphone to care.

"The wayward Sisters, hand in hand, Posters of the Sea and Land ..." he whispered to Lisa.

She understood the allusion to the weird sisters immediately. Any literature pertaining to murder she had read an infinite number of times. She grinned. "Fair is foul, and foul is fair ..."

Riddel Building loomed in front of them. It was a diabolical structure of decaying stone, crooked gutters, and treacherous turrets. The roof was a nesting site for seagulls. Burt Sweeny slouched against the door of the Security Office, smoking a cigarette. Sad, sad night, Jay recalled. He and Will had to break the horrible news to Burt about his wife Debbie.

They followed Hank Stupens up two flights of stairs to the second floor, down a grimy hallway that once was occupied by the ROTC, and around the corner to Room 205. A paper taped to the door read: Dr. Nina Vega, Assistant Professor of Sociology. Jay puzzled over it. Why was that name so familiar?

"Mary, I told you it was Griffin Blake." Dean Hinkie rapped smugly on the door next to Vega's office.

Stupens opened the door to 205 with his master key.

Jay stepped into the office and grimaced. The room had a mildew odor. "What is this?" Funnel spiders, funnel-shaped pits in the forest, and now this, funnel-shaped heavy-duty plastic draining rainwater into a plastic trashcan.

"That's why we call these offices the Rainforest," Stupens said.

"I'm working tirelessly to find a donor to replace this roof," Blodgen said. "Fund-raising is such an exciting challenge!"

"How did *this* ever get by the Accreditation Board?" Wines said incredulously.

"*You've* never seen this before?" Jay was equally astounded that the academic dean was unaware of her faculty's shitty working conditions.

"No. Why would I?" Wines said indignantly.

Jay frowned again. "How *did* this by an accreditation board?"

Many people were very allergic to mold spores, Laura being one of them. And the whole building was covered in dust. Not to mention water-borne hazards associated with stagnant water. He peered into the plastic trashcan. It had been emptied recently. He turned to Stupens for an explanation, but the man shrugged and deferred to his boss once again.

"We were having problems with the plumbing in the men's room last spring," Blodgen said. "We closed down this building during the board's visit. The men's rooms were renovated over the summer so they're pristine and lovely now. Salmon pink speaks to a sense of physical tranquility."

"Lisa, take some pictures of this office," he said. "I want to see the other offices."

Stupens opened them. The office next to Vega's on the right was covered in pictures of Fidel Castro, Che Guavara, Catalina Adrianzen, Salvador Allende, and the like. It was Brad Smyth's. Jay knew Brad from around the village. Brad was one of Gary Smyth's sons, from the Smyth Family Marina. The Smyths were one of the original pyrate families that founded River Glen, along with the Collinses, Wilkinses and the Allaways.

The office on the opposite side of Vega's belonged to Griffin Blake who seemed a bit of a neatnik. The two sociologists Blake and Vega had decided to arrange their offices identically by using a bookshelf to separate their desk from the space where they met with students.

Jay made his way down to the end of hallway where Stupens stood by the door. The sign on the door read Levon Bakanian, PhD, Associate Professor of American History. "Open it."

"I'd rather not," Stupens said.

"Why not?"

"Okay, but be careful." Stupens cracked open the door.

Jay peeked through the opening. Lisa craned her head around his to look as well. The walls were covered with pyrate posters, maps, and flags, but the air swarmed with bees. "Jesus!" He slammed the door closed.

"What?" Blodgen asked.

"The bees," Stupens said irritably. "They're back."

"Oh dear, those tiresome bees," Blodgen sighed. "Call the exterminator again, Hank. Today, if possible so they're gone by tomorrow. We don't want any students getting stung."

He and Lisa returned to Vega's office and circled it one more time. "Ms. Wines, I'm going to need any files on Bob Randolph that you may have."

"Doctor," she snapped.

"What?"

"Doctor or Dean Wines," she said.

Jay scowled. "Is there anything else any of you can tell me about Bob Randolph?"

"I liked Bob," Hinkie said. "Great teacher. The students loved him."

Paco gazed into Vega's trashcan. "Where did Randolph go after he retired?"

The administrators looked blankly at one another.

"Sadly we sometimes lose touch with our dear colleagues once they retire," Blodgen said.

"Bob had an RV that he drove to different locations to collect bugs," Hinkie said. "I do remember that. He loved that RV."

"You're right, Lana. He did," Blodgen agreed.

"Do you know how Randolph might have known Henry Herssen?" Jay asked the group.

"Who's Herssen?" Wines asked Blodgen. "Was he here before my time?"

"I don't remember a person named Herssen working here," Blodgen said. "But my memory's not what it used to be."

"No, no, Mary. Herssen's place is where the police found the bodies. Aren't you following this on the news?" Hinkie turned to Jay. "Do you think that Bob had anything to do with those murders by the cliffs?"

"Shame." Lisa lifted bits of a shattered coffee mug from Vega's trash. She scanned the floor for fragments of pottery. Her eyes travel up the back of the bookshelf. "Dr. Vega broke her coffee cup."

"And a lovely southwest design at that," Blodgen said. "Gloria, let's order her a new one. From my budget. As compensation."

"Compensation for what?" Jay asked.

"Dr. Vega had a bit of a mishap with a slate from the roof," Blodgen said.

Lisa Paco snapped one more photo of Nina Vega's office with her iPad before Hank Stupens closed the office doors and they left the Riddel Building.

Jay and Lisa swung by the Administration Building where Dean Wines gave them a file folder on Bob Randolph and a list of faculty names and addresses going back forty years. The disparity between the dirty, mildewed faculty offices in the Riddel Building and the pristine mahogany-walled offices of the deans was staggering. They left the building and passed the dean's reserved parking spaces en route to their police cruiser. Just as Jay suspected, President Blodgen drove a college-leased luxury car, a Lexus. Lana Hinkie drove a Mercedes Benz, and Gloria Wines an Audi sports car convertible.

"I should have gone into college administration," he said facetiously. "I would have bought myself a Lamborghini."

"Me, a burgundy Jaguar Mark 2 like Inspector Morse's," Lisa said. "Where next, sir?"

"Headquarters. I want us to pour through everything related to Bob Randolph. His spider containers were in Herssen's shed. I want to know why. Let's also try to reach his colleague David Towers at UMES."

They climbed into their cruiser in the visitor's lot.

"I think we should stop by and talk to Nina Vega first." She scanned the faculty addresses. "She lives close by, at the Driftwood Apartments."

"Why?"

"Here's why." Lisa opened the photos on her iPad. "These are the pictures I took of Vega's office. The furniture had recently been moved because the imprints in the carpeting were still fresh. See? There."

He leaned across the front seat.

"The bookshelf had been against the far wall. There. But it had been moved to form the partition. Look there." She enlarged the image of the bookshelf. "Something, like a

8x11 document, had been taped to the back of the bookshelf. You can see the border of scotch tape. There. The document had been removed very recently because fragments of scotch tape still remained on the floor. They hadn't been vacuumed up yet. I noticed the tape fragments when I was looking for the pieces of the broken coffee cup. There were no pottery shards on the carpeting. That cup broke when someone tossed it into the trashcan, perhaps intentionally. All the shards were in the bottom of the trashcan."

"So where's the document?"

"There." Lisa pointed to a photo of Vega's desk that was covered with books and papers.

He squinted at the iPad. "Can you see what it is?"

She tried to enlarge the image, but there was no clarity. "This camera doesn't have enough resolution."

"We're still on campus. Let's go back for it."

"It's long gone by now."

Jay's eyebrow rose. "Meaning?"

"Look." She swiped to the last photo taken in Vega's office. "Just as we were leaving, I took another shot of the desk."

He stared at the image. The corner of the desk where the document had been was empty.

"Any one of the Weird Sisters could have slipped the document into their purse," she said. "Or, the Weird Sisters or Hank Stupens could have slipped it into a drawer or onto a shelf for later retrieval. But the fact of the matter was that the document was there, and then it wasn't."

"A document doesn't vanish into thin air by itself. It had help."

Jay jumbled the car keys in his hand, thinking. The group of them had moved in and out of Smyth, Vega, and

Blake's offices for about fifteen-minutes, and then ever so briefly peeked into Bakanian's bee-infested room. Vega's office had remained open for the entire time. When they had walked en mass over to the Administration Building, the three women carried purses, but Hank Stupens only carried a ring of building keys in his hands. One of them had lifted or hidden the document. That fact was clear enough. By now it had likely been run through an office shredder, never to be seen by human eyes again. At least Nina Vega would be able to tell them what it was.

Ah, yes … now Jay remembered where he had heard the name Nina Vega. Vega was on the boat with Alex when they discovered the bones in the cliff. He had even seen Vega briefly when Alex helped her out of her pickup and led her into the cottage on the day of her injury. And Julia had mentioned making breakfast for Alex and a girlfriend. The friend had hurt her hand in freak accident and had had trouble eating the pancakes that Julia had made them. Crazy small world, River Glen.

So far, so good, Nina Vega told herself. She and Griffin Blake had survived compatibly for nearly a day. It was a good idea mentioning to him that she needed an apartment mate to share expenses. They had agreed to give the living arrangement a go for a month. If incompatible, they would cut their loses and move on. A month would give Griffin time to search for another place. He had moved his camping cot and bags into the spare bedroom the evening before. His only conspicuous quirk was his germaphobia. He had scrubbed the whole apartment with disinfectant wipes despite her telling him that she had already done the bathroom and kitchen.

'No, she had not done the doorknobs, the banister to the upstairs, or the light bulbs in the lamps hanging over the kitchen island.' If cleaning the apartment once again would give him peace-of-mind, then knock yourself out. Better compulsively neat than a slob like that shithead Ricardo, who had expected her and his sisters to wait on him hand and foot.

That morning, while Griffin headed out to the farmers' market for fresh fruit and produce – he only ate paleo and organic – Nina decided to make pan dulce. Her mother was a master baker and taught her and her sister Juanita her craft. It wasn't the easiest task in the world to knead dough with one hand, but baking always soothed her. The Pendejo Ricardo had not contacted her and she was not about to contact him. Griffin had been a pleasant distraction and had great taste in music. She admonished herself for stereotyping, but she half-expected his music collection to contain Cher, Mariah Carey, the Bee Gees and other artists that she supposed gay men listened to; instead his CDs contained Neil Young, the Cure, the Red Hot Chili Peppers, and Death Cab for Cutie.

Nina's doorbell rang. Maybe Griffin had forgotten his apartment key. She peered through the peephole. It was a stern man with snow-white hair, and a petite uniformed police officer with thick glasses and shoulder-length brown hair. Oh my god, had something happened to Juanita? Why else would the police want to talk to her? Nina's stomach knotted as she opened the door.

"Dr. Vega, I'm Detective Braden, and this is Detective Paco."

Braden looked vaguely familiar but from where? From the hospital's ER when she was out of it? "Have we met before?"

"No, not formerly, but I was at Julia Hale's house when Alex brought you home from the hospital."

"Julia Hale?"

"Alex's grandmother."

"Oh, I remember now." Pancakes, sultans, jeweled spiders – throbbing hand.

"Are you feeling better? How's your hand healing up?"

"It's getting better. Is everything okay with Juanita? She hasn't been in a car accident or anything?"

"Who's Juanita?"

"My sister who lives in Houston."

"Juanita's fine as far as we know."

A car door slammed in the parking lot. Griffin crossed the parking lot with bags of groceries. He slowed when he saw the cops.

"Can we come in for a minute?" Braden asked. "We need to ask you some questions about your office at Tolchester."

"Yes, of course." Nina stood aside and let the two detectives and Griffin enter. "I'm so relieved. I thought that something had happened to Juanita. She has two small children ... I'm sorry, I'm rambling. I'd offer you a chair, but we're still moving in. I haven't bought furniture yet."

Griffin dropped the bags on the kitchen island and returned to the living room.

Braden turned toward Griffin. "And you are?"

"Griffin Blake, Nina's apartment mate." He offered his hand to the cops. "I work with Nina at Tolchester."

"You have the office next to hers," Braden stated.

"Yes. Has something happened there?" Griffin asked.

"No. We're making inquiries about Bob Randolph who previously occupied Dr. Vega's office."

"Yes, his plate's still on my door."

"And yet he retired six years ago. Do you know why no one occupied it before now?"

She shook her head.

"And you?" Braden asked Griffin.

"No clue. We're both new. Our first day is tomorrow."

"And you two recently rearranged your offices in the same way," Braden continued.

"Yes," Griffin said.

"When?"

"Yesterday afternoon."

"Something was taped to the back of your bookshelf, Dr. Vega."

"Yes."

"I pulled it off," Griffin said.

"What was it?"

"It was a report from the Finance Committee, written six years ago," Griffin replied.

"What did it contain?"

"We just leafed through it," Nina said. "It was just columns of numbers. Then we got busy moving things again. We decided that we would look at it later. It had to be something interesting if it was hidden away like that."

"Who wrote it? Did it say?" Braden asked.

"Yes, the committee co-chairs. Bob Randolph and the business professor who occupied my office, Sheila Myers," Griffin said.

Jay dropped Lisa off at headquarters with orders that she and Will were to contact Drs. Bob Randolph, Sheila Myers, and David Towers. In an age of smartphones, conversations with all of them should be completed by day's end, even on a Sunday. The facts about this case were multiplying faster than could be imagined. Bones, funnel-shaped pits, spider containers, mysterious finance reports. None of it felt right. He headed to the Smyth Family Marina where Brad Smyth lived. He passed behind the Nauticus to reach the marina, and parked next to the boat ramp. It started to drizzle as he walked down floating dock B. He passed the Carver 38 *Margaritaville*, the Albin aftcabin *Mistress*, the Ranger Tug 32 *Crabby One*, and the magnificent motor yacht *Knot-A-Care* from South Beach. He glanced up at the yacht, hoping to catch a glimpse of the strawberry blonde who climbed around the boat all summer, clad only in a string bikini. Sadly, she was nowhere to be seen. The light rain probably drew her indoors.

Brad Smyth's Gibson houseboat *Banana Republic* floated at the end of the dock. Brad and his wife Judith Ann, the librarian at the historical society, were sitting under an awning on the deck having a late breakfast. Their toy poodles Rocky and Adrian sped down the dock and jumped up and down Jay's leg until Judith Ann called them off. The dogs were the terrors of the dog park; their yips and nips annoyed Miranda to no end. If the poodles mysteriously went missing, Jay was sure that he would have to arrest Julia.

Brad pulled another patio chair to the table, and offered him a Bloody Mary and bagel. He declined the Bloody Mary as he was on duty but said 'yes' to the bagel and a glass of orange juice. Then he asked Brad about Robert Randolph.

"I knew Bob as much as one knew a professional colleague," Brad said. "He was an outstanding scholar, a full professor. He was an expert on the venom glands in spiders and the mechanisms of venom secretion."

"Do you know his colleague David Towers?"

"Yes. I met Dave when he visited the campus to discuss data with Bob. Bob was also an excellent teacher and had won the college teaching award on several occasions. He taught General Biology and Invertebrate Zoology."

"His committee work?"

"He was an active member of the faculty senate."

"Finance Committee?"

"Sorry, I don't know for sure. But that would seem a logical fit because Bob was committed to administrative transparency."

"Is there a wife? Children?"

"Nope. Bob was a bachelor. He often visited a sister for the holidays."

"Are you in touch him? Is he still in the area?"

"I have no idea where he settled after he retired, but he had mentioned traveling around the country in his RV."

"So you haven't seen him at all since he retired?"

"No, but I wished we'd kept in touch. He was a great guy. He's sorely missed."

"And no one's occupied his office during the past six years?"

"No. Probably because of the leaky roof. Our blood-sucking administration only hired adjuncts and paid them slave wages, until recently. Then the Accreditation Board gave them a scathing evaluation that forced them to hire a new group of full-time faculty. There was no other office space available so the deans assigned them to the Riddel

Building. Blake, Vega, Trent, Bakanian, Yulak, the whole lot of them, went into the Rainforest. It's nice to see new faces. They seem like a good group."

"And Sheila Myers?"

"Another full professor on my hall. Sheila and Bob retired the same year. The two of them were inseparable. They wandered between their two offices all day, talking politics and sharing types of tea. She was widowed. I half suspected that she and Bob might settle down together, but they kept it professional."

"She taught ...?"

"Business Ethics and Forensic Accounting. But she wasn't a popular teacher like Bob was. In fact, her courses had a very high attrition rate. She was a stickler for detail, an absolute perfectionist. I liked her. She was extremely knowledgeable and a competent scholar. But the students saw her as an irascible old witch. And her appearance matched."

"How so?"

"Her wrinkles had wrinkles. Her warts had warts. She had fiery red hair, her one vanity, which she continued to dye even into her sixties. And she was deformed, a hunchback."

"What did Bob look like?"

"A giant. A basketball player in college. He was six four or five. He loved talking basketball. His hip progressively deteriorated in later years so he walked with a cane."

Jay nodded. Dean Hinkie had also mentioned Bob's cane. "When was the last time you saw Sheila or Bob?"

"At the campus retirement party President Blodgen held for them and other senior faculty who were retiring that year. The party was held in Blodgen's sunroom." Brad shrugged.

"I guess that's all I can tell you. Both Sheila and Bob were nice folks, good colleagues."

Jay swilled down the last of his orange juice and stood. "This was really helpful. If you can think of anything else, give me a buzz."

"Will do."

"And thanks for the breakfast. I notice you're not dressed as a communist dictator today." He'd seen Brad, dressed in olive drab guerilla attire, dining with Judith Ann at the Dockside Café on a number of occasions after work.

Brad looked down at his shorts and t-shirt and grinned. "I only wear my junta wear during the work week. The outfits go right up Dean Wines' ass. She's an insufferable religious conservative. My communist revolutionary persona ensures that she leaves me alone and doesn't ask me to be on any useless committees that she chairs. It leaves me time to write my books."

Jay chuckled and pulled his raincoat hood over his head. "Academics. Too clever for their own good."

Brad smirked. "Some of us anyway."

Alex Allaway was astounded at her own stupidity. Her parents Colin and Carole were an architect and lawyer, respectively, so they must have had an inherent level of intelligence. It seemed unlikely that there was a genetic basis to her idiocy. It had to be environment factors. That was it. Not nature; it was nurture. It was her inhaling second-hand weed smoke from Papa Randy and Old Ben's bong or joint during her infancy and childhood. Yes, that was it – arrested development during critical formative years. When she first saw Will, it was at the bus stop; she was a second grader and he was in kindergarten. Because she got held back twice, once in elementary school, and again in junior high – though Randy was partially to blame for that – she and Will ended up graduating in the same class, even though she was two years older. Definitely ... the second-hand weed smoke was the reason for her ditziness, her being punctuality-challenged, her inability to match clothes ... and blurting out moronic things in public!

"Alex, can you tell me where you read about the island where Giles Hale hid his and Allaway's family on the night he murdered the Whitbys?" Levon Bakanian had asked on her front step. "I've never read that before. Has a new document been discovered? I'd love to read it."

Jesus Christ, did she step in it this time!

She knew exactly where she had read it. But the source could never, ever be revealed as it would incriminate Julia and Aunt Beatrice in Aberdeen, incriminate all of them ... the secret society of pyrates in River Glen ... it would acknowledge the existence of the River Glen treasure.

Instead, she had stood there with her hair in disarray from the fencing mask, her t-shirt sweaty from the sword-play while Water Boy gnawed her shoelaces. Levon had looked awesome in his tropical shirt with Ford Woodies and palm trees. Like she wasn't flustered enough ... Levon's was the same aphrodisiac aftershave that Will wore ... that drove her wild. At that moment she couldn't get inside fast enough, have a swig of rum, eat a Twinkie, and take a cold shower.

She had hemmed and hawed, then stuttered a bit, while shaking Water Boy off her shoelaces. Finally she concocted a bullshit response.

"I think I heard that on a ghost walk years ago. They have these creepy ghost walks every October through the graveyard and the village. But who knows what's true? I think those guys make up a lot of stuff to make the story more authentic."

"Ghost walks sound like fun." Levon had smiled his dashing smile. His white teeth glowed bright white, his blue eyes glowed bright blue. "Maybe we could go on one this fall?"

"Sorry. But once was enough for me. I have a low threshold for terror. They have some guy dress up as a headless Charles Allaway who staggers from behind the gravestones. Everyone screams at the top of their lungs. I can hear the shrieks every Halloween, even from here."

Levon laughed. "That is scary. Maybe we could just take a walk during the daylight so you can show me the old headstones. Maybe tomorrow? Maybe get some food after?"

Alex had balked. Over Levon's shoulder, Julia was smoking and pacing the porch. She could already hear Julia's warning: "Watch your back, lass, be careful, watch your back."

Where was Will? There was still no response from him, even after three texts. Whatever he had to say, he was dithering; he was too pained to tell her. She glanced back at Julia. It was definitely not cool having her grandmother live next door, surveilling and opining on her every movement. Levon was a harmless historian. She could befriend whomever she wanted. It was none of Julia's goddamn business.

"Alex, could we take a walk to the headstones tomorrow?" Levon repeated.

"Yeah. Okay."

"Great. At noon?"

"Okay. Noon's fine."

Then Levon had completely disarmed her. He lifted her hand to his lips. "I'll look forward to it." He departed with a pleasant wave.

Jay returned to headquarters to find Lisa, Will, and Denny the state trooper standing in front of Will's laptop. Their eyes were fixed on the spiraling storm that had passed Bermuda and was racing toward the Atlantic coastline.

"Winds at ninety-five miles per hour. It's now officially Hurricane Beau," Lisa said.

"Yeah, yeah." Jay moved in front of the crime board. Rain and wind were irrelevancies when he had five bodies in various stages of decomposition to identity and a sick bastard to catch. He was almost certain of the identity of Female 2 and Male 1, but he wanted to see what his young colleagues had found. "Any word from Sheila Myers or Bob Randolph?"

"No," Lisa answered.

"Hmm."

"The phone company has no record of either of them having phones in years," Lisa said. "I spoke with Bob Randolph's research associate David Towers. He's also retired and lives locally in Queen Anne. I emailed Towers an image of the dead spider you found in the shed. He said that it was definitely an *Atrax* and a male, though significantly larger than most he'd seen. He and Bob Randolph worked on the mechanism of envenomation together for over three decades. The spiders produce a venom called delta-atracotoxin or robustoxin. He was shocked that there was an

Atrax found outside of a laboratory. These are controlled animals since they're not a local species. They're found only in the area surrounding Sydney, Australia. They're actually called the Sydney funnel-spider. It's the male spiders of the species that are the most toxic. Most bites are by males who wander out of their nests searching for females. Females don't produce enough venom to cause death. The bite, he said, is very painful due to the large fang size, and the acid in the venom. People rarely die of these bites anymore since the production of the anti-venom."

"When was the last time Towers saw Randolph?"

"Six years. Towers had meant to go to the retirement party for Randolph at the college, but his wife got ill and he couldn't make it. He was saddened that Bob hadn't kept in touch. He said that it wasn't like Bob not to return his emails or texts. They'd been close collaborators for decades. Bob was supposedly heading south in his RV to collect black widow spiders in the southern states and bring them back to Towers' lab."

"Did you check on Randolph's sister?"

"Yes. Eve and brother-in-law, Kenneth Cupper, live in Myrtle Beach, South Carolina. Will spoke with her."

Will flipped through his notes. "Randolph was supposed to have visited Eve in Myrtle Beach, but he never appeared. Eve filed a missing person's report when he didn't show up. Randolph had called her from the Big Meadows campground in Shenandoah National Park. He told her that was going to drive down the Skyline Drive south, then cut over to the coast to see her. Local police interviewed a park ranger who had reported seeing a tall man with a cane walking around the Big Meadows campground in the evenings. Randolph's

RV was then seen on a security camera exiting the park onto Route 211, heading west toward Luray."

"Not east toward the coast? You're sure?"

"Yes, sir."

"Where was Randolph seen next?"

"Nowhere after that."

Jay's gaze returned to the photographs of decomposed bodies taped to the crime board.

Female 1 age 20? 4 yrs in ground
Female 2 age 65? 6 yrs in grd
Male 1 age 65? 6 yrs in grd
Male 2 age 40? 20-25 yrs in grd
Male 3 age 40? 20-25 yrs in grd

"But Randolph's RV was located months later, without plates, in the back of a junkyard near Front Royal, Virginia," Will said. "The only prints on it were Randolph's."

"Do you have footage of the RV leaving the park?"

"Yes. The Virginia state police had it filed under Cold Cases." Will turned his laptop. "Here."

Jay leaned toward the laptop. The driver was wearing sunglasses and a black hoodie, gender unidentifiable. The time stamp read June 13 4:32 pm, six summers before this one. "No one wears a hoodie in Virginia in June," he grumbled. "My hunch is that that's not Bob Randolph." He walked to the crime board and tapped his pencil next to *Male 1 age 65? 6 yrs in grd*. "But that is."

Perhaps Levon wouldn't notice if one of her socks was red and the other was brown. Many males had red-green color blindness; Alex could only hope that he had that sex-linked trait. She had spent the last few minutes on her hands and knees by the washer and dryer, searching for the missing socks, but they had vanished. Was it an electromagnetic force attracted to the static-cling in socks that pulled them into a black hole of missing socks, or simply a washing machine gremlin with a voracious appetite for elastic polymers? And why did the gremlin not eat two of the same color? Why just a red and brown, or a blue and a yellow? Was this intentional, done to frustrate her and leave her with no choice but to wear mismatched socks on any given day? A knock at her cottage door distracted her from pondering the issue. She opened the door.

"Hey, Levon. Come on in. I'm almost ready. I just need to find my shoes." She circled the living room in her stocking feet. "Water Boy uses my sneakers as chew toys. He has a weird oral fixation that compels him up to chew everything up."

"It's raining. You might want to wear boots."

Levon was wearing a raincoat and rubber walking shoes. His socks matched. No sock gremlins in his apartment.

"Oh, okay. My boots are probably in my bedroom." She started toward the back of the cottage.

"They're there." Levon pointed toward the foyer.

Her boots were neatly placed next to her half-eaten flip-flops. Will must have done that in an attempt to help her organize. He always did small kind things ... like remove her salt and pepper shakers from the living room floor and return them to the kitchen table ... pick up her bra and thong from the hammock outside and put them in the dirty clothes basket. Wordless, helpful things. She had found the perfect man – no texts at all from him that day – and lost him.

She tugged on her boots and raincoat, then strapped Water Boy into his raincoat and attached his leash.

They set off. The River Glen cemetery was a short walk, up the river road in the opposite direction to the Point, in a dense forest. By the time she and Levon passed under the wrought iron entryway the drizzle had become a steady rain. Levon did most of the talking – about his research in an archive in Madrid for his recent manuscript on the disappearance of Juan Carlos del Castillo and the sloop *Tereza* once in the Chesapeake. Had the crew died of a highly contagious infectious disease, a 17th century plague? Or had they been slaughtered by Nanticokes, Choptanks, Pocomokes, or another indigenous tribe?

How had an entire ship of pyrates up and disappeared?

Alex listened half-heartedly because she was feeling glum about life in general … about Nina's lost finger, absent texts from Will, bodies in the cliff, odd socks, and the impending storm. She hated to be the pessimist, but she had never noticed headstones of any Spanish pyrates in the cemetery. If there had ever been Spaniards in the upper Chesapeake, they might have sailed up the west side of the bay, without noticing the Glen River to the east. But she was willing to have a look. She glanced at her cell phone once again. Still no word from Will.

It really was nothing, she told herself. Will was bogged down with the skeletons in the cliff. He was very busy catching a serial killer. There was no other woman. She had a minimal level of attractiveness; she vaguely resembled Julia who was in-your-face gorgeous. She was a scrawny, gawky copy of her grandmother. A number of men in River Glen had asked her out before she started seeing Will. But that was because she was the only single woman in River

Glen under the age of sixty. Everything was fine with Will; he was just too busy to call. After the history walk through the cemetery with Levon … that's all it was after all, not a date, just a history walk … she would be an adult and invite Will over to dinner. She would tell him her true feelings, and propose the idea of co-habitation. Maybe if the rain stopped, they could take a walk into the woods behind her cottage and he could indulge her peculiar fetish – outdoor sex. Will was always a good sport about it. All would be settled.

"All of the pyrate gravestones are in the back," she said.

She approached a marble obelisk. It read Todd and Janet Allaway, and the next line, David and Debra Allaway. Under the name of her great-uncle Jason Allaway, who was killed in Vietnam, were letters carved into the stone from the summer of 2017. "Randall Allaway, my grandfather," she told Levon. "My father Colin was buried in Philadelphia, with my mother Carole, and her family." The flowers at the base of the obelisk that she and Julia delivered monthly were old and dry and needed replacing.

She and Levon wound through trees and gravestones, moving back in time through the 1800s, 1700s, to the 1600s. In the back corner, bordered by a crumbling stone wall, the oldest headstones appeared like an old man's teeth, chipped, cracked, and toppled. Many inscriptions were shrouded with moss, others worn away by the revolutions of time.

"Here's the pyrate burial site," she said.

"Spooky."

"Yeah, especially in the rain. You can see that the pyrates had developed an organized society since they were cutting headstones for one another."

"All the same names all over the place," he observed. "Allaways, Wilkins, Collinses and Smyths. All pyrates from the *Raven*."

She stopped in front of one singular stone. "Look at this one. They always keep this headstone clear of moss for the ghost walks." She shuddered; she had an inexplicable feeling of being watched. She searched the misty forest but saw no one. She and Levon were completely alone.

Levon read the epitaph aloud:

Charles Innes Allaway
1663-1694
Here lies a pyrate rotten and dead,
Rest for eternity without ye head

"Incredible!" he said. "Incredible to have read about this murder and then see the headstone of Charles Allaway with my own eyes. It gives the decapitation a horrible immediacy."

She pointed to another gravestone. "Look there."

Neville Whitby
Wife Emmaline
Children John and Sara
Memento mori 1694

"Those four murders were the handiwork of Giles Blood-hand," she said grimly. "The Avenger."

Wind and torrents of rain lashed Alex and Levon on their walk back from the cemetery. Water Boy whimpered the whole time. Alex begged off on lunch with the excuse that she needed to fix the lines on the *Vital Spark* before the gales became dangerous. Alice Hoffman, who owned the Dockside Café, was gossipy and would inevitably tell Will's mother Belle Wilkins, aka the village busy-body, that she had lunch with Another Man. That's all she needed; another reason for Belle to hate her. Besides, Levon didn't seem particularly interested in lunch with her after all. Her carrying of Water Boy's plastic bag of poop back from the graveyard was certainly unappetizing. Or maybe it was her mismatched socks, in case he wasn't color blind. It could be any of a thousand things. Before Levon left, he asked her once again about Giles Hale's sequestration of the Hale and Allaway families on an island while Giles returned to slay the four Whitbys.

Best to stick with the same story from the previous night. "I must have heard it on a ghost walk."

"Do you remember when?"

"Maybe when I was in junior high school?"

"Do you remember the name of ghost walk company?

"Who knows? Tour companies come and go."

The responses seemed to satisfy him. He left with a "thanks for the walk," and a wave. His car disappeared down the river road.

From Levon's perspective, the graveyard walk had been hugely helpful in his research on Juan Carlos del Castillo. Two tantalizing bits of information had been uncovered at the pyrate burial site ... tangible proof that the Spanish, or at least two Spaniards, had made it this far up the Chesapeake.

First, the headstone of Barnaby Wilkins, the young carpenter on the *Raven*, revealed that he had a Spanish wife named Consuela. Second, they had located a gravestone that belonged to one Diego Alvarez del Castillo who died in 1698 at the age of twenty-eight.   Alex had never noticed that particular gravestone because it was in the far corner, off by itself and partially overgrown by a rhododendron bush. Juan Carlos and Diego Alvarez were both from Castillo.   Could they have been related? That coincidence thrilled Levon.

Once at the cottage, Alex removed Water Boy's raincoat and dried him off. She gave him a peanut butter-filled bone to gnaw on for the afternoon while she ate a lunch of Twinkies. To remove the chill of the walk, she made herself a rum drink and slid into a bubble bath.

"Ah, heaven." She leaned her head back and closed her eyes.

Diego Alvarez was not a pyrate on the *Raven*; of that she was sure. Before moving to River Glen, Julia and her Aunt Beatrice had worked diligently to transcribe and digitize Giles Hale's memoir that his father Sir Edmund Hale had urged him to recount upon his return to Scotland.   The account of Giles' extraordinary adventures in the Americas was incredible in detail. After all, Giles had been too ill to occupy himself with work, and spent endless hours talking to Sir Edmund and his scribe. Giles was in a race against time. His hardships at sea, battle wounds, and tropical diseases were wasting away his frail body.

Giles' memoir included vivid descriptions of the treacherous pyrate enclave of Avispero (aka The Hornet's Nest) on an undisclosed island in today's Bahamas, and life aboard the *Raven*. The looting of the treasure from *El Espíritu de la Virgen*, the mutiny that led to the death of the cruel Captain Dodd, the *Raven*'s flight up the Atlantic seaboard, the acquisition of the indentured women at the Virginia tobacco farm, and their settling in the hidden river on the upper Chesapeake, all occurred in 1688. Included in the memoir were the personalities of the original settlers of River Glen, in short, the entire crew of the *Raven.*

The pivotal events in the creation of the Giles Blood-hand myth occurred in 1694. The pyrates and their brides had lived on the banks of the Glen River for six peaceful years, starting in 1688. During these years families had formed and children were born. Then Emmaline Whitby poisoned Abigail Collins and Tess Smyth, the wives of Huw Collins and Angus Smyth. Emmaline and her husband Neville vehemently denied the accusation, yet the poison foxglove was found in the Whitby's hut. The verdict of the village tribunal was that the Whitbys be banished from River Glen. That night in a rage, Neville murdered Charles Allaway who headed up the tribunal, and jammed Allaway's severed head onto a pike in front of the tavern run by Giles and his wife Kathleen Noonan. Gold from the village treasury was also missing.

Alex reached for her Baltimore Ravens mug sitting on the lid of the toilet. She took a long ponderous sip of rum and coke.

"Spotting Allaway's head on the pike, Giles feared for the safety of Allaway's wife, Shannon and children, and rowed them and his own family out to an island for safe keeping."

This is where Alex had read this – in Giles' memoir that Julia and Aunt Beatrice had digitized. She, Julia, and Beatrice had copies of the document in their assorted laptops, while the original manuscript crumbled away in a safety deposit box in Aberdeen, Scotland.

After hiding the two families on the island, Giles had returned to River Glen and hunted down the Whitby family as they attempted to flee with the *Raven's* treasure. He caught up with them at an area now known as the Point. It was a very busy night for Giles Hale. After the slaughter, he rowed the Allaways back to the village, where the widowed Huw Collins and Angus Smyth promised to care for Shannon and her children. Giles returned the stolen gold to the village treasury. But River Glen would never be safe for Hales, not as long as the drunkard brother Conal Whitby still lived. Giles and Kathleen sailed their family up the Elk River. They eventually abandoned the skiff and traveled north by foot to the pyrate town of Philadelphia to await passage back to Scotland. The Hale family arrived in Aberdeen in the spring of 1695.

Alex mentally reviewed the timeline of events once again, but never, she was sure of it, was there a mention of a Spaniard named Diego Alvarez. But that was not surprising. When Diego Alvarez had contact with the pyrate village of River Glen, it was probably years after the Hale family had fled River Glen in 1694. Diego Alvarez had died in 1698 and a villager had cut him a headstone. That much was known. Was Alvarez traveling alone, or with Captain Juan Carlos del Castillo and the crew of the *Tereza*? Levon seemed convinced that he was crew on the *Tereza* since those pyrates were from the Castillo region of Spain. Alvarez died at the age of twenty-eight. Of what? Nothing specific was mentioned on his gravestone. Illness? Murder? What?

Will could hardly believe his eyes. Now it would be impossible to think straight for the rest of the afternoon, if not the rest of his life. He was supposed to be researching a business professor named Sheila Myers that Jay had some hunch about, but how could he possibly think now? Last night a dark stranger was kissing the hand of Alex under her front door light, and now his cell phone had a text message that read: *Will, can we meet at my place for dinner tonight? There's something I want to talk about. Oh BTW I love you. In fact madly.*

Will's eyes were glued to the text. Permanently. Forever. He blinked back tears. Thank you God that a member of Zera Lim's CSI team had found his cell phone in the bottom of the funnel-shaped pit! This was one text that would never be deleted. Upon his death, he would instruct the village lawyer James Collins to have him buried with this same phone, with this same text message in his suit pocket.

Maybe he and Alex would have to purchase two minivans to hold all of *their* children, and build additions onto *their* additions, until the additions snaked across Alex's (*their!*) backyard, all the way to the forest and to the old greenhouse where Randy and Old Ben used to grow marijuana. If *their* family went to Disney World on vacation, should they stay at the Caribbean Beach Resort, or camp at Fort Wilderness? Carly and Alex were of like minds. They would probably opt for the Animal Kingdom.

"How are we doing with Sheila Myers, Will?" Jay said.

Maybe he had been gazing at Alex's text – her proclamation of love – for too conspicuously long. "Fine, sir. I'll be able to give you an update in a moment."

Will rose gingerly, reached for the crutches, and hobbled to the men's room. He prayed that Denny not engage him in chitchat about his wife's new invisible braces while standing at the urinals. He pushed through the bathroom door. He sighed audibly; the bathroom was empty. He whipped the phone out of his pocket and tapped with shaky fingers his response to Alex. When he had played tight-end for the

University of Maryland and caught a game-winning pass in the end zone, he was too shy, too inhibited to spike the ball like Rob Gronkowski, or make a Superman-like gesture like Cam Newton, or do a chicken-dance like other showboaters in the NFL. But he had his own victory dance, performed later when alone in his dorm room. It was the dance of ineffable joy. He couldn't help himself. He hopped around the men's room on his one good foot; one fist pumped the air while he clung onto his crutch with the other. He bent his head back and shouted in silent delight into the fluorescent lights. Who knows how long it took to compose himself? He splashed cold water in his face and dried himself off with a paper towel. He was a detective, he reminded himself, working on five gruesome murders ... but he was so happy! He looked in the mirror and positioned his thrilled face into the most serious, no-nonsense-cop-expression possible. He pushed through the door, prepared to tell Jay about Sheila Myers.

Alex couldn't believe it. She had done it. She sent the text to Will that she had wanted to send for two years. Perhaps it was the liquid courage in the rum, or the eerie flickering on and off of the lights due to the storm, or finding the rare Spanish gravestone that impelled her. Whatever the impetus – it was done! Her commitment issues had nothing to do with Will but had everything to do with Randy who raised her. Her grandfather had been married five times after his first marriage to his one true love Julia. Each subsequent marriage was shorter, more miserable and ill-fated than the one before it. Alex had witnessed the initial euphoria, the stages in between, to the final malaise during the packing and departure. The marriages were for her benefit, she supposed, to provide her with a mother figure since her mother and father were murdered by the deranged Whitby brothers. Randy's strategy was unnecessary. Luna the Psychic was an excellent role model. Alice Hoffman from the Dockside Café had taught her to how to make hush puppies and Swedish pancakes, and Judith Ann Smyth showed her how to water ski.

For agonizing moments of unknown, Alex walked wet circles around her bedroom, imagining a thousand scenarios of why Will wasn't responding. It was probably Jay's fault. He hated when Will or Lisa Paco used their cell phones for personal things while at work. Then her phone vibrated. Finally, a text back from Will.

I count the minutes til dinner. Oh BTW I love you too. In fact madder than madly.

"Yes!" She whipped off her towel and looped it wildly above her head. The swirling motion knocked her plastic pyrate sculpture off the wall. It crashed onto the wood floor and the crossed bones broke apart from the skull with the eye patch. Who cares? She could get a new sculpture when she and Will took Carly and their dozens of children to the gift shop at the Pirates of the Caribbean store at Disney World.

Now what to do? It would be hours until she would see Will. Watch TV? She picked up the clicker. The storm was scrambling the satellite reception so only frozen lines appeared on the screen. She flicked it back off. Now what? Facebook? No ... boring. You Tube? She had watched all of the Flipper re-runs. Prepare a celebratory dinner? Yes, that was it! And get some wine in the village. Yes! And visit James Collins who volunteered at the archives of the River

Glen Historical Society. He and Judith Ann, the librarian, had worked tirelessly to organize and digitize the historical records there. Maybe James could tell her something about a Spaniard named Diego Alvarez.

Alex peered out the window. The wind and rain had picked up. She pulled on her clothes, and then her oilskins and boots.

"You stay here, Water Boy. The storm's too bad." She unlocked the dog door. "If you need to pee, your door's open. But you come right back in." He understood English perfectly. He made no movement to go out in the rain.

"I'm going to James Collins'. Then to the Dockside Café to get crab cakes for dinner, and then I'm getting wine. You stay right here until I get back."

Water Boy listened with minimal interest; the peanut butter-filled bone was too wonderful.

The one thing that Pamela Dodd could not tolerate was disloyalty, from her subordinates at the modeling agency, her friends ... and especially her boy toys. Levon Bakanian had failed to rally in defense of Turtle Island. She – alone – had to repel that father and son from the beach. She had expected that Levon would have raised a metal detector and shaken it in the air, next to her with the threatening spade. She had expected that they would be a united front. But nooo! Instead the Pussy backed away and stared down at his shuffling feet. Then there was his misplaced sense of humor. How was uncovering a fucking Eiffel Tower and toy treasure chest anything less than infuriating? Instead he had laughed ironically when the items were pulled from the sand.

It was not fucking funny!

That local yokel who lured them to Turtle Island was probably watching them from afar with binoculars, muffling her laughter with her hands. Shit, that bitch had probably filmed them! At any second the film might appear on You Tube, with a mortifying title like The Sucker Treasure Hunt! How was she going to explain that to the girls at the South Beach Club? The only things obtained from that humiliating day, besides worthless sandy trinkets, were countless mosquito bites, poison ivy down both legs, and the realization that her treasure hunting partner was less than useless! The poison ivy had just started to blister; the itching was driving her insane. She tried to calm herself by listening to her favorite Tchaikovsky CD – perfect mood music for the crazy storm – but nothing was working.

She paced the boat salon, seething. That redneck crabber Alex Allaway was going to pay!

Allaway's name was easy to find as Pam had seen the *Vital Spark* tie up at the town pier and deliver crabs to the Dockside Café and the Nauticus numerous times. All Pam had to do was walk into Harlow's Pub, bat her eyelashes at the bartender Miles Harlow, and ask him if that crabber on the tugboat might sell her crabs for seafood quiches.

"I bet Alex would," Miles had said. "She knows all of the best crabbing places and sells the largest, freshest crabs."

"Alex what?" She had coyly sipped from a mimosa. She could justify the drink as it only had 75 calories and 0 grams of fat.

"Allaway."

Allaway? Pam's hair bristled. A relative of Charles Allaway that was beheaded by Neville Whitby in 1694? Granddaddy Dodd's chronicle said that it was Giles Hale,

Neville and Conal Whitby, and *Charles Allaway* that had cast him overboard. Another reason to hate that bitch.

"How fascinating! Miles, you're a wealth of knowledge." He would fall for the flattery. She knew the answer to her next question, but she just needed confirmation. "Is she any relation to Charles Allaway from the Giles Blood-hand legend?"

"Yep. There used to be a ton of Allaways in this town, but they've all died out. She's the last living Allaway around here. Here's the interesting thing. She's also a Hale, a direct descendant of Giles Blood-hand."

"Really?" Pam smiled encouragingly. Bartenders were the best source of local gossip and men in their fifties were highly susceptible to attention from younger women, especially hot ones like her. Men were ridiculously weak and easy to manipulate.

"Yep. Pyrate blood flows in that girl, from both her grandparents."

Therefore that pyrate girl would be privy to both Allaway and Hale family documents concerning the whereabouts of the Dodd treasure. How very, very interesting!

A knock at her sliding glass door returned Pam to the present. The disloyal Pussy was standing in his raincoat and rubber rain shoes on her deck. Over his shoulder, in the distance the *Vital Spark* was tethered at that cottage near the Point. She had surveilled that cottage last night with her high-powered binoculars. She had witnessed the sword play between Alex and the older woman who lived next door. The two women were carbon copies of one another. If Alex had the name Allaway that meant that she was an Allaway from her paternal side. Therefore the older woman, clearly a grandmother, must be a Hale! And as a Hale that woman would have access to Hale family documents, and know the whereabouts of the Dodd treasure! There were two sources from which she could ... *extract* ... information.

Last night Pam had witnessed the incomprehensible. Levon Bakanian's car had appeared at Alex Allaway's cottage. He knew her? Yes, it *was Levon* who got out of the car! Never once did he mention that very critical fact, never once during the champagne, the hot tub, rolling in the silk sheets ... that double-crossing, traitorous ... she couldn't find the words to articulate her rage. Shit! He had kissed Alex's hand! Alex was a low-life Googan! True, the crabber was pretty, in fact, very pretty. Had she and Alex met under different circumstances, her modeling agency would have offered Alex a contract. The jet black hair and fluorescent green eyes were a stunning combination. But the Googan had no fashion sense. Alex obviously shopped in the little boy's department at Kmart.

Levon Bakanian was a duplicitous bastard! What if Levon and Alex were in cahoots? Yes, that was it! Levon had used Pam to gain information about the scope of the treasure from Dodd family papers. She had fallen for it! In good faith, she had shown him the Dodd .pdf in her laptop! What a fool she was!

'Do I even unlock the glass slider to let Levon in from the rainstorm?' Hmm, let's hear him out. Pretend to know nothing.

"Levon ..." She opened the slider. "What a pleasant surprise."

He panted with excitement. "Pam, it's been a day of amazing breakthroughs with my research!"

"Really?"

"First, that woman who mentioned Turtle Island at the talk on Friday. I tracked her down. She's a friend of Nina's, a colleague of mine at Tolchester College. She heard the information about Giles taking the Allaways and Hales to an island on a ghost walk."

Sly of him not to mention Allaway's name. Just a friend of Nina's. She would let this pass. Best to let him spill his guts. Spilling guts … hmm. "A ghost walk?"

"Yes. They have these ghost walks into the cemetery every Halloween where the tour guide tells the story of Giles Blood-hand. I walked to the cemetery with Nina's friend. They were there! The Whitby family gravestone, and Charles Allaway's gravestone. I saw them. Look!" He pulled his cell phone from his raincoat pocket and swiped the photos in front of her eyes. "But here's the big news. We discovered a gravestone from a Spaniard named Diego Alvarez, hidden way in the back, covered by a bush. I just knew it! I had a feeling that Juan Carlos del Castillo and his crew had made it this far north."

"Wow." Ghost walk, right. He was feeding her a crock of lies.

"Why wouldn't the Spanish crew have stopped in River Glen to resupply? It was a thriving, self-sufficient village by the mid-1690s. And pyrate communities, the pyrate brethren often helped each other out. That was the pyrate way. Now if I can just find some corroborating document. Maybe at the archives at the historical society –"

"I'd love to see the gravestones. Let's go."

"Now? In this storm?"

"Sure, why not? You already have on your raingear. I'm a boater. A little water means nothing to me."

"But the winds?"

She laughed. "These little gusts?"

"Pam, it's a hurricane."

"A walk through the graveyard will be fun. Let me get my raingear. I'll be right back." She hurried to her cabin and opened her closet. "Pyrate communities, the pyrate brethren often helped each other out. Wrong, pal. It's the pyrate way, the Dodd way, to punish disloyal pricks."

Alex pulled the drawstring of her raincoat so tight that only her eyes were visibly from her hood. No one but her was fool enough to be out in such weather. She saw no one else as she walked up the river road, passed over the River Glen bridge, and walked up Main Street. Nor did a single car pass her on the road. Alice Hoffman would need to wrap the crab cakes in two plastic bags, at least, to ensure that the dinner not get wet on her walk home. Alex fought through the winds up Skipjack Road to James Collins' mansion on the bluff. The Maryland State flag, pyrate flag, and American flag snapped on the flag pole in his front yard. She pounded on his skull and cross bones door knocker.

Alex loved visiting James for one single reason; he was a nautical history freak so his home was filled with antique sextants, figureheads, ship's wheels, old globes, anchors, and the like. The rafters were laden with fish nets, oars, and rowboats. The expansive rooms smelled like teak and candles.

She was a distant cousin to James. That was because Emmaline Whitby's poisoning of Abigail Collins and Tess Smyth with foxglove left Huw Collins and Angus Smyth widowers. And Charles Allaway's beheading by Neville Whitby left Shannon Allaway a widow. Due to a shortage of women in the nascent village, Shannon had lived with two husbands at once, Huw and Angus. It was a harmonious threesome and she produced many children by both men. This meant that Shannon Allaway was the great great ... and so on ... grandmother to the Collinses, Smyths, and Allaway families. Alex and James were related by a common ancestor in the late 1600s.

She knocked again.

James finally answered. "Alex? A nice surprise. Come in. Let me get you something warm. Tea? Coffee? A glass of wine?"

"No, I can't stay."

He gestured her inside. "At least come in for a moment to get out of the storm."

"Okay. I was at the graveyard today with Levon Bakanian, the new history professor at Tolchester."

"In this mess?"

"We went out before the rain got heavy. He's trying to track down anything related to the pyrate Juan Carlos del Castillo."

"Yes, I remember Juan Carlos from Levon's talk on Friday night."

"I was wondering if you and Judith Ann had come across anything in the archives related to Spanish pyrates in the area. There was a gravestone for a person named Diego Alvarez."

James was silent for a moment. "Sorry. It's not ringing any bells. You might want to check the chronicle written by the Spanish priest Brother Guillermo who was on the *Raven* for a brief period of time. Judith Ann and I have organized everything from World War I and II, and we're just starting the Civil War, but hardly anything's been scanned or transcribed from the colonial period.   Most of the senior citizen volunteers have good intentions, but they're old and computer illiterate so little's getting done.   They use the historical society as a social center to gossip and drink tea all day.   We decided not to load files onto the website until they're digitized, but I have the pyrate era files in my laptop. Do you want to have a look at Guillermo's chronicle?   He's the only Spaniard who comes to mind."

"Sure."

"Let me take your coat."

Water had dripped from her raingear onto the stone floor of the entryway. "Thanks." She handed him her raincoat, and stepped out of her boots and rain pants.

"Are you certain I can't get you some tea?"

"Okay. Tea would be great."

"My laptop's in the kitchen."

She followed James to the back of the house where the kitchen adjoined a living room and a bar. He put on a kettle. The kitchen counter was covered with vegetables, eggs, and cheese. A butcher knife sat next to a cutting board.

"What are you making?"

"Quiches.   There's nothing else to do but cook since I'm not getting the Ravens-Dolphins game.   Were you getting satellite reception at your place?"

"No."

While searching his laptop for the document, James glanced up and smiled at her twice.   She smiled back reluctantly.   She went to James' house for his annual Christmas party though never alone.   She was always with Julia.   James adored Julia; every man on the planet was infatuated with her grandmother.   Alex crossed the living room to a plate glass window and pressed her eye to a telescope. The Chesapeake was speckled with white caps. She swiveled the telescope toward the harbor. Most boats at the marina had been pulled from their slips in preparation for the storm. That obnoxious yacht *Knot-A-Care* was still at its slip. It was late August. Shouldn't that bitch be heading south by now? With any luck, Ms. *Knot-A-Care* would head out to the bay, be capsized by a wave and eaten by a ferocious bull shark that had a taste for Floridians. One could only hope.

"It's getting bad out there," he remarked. "The storm's taking Track Two. It's supposed to make landfall sometime tonight. Here. I found it. But it's badly faded. Let me know if you can make heads or tails of it."

The kettle whistled.

She returned from the window and climbed onto a stool at the kitchen island. He turned the laptop toward her. She leaned toward the screen. "Whoa, it is badly faded."

He placed a tea cup and assorted tea bags next to her. "That's why we're racing to get these documents digitized, before the ink vanishes completely. But at least it has been scanned. It's a start anyway."

"The priest's handwriting is all over the place."

"Because he was an alcoholic. He and Conal Whitby, the only Whitby to survive Giles' massacre, were allegedly drunk around the clock."

"How long is this document?"

"Long. Over a hundred pages. I've only read the beginning of it. If I read everything at the archives, I'd get nothing else done."

She groaned. "His handwriting is atrocious. It will take me forever to read."

He diced a green pepper with the large knife. "Email it to yourself. Then you can take your time."

"Good idea. The best thing to do is just look for the names Juan Carlos del Castillo and Diego Alvarez. Then read it later for the details."

"That sounds like a good plan."

James suddenly tossed the butcher knife into the air. It flipped and glinted under the kitchen lights. His hand darted upward like a striking snake; he plucked it from the air by its handle. He smiled at her ... again ... and resumed dicing the green pepper.

O – kay. That was weird. A very disconcerting display by the innocuous James Collins. Everyone knew a person like James. He was invited to all of the parties yet he was overall forgettable. He was never flamboyant, nor was he dull. Not handsome, nor homely. Pleasantly average. Probably in his late thirties, possibly forty. A receding hairline, thinning brown hair. Not tall, not short. Not thin, not fat. Despite them growing up in the same village, she had never given James much thought, because he was older than her so they were not schoolmates. The old bitties considered him as the most eligible bachelor of River Glen because he was intelligent, had a law degree from some Ivy League school that she couldn't remember, and had inherited his father's wealth and successful law practice. She danced with him annually at the Giles Blood-hand Festival, but that was true of every other man in the village. He had been helpful to Julia in settling Randy's estate, and again when Ben Hancock had contacted James with the instructions to sign the cottage over to her.

Innocuous James Collins. An Everyman in preppy, pressed clothes. That's how she would have described him until she witnessed the demonstration with the knife. Why had he done that? To show-off, or terrify her? Was it a subtle threat, or a warning of some kind? What! She glanced slowly around the room, trying not to be too obvious, only to notice that there were knives and swords of all types scattered amidst the clutter of nautical memorabilia. In fact, razor-edged weapons were all over the living room and kitchen. The speed and skill at which he snatched the knife from the air, missing the blade entirely, was certainly meant to impress but instead it unnerved her.

There was a serial killer murderer in their midst, now referred to as the Cliff Top Killer. Will told her nothing about the crimes – he never did – yet the villagers were eyeing each other with varying degrees of suspicion. Perhaps it was James Collins that had been cutting up bodies, then stashing them in a mass grave at Henry Herssen's abandoned property? What did she really know about her distant cousin? Through the village rumor mill, she had heard that the bodies had been placed in the mass grave over a twenty-year period of time. All attention was focused on the fisherman Henry Herssen, but what if it was a polite, mild-mannered attorney who was oddly adept at handling dangerously large knives? James would have been in his late teens at the time of the first murders. And he was definitely the most intelligent of all of the villagers. He would be able to carry out an undetectable crime.

She chugged down her tea. "I should be getting home. To take Water Boy out."

"How about I drive you home?"

Typhoon winds and rain seemed preferable to a ride in a BMW Z4 Roadster with a knife freak and possible serial killer. "Oh, thanks, I'll walk. Besides, I need to stop at the

Dockside Café to pick up some crab cakes." She hurried on her raingear.

"Alex?"

"What?"

James gazed into her eyes and flashed her a tacit smile. "Oh, nothing. Just be careful in these winds. Be careful on that bridge."

A small step forward. Jay added Bob Randolph's name to the crime board.

Female 1 age 20? 4 yrs in ground
Female 2 age 65? 6 yrs in grd
Male 1 age 65? 6 yrs in grd **Dr. Bob Randolph**
Male 2 age 40? 20-25 yrs in grd
Male 3 age 40? 20-25 yrs in grd

The arthritic hip and significant height of that victim were suggestive of Male 1's identity. Four more bodies still to go. And still no goddamn clue to Henry Herssen's whereabouts. Eve, Randolph's sister in Myrtle Beach, had gone to a police forensics lab that afternoon to offer up a blood sample. A DNA match between Male 1 and Eve would confirm that victim's identity. Bob Randolph had been seen by a park ranger at the Big Meadows campground on the Skyline Drive, but how did his body get back to River Glen? Was he transported back to Herssen's property alive or dead? Every revelation opened up more questions, and the minds of Wilkins and Paco were anywhere but on this case!

Millennials ... distracted by anything technological. Cell phones to that generation had become another appendage.

Will, who had been pensive and withdrawn all morning, had received a text and could no longer sit still in his chair. It was certainly a sext from Alex that caused him to look at the wall clock every five seconds. It was awkward that he and Will were dating women from the same family. But in a village where everyone was related and options were limited, that was inevitable. Will glanced at the clock again. Yes, it had to be a deliciously salacious text.

And Lisa Paco, Millennial Number Two, had been on her computer with Norman from IT, running a background check on the man who owned the sewing store. Why? Then Lisa had wasted precious time checking out Stanley, the man who delivered groceries to the elderly and sick in the village, all while she stretched her gum from her mouth to her laptop, then slurped it back in her mouth like a spaghetti noodle. Why the fascination with Stanley? Stanley was one of the nicest, most earnest men who ever walked the planet. He coached little league and organized the Go Green initiatives in town. Highly doubtful that he was a serial killer. Besides, Stanley had only moved to the area with his wife and sons from Omaha, Nebraska, three years before. It was unlikely that he had been commuting between here and Omaha to bury bodies in a cliff. There were certainly abandoned fields and woods around Omaha to bury bodies if he felt compelled to. The whole thing was absurd.

Jay searched his desk drawer for an aspirin. "Okay, Will, tell me what you have on Sheila Myers."

"I have a very bad feeling about this, sir. It's another situation like Bob Randolph. She took a trip shortly after she retired and ..."

"Disappeared."

"Yes."

"Where this time?" He tossed down an aspirin with cold coffee.

"30th Street Station in Philadelphia."

"Six years ago, right?"

"Yes. Two weeks after Bob Randolph. It wasn't on the radar screen of the River Glen PD because she disappeared in Philly so it was handled by their detectives. Here's what they sent me."

He and Lisa leaned toward Will's laptop.

"Myers boarded a bus for Philly at the River Glen bus station there. She paid for the ticket with her credit card." Will pointed. "That's her there, caught by a security camera."

Myers was a hunched, old woman pulling a rolling suitcase. She wore a green rain coat, and the flaming red hair that Brad Smyth had described was visible from under a brimmed rain hat. Her face was concealed by sun glasses. She wasn't close enough to the security camera to see the wrinkles upon wrinkles, or warts upon warts that Brad had mentioned. The weather at the bus station appeared to be sunny which explained the sun glasses. Perhaps rain was in the forecast for her final destination.

"Here's Myers again in 30th Street Station, buying a cup of coffee and a bagel," Will said. "Again, the purchase showed up on her credit card at the same time she appeared on the security camera. Then she walked outside, waited by the curb and got a cab toward Center City. She was spotted again, browsing the booths in the Reading Terminal Market. She headed toward the women's room, and wasn't seen again. But her suitcase was found in a bathroom stall. It had been rifled. Everything in it stolen. A dirty syringe was found in the same stall. Philly PD figured that she had stumbled upon someone who was shooting up."

"And the prints on the suitcase matched Myers?"

"Yes. The Philly detectives came down to River Glen and searched her townhouse. The prints on the suitcase and her house were a match."

"Any prints on the syringe?"

"Yes, but they didn't match Myers' prints, and they're weren't on file."

"Family?"

"She had been widowed for years from Morton Myers, a CPA. They met and married when they were in their twenties and getting their MBAs. There were no children. She has brothers and in-laws in Hartford, Connecticut. That's where she's originally from."

"The brothers were interviewed by the Philly PD?"

"Yes. They had no knowledge of her taking any trips. After she retired, she was planning on finishing up a book on Forensic Accounting that she'd been working on."

Lisa grabbed a pen and hurried to the crime board. "Zera said that Female 2 had thoracic kyphosis."

"What?"

"Thoracic kyphosis. She was a hunchback like Quasimodo." She pointed to Sheila Myers's hunched frame boarding the bus. "See!" She scribbled a new name onto the crime board.

Female 1 age 20? 4 yrs in ground
Female 2 age 65? 6 yrs in grd **Dr. Sheila Myers**
Male 1 age 65? 6 yrs in grd **Dr. Bob Randolph**
Male 2 age 40? 20-25 yrs in grd
Male 3 age 40? 20-25 yrs in grd

SPIDER

CHAPTER SEVEN
Monday

Nina dragged the plastic trashcan to the ladies room in the Riddel Building. She had decided not to dress up for the first day of classes; first, because it was pouring out and she didn't want traipse through puddles in pumps, and secondly because water would be streaming down the plastic funnel all day and she would be making repeated trips to the bathroom. She was right about that. When she came to campus for her eight o'clock class, the trashcan was nearly a quarter full. Progress. She was able to lift the trashcan over the sink in the ladies *by herself* because Griffin had re-taped her hand leaving her pointer finger and thumb exposed. Her hand was no longer a non-functional gauze club but a crab claw. And he didn't squirm and turn white like Alex did when he saw her hand. In fact, Griffin told her that his grandmother had had her foot amputated due to diabetes and functioned satisfactorily with an artificial foot. If Griffin's grandmother in Dearborn, Michigan could walk her dachshund and ballroom dance with an artificial foot, then she could empty a trashcan of water with a missing finger.

Nina watched dusty water swirl down the bathroom drain. Everything about the town of River Glen was plain bizarre. First, the speeding yacht and the bones in the cliff. Then her finger, the mysterious finance report and the cops appearing at the apartment. She returned to her office, and put the plastic funnel back into the trashcan because at Tolchester College that was the normal thing to do in one's office. The gutter outside was clogged so water cascaded down her window pane. She felt akin to the Munro sisters in *The Last of the Mohicans*, hiding behind the waterfall from the pursuing Hurons. Now more River Glen bizarreness, a hurricane.

Yesterday she and Griffin had made the most of the storm. After the cops left, Griffin ran out to Walmart to buy a flat-screen TV and a DVD player. By then, the rain was really coming down. After he finished rewriting his syllabus – with all the new instructions from Dean Wines – he asked if she wanted to watch DVDs and drink wine. Why not? Her syllabus was already done as she was a typical compulsive Type A academic; she had also reviewed her lecture notes for SOC 101 for her Monday morning class. Then Griffin did the unbelievable. He asked her what *she* wanted to watch. Had it been Ricardo, she would have been told that they would be watching a Bruce Willis or Arnold Schwarzenegger movie, or Ricardo's favorite, *Rambo*.

She had told Griffin that she loved Meryl Streep movies.

"So do I. I have *The Devil Wears Prada*." He rummaged through his box of DVDs.

Sprawled on blankets and pillows on the living room floor, they had watched Meryl, followed by *Master and Commander*, as they both loved sea stories and Russell Crowe movies. The microwave popcorn did little to absorb the wine and they became giddy as the rain and wind shook their apartment. For some reason – probably the second bottle of wine – they decided upon Christmas movies. They made it all the way through *The Nightmare Before Christmas* and started *How the Grinch Stole Christmas* when the power went off at the second the Grinch's sled was poised precariously at the top of Mount Crumpit. The power had remained off for the rest of the evening. She headed up to bed since she had an early lecture while Griffin remained downstairs to swab the kitchen counter and bannisters by candlelight.

Nina's eight am lecture that morning had gone fine. The computer and projection system in Learning Lodge #3 – in actuality just a trailer – where she was assigned to teach had miraculously worked so she had been able to review her syllabus policies and start on the introductory concepts, social institutions, patterns, and processes. The plinking rain on the metal roof sounded like they were in a tin can so she had to yell to be heard. The students seemed minimally interested in the course content, and for much of the hour they stared into their smartphones. Likes on Facebook were more important than the topic of social stratification.

She doubted that any students would come to her office hours on the first day of class, but she left her door open anyway. Music from a Caribbean steel drum band came from Brad's office which put her in a festive mood despite the rain. That morning Brad had dressed in a red beret with a metal star pin, olive drab military attire, and combat boots. He was Che Guevara.

Around noon disgruntled voices traveled from the stairwell. Nina poked her head into the hallway. Brad hopped to attention, a saluting hand over his eyebrow.

"Dean Wines, mi hermana de la revolución. Comrade Stupens. Buen semestre!" he said in a fairly convincing Spanish accent.

"Good semester to you also, Brad," Gloria Wines said tiredly. Her hair and the cuffs of her suit pants were soaked.

Hank Stupens grinned at Brad over Dean Wines' shoulder.

"Is Levon Bakanian here?" Wines asked. "He didn't show up for his morning classes. Annoyed students have been at my office all morning."

Brad stood at ease. "No, camarada, the only ones here are Professora Vega and me."

"Oh, hello, Nina. How's that hand?"

"Getting better, thanks."

"Have either of you seen Levon this morning?"

She and Brad shook their heads.

"Hank, let me into Levon's office," Wines said. "Are those bees gone yet?"

"Yes, the exterminator was here yesterday." Stupens rolled his eyes at Brad. "Again."

Wines peeked apprehensively into Levon's office and sighed. "He's not here. How exasperating. Hank, can you get one of your guys to vacuum up the dead bees?"

"Yes, of course."

"Send someone over to check Levon's apartment. He lives at the Driftwood Apartments."

"Yes, of course."

Wines zipped up her London Fog raincoat, and she and Stupens disappeared down the hallway.

Nina returned to her office and sat down at her desk. The lights flickered on and off so she unplugged her laptop and CD player from the wall. Lightning cracked directly over the Riddel Building. She leapt from her chair. Seagulls took flight, and shrieked outside her window.

"That was right over our heads!" Brad dashed into her office. "Nina, are you okay?"

"That was way too close!"

He froze. "What the hell!"

"What?" She spun.

Scampering down her office wall was a massive black spider.

"Faculty prima donnas." Hank Stupens climbed into the Tolchester College pickup truck. "Now, on top of everything else, my job is to track down a fucking pretty boy."

Levon Bakanian was too good-looking for his own good. All Hank had been hearing from the women who worked in the cafeteria and the cleaning woman assigned to the Riddel Building was about 'that gorgeous new professor with the black hair and blue eyes.' Half of the female maintenance staff had shown up at Bakanian's talk on Friday night ... like any of them really gave a shit about pyrate history. Bakanian was a skinny wimp. No way could Bakanian bench-press one eighty-five like he could. The new protein supplements from the vitamin shoppe, expensive as they were, were really paying off.

Hank turned up his windshield wipers to the highest speed but it was pointless. He could barely see a thing as he drove along College Avenue. Fortunately the Driftwood Apartments were not that far from campus. This was a fucking waste of his precious time, he had told Gloria. Bakanian had probably overslept after a weekend of carousing with beautiful babes. Bakanian would probably answer the door, dressed in his boxers, red-eyed and hung-over, with a scantily-clothed chick on his sofa. Then Bakanian would concoct some lame-ass excuse ... I have a sore throat ... my cat was sick ... that he would have to take back to Gloria, who would stuff a bonbon in her mouth and mutter an aggravated "Faculty. What am I going to do with them?"

"The fucking faculty gets away with fucking murder," Hank growled. While the professors were taking last minute summer holidays and Mary Blodgen was brushing up on her Italian in Rome, he was towing trailers across a steamy field and overseeing the grout of salmon-colored bathroom tiles ... while he should have been trout-fishing in the Poconos!

He half-expected to see a bright red Corvette in Bakanian's parking space, but instead it was empty. He pulled up the hood of his raincoat and dashed to the overhang at Bakanian's apartment door. He pushed the doorbell and waited. Nothing. He huddled into his shoulders to protect himself from the lashing winds. He pushed the bell again. Still nothing. He peered in the front window, but the Venetian blinds were closed. Fuck it ... he didn't have all day to look for errant faculty members! Bakanian probably went to New York City for the weekend and was having so much fun with the lap dancers that he forgot to come home. Hank reached for his ring of building keys. It had been one of Mary Blodgen's brilliant ideas to buy a block of apartment buildings for the new faculty to live in. "So they can bond." He stepped inside. This was one of the two bedroom units. He knew the floor plan of the apartments all too well since Blodgen had him oversee the installation of the kitchen cabinets and bathroom vanities. What the fuck didn't she have him do?

Unpacked boxes were scattered around Bakanian's living room.   The kitchen counters were clean and tidy.   Hank glanced through the back slider to a patio with a new propane grill where the professor would be entertaining throngs of beauties.   He climbed the stairs.   The bathroom was as clean and orderly as the kitchen.   In the bedroom was a bed.   Of course it would be a king.   He checked his watch. What a fucking waste of time!   If he hurried, he might be able to get in a workout during the lunch break.   The one good thing about Hurricane Beau was that it was keeping the students in the dorm.   He should have the free weights all to himself.

Hank shut the door behind him and dashed back to the truck. The only noteworthy thing to report to Gloria was that Bakanian's bathtub and sinks were all bone-dry. One thing was certain. Dr. Bakanian had never come home last night.

The spider reared up on its hind legs, its pelipalps and forelegs flailing.

"Jesus Christ!"   Brad jumped backward. "It's going to attack!"

Nina cowered against her desk. "What kind is it?"

"I have no clue! I've never seen such a beast. I've lived here all my life. I've never seen a spider that size!"

"We have tarantulas in New Mexico that are much bigger than this. But they're pretty docile if you don't bother them. This one seems so angry, so aggressive."

Brad anxiously searched the office. "Let me find something to kill it with."

"No, let's see what it is. My friend Alex is a biologist. She'll know what it is."

"Alex Allaway?"

"Yes. She was my roommate in college."

"Small world. I know Alex. Randy Allaway and I were good friends. You're right. She knows everything about every animal in these parts."

"We need to put it in something secure." Nina scanned her office. "I don't have anything."

"I have a peanut jar with a lid, but I'll need to dump out the peanuts." Brad scurried to his office and returned a moment later. "I hope it doesn't jump and bite one of us."

"I never saw a tarantula jump. Most people think their bite is deadly, but it just feels like a bee sting."

"Were you ever bitten?"

"No, I never got that close to them. But I have seen them in the desert."

"Okay, here goes." He tiptoed forward, then slammed the jar against the wall. The spider climbed up to where his hand pushed down on the glass. "Quick, Nina, hand me the lid!" He tilted the edge and shoved the metal lid onto the mouth of the jar.

"Screw it on tightly!"

"Definitely!" Brad held the jar in front of their two faces. "That's the meanest bastard I've ever seen."

They gazed at it with a dreadful fascination. The spider pushed its black fangs outward and attempted to bite them through the glass.

"Just what we need!" Jay slammed down the phone on his desk.

"What, sir?" Will asked.

"A missing person."

Lisa looked up from her laptop. "Who's missing?"

"A historian from Tolchester College. Levon Bakanian. That call was from Gloria Wines. I remember his name. He had the office with the bee infestation."

"And the pyrate flags," she said.

"Bakanian never showed up for his classes this morning so Hank Stupens went by his apartment to check on him. He wasn't there."

"Maybe our murderer has struck again!" Lisa popped another piece of gum into her mouth.

Jay moved in front of the crime board. "Thank God for Zera Lim."

Female 1 age 20? 4 yrs in ground
Female 2 age 65? 6 yrs in grd **Dr. Sheila Myers** √
Male 1 age 65? 6 yrs in grd **Dr. Bob Randolph** √
Male 2 age 40? 20-25 yrs in grd
Male 3 age 40? 20-25 yrs in grd

Zera's team had burned the midnight oil. The check marks signified DNA matches between Male 1 and Eve Randolph-Cupper in Myrtle Beach, South Carolina. The same was true of Female 2 and Sheila Myers' brothers in Hartford, Connecticut. But three bodies remained unnamed. And now a name – Bakanian – without a body. Jay hated jumping to conclusions, but too many threads led to Tolchester College. Something was terribly amiss there, but what was it? Bob Randolph. Sheila Myers. Now Levon Bakanian. An Australian funnel spider in the woods. A missing finance report.

Jay returned to his desk and took a sip of coffee. Putrid. Too watery. Not worth drinking. He backhanded the

Styrofoam cup off his desk and into the trashcan. The secretary Cloris had been instructed by their police chief to save money by cutting back on the coffee scoops going into each pot. On top of his sciatica that the rain exacerbated, his back throbbed. He opened his desk drawer. His bottle of aspirin was empty.

Jay's plan last night, after an endlessly long day at work, was to spend the evening pressed against his Scottish lovely while the rhythm of the rain lulled them to sleep. Instead, when he had dropped by his house to shower and change, he had discovered that his sump pump had failed and his basement was filling with water. He struggled on his hands and knees in inches of rising water to fix the pump on his own, but he was hopelessly inept at all things mechanical. The lights had flickered on and off so electrocution seemed inevitable; he had finally called a plumber. After the plumber left with his seven hundred dollars for the emergency call and installation of the new sump pump, he grumbled a "fuck everything," dropped into his recliner, and drank himself into a scotch-induced coma.

Now on top of everything ... his sciatica, sore back, rancid coffee, hangover, Hurricane Beau taking a track that promised to wash away River Glen, three unidentified corpses on the crime board ... was a missing person. Shit, life was good.

Lisa's phone vibrated. She read the text and pumped her fist into the air. "Woo hooty hoo! She didn't do it! She's not a psychopathic murderer. She really does have MS. That was her doctor. He said definitely yes! She had no idea where the Big Meadows campground was, or the Reading Terminal Market. I know she wasn't lying. I can tell. She never lies. There's no way she had time to kill Levon

Bakanian because she and Aunt Helen have been playing Scrabble all weekend."

Jay's head pounded. "Who the hell are you talking about?"

"My mother!

"You thought your mother was the killer?" he said incredulously. "That's why you've been chewing ten packs a day?"

Lisa scrawled another name on the crime board.

Female 1 age 20? 4 yrs in ground

Female 2 age 65? 6 yrs in grd **Dr. Sheila Myers** √

Male 1 age 65? 6 yrs in grd **Dr. Bob Randolph** √

Male 2 age 40? 20-25 yrs in grd

Male 3 age 40? 20-25 yrs in grd **Owen Paco**

"I need to see Zera!" Lisa grabbed her raincoat. "I need to give her a blood sample."

"An uncle, a cousin?" Will guessed.

"My father!"

Will felt the needy stare of Cloris boring into him, but he refused make eye contact. If he stared intently at his computer and appeared to be in the thick of the murder investigation, Cloris would not tell him about Sylvester's food allergies. Yesterday for twenty interminable minutes, she had lectured him on the composition of Mr. Friskies, compared to Uber Kitty and Fish Fiesta. Desk duty was sheer torture! Lisa and Jay were out interviewing murder suspects while he was hearing about the fiber and protein content of dry- versus moist cat foods. Jay had left him with various assignments, first to check out anything and everything about Owen Paco, and then track down the recent activities of the missing historian Levon Bakanian – when all he wanted to do was relive his evening with Alex.

The evening was that perfect.

In addition to being buried with his cell phone that contained Alex's proclamation of love, he would now instruct James Collins to have him buried with the napkin from their crab cake dinner. There was nothing remarkable about the napkin. It was simply white paper with red stains from when Alex knocked over the cocktail sauce, but it was a physical reminder of their first night as A Couple. He had been upgraded from a friend-with-benefits to Partner. Better still, she was interested in tango lessons. In fact, very interested, because Alex was obsessively competitive with Julia. She wanted to fence better than Julia; now she wanted to tango better.

Alex had been as nervous as he was for their weighty dinner conversation. She had burned the crab cakes and drank her wine too fast so that she was soon giggly and amorous. Her amorous gene had been inherited from Randy the Casanova of River Glen. Before they even got to pie and ice cream she wanted to tango in the kitchen. The next thing he knew their clothes were dropping to the linoleum floor. One thing led to another in the kitchen, living room, and bedroom. He rose to the occasion each time – he always did where she was concerned – despite the hindrance of the hard cast and his achy ankle.

They finally settled themselves long enough to talk about his and Carly's move to the cottage. He and Alex were in total agreement about everything. They could set up Carly's plastic *Frozen* tent and sleeping bag in the living room until the addition was completed.   Carly would love indoor camping with Peppy and Water Boy.   One long addition heading out in the direction of the grow house would be preferable to one projecting off the side of the cottage toward Julia's place.   The addition with multiple bedrooms would accommodate their numerous children.

Enough daydreaming ... back to work. Will typed Owen Paco into his laptop. Whoa. A ton of hits in the police database came up.   No wonder Lisa never mentioned him. Owen was in that gang of slimeballs that hung out at the Lame Dog Saloon.   The group consisted of mean-spirited mental defectives who had been apprehended for a variety of idiotic, petty crimes.   Lisa had clearly inherited her keen intelligence from Wanda. Owen had violations for DWIs, battery, fencing stolen property (microwave ovens, go figure), and distributing meth. His profile photo showed a pair of boxing gloves tattooed to his neck.   Lisa lacked Owen's protruding brow ridges, sprawling nose, and thick, uneven lips. Owen's profession was listed as a landscaper. Where? Nothing came up in the police files. Ugh ... that meant checking tax records, if the thug had even paid taxes.

Owen Paco was one of two men that been buried in the cliff twenty years ago when Lisa was about ten. She had mentioned a knock-down-drag-out-brawl between Wanda and Owen at the same time he vanished from their lives. The fight was what led Lisa to suspect her mother. Will opened up the IRS database and waited for his search query to be processed. Cloris' desperate eyes boring into him – once again – prompted him to lean across his desk as though a vital clue was to appear on his laptop at any second. Why couldn't he be out with Jay interviewing potential serial killers! He could keep up with Jay, even on crutches; he was sure of it.

Owen Paco's tax returns appeared on the screen. Small miracle. The man had filed his taxes. Incredible! Will's hand jumped to his cell phone.

"Sir, guess where Owen Paco was employed as a groundkeeper?"

Jay responded immediately. "Let me guess. Tolchester College."

"Bingo."

Zera Lim bandaged up Lisa's arm and left with the vial of blood for the back lab. Lisa dropped her head against the wall. She exhaled. An incalculable burden had been lifted from her conscience; now her mind was unfettered. She could think clearly again and put this creepy serial killer behind bars. Despite Hurricane Beau that nearly blew her car off the highway, she was having a perfect day. She was no longer withholding evidence from her awesome colleagues. Now the case would be given her all. A definite pattern was emerging.

All three victims identified so far were associated with Tolchester College – Professors Randolph and Myers, and Paco, a landscaper. The evidence suggested that the killer had followed Randolph and Myers to sites away from River Glen, possibly to deflect attention away from the college. This suggested that the killer knew them both. Perhaps the professors had even mentioned their intended destinations to the killer. The two professors were possibly murdered in the Shenandoah National Park and Philly, respectively, then their bodies brought back to River Glen for burial.

Very odd. Why go to all that trouble?

Why not leave the bodies at the site of the killing?

Goosebumps rose across Lisa's skin. The chair with the straps in the funnel-shaped pit in Herssen's forest implied that the victims had been restrained. What if Randolph and Myers had been brought back alive, then tortured in that chair? Another odd thing ... the bodies exhibited no signs of physical trauma. No stab wounds, no points of bullet entry, no garroting, no nothing. And Sheila Myers would have been seen being dragged out of the women's room at the Reading Terminal Market if that's where she was in fact abducted.

Who would kill two faculty members? A disgruntled student who had received Fs by both of them? A fellow faculty member? By all accounts Randolph and Myers were collegial, well-respected colleagues. And how is the missing finance report mixed up in this whole business? Is it relevant or just a peripheral matter? Perhaps one of the deans simply picked it up because they didn't want financial data laying about, nothing more. The deans would have to be asked.

Lisa walked into the morgue where the bodies were stored. She pulled her father's corpse from the metal cabinet in the wall, and lifted the sheet. She studied his face, now a skull with leathery patches of skin.

She felt a gentle hand rest on her shoulder.

"Are you okay?" Zera asked.

"Yes. I feel nothing but relief. For twenty years, my mother and I were living in fear that he might return. Our life became so happy, so tranquil after he left. But his death doesn't make sense. I can imagine a pissed-off, psychotic student killing his or her professors. That certainly wouldn't be a first, but why also kill a landscaper? Landscapers and professors don't exactly run in the same circles."

"But Henry Herssen, or whoever, killed and buried your father over twenty years ago, and Randolph and Myers six years ago in the same mass grave. That is a certainty."

Lisa pushed her father's body back into the wall cabinet, and pulled out the shelf containing Female 1, the twenty-year-old with the crushed bones.

"Zera, I think I know who this is. Four years, when I was at the police academy in Sykesville, a Tolchester student disappeared. I remember my mother telling me about it. The girl's name was Amanda Lamont."

"Four years ago," Zera said to herself, "was another lifetime ago." She opened her laptop to search for the case file of Amanda Lamont. Four years ago, Hideo, her husband of nearly thirty-years, had informed her over breakfast, in a voice as nonchalant as mentioning the day's weather, "Zera, I want a divorce. I want to marry Sierra."

Sierra? Who the hell was Sierra? No one in their circle of friends was a Sierra. Ah, yes, of course … the new member of his firm, the twenty-something Sierra.

Zera had clamped her hands around her coffee mug to quell the shaking; her knees jittered under the table. The prospect of sifting through the memories of where they had raised their two children and dividing up the spoils accumulated over decades in their Georgetown townhouse was too daunting. Despite her confusion, the single wisest thing she had ever said tripped off her tongue. "Take whatever, but the dog is mine."

Two weeks after the blindsiding revelation, she had an interview at a coroner's office on Maryland's eastern shore. Two weeks after that, she and her beloved elkhound moved from Washington, DC to a village called River Glen, notable only for its annual pyrate festival. Two weeks after her move, a hard-boiled Baltimore detective named Jay Braden joined the River Glen PD. "His wife is different," said her curmudgeon of a boss. "Different" was code for mad as a hatter.

Zera read through the Amanda Lamont case. No wonder she had never heard of Lamont. The girl had disappeared before she and Jay had arrived in River Glen. Both Lisa and Will would have still been at the police academy. She read on: the case was a study in conflicting information. A 4.00 GPA student majoring in Economics and heading for a graduate program at Rutgers allegedly gets pregnant by an agricultural worker and runs off with him to Central America. Zera knew full well that the heart leads people down strange alleyways, but Amanda's parents in Topeka, Kansas vehemently denied the story. It was completely implausible, Edward and Nancy Lamont had insisted. In fact, preposterous. There was no Guatemalan boyfriend, no pregnancy, no secret marriage. It was foul play, plain and simple. Amanda had been abducted, the parents contended.

On the day of her disappearance, Amanda had been dropped off at an intersection outside the town limits of River Glen with an empty can to collect for pediatric cancer. PedCan, affectionately named by the students, was the annual fundraising effort. It was a Saturday morning in April, four years before. The canning event entailed students collecting change from drivers when stopped at the red light. The intersection where Amanda's roommate Missy Clarke had dropped Amanda at was at Bayside Road and Gull Drive. Because this was a quiet intersection, only one student, Amanda, manned the stop, rather than two or three students assigned to busier roads. When Missy returned at noon to pick up Amanda, there was no sign of Amanda. No cup, no change, no nothing.

Numerous people on campus had been interviewed: Missy Clarke and the girls on Amanda's dormitory floor, Dean Hinkie whose department sponsored the event, and Hank Stupens who brought boxes of empty cans to the Student Union building to distribute to the student volunteers on the morning of the event. A few students corroborated the story about Amanda having a boyfriend off-campus because she never attended campus parties and often disappeared on Friday and Saturday evenings. Amanda had told Dean Hinkie that she was bringing "a special someone" to the Spring Formal but did not mention the individual by name. Hinkie had heard mention of a boyfriend that worked on a nearby farm.

Hinkie also mentioned to the detectives that a list had been distributed among the students – for safety purposes – listing the participants' cell phone numbers and locations where they would be dropped off. This meant that anyone with that list would have known Amanda's canning location, and that she would be alone at the intersection of Bayside and Gull.

Initial suspicions fell on Missy Clarke who had lost to Amanda in the election for the Student Government president, but Missy had an alibi. She was working in the campus tutoring center for the entire morning that Amanda disappeared.

Dean Hinkie also had an alibi. Once the students dispersed to their intersections, instead of awaiting the students safe return, she left for the Tidewater Greens Club where she played the back nine and had a leisurely brunch with three women on her golf team.

Hank Stupens was also interviewed because he had been present at the Student Union building when the cans were distributed. "Yes, I know who Amanda is. She attends every event," he had reported. "The boxes of cans for the PedCan event are taking up too much space in my maintenance shed." He had never heard of a boyfriend; why would he? "I spent the morning cleaning the windows in President Blodgen's sunroom," he had grumbled. "I was supposed to be fishing."

Mary Blodgen had also been questioned. "I know Amanda very well," she had told the detectives. "I worked closely with Amanda and other members of the Student Government on a number of important issues, like improving the Wi-Fi in the dorms and increasing the number of parking spaces in the commuter lot. Amanda was an exemplary student. She was wonderful to work with and had a promising future as an economist."

"Any knowledge of a boyfriend on a farm?" the detective had asked.

"No," the president said, "but rarely do I discuss personal matters with the students."

On the morning of the PedCan fundraiser, Blodgen had been repotting begonias in her basement while Hank was washing windows in her sunroom. "I have quite the green thumb," she had cheerfully told the detectives.

Zera clicked open the file on Female 1. This victim had no surgical incisions, no indications of pregnancies, and excellent teeth that had been straightened by braces. This victim had her pelvis and rib cage crushed – most intentionally – under the tires of a car, possibly at the intersection of Bayside and Gull while fundraising for pediatric cancer.

"Shh! Wait!" Lana Hinkie extended her arm in the direction of the doorway. Jay followed her order and halted, but Lisa was sure that his blood was steaming.

President Blodgen was poised, putter in hand, on Hinkie's office putting green. Her putter clicked against the golf ball; it rolled down the green, circled the cup and spun on to the oriental carpet.

"I'm hopeless," Blodgen laughed. "I'll never make it to the LPGA tour this way."

Hinkie retrieved the ball. "That's because you refuse to hold the putter as I instructed. You're absolutely unteachable." She tapped the green with her Prada lace-up Oxford shoe. "Check this out, detectives. This proprietary aerated polymer exactly simulates the grain of a real putting green. Step on it. It even replicates the soft feel under your feet. I ordered the green with the fast, championship stimp. We can always dream."

Lisa had never been on a golf course, although she was quite expert at Swashbuckler Island miniature golf. She and Aunt Helen were almost always under par. She had even mastered that tricky water hole with the ship entangled in the octopus' tentacles. She stomped across the synthetic green. "Oh, so this is what it feels like ..."

Jay grimaced at her and anchored himself obstinately in the doorway. It was only mid-morning and his patience was taut. "When's the last time you two saw Levon Bakanian?"

"We attended Dr. Bakanian's very interesting lecture on Friday night," Blodgen said. "It's an eons old tradition that the new faculty members give a research lecture when they arrive. Dr. Bakanian was first in the queue. We do this for many reasons. First, it gives the young faculty practice for giving talks in larger forums, like research conferences. Second, it allows the college community to see the research interests of our new faculty, for purposes of building new collaborations. I'm a huge supporter of interdisciplinary partnerships among our faculty. How I wish I'd kept up with my botanical researches," she said wistfully. "But no time to dwell in the past. Administration was my calling."

"And Bakanian lectured on?" he said.

"His historical research on two pyrates, the Scotsman Giles Hale, and a Spaniard Juan Carlos del Castillo."

Jay rolled his eyes at Lisa. He hated everything about the River Glen pyrate legend. The Giles Blood-hand festival was his least favorite event of the year. Their small police force had the herculean task of keeping in line the inebriated masses from Baltimore, Philadelphia and Washington, DC, who descended upon their village. Last summer a group had decided to peel off their skull and cross bone hats, peg legs, and wench dresses, and leap naked off the town pier. The police had spent the evening passing cups of coffee through the bars of the holding cell while the wet pyrates tonelessly crooned the entire repertoire of Jimmy Buffett and Bob Marley songs.

"Was there anything noteworthy, different, out of the ordinary that occurred at the lecture?" he asked.

Blodgen looked curiously at Hinkie. "I can't think of anything. Can you Lana? It was very well-attended as campus lectures go. Because everyone's fascinated by Giles' treasure. Do you think there's treasure in River Glen, Mr. Braden?"

He frowned again. "The whole thing's an advertising ploy to attract tourists to River Glen. I'd like the security footage from the Friday night lecture."

"We don't have security cameras in the lecture hall," Blodgen said. "Only in the entryway to our auditorium building. I'll call over to Burt Sweeny in the Security Office to make you a copy of the footage."

"That would be appreciated." Jay headed out the door. He turned in afterthought. "Four missing persons connected to Tolchester College."

Blodgen was taken aback. "Four?"

"Levon Bakanian, Bob Randolph, Sheila Myers and Owen Paco."

"I'm aware that Levon did not show up to teach today, but that was Dean Wines overreacting again. He'll turn up any moment now. Let's keep the right thought."

"But there was no sign of him at his apartment. Why does Hank Stupens have keys to the Driftwood Apartments?"

"Because the college owns the property. It was a wonderful investment opportunity."

"Your thoughts on the disappearance of Bob Randolph and Sheila Myers?"

Blodgen leaned against Hinkie's mahogany desk and nodded pensively. "Yes, the police did inform us of that. They went missing after they'd retired, when they were traveling abroad, I believe."

"Not abroad, Mary," Hinkie interrupted. "Locally. Bob was traveling in Virginia, and Sheila was in Philadelphia. I worked here when that happened. I was interviewed by the detectives."

"Yes, yes, so was I, but those events had nothing to do with Tolchester, Lana. It's very important that those incidents not be connected to Tolchester. It's bad publicity. We run almost entirely on tuition dollars. Unfortunately we don't have the endowment of a Harvard, Yale or Penn. But who knows? Hope springs eternal. If one is patient, who knows what might spring from our brave garden. A generous benefactor might appear at any moment." Blodgen's forehead knitted in thought. "Who was the fourth person you mentioned?"

"Owen Paco. A landscaper that worked here between twenty and thirty years ago."

"That was before I was an administrator here. Sorry, I don't remember him. Lana, have you ever heard of this man?"

"That was before my time also." Hinkie hunched forward with a titillated grin. "What did Mr. Paco do that you're looking for him?"

"He hasn't paid his taxes in a few years," Jay said evasively.

"Five missing persons, actually," Lisa interjected. "There was Amanda Lamont. What do you think happened to her?"

"I remember Amanda very well," Blodgen said. "She's probably making babies in Honduras with her husband. We've had a number of students get pregnant, then leave school to begin families. Additionally, a number of our international students, particular females from Asia and the Middle East, have returned to their home countries for arranged marriages. Sadly many of them never return to Tolchester to complete their educations. Tolchester has been making huge strides recruiting international students. This has been one of Lana's greatest accomplishments. Increasing the numbers of diverse students and faculty is a top priority in our Strategic Plan."

"Guatemala, Mary," Hinkie said. "I'm sure that Amanda had said that the boyfriend was Guatemalan."

Blodgen stepped back onto the putting green. "Guatemala, Honduras. Same difference."

By late afternoon the medical examiner from the State of Kansas and Zera Lim had found that the DNA from Amanda Lamont's parents matched the DNA from Female One with the crushed rib cage and pelvis. The DNA from Eve Randolph-Cupper in South Carolina matched Male 1; the DNA from Sheila Myers' brothers in Connecticut matched Female 2; and the DNA from Male 3 was a match to Lisa Paco's. The check marks behind the name indicated a genetic match.

Female 1 age 20? 4 yrs in ground **Amanda Lamont** ✓
Female 2 age 65? 6 yrs in grd **Dr. Sheila Myers** ✓
Male 1 age 65? 6 yrs in grd **Dr. Bob Randolph** ✓
Male 2 age 40? 20-25 yrs in grd
Male 3 age 40? 20-25 yrs in grd **Owen Paco** ✓

The positive IDs on the crime board should been heartening, but Jay sulked. There were no still leads to the whereabouts of the prime suspect Henry Herssen. None whatsoever. Herssen was still somewhere, writing checks to pay his property taxes. Amanda Lamont was likely run over a car during the PedCan event, but the four other victims had no signs of injury. And who was Male 2?

Worse, where was Professor Bakanian? If Bakanian proved a sixth victim, this suggested that Herssen was still in their midst. Had Herssen assumed a new identity? Who was he? Where was he? What might Bakanian done to have provoke him? The pyrate historian had been in town for only two weeks. Uniformed patrolmen had gone door-to-door at the Driftwood Apartments and through the village of River Glen with a photo of the scholar, but no one reported seeing him recently. The manager of the Nauticus confirmed seeing Bakanian having lunch at the tiki bar the previous week. The security camera on the River Glen bridge had captured Bakanian's green SUV crossing the bridge throughout the weekend. The footage on the security camera put Jay on edge. Three times the SUV had turned in the direction of the river road, toward Julia and Alex's homes, the last time on Sunday afternoon. One thing was clear. As of Sunday afternoon, Bakanian was still in the area of River Glen. And then he vanished.

Jay pulled his chair next to Will and Lisa who were replaying the camera footage from the auditorium at Tolchester College. At 7:10 pm last Friday night Levon Bakanian and a paunchy man entered together. Will and Lisa had identified the other man as Gabe Issacs from IT Support. Issacs and Bakanian had shown up early to set up the computer and projection system. People had strolled into the auditorium from 7:13 pm to when the lecture started at 7:30 pm. A number of people were recognizable. Burt Sweeny and Burt, Jr., dressed in a pyrate costume, were the first to show up. The strawberry blonde babe from the *Knot-A-Care* wandered in, followed by James Collins and Judith Ann Smyth from the River Glen Historical Society. President Blodgen, Dean Hinkie and Hank Stupens came in a few minutes later. Also, in attendance were Nina Vega and Griffin Blake. The foyer was silent until 7:43, when Alex Allaway rushed in, motorcycle helmet in hand. There was no activity in the foyer until 8:33 when the lecture was over when the same crowd left. Alex, Nina and Griffin left together. So did Blodgen, Hinkie, and Stupens. Gloria Wines had never made an appearance that evening. The strawberry blonde left last, suggesting that she had remained to talk to Bakanian. Around 8:41 Issacs reentered to shut down the equipment. Issacs and Bakanian exited from the front entrance together.

"Ooh la la ... Bakanian's hot," Lisa said. "Real eye candy."

Jay glanced askance at Will. Perspiration covered Will's forehead. No way Will didn't recognize Bakanian. He was the same man in the tropical print shirt who had lifted Alex's hand and pressed it to his lips on Saturday night, when Will had said to him, "Um, maybe you should drop me at my place."

"Goddamn rain ... goddamn windshield wipers ... completely useless." To use one of Julia's phrases, Jay couldn't see a bloody thing. It was a miracle his car wasn't in a muddy ditch. "And goddamn pyrates. Every horrible thing that happens in this town has to do with Giles Hale, Charles Allaway, and the pyrates of the *Raven*. Those pyrates cursed River Glen."

Jay pulled into the Smyth Family Marina, murmuring to himself. Had it not been for that blood feud between the Allaways and the Whitbys, Laura might still be alive. But would she? Twice she had tried to take her own life. No one ascends from such a deep chasm of madness. Do they? If she was still alive, would she even recognize him?

The bullet that Clyde Whitby shot into Laura's brain killed her instantly. Jay was sick with guilt every time this thought crossed his mind, but had Whitby's bullet put her out of her misery? Had Laura goaded Whitby, provoked him? What had transpired in her last moments on Mutter Island? Laura had an exceptional quality that only the mad possess – a disregard of fear.

The stolen finance report in Nina Vega's office had originally led Jay to believe that financial malfeasance at Tolchester College was at the center of this case. Now the missing Bakanian added a new, befuddling dimension to the murder investigation. Was this case instead linked to the elusive treasure of *El Espíritu de la Virgen* that the pyrates of the *Raven* had stolen?

If someone, once and for all, could find that goddamn treasure, he would not have to step between treasure hunters slugging it out over a plot of sand filled with beer cans. Nor take a report from an irate redneck whose metal detector had been stolen from the bed of his pickup truck. In the last incident, a man who had set off to find 'the X marking the spot' returned to the beach to find that a local fisherman had found his wife's G-spot.

Jay castigated himself ... what was he thinking? "There is no treasure; it's merely a legend concocted to lure tourists to the village. No, no, no, there is no fucking treasure in River Glen!"

He pulled up the hood of his rain coat and rushed across the parking lot to the marina store. He pressed his face against the plate glass window while hurricane winds whipped his coat against him. The front door of the store was locked and the lights were off. Rain blew horizontally across the floating docks. The *Knot-A-Care* was gone from its slip. Shit – more time wasted. Detective work was a methodical, often banal, plodding forward until a bit of evidence or combination of evidence made everything clear, but his thoughts reeled as though a behemoth from the deep grabbed his fishing line and yanked it from his grasp. This case was moving anywhere but forward. A headache pulsed behind his temples. He glanced at his watch. Two hours to go until he permitted himself the first scotch of the day.

Most of the boats had been pulled from the slips; others had departed the marina to avoid a pummeling against the docks. The *Knot-A-Care* had obviously chosen the latter option. The typically bustling marina was devoid of life. He passed through the boathouse and found Gary Smyth in the back office, collapsed in a chair.

"Sorry, Jay," Gary said preemptively. "I can't pull your boat. I've been pulling boats 24-7 for three days. My back's frozen. There's cold ones in the fridge."

Jay looked longingly at the refrigerator. "Can't. On duty." A cold beer would be perfect at this moment. His shoes, socks, and pants legs were drenched. If he could be anywhere at this moment, it would be in chest-deep hot water, his legs around Julia's waist, passing a bottle of Royal Lochnagar back and forth through the steam. Instead he had spent the day running between air-conditioned offices and pounding rain, getting absolutely nowhere. His throat was on fire ... fuck, he probably had strep. He eyed the fridge once again.

"Yeah, okay. Beer's good for sore throats. I'm looking for the woman on the *Knot-A-Care*. When did she leave?"

"Don't know for sure ... wasn't paying much attention. I've been madly pulling boats."

"Who is she?"

"Pamela Dodd. She comes here every summer to treasure hunt. She's a regular. A good customer."

According to Will, it seemed that Pamela had almost swamped Alex Allaway's tugboat the week before. Alex's reappearance in this investigation was unnerving.

"This man's gone missing." He handed a photograph of Levon Bakanian to Gary. "Have you seen him around the marina? Talking to her?"

"Yup. And a lot of other men. Some twins last week. She likes her in men in twosomes."

Jay stuffed the photo back in his raincoat. "Do you remember *when* you saw this man?"

"Sorry." Gary shook his head. "I was running around like a chicken with its head cut off trying to get as many boats out of the water as possible ... maybe Saturday, maybe Sunday."

"I'm going to need the footage from your CCTV."

"Sorry, no can do. Before the storm rolled in, I turned off the power to the dock and slips. That's all I'd need – live wires and cables dropping into the water."

"But you're sure you saw them together?"

"Yes, definitely. And so did my daughter-in-law Judith Ann who lives on the same dock. She found it humorous that Pamela sent the twins packing, only to replace them with another handsome playmate the following day."

Lisa insisted on going to the Lame Dog Saloon with Jay, despite his warning that the place was "a disease-infested cesspool." Owen's sordid personal history intrigued her. Jay rarely carried a gun, but he fastened his shoulder holster under his raincoat before he entered the saloon.   If he thought that a firearm was necessary, then she would do the same.   Jay could have been an actor, she decided.   If the situation warranted it, he would morph into the sickest uber cop imaginable – Psycho Cop – which scared the shit out of the most hardened criminals and yielded immediate results. If he was going to transform into Psycho Cop, it would happen here in the Lame Dog Saloon.   She couldn't wait. This situation warranted three pieces of gum.   She chewed excitedly.   If she could just record the Jekyll and Hyde transformation of her most awesomely cool boss and post it on Facebook, she would get a zillion Likes ... except that her awesomely cool boss would go ballistic.   He was still hung over.

"Brace yourself for the revolting, Lisa." Jay looked warily at the doorknob.   "Who knows what disgusting infection or plague I'll contract by touching it."

The noise stopped as soon they entered.   The place was as vile as Jay said it would be ... a dingy rats' nest that the police had cleaned out twice since her employment at the River Glen PD.   The gray air was lit only by neon beer signs and smelled of urine, body odor, and cigarettes.   Lisa's stomach quaked.   The few occupants leaning over the pool tables and slouched at the bar were a primitive form of hominid ... something below *Homo sapiens.*   The long-time owner Lanny Landry took one look at Jay, spit, and disappeared down a hallway.

Improvisation was Jay's most impressive skill; he lifted an eight ball and cue ball from a pool table, grabbed a towel from behind the bar, and dashed down the dim, trash-laden hallway. She followed, glancing behind to see if anyone, some thug or henchmen, was coming to assist Landry. No one was. The drug-addled whores were too interesting to the troglodytes.

They found Landry behind his desk, cramming papers into a shredder. Jay laid the bar towel across the desk and placed the white and black pool balls in its center.

"Ain't telling you fuckin nothing." A cigarette dangled from the corner of Landry's mouth. Ashes dropped into the shredder as he hurried papers into the grinding blades.

"Yeah, you will, Lanny." Jay pulled a mug shot of Owen Paco from his raincoat pocket. Unfortunately no photos were known to exist of Henry Herssen.

"Ain't done nothin' so get the fuck out."

"You're going to tell me about this man."

Landry's protruding frog eyes moved across the photo. "Don't know him."

"You've owned this bar for ages. He was a regular here about twenty to thirty years ago."

"Don't remember."

Jay lifted the corners of the towel around the pool balls and spun the towel, pressing the balls together into a hard knot. Lisa was mesmerized. Improvisation! Jay was the boss! He swung the knot of balls into a glowing Pabst beer light. Plastic and glass sprayed the desk.

#woohooty #PsychoCoparrives!

"Fucker! That was my dad's!"

"Sentimental are we? This one?" Jay pointed at a Miller sign. "Mom's?" He whacked it. Shattered glass and plastic rained onto a tarp covering boxes. He shoved Landry aside, and kicked the shredder's power cord from the electrical socket. "After I smash up your family heirlooms, I start on you, Lanny."

"Don't know the fucker!"

Jay swung the knot of balls in the air and smiled menacingly at Landry. "Knee caps, face, or wrists? You decide which I break first. Don't say I'm not fair."

"Okay ... okay ... it's Owen Paco! That asshole left without paying his bar tab!"

"You're doing great," Jay said. "Wrists just came off the I'm-going-to-break-it list."

"Dealt a bit ... painkillers ... some meth." Landry's eyes dizzily followed the swirling knot of balls.

"Paco's companions?"

Landry paused.

"Companions." Jay glanced impatiently at his watch.

Landry stalled again.

"Ouch. The wrists went back on the list. How are you going to roll those kegs around without knee caps and wrists?" He turned to her. "This is going to get bloody, Sergeant. I don't know if you want to watch this."

Lisa chewed frenetically. "I definitely wanna watch this."

Jay stepped threatening forward.

"Okay, okay! The fisherman Herssen was okay. Just a silent guy. Just drank beer, said nothing. But Herssen's companion was insane ... a psychopath ... worked here briefly ... took a meat cleaver to the cook ... whacked off part of his hand ... please ... please ... don't tell me that Rick Sarova's back in the area!"

Jay Braden's impulse was to stomp on the gas pedal and tear through the village, tires squealing. Julia Hale had that effect on him. It had been days since he had seen her. A hot meal, gargantuan glass of scotch, hot bath, and Julia would realign his world. No, Julia before the hot meal. Maybe he would make love to her on the living room sofa, or on the soft rug by the fireplace, if she was agreeable. Agreeable? … she was always agreeable. Instead, his police sedan inched across the River Glen bridge as a torrent of water rushed feet below the metal girders. He accelerated again when he reached the river road, despite high water slapping against the banks.

Shit. What now?

He backed off on the gas pedal. A bunch of cars were parked between Julia and Alex's houses. One was Will's, but the others were unfamiliar. Was Alex having a hurricane party? The locals used any occasion, festive or somber – a pyrate massacre was a case in point – to party.

Jay trudged up Julia's porch steps. The chimenea blazed so he paused to warm his rain-shriveled hands. Julia and Royal Lochnagar were the singular objects in his universe at the moment. He pushed through the screen door that she always left open for him. A fire crackled in the fireplace – oh, to see Julia naked by the fire! But instead voices, not lovely lilting ones, but bland American ones, came from the kitchen. His hopes fizzled. The kitchen was brightly lit. Huddled around the kitchen table were Julia, Alex, Will, Brad 'Che Guevara' Smyth, Nina Vega, and Griffin Blake.

"Take a look at this, sir!" Will slid aside to let him see.

SPIDER

In a peanut jar was a black spider. At the sight of him, it reared back on its hind legs and spit venom at the glass.

Now Nina was really spooked. The whole day her missing finger had hardly crossed her mind. It wasn't bad enough that a giant spider – that turned out to be venomous! – climbed from a crack in her office ceiling and Levon Bakanian was missing, but now Detective Braden didn't want her and Griffin returning to their apartment. Clearly the murder investigation, though Braden couldn't elaborate, had something to do with the finance report that she and Griffin had found stuck behind her bookshelf. Until the murderer was caught, Braden insisted that she and Griffin go only to campus to teach their classes, then return directly to the village. She and Griffin had bonded in their short time as apartment mates and wished to stay together. Since Will and Carly had begun to move into Alex's cottage, it would be too crowded for Griffin and her there. Will suggested his mother's house, but Julia nixed the idea.

"Belle's a big-mouth and busy-body," Julia said. "Everyone from here to Edinburgh will find out that she has two individuals staying in her spare bedrooms. Jay…"

He was transfixed with the spider furiously pacing the jar.

"Jay, lad …"

"Hmm?"

"… how about you stay with me, and give Nina and Griffin rooms in your house? Your housekeeper's there to watch over them. No one but a nutter would attempt to break in with a police officer about."

"Life does not get better than this!" On Lisa's desk was a bag of Cheetos, a caffeinated soda, and an apple because Wanda insisted on fruit with each meal. Sustenance to work late, her computer – a portal into the netherworld of the diabolic and demented – and a complicated crime to solve. This was why she chose a career in law enforcement. This was why she was a goddess of crime-fighting. #lifecouldnotbebetter Will, Jay, Cloris, and Denny had left for the evening. It was just her, Norman from IT, and state troopers on the night shift. Besides the murders and the missing professor, the newest concern was the River Glen bridge. Since the hurricane had parked itself over the northern Chesapeake, the river had risen dangerously high and threatened to wash away the bridge. Police cruisers were positioned on either side of it, monitoring its foundation.

Whoever Rick Sarova was, he terrified Lanny Landry to this day. After uttering the name, a green-faced Landry had dropped into his chair.

"Evil, evil, pure evil."

"What else, Lanny?" Jay had asked.

"Don't know. Sarova disappeared years before Herssen and Paco stopped coming by. Don't know nothin' else. Don't ask me, don't know."

The name had appeased Jay because he dropped the sling of pool balls onto Landry's desk. "When was this?"

"Who knows? Maybe twenty-five years ago, maybe longer. I'm trying to forget. Then Herssen and Paco took off a few years later. Has Sarova come back?"

"Don't know." Jay lifted the tarp covered with shards of glass from the broken beer lamp.

She and Jay had recognized the boxes immediately – the flat-screen TVs stolen from the Walmart earlier that summer. This delayed them until a police van arrived to take the TVs and Landry back to headquarters for processing.

Lisa stuck her gum to the corner of her desk, tore open the Cheetos and stuffed a handful in her mouth. Her fingers danced over the keyboard. She typed Rick Sarova into the police database. If this guy was such a monster, then certainly something would turn up.

Odd ... nothing.

She typed Richard Sarova and waited. Still nothing. Ricardo Sarova? There was absolutely nothing in the police or FBI files on a Rick, Richard or Ricardo Sarova.

Sarova, Sarova ... the name looked familiar, but where had she seen it?

Lisa munched down more Cheetos and reached for the Tolchester folder. President Blodgen had the Chief Financial Officer print out the financial information for the college for them. Nothing seemed amiss, but it was not difficult to doctor books, if one wanted to.

Norman in IT, a master of the spreadsheet, had reconfigured the Tolchester staff and faculty list for her in reverse chronological order according to date of employment. Some of the names she recognized. Drs. Nina Vega, Griffin Blake, and Levon Bakanian were at the top of the list as they had been hired most recently, this same summer. Six years before appeared the name of Dr. Gloria Wines; that same year was the retirement date for Drs. Bob Randolph and Sheila Myers. Fifteen years before Dr. Bradley Smyth was hired. That same year Hank Stupens came onboard as a maintenance man and groundskeeper. Twenty-five years before, Dr. Lana Hinkie joined the faculty as an

Assistant Professor of Communications, and Mary Blodgen was hired as a Laboratory Instructor in Botany and a tutor in the Tutoring Center.

Eureka.   Thirty-five years ago two landscapers were employed concurrently for three years.   Owen Paco and a female named Ricarda Sarova.

But it wasn't on this spreadsheet that Lisa had seen the name *Sarova*. Her memory was close to photographic. *Sarova* had been seen before in a different font.   This spreadsheet was in Helvetica, but she had seen the name written as Sarova, RD in a font like Times Roman.

#pacoisgenius!   She clicked into a search engine and typed Robert Randolph *Atrax* publications.   A long list of manuscripts appeared, all of which were written by both Drs. Robert Randolph and David Towers at UMES.   Thirty-four years ago a single publication, "On the preliminary mechanism of venom secretion in *Atrax robustus*," had been co-authored by Randolph, RA, Towers, DX and ... hmm fascinating ... one *Sarova, RD*.

"Julia and Royal Lochnagar are out of reach for another night. Just fucking kill me. I'm getting too old to be slogging around in rainstorms late at night. Detective work is a young man's game," Jay told himself. He should have been laid by now and settled into the pillows, watching the Orioles-Braves game. Instead, he had dropped off two young professors at his house, and was now en route to a secret meeting with Burt Sweeny at Tolchester College. He had nothing against Burt; in fact, he liked the man. It was just that Burt brought back bad memories.

After Laura's murder on Mutter Island, he admittedly went off the deep end. Every evening had been spent on his deck, swilling down pitchers of gin and tonics, chain-smoking, and staring numbly at the river where Laura loved to swim. At work the following day he was too incapacitated by a blinding hangover to do much else but listen to Cloris talk about Sylvester's catnip trips. This continued for weeks until his captain and a police psychologist appeared at his desk. His choices were: early retirement (not so subtle code for termination), or attend AA meetings, or grief counseling. His first impulse had been to say fuck it and quit on the spot, except that at his extraordinary rate of Tanqueray and Marlboro consumption, he would be broke by year's end. The grief counseling seemed the lesser of the three evils and entailed two nights a week of sitting in a smoke-filled room of human misery, hearing about ... a teenager dying at a rave, a daughter killed by a suicide-bomber in the Middle East, a senile grandmother drowned in the bay, a husband losing his job and overdosing on pain medication. In Burt's case, it was his wife driving head-on into a tree.

When he was called upon to speak, he froze. Where ... how ... to begin ... to articulate the jumbled emotions one feels for a mad wife killed by a psychopath on a beautiful summer day?

One consolation of grief counseling was that Dr. Mullen, who ran the sessions, had great legs. Twice he had asked her out for drinks after the meetings and twice she reminded him that she was married.

At the first meeting, Jay had picked a seat by Burt and the ash tray. He, Burt, and a firefighter chain-smoked throughout the meeting, and after went to Harlow's for beers. That's how he was able to contact Burt that evening; he and Burt had exchanged phone numbers.

Jay left his police sedan at his house after dropping off Nina Vega and Griffin Blake, and instead drove Laura's black convertible to Tolchester College. It was around ten pm when he pulled into the parking lot of the Riddel building. Something about that building felt wrong, but a poisonous spider – from Sydney, Australia of all places – crawling into Vega's office made his internal alarm system go haywire. The spiky turrets of the building disappeared into the fog. It was a remarkably tall building to house only two floors. There had to be another floor or floors under those turrets. Burt's silhouette, holding a cigarette away from the dripping eaves, waited for him.

Jay grabbed a flashlight from the front seat and climbed from the car. "Thanks for meeting me."

"Su – sure, no problem."

Burt pulled a flashlight from his raincoat and they entered the building through the front door. They climbed to the second floor. "It's gotta be this way, Jay." They headed in a direction opposite to the faculty offices. "I have a master key to all the buildings."

"Who else does?"

"A lot of people. All of us security guards."

"That's how many of you?"

"Only three. We're short staffed."

"Know that feeling."

"And the maintenance staff and the administrators. A lot of people."

"Can you get me a list?"

"Yeah, sure. If there are stairs, they gotta be in here."

Burt moved his key toward the lock.

"Wait. Here, put these on." He handed Burt latex gloves. "Then we don't leave prints in case CSI needs to dust later. What's in here?"

"Don't know."

He grimaced.

Burt shrugged. "We were told to never go in here. Unstable floor, rotten beams apparently."

"Who told you that?"

"A guy on the construction team that surveyed this building. He told us to leave that room and end of the building alone until it could be stabilized."

He grimaced again. "I want to see for myself."

Burt moved the key toward the lock. Nothing. The key wouldn't budge. "Th - this key's supposed to open all the campus doors!"

"Except this one." Jay pulled his MiracleKey device from his pocket. A perk of his thankless job was cool devices. He pushed open the door. The absence of a squeak indicated that it was opened often. He inched his foot forward, then stomped. The sound of secure planks resonated under his foot. "There's nothing wrong with this floor."

He decided against flipping on the overhead light and alerting someone outside to their presence. Instead he shone his flashlight beam around. The room was full of filing cabinets. He opened one up. Decades and decades of personnel folders, from the 1950s through to the 1990s, before the age of computers and digitized documents. Behind a stack of chairs was a door.

"Maybe our stairway, Burt."

They slid the chairs aside. Again they were impeded by a lock. He pulled the MiracleKey from his pocket again. The door creaked open and they leaned into the crack. Yup, just as predicted. A stairway climbed into the darkness.

Jay had dragged Burt into this mess; the least he could do was go first.   He crept up the stairs, his flashlight twitching nervously. Spider webs grazed his face; he batted at the dark.   The wood planks groaned under their wary footsteps. He and Burt gazed over the top stair. It was one giant room. Jay exhaled. So far, so good. The attic was silent except for the *plink plink* of dripping water. Buckets had been placed around the room to catch the drizzles leaking through the old roof.   He directed his light into a bucket.

Plink. Plink.

"Not very full. This was emptied recently."

"This place has a b-bad feeling, Jay."

"No shit."

Burt moved his beam toward the staircase. "I'm I'm gonna watch the stairs."

"Yeah, good idea."

Plink. Plink.

The floorboards were slick under Jay's shoes as he passed by dusty classroom furniture. "Ahhchoo!"

"G-god bless you."

"Thanks."

Jay's head swiveled from side to side. He checked over his shoulder countless times. Burt responded each time with a reassuring thumbs up. Good man, Burt. Debbie's was a terrible crash.   She must have died instantly.   Laura and Debbie had that in common. Jay tiptoed on. He didn't recall the building being so interminably long. His heart pounded, and his ears strained for noises other than *plink plink*. At any second a demon might lunge from the darkness. After a seeming eternity, he arrived at the area over the faculty offices.   It was possible that he was standing over Nina Vega's office.   A table was pressed against the wall.   He swiped his finger across it.   All of the attic furniture was covered in dust, yet this table was perfectly clean. Whatever was on it had been removed very recently, probably when he and Lisa appeared on campus.   He shone his beam at the floor. Weird. Dried out cockroaches, crickets, and earthworms dotted the floor around the table.   Worms? Worms would not have gotten to an attic on their own.   But the rest of the attic floor was devoid of bugs.   The critters were only around the table.   He pulled his cell phone from his pocket. Thank you, God ... cell reception. He typed into a search engine: What does *Atrax robustus* eat?

Answer: insects and small lizards.

He swept the flashlight beam over the floorboards around the table. Wait, what was that?

A glint.

He peered downward. A shiny object was lodged between two floorboards under the table. Shit. This meant getting down on his hands and knees and crawling underneath. With his dismal luck, a funnel spider escapee was hiding on the underside of the table, would drop into his collar, and plunge its fangs into his neck.

He typed: What are the symptoms of an *Atrax* bite?

Christ, no way ... increased salivation and lacrimation, tachycardia, hypertension, dyspnea, pulmonary edema, increased intracranial pressure, and mental disorientation.

He bent down and pried the shiny object from the crack. It was a syringe. He had seen one just like it, very recently, in a photo from the Sheila Myers case. That syringe had been found in a stall in the ladies room at the Reading

Terminal Market in Philly. He yanked a plastic bag from his pocket and stashed the syringe inside. More work for Zera's team.

Something else caught his eye. It was stuck between the ends of the floor boards and the wall. It was a plastic animal container, identical to the ones in Herssen's shed. He hesitated, lest the crack be a nest of poisonous spiders. He had no children, no wife. If he died tonight, no one but Cloris – because he tolerated her cat stories – would miss him. Julia was so stunning; another boyfriend would be warming her bed by week's end. What the hell ... he reached into the crack.

Jay exhaled loudly. His hand returned from the crack unscathed. There was black writing – a name – on the plastic container. The container must have fallen off the table and cracked open. Its occupant had escaped and scurried down Nina Vega's wall. The occupant, that now resided in a peanut jar on Julia's kitchen table, was named Brutus.

Spider sat in the corner of the commuter student parking lot, concealed by the hood of a black raincoat. The rain made it impossible to see through the windshield so she leaned with binoculars out the car door to see who it was that Burt Sweeny was meeting. How interesting! It was Jay Braden, with the snowy white hair and implacable blue eyes.

"Sweet creature!" said the Spider, "you're witty and you're wise, How handsome are your gauzy wings, how brilliant are your eyes!"

How interesting that that the sweet creature not go through the normal channels and contact the administrators or Hank Stupens, if he wanted to visit the faculty offices once again. Interesting.

Spider checked the time and sipped a latte. After about a half an hour, Braden exited the building and climbed into his convertible. The convertible left the Riddel building parking lot and turned onto College Avenue. Spider followed, keeping a smart distance. Braden drove down the coastal road into the village of River Glen and paused at the entrance to the bridge. There was a flash of blue and red lights, police cruisers having blocked traffic on the bridge. Spider turned off near the bluff and pressed binoculars to her eyes. The officers recognized Braden, waved him through, and his car motored across the bridge. He disappeared down the river road, heading toward the Point. Spider checked the time and turned back up the coastal road.

"So he wove a subtle web, in a little corner sly, And set his table ready, to dine upon the Fly."

By the time Jay arrived back at Julia's house it was too late to dine. He was secretly thrilled at her suggestion to cohabitate while Vega and Blake took the spare rooms in his house. This would be an interesting experiment. He had only lived with one woman, Laura. Then he was alone, a widower, a term that nauseated him and implied a man whose shelf life had expired. He was not meant to be a solitary creature. A woman's companionship was the finest thing in life.

Julia moved Brutus' jar onto the windowsill over the kitchen sink. "He's utterly unappetizing as a centerpiece for the table."

"Utterly," he said, heading to the bathroom.

After a hot shower, he returned to the kitchen and tossed back a glass of scotch to dampen the sciatica and the ache in his lower back from crawling around in the damp attic. He sipped his second drink while studying the spider on the windowsill. Yes, definitely. Brutus was utterly unappetizing. It would be a liquid dinner. Bakanian was missing, and Randolph, Paco, Myers, Lamont and an unidentified male were victims of this killer. And there might have been another.

As he was leaving the Riddel building that night, Burt grabbed at his raincoat sleeve. "J-Jay ... Debbie always drove so slow, so cautious. I think something scared her ... t-terrified her that night."

That was the tipping point. Jay's thoughts reeled. That day evidence had appeared faster than his brain could process it ... sleep, if he could just get some sleep. He stepped over Clark and Miranda who were curled together on the bedroom rug.

He placed his scotch on the bedside table. "I'm so exhausted."

"Then come to bed, lad." She pulled back the sheet.

Lad ... she called him lad! And her summer nightgown was translucent. He was not *that* exhausted. He fell into Julia's warm arms and pressed his mouth on hers. A woman's companionship was the finest thing in life.

CHAPTER EIGHT
Tuesday

Pamela Dodd washed her hands again. Maybe if she used the peppermint-scented hand soap that she typically used during the Christmas holidays, the smell would go away. She scrubbed and scrubbed, then rinsed and sniffed at her fingers. She frowned. She turned on the lights over her sink because the galley was dingy and grey that morning. The weatherman reported that the worst of the storm was over. Hurricane Beau had moved northwest and was breaking up over central Pennsylvania. By tomorrow there would be blue skies over the Chesapeake and it would be bikini weather once again.

"Ugly and plain." She examined her fingernails. Last night she had removed her red fingernail polish. Her hands looked hideous without the polish. "Wait ... what was that? Blood behind that nail?"

She flipped on the lights over the galley table. How did she miss that? She dashed to the silverware drawer. With the tip of a steak knife, she scraped and scraped the blood from behind her thumb nail. That horrible smell reappeared. She sniffed at the hands. No, not again ... that dreadful odor! She jerked on the faucet and scrubbed her hands. She rinsed and sniffed, and scrubbed and scrubbed her hands once again.

Some people were blessed with good-looks, a sense of humor, athleticism, or creativity. One of these features set a person apart from the Everyman, but Julia was blessed with all of them. Yes, she was perfect in every way. But her most exceptional quality was her musical lilt. Jay easily envisioned an entranced London audience – as Julia played Desdemona, Ophelia, or Lady Macbeth – hanging on her every word when she was an actress for the Royal Shakespeare Company. It made no difference that that morning she was chattering about the thoroughly mundane ... the weather, the bridge possibly collapsing, or how he took his coffee. The words hurricane, girders, and creamer floated off her tongue like sparrows on a summer breeze. And his sciatica hardly hurt. He kissed Julia's perfect mouth, grabbed a travel mug of her perfect coffee, and set off to his house for a fresh change of clothes and to check on Nina Vega and Griffin Blake.

When he arrived home, Mrs. Pulacki whom he had hired years ago to watch Laura, was preparing breakfast for Nina and Griffin. It was strange to see young people in his house because the usual visitors were Mrs. Pulacki's ancient sister and friends from their book club that congregated on his deck. Had he and Laura had children, they would have been the age of Nina and Griffin. Nina was a pleasant black-haired, black-eyed woman, and Griffin had the lanky body of a cross-country runner. They had Monday-Wednesday-Friday teaching schedules, they told him, so there was no need to go to campus since it was a Tuesday. They had their laptops; they could work from the house. That was good news. If everyone would stay at the house together and keep an eye on one another, he said, it would give him peace of mind. Yes, it was another of Julia's perfect ideas for the group to occupy his riverfront house and watch over each another.

Jay climbed into the police sedan and looked warily across his front seat. The peanut jar containing Brutus was seat-belted into the passenger's seat. The jostling car ride from Julia's house had awoken the spider; it postured ferociously and scraped its fearsome black fangs against the glass. Jay's plan was to drive very carefully to headquarters. All he needed was for someone to rear end him and shatter the jar, causing Brutus to scurry across the dashboard, leap onto the steering wall, chomp into his hand, and inject a deadly amount of atracotoxin, or whatever the hell Lisa had called the venom. At least he would die a happy man, delighted by Julia's bawdy words and sizzling body the night before.

Jay entered headquarters to find Lisa and Will talking to an elderly African-American man with white hair and wired-rimmed glasses. It had to be Bob Randolph's colleague Dr. David Towers from UMES who had come to get the spider. He could not hand Towers the jar fast enough.

Towers' eyes widened. "This is definitely an *Atrax robustus* and a huge one! A male."

"Named Brutus," he said sardonically.

"I've never seen one of this remarkable size." Towers tilted his head and studied the spider. "Something about this one is different. First, I've never seen one this active and exhibiting so many threat displays. The males are only active when searching for females to mate with, otherwise they're fairly shy. And the chelicerae ..."

"The what?"

"The mouthparts that house the fangs are enlarged. I have no clue why. I'd have to open him up to have a look." Towers shook his head in bafflement. "There." He pointed. "The exoskeleton on both chelicera has been damaged, punctured."

"By what?"

"Maybe a syringe. The wounds have been sealed by scar tissue."

"Are you telling me that someone's been injecting something into the fangs of this beast?"

"No, the puncture marks are upstream to the fangs. Someone's been injecting something into the venom gland."

"Ricarda Sarova was a co-author on one of your early papers with Bob Randolph," Lisa remarked.

"Yes, thankfully only one," Towers said grimly. "I didn't want to put her name on the paper at all because her work was shoddy and inaccurate. In the end, Bob and I had to redo all of her experiments and correct the data tables that she had worked on."

"Was she a scientist?"

"No, a scientist-wanna-be. She worked at Tolchester as a landscaper and pestered Bob about her getting a job in his lab. But Bob had no lab facilities at Tolchester so we performed all of the experiments at my lab at UMES. One summer he brought her along with him to work on the mechanism of venom secretion."

"When was this?" Jay asked.

"Decades ago when Bob and I were just starting out as assistant professors. Bob was quite enthusiastic about working with his undergraduates.   He thought that by working with Ric it might encourage her to go to college and get a biology degree.   He had a lot more patience with students than I ever did. I couldn't stand her. She was off-putting, an arrogant know-it-all.   From her work as a landscaper, she believed that she knew everything about everything.   She was an expert on plants and animals, she used to say. I knew her work was falsified. No one could generate so much data in such a short period of time. When Bob and I replicated her work, we found that her results were completely bogus. I wanted to fire her immediately, but Bob had a more generous spirit and let her stay on for the rest of the summer to care for and feed the spiders."

"How did she take that?"

"Not well. The demotion made her angry. She was surly and aloof for the rest of the time. She did not take criticism well, which was surprising."

"Why?"

"She was an adult in her mid to late thirties. I would have expected a more mature response from someone that age."

"Then what?"

"The summer ended and she thankfully went away but not before stealing some spiders."

"She stole your spiders!?"

"Yes, and these are regulated animals that can only be used for medical research. Bob and I used to milk the atracotoxin from the spiders so that neuroscientists could study the effect of the venom on neuronal activity. Other colleagues of ours used the atracotoxin to produce the anti-venom. Bob tried to contact Ric about the missing spiders, but she had quit her job at Tolchester at that same time ... when she got pregnant."

"Do you know the name of the father?"

"No, sorry. A fisherman that she lived with. That's all I remember her mentioning."

"Henry Herssen?"

Towers shook his head. "Sorry, it was over thirty years ago."

Jay turned to Lisa and Will. "I want you to check out every elderly woman associated with Tolchester College."

"Don't bother," Towers said. "Ric Sarova's buried in the River Glen cemetery. She and the baby died in childbirth."

Jay's heart was heavy with guilt. Every time he visited the River Glen cemetery he brought flowers. Instead he paused in front of Laura's gravestone empty-handed. Laura would forgive his oversight and empathize with his mounting frustration; this case was all about chasing ghosts. The quiet, unassuming Henry Herssen and the wicked Ricarda Sarova, Jay surmised, were living under assumed names on the outskirts of River Glen and exacting revenge – death by spider bite – on individuals who had wronged them. Then he had imagined that the couple wasn't sedentary at all ... not farmers or fishermen living off the grid ... but truckers who would rumble into River Glen to kill their victim, then bury the body under Herssen's floorboards and depart for places unknown. That hypothesis no longer made sense. Sarova had been dead for over thirty years. Owen Paco and an unidentified male had been killed around twenty years ago, Randolph and Myers six years ago, and Amanda Lamont four years ago. Sarova could not have been involved; she was long dead. They were back to square one. Henry Herssen was still paying his property taxes. But who was he associating with at Tolchester College that was housing poisonous spiders in the attic of the Riddel building?

After slogging through the wet grass, Jay finally found the Sarova headstone.

Mother and son
Ricarda Darlene Sarova 1953 – 1985
Henry Paco Herssen 1985

The infant Henry had died with Sarova that same day. The boy's middle name raised another question. According to Lanny Landry from the *Lame Dog Saloon*, the threesome was inseparable. Was the infant named after the friend Paco, or was the boy's paternity ambiguous? Had Sarova named the boy after the two possible fathers? That answer would remain unanswered for now, because the circuitous legal paperwork for an exhumation might take weeks, even months, and he didn't have weeks to catch this killer.

According to Professor Towers, when the Randolph, Towers, Sarova paper had been published in the *Journal of Arthropod Physiology*, Randolph had tried to contact Sarova about the good news only to find out through the Tolchester landscapers that she had died.

"Sir!" Lisa shouted.

The morning mist made it impossible to discern her exact whereabouts. "Where are you?"

"In the back! By the pyrate gravestones!"

Lisa's voice had an agitated edge to it. She had definitely found something. "Coming!" He hurried between the headstones from the 1900s, through the 1800s and 1700s, to the crumbling ones from the late 1600s.

He had been back to the pyrate burial site only once before. The first autumn that he and Laura moved to River Glen, she had insisted that he take her on a ghost walk. It had been a disastrous idea; he knew it full well at the time. Already Laura's behavior had become volatile and erratic, which was why he had moved them from the chaotic city of Baltimore, where he had been battling drug lords, to the serene village of River Glen.

"We'll meet our neighbors!" Laura had handed him a glossy brochure that she picked up in town.

The ghost walk had been a ridiculously expensive package deal: a seafood dinner at the Nauticus, assembly on the town pier and walk down the river road with the Grim Reaper tour guide, all culminating with fireside drinks afterward at Harlow's Pub. He hadn't the heart to tell Laura that their companions on the ghost walk would be tourists from Wilmington, Annapolis, and Philadelphia whom they would never see again, and he was right about that. The only neighbor that they had met was Luna who was distributing pamphlets about psychic readings on the town pier. But the ghost walk had not been a total wash. In fact, there had been some plusses to the evening; the seafood dinner at the Nauticus was exceptional, the Grim Reaper was an animated tour guide with a great knowledge of local history, and Miles Harlow had an excellent selection of scotch. The down-side was that the headless pyrate Charles Allaway, who had popped from behind a gravestone, was terrifyingly realistic so Laura had insisted that he buy her a telescope (another painful hit to his wallet because she wanted the high-end model) to watch for the ghost ship *Raven* sailing up the Glen River to retrieve the missing gold.

"There is no treasure in River Glen," he uttered to himself for the umpteenth time. He passed through a gap in the collapsing stone wall. A trial of footprints in the soggy ground had led Lisa to a lone gravestone set apart from others. It was half covered by a rhododendron bush.

Diego Alvarez del Castillo
1670-1698

"What?"

"Someone drove a car back here." Lisa pointed to tire tracks.

"That's no small feat in this mud."

"Wide tire tracks. Maybe a jeep or SUV." This time she pointed to the Alvarez headstone. "The hurricane didn't wash all of it away."

He knelt on the wet ground. "Shit! Text Zera. She needs to send her people over here now."

"On it!" She smacked her gum vigorously.

"This is going from bad to worse. We're going to have question Alex Allaway. She was in the graveyard over the weekend. She told Will and I this last night when I informed Nina Vega and Griffin Blake that their colleague was missing."

Jay felt vaguely sick. Congealed on the edge of the Alvarez headstone was a clot of bloody skin with short black hairs. Levon Bakanian had short black hair.

Nina needed a quiet moment to herself. She was supposed to be working on her Rhode Island fisheries manuscript at Detective Braden's dining room table, but instead she paced his back deck. How she could concentrate at a time like this? To distract herself, she pressed her eye to the large telescope. Focus, focus. Focus on the scenery. When she swiveled the telescope to the right, she saw the Glen River disappear around a bend; to the left was Alex's cottage, Julia's house with the dock, and the village center built around the piers. When she directed the telescope skyward, she saw breaks in the ragged clouds and glimpses of blue. Finally – blue sky after days of torrential rain.

Prior to her move to River Glen, her life had been quiet and orderly. After all, she was an academic who spent most of her time behind a computer or in the library. She had lived a placid life with Juanita and her mother, until pancreatic cancer took her mother in less than a month. That was the single trauma of Nina's life, the death of her mother who had been only forty-eight. Ricardo and his family were anything but tranquil, but Nina's strategy for those visits had been polite detachment, avoidance of the kitchen where Abuelita and Mamacita conspired against her from dawn to dusk, and solitary walks around the ranch with the dogs. But since moving to River Glen, there was a catastrophe at every turn. Now she was hiding out in a detective's riverfront home all because she and Griffin had found a mysterious finance report taped to the back of her bookshelf, and a deadly spider had climbed down her office wall.

Last evening Detective Braden had kindly offered up his home, showed them the liquor behind his bar, and pointed out the spare bedrooms. Nina suspected that his willingness to give up his house had as much to do with their safety and security as it did with his attachment to Julia.

At Julia's kitchen table Alex had peered at the snarling spider and said that it was not indigenous to this area. But after that, Alex seemed only interested in getting Will back to her cottage. A possible murderer in River Glen had put everyone on edge.

After Braden had dropped them at his house, she and Griffin explored the upstairs. It was Griffin's suggestion that they sleep in the same room; that way the murderer couldn't slip in and kill one of them in their sleep. It seemed a good idea at the time. She had slept in the proximity of others ... who hadn't? As children, she and Juanita had shared a bunk bed in their apartment. She had slept in tents during camping trips with her church youth group, and she had a number of roommates during college. Sharing a bedroom with a colleague was admittedly awkward, but justifiable for safety reasons. Griffin, she had supposed, was gay. He had Pride written in rainbow colors on his door. He researched gay health clubs. Other than Braden's master bedroom, their room choices were one with a king-sized bed and one with a single-bed. They opted for the king-sized bed as it would give them space. After Griffin swabbed down the bedroom furniture with disinfectant wipes, they had shared a bottle of wine at Braden's bar, took hot showers, and climbed into bed. Though she was no expert in psychology, she did know that stress and lust were coupled phenomena. The stress-lust effect kicked in ... with ferocity.

She supposed wrong; Griffin was not gay.

First they ... then they ... next they ... how did Ricardo not know how to do that, or that? *Or that!* After the nth wave of pleasure rippled through her – no, they were far from ripples, there were tidal waves – it seemed likely the River Glen medical examiner might be investigating another death the next morning ... her own ... death by rolling waves of orgasm. The night wasn't just a one off. The rapture continued that morning and might have gone on indefinitely had not the housekeeper Mrs. Pulacki fried up bacon and played a Kenny G CD in the kitchen.

Nina pulled her eye from the telescope and dropped into a chair next to the propane grill. My god ... what had happened? The stress-lust effect was precipitated by an insane murderer in their midst. Insane murderer ... now she was thinking in redundancies. What murderers were sane? She was completely confused. She was a good Catholic girl; her mother had raised her and Juanita strictly. She had known Griffin for what – a week? Of course she had slept with Ricardo because she was going to marry him. But sex with a colleague? And the guy in the next office? She so knew better! Now it would be impossible to concentrate at work. She would never get her research done, or the manuscripts from her dissertation written. Tenure, forget it. Every time she might pass Griffin in the hall while emptying the water from her rain funnel, or might sit in a Sociology Department meeting with him, all she would be thinking about was his lean body between her convulsing thighs.

The slider opened behind her. It was Griffin, smiling his carefree smile. He knelt between her knees. "Mrs. Pulacki just left to get groceries. I was wondering if you wanted to take a break from your writing."

Nina's answer came in nanoseconds. She flung her arms around his neck and pulled his mouth onto hers.

"Voila. Done." Alex Allaway attached the herring migration report to the email to Mr. Ward in Annapolis, and hit SEND. Each year the reports to her boss were improving, the text supported by detailed tables and graphs. In the few years since taking this job at the marine station, she had located the best waters and marshes to sample in and worked with the most knowledgeable fishermen and fisheries experts on the bay. She had the best job ever.

"Water Boy. Treat." At the magical T word, the Labrador retriever sprang from his dog bed and dashed across the lab. She tossed him a beef-favored chew stick before heading to the hot water dispenser. "We celebrate." She stirred a packet of hot chocolate into her skull and cross bones mug and pulled a canister of Cool Whip from a rusty fridge that smelled more like bait than human food. She squirted whipped cream into her mouth. "My treat for a job well done." She spiraled a cone of cream onto her hot chocolate. Mug in hand, she peered out the back window. At the rickety dock the *Vital Spark* was tied to the cleats. The rugged little tug had survived the hurricane with not so much as a scratch. The sky was still overcast, but the clouds were starting to break up. It would be a perfect afternoon to check the crab pots. Due to the storm the crab pots hadn't been checked for days. The pots would be bursting. She sent a text to Alan and Jacob at the Nauticus, and the Hoffmans at the Dockside Café telling them to expect a delivery of blue crabs by the end of the afternoon.

Her next text went to Nina. "How's the hand feeling? Are you up for eating crabs at my place tonight? I'll peel. I should be bringing in a giant shipment."

Maybe she should drop off crabs with Will's mother Belle, as a peace offering of sorts. Will and Carly's move to her cottage was, in Belle's mind, entirely her fault. The move had gone smoothly, despite shuttling of their belongings from the car to cottage in the rain. The plastic tent sleeping arrangement in the living room delighted Carly. The girl had fortuitously inherited John's happy-go-lucky demeanor and not Belle's bossiness.

Alex checked the time. It was the first time in weeks that she had mental downtime at work. How to kill a few hours before taking the *Vital Spark* out to the crab pots? There were beakers and graduated cylinders in the sink that needed cleaning, and the weather station on the roof got bent during the hurricane; those chores needed to be tended to but later. She was 50% pyrate after all. More interesting things beckoned. She settled herself at her laptop and opened up Brother Guillermo's chronicle given to her by James Collins.

It was slow going through the faded, drunken handwriting of the Spanish priest. Worse, it was written in old English. Guillermo's account was biased toward the Whitbys due to his close friendship with the Scotsman Conal Whitby, the only Whitby to survive Giles Hale's wrath. The priest and the Scot had lived together on the outskirts of the village. Names of all of the usual suspects, Smyths, Collinses, Wilkinses and Allaways popped up throughout the chronicle. By the late 1600s River Glen had become a thriving, self-sustaining community of fishermen, carpenters, and farmers. Shannon Allaway took over the running of Giles and Kathleen's tavern. There were increasing references to traders, mostly Dutch, English, and French, and Nanticoke Indians passing through, suggesting that River Glen was no longer an isolated community.

In the July of 1698 Guillermo wrote that a battered sloop appeared at the mouth of the Glen River, a ship called *Tereza*.

"The *Tereza*?"

Water Boy's head jerked up from his chew stick and he briefly stopped his gnawing.

She read on, transfixed. The traders on the *Tereza* were from Castillo. The captain was one Juan Carlos and his cousin was Diego Alvarez. "Traders, yeah right, Water Boy. They were no traders. The *Tereza* was a pyrate ship. Anyone who knows anything about pyrates know this."

This was just the evidence Levon Bakanian was looking for! This was why he had moved to Tolchester College from UVA ... to discover historical gems of information in the local archives. The night before Jay had mentioned to everyone around Julia's kitchen table that Levon had not showed up for work. Nina and Griffin had been to Levon's Friday night lecture, they had told Jay. They also reported that Levon's car had been gone for much of the weekend, but they saw it briefly on Sunday morning. Alex had confirmed that she also saw Levon at the lecture, and he had stopped by her cottage on Saturday evening to invite her for a walk to the graveyard. On Sunday, in the rain, she, Levon, and Water Boy had walked to the graveyard to visit the pyrate gravestones. They had found the headstone of Diego Alvarez, which delighted Levon. She never saw him again after the walk.

Weird that Levon would have skipped work. He had swarthy good looks, but nothing indicated that he was irresponsible, an errant playboy or wastrel. He seemed earnest and scholarly, much like Nina and Griffin. Though Will and Jay never talked business around Julia and her, she had the distinct impression that the Cliff Top Serial Killer had been settling old scores over many decades. Levon had only been in town for a few weeks; it seemed improbable that he would have met up with and provoked the killer in such a short time. She would keep the right thought ... pray for

Levon's safe return.   His absence was probably nothing. Maybe a new archival find drew him away from River Glen. Maybe he had a girlfriend back in Virginia.

Levon had come to River Glen to find Juan Carlos del Castillo ... and Juan Carlos had been found in Brother Guillermo's chronicle.   Wherever Levon was, he should know. She pulled her cell phone off her desk and typed a text.

Levon, Amazing news. Juan Carlo del Castillo was in River Glen! Diego Alvarez was his cousin! Let's meet so I can give you the file. Alex

Pamela Dodd scrubbed her hands – once again – under her galley faucet. Why couldn't she remove that goddamn blood from behind her fingernails, those blood stains from her hands! Levon Bakanian's cell phone vibrated. She dried her hands quickly and read the text.

Levon, Amazing news. Juan Carlos del Castillo was in River Glen! Diego Alvarez was his cousin! Let's meet so I can give you the file. Alex

"Fuckers!" Alex Allaway and Levon Bakanian had been in cahoots! The text was tangible evidence that those two had been partners in acquiring documents about the pyrates of River Glen. She'd been used! She'd been played for a stooge! Bakanian had paid for his disloyalty; soon the Allaway bitch would pay for her treachery.

Think, Pam, think. She had a staggering IQ, unquestionably higher than the village idiots of River Glen. Her parents had had numerous intelligence tests conducted on her when she was a girl, which was why they had sent her to the best prep schools and universities in England. The plethora of childhood tests had sparked her interest in psychology.

It was clever to have rid herself of that traitorous Levon Bakanian. His death was his own stupid fault. He presented the opportunity and she seized it. It was that simple. He had bent down next to the Alvarez headstone to remove moss encrusting the lettering, while her hand slipped into her raincoat pocket for the wrench. The exposed back of his head was too tempting to resist. The first blow thrust him into the edge of the gravestone. At that *whack* of metal against bone, unexpected heat flashed between her thighs. *Whack* – another sensuous pulse. *Whack!* What a fucking turn on! *Whack! Whack!* By the time her task was done, she had worked herself into a heaving froth. It took a while to settle down from the frenzy and drag his body to the car. More fortunate luck. The hurricane had kept visitors from the graveyard. She had waited for the cover of night before driving Bakanian's SUV to Guyton Cliffs where she watched the rear bumper disappear over the black edge. The lashing rain had washed the blood from her raincoat. And all the training on the treadmill had really paid off; she was hardly winded during her run from the cliffs back to the village.

It was also clever to have moved the *Knot-A-Care* from the marina that night because the hull would have been battered against the floating dock, despite its industrial-grade fenders. By midnight, the yacht had tugged gently on its mooring lines, shielded against the winds by marsh grass in a secluded estuary. She had sipped white wine while soaking in her hot tub. The wine could be justified because more than one hundred and twenty calories had been burned that day while she lugged Bakanian's body into his car and jogged back from Guyton Cliffs. It was in the hot tub that she first noticed that stubborn blood stain. She scrubbed her hands. Ugh ... so frustrating! How to get rid of that damn spot!

Pam's attention returned to the text. *Levon, Amazing news. Juan Carlo del Castillo was in River Glen! Diego Alvarez was his cousin! Let's meet so I can give you the file. Alex*

Her first thought was to send a text saying, *"I'm free now. Where are you?"* But if Levon had been reported as missing, which was a certainty by now, his cell phone activity was being monitored. Did the police have the ability to triangulate precisely on the location his phone? Yikes! His phone had to be dumped immediately.

Levon had insisted that Allaway had learned of Giles' island hideaway from a ghost walk. He was a moron to have bought that bullshit.

"Allaway is just a harmless marine biologist," he had let slip.

Allaway definitely knew the whereabouts of the *Raven*'s – Dodd's – treasure. Since another document had been uncovered, Allaway might know the whereabouts of the treasure of Juan Carlos del Castillo also. Two treasures were ripe for the picking! That marine biologist-Googan was going to take her to both of them. There was only one place in River Glen where marine biologists might be employed. Pam Googled the River Glen Marine Station. How convenient. The marine lab had a staff of one. It was the middle of the day in the middle of a work week. Allaway should be at work and alone.

Pam hurried to the transom, lowered the *Zodiac* into the water, and dashed back inside. She tossed rope and duct tape into her backpack, and opened her safe where her pistol was stowed. It would be so much fun if her firearm was a cool blunderbuss, but all she had was a boring Glock. What the hell ... a Glock would do. Like all stealthy pyrates, her attack would be by water.

Alex checked her cell phone. Still no response from Levon but Nina responded with a 'yes' for a dinner of steamed crabs. She returned to Brother Guillermo's chronicle while Water Boy gnawed at his chew stick. According to the priest's account, the villagers of River Glen were leery of the traders of the *Tereza* because grim-faced guards had been posted on their sloop and the Spanish sailors were only allowed to drink in Shannon Allaway's tavern in shifts. What was so valuable on the *Tereza* that it required round-the-clock defense?

Huw Collins, Angus Smyth and the other villagers feared the worst so they stashed weapons strategically around the village. The *Raven*'s cannons were hidden in the brush at the forest's edge. Feigning drunkenness, the villagers lingered around the tavern – maintaining their own vigil of the *Raven*'s treasury in the tavern storeroom. Had the Spaniards heard of the extraordinary wealth in River Glen, the treasure stolen from *El Espíritu de la Virgen*? Did the Spaniards know that the hard-working husbands and fathers had once been cut-throats from the *Raven* ... that their wives were murderesses, whores, and pickpockets from the slums of Dublin and London? Years before the *Raven* had melted into the landscape, its wood beams forming the tavern, smithy, and cabins. No physical evidence was left in the village to reveal that they themselves had once been pyrates and killers.

Was it true that the crew of the *Tereza* was merely making repairs and resupplying for a journey to the cold waters of New England? Or was it a ruse? Was their true intent to steal the *Raven*'s booty? The villagers suspected the latter. They sold the Spanish traders goats, pigs, grain for bread, cloth for sails, new barrels and lumber but anxiously awaited the *Tereza*'s departure into the mist of the bay. For the weeks that the Spaniards roamed the village, the atmosphere was thick with apprehension. Hands hovered near sabres, and children clung to mother's skirts.

Hushed grumbling amongst the Spanish crew while they huddled over their mugs in the tavern heightened the tension. Was something afoot on the *Tereza*? A power struggle? A mutiny in the works? An impending attack on the village treasury?

As long as the violence remained offshore on the *Tereza* and no harm came to the women and children in the village, the sales to the Spaniards could continue, but if blood were to flow it was war ...

Then it happened.

Furious shouts erupted into the summer night. Boots pounded across the decks of the Tereza.

"Dónde están? ... quien? ... la Condesa y Diego ... el oro? ... robado!"

The Spaniards spilled over the gunwales into their skiffs. Their oars stabbed at the water, but at the town dock, they were halted by blades and gun barrels. The villagers were poised and readied for the assault.

"Diego y la Condesa! Dónde están? Dónde están?" Juan Carlos screamed from his skiff.

The villagers clenched their weapons. "Guillermo, what are they saying?" Huw Collins cried. The villagers parted and the priest stepped toward the edge of the pier.

"Un bote falta!" shouted a sailor from the Tereza.

"A boat's missing," the priest translated. "We didn't take it! No tenemos!"

"Me no refiero a usted ningún daño!" Juan Carlos screamed. "Solo quiero la niña and my primo, Diego!"

"He means us no harm. He only wants the girl and his cousin Diego," Guillermo said.

"What girl?" asked the teenager Barnaby Wilkins.

"They not be 'ere. We haven' seen 'em," Angus Smyth shouted.

"Sólo quiero buscar," Juan Carlos replied. "No mas!"

"He wants a look. Nothing more," the priest said.

"Caballeros, sólo quiero buscar," Juan Carlos repeated insistently. "Mi propiedad fue robada. Por favor!"

"He just wants to look," Guillermo explained. "His property was robbed."

The villagers formed a twitchy huddle. Who's the girl? What was robbed? They crouched defensively on the pier once again.

"If a single woman or child is touched, you all die," warned Huw Collins.

"Si alguien es táctil, todo muere ..." Guillermo said.

"Sí, sí!" Juan Carlos bowed gracefully. "Gracias, caballeros."

The Spaniards clambered up the trails into the woods. Torch-lit boats disappeared up the Glen River.

The villagers also disbanded. Some paced the pier while others guarded their cottages and the tavern. But all whispered ... Oro ... I 'eard ... oro.

"This be awesome, laddie," Alex said, imitating Julia's brogue. "We need mood music." She opened her nautical music playlist and selected the soundtrack from *Master and Commander*. "The Far Side of the World" theme wafted from the laptop speakers. "I sooo know what's coming. Once pyrates, always pyrates."

The single Spaniard positioned at Tereza's bow pressed a spyglass to his eye and watched the boats row up the black river. Barnaby Wilkins silently swam to the sloop, climbed the ropes in the stern, and slipped into the hold.

"Thars chests, tobacci, and rum!" Barnaby announced to his elders upon his return. "These be no traders. These be pyrates!"

At dawn a sharp keen rose from the headwaters ... a wail so doleful that the stars shuddered and retreated into an orange sky. As the sun peeked over the trees, the boats rowed solemnly toward the village.

"Traidor," Juan Carlos snarled. He dumped the limp body of Diego Alvarez into the pilings of the dock.

A blood-stained teenager bolted to her feet, rocking the boat. "Ayudameeee ..." Her desperate appeal was directed at a pregnant Shannon Allaway holding a blunderbuss in hand. Juan Carlos struck the girl's face and shoved her into the boat.

"Ye leave the lass 'ere," Shannon called to Juan Carlos.

A defiant guffaw erupted from his throat.

Shannon pointed the blunderbuss at his chest. "Leave 'er."

"Mujeres," Juan Carlos scoffed.

"Capitán, rot en 'ell." Shannon pulled the trigger. Juan Carlos' chest was torn open; he collapsed into the boat.

"Oh, this is too good!" Alex cranked up the volume. Her hands tapped to the rhythm of the drums in the soundtrack.

Water Boy lifted his head, his ears pricked. His chew stick dropped to the floor.

"Jump, Countess!" Barnaby shouted.

"No puedo nadar!" she screamed back.

"Jump!"

Deafening explosions ripped the dawn as the Raven's cannons raged. Tereza's splintered hull rained into the shallows. Her mast cracked and plummeted onto the deck, crushing the lone sentry. The girl flung herself overboard. Barnaby dove after her. The Spaniards in the skiffs scrambled for their guns. But it was too late. The villagers opened fire. When the slaughter was over, skiffs manned by deadmen floated next to the dock. Tereza creaked and smoked in the morning mist.

Water Boy growled.

"I'll take you out to pee in a minute," Alex said. "I'm just getting to the part where the Countess tells the priest about Diego Alvarez's murder." She leaned toward her laptop. Brother Guillermo had drawn a crude map where Alvarez had been killed for stealing the girl and *Tereza*'s treasure. From the looks of the map, the missing gold had been buried upstream beyond Turtle Island, in that mosquito-infested swamp called the Devil's Spit.

Water Boy sniffed the edge of the back door.

"Okay, okay, I'll take you out. But we're avoiding the marsh because I'm not picking ticks off you all day."

Alex rose and froze at the window. A *Zodiac* was tied to the dock behind the *Vital Spark*. Had someone stopped by for gasoline? She had once given gas to two bass fishermen who ran out while fishing in the marsh. This was an expensive *Zodiac* with all the bells and whistles. Only one person in River Glen had the cash to afford such a boat. Alex circled the lab, looking from window to window. Ms. *Knot-A-Care* wasn't on the dock, or in the marsh to the left or the right, nor in the gravel parking lot in the front. The only people who ever visited the lab were Mr. Ward, an ornithologist from the University of Delaware, and fisheries biologists from the University of Maryland. No one ever came to the lab unannounced. Alarm bells chimed in her head. She circled the lab once more, but there was still no sign of the Floridian outside. Bakanian was missing; there was a serial killer in River Glen. Everything felt off kilter. Still ... if she called 911 and asked for Will and Jay and they dashed over here only to find that the woman wanted to use the restroom, she would look like a paranoid idiot. It was nothing. Maybe the woman was lost in the labyrinth of the marsh, or wanted to refill water bottles, or needed to pee. Really, it was nothing. There could be a thousand harmless reasons why the *Knot-A-Care* bitch was here.

'I'll just see what she wants. Then get rid of her.'

Alex pushed open the screen door and stepped tentatively outside. A glint of metal flashed in her peripheral vision – a crack of her skull – blackness.

Will hung up the phone. "Sir, that was the fisherman Byron Smyth."

"What now?" Jay slumped in his chair.

"Unusual shark activity."

"Sharks? So we have a rogue great white in the Chesapeake devouring bathers? That's all we fucking need."

"No great white. Byron reported a frenzy of sandbar sharks at the base of Guyton Cliff."

"Then call the Coast Guard. This isn't our jurisdiction."

"Byron went over the area with his side scan sonar. He thinks there's a car down there."

"Good afternoon, spiderlings.   Lunch time." Spider shook a bag of crickets.   Long ago she had a dilemma – to name her babies after great scientists like herself, or after great leaders?   She had finally decided on leaders.   The names Caligula, Adolf, and Talat were printed in black pen on the plastic containers on the worktable. "Sadly Brutus is no longer with us. The storm must have frightened him. A few more experiments, boys, and our work will be done. Then it's time to write my magnificent tome, my opus." Spider stopped at the last container labeled Vlad the Impaler.   She pressed her face to the plastic and smiled affectionately. "Vlad, I'm depending on you."

Zera Lim yawned.   "A fifteen-minute cat nap is all I need." She closed her office door. The last hours had been spent analyzing the chemical from the syringe in the Riddel Building attic, and pulling hairs and blood off a headstone in the River Glen cemetery. Too many moving parts in this investigation, too many bodies, too many anomalies, too many dead-ends. She removed her sneakers and dropped onto the leather sofa. This endless investigation had caused her to miss the trip to Whale Wall in central Pennsylvania with her rock-climbing club. If they couldn't wrap up this case by the weekend, she would miss her granddaughter's third birthday party in Alexandria, Virginia. The upside to skipping that event would be that she wouldn't have to make small talk with Hideo and Sierra. The couple would, like at all family gatherings, play their parts of wedded bliss, despite the fact that they were in marriage counseling because of Sierra's affair with her yoga instructor. And Hideo would try to corner her and whisper, "Zera, honey, I made a terrible mistake ... can we talk? Maybe lunch somewhere?" Her response was always the same, an uncompromising "Get lost."

She squirmed on the sofa. An uncomfortable lump in the cushions under her hip threatened to roll her over the edge. If, for one evening, she could sleep in her own bed ... eat her own healthy food ... soak in her own tub ... finish that wonderful book on the best climbing sites in the Catskills. But for now, if she could doze for fifteen minutes ... for fifteen minutes, close your eyes, for fifteen minutes, don't think about work ... Her mind jumped back to the syringes.

Peculiar thing, those syringes. In the Sheila Myers' case, the Philadelphia detectives had located a syringe in the bathroom of the Reading Terminal Market, where Myers was last seen. It didn't contain a narcotic or other street drug that an addict might be injecting. Instead it was an anabolic steroid. The syringe that Jay had found between the floorboards of the Riddel Building attic also contained a testosterone-derived growth hormone, but it was a slightly different chemical and of a higher potency. Professor David Towers, upon opening Brutus' venom glands, had discovered a huge proliferation in the epithelial cells that produced the venom. Not only were the epithelial cells increased in size and number, but within the cells, the vesicles storing the atracotoxin were enormous and packed against the cell membrane, nearly bursting and ready for release. Someone had been conducting very bad science, deadly science, creating hyper-aggressive spiders capable of secreting copious volumes of venom.

Someone in River Glen had been creating super spiders. A scientist? A scientist wanna-be? Ricarda Sarova, that Jay had told her about, seemed the obvious culprit, except that she was dead.

Who could nap at a time like this? Zera slung her feet off the sofa and headed to her coffee maker. Strong Sumatran would do the trick. While the coffee drizzled into the pot, she opened her laptop. The doe-eyed giant Will Wilkins, confined to desk duty with a broken foot, had been busy. His hunch was that the unidentified forty-year-old male who had been buried with Owen Paco, was not killed by Henry Herssen, but *was* Henry Herssen. This had impelled Will to contact Herssen's estranged sister in Cleveland, Ohio. Winifred had not heard from her younger brother in over four decades. They had lost touch when Henry took up with Ricarda Sarova, who the sister claimed was "sinister, dangerous, and all together horrible." Winifred had volunteered to give a blood sample to the medical examiner at the Cleveland PD.

Zera yawned again and scanned her inbox. Yes, finally ... a file from a Cleveland forensics lab. She studied the data from Winifred Herssen's blood proteins and DNA and compared them to her results from Male 2.

Will's presentiment was spot-on. She sent him a brief email, the subject line reading "Right on target." She filled her mug and checked her watch. The caffeine in her coffee, if she downed the entire cup right now, wouldn't be entirely absorbed across her GI tract- and cell membranes and have an effect for at least thirty minutes. How was she possibly going to stay awake for that long? There was a knock at her door.

"Come in."

Albert, the assistant pathologist, poked his head in. "The Underwater Recovery Team found the car at Guyton Cliffs. It was Levon Bakanian's SUV."

"And Bakanian?"

"He's in the back room and he's not pretty."

Will Wilkins read Zera Lim's email and lifted himself out of his chair. He hobbled to the crime board, and filled in the last name and added the check mark that indicated a conclusive DNA match.

Female 1 age 20? 4 yrs in ground **Amanda Lamont** √
Female 2 age 65? 6 yrs in grd **Dr. Sheila Myers** √
Male 1 age 65? 6 yrs in grd **Dr. Bob Randolph** √
Male 2 age 40? 20-25 yrs in grd **Henry Herssen** √
Male 3 age 40? 20-25 yrs in grd **Owen Paco** √

Jay balled his fists in his pockets. "Our killer's not young. If the killer was a contemporary of Herssen and Paco, that person's now in their sixties or seventies."

"Unless the first killings were conducted when the killer was a teenager," Lisa said. "That would make him or her in their forties or fifties."

"Still old," Will said.

"Thanks, pal," Jay said.

Lisa's computer chimed. "This is odd."

"What?"

"It's from Norman in IT. He's picked up activity on Levon Bakanian's cell phone."

"But Bakanian's on Zera's table," Jay said.

Lisa stretched her gum from her mouth and shot Will a sidelong glance.

"What?" Will said. "It's from Alex, isn't it?"

Lisa slurped the gum back into her mouth to stall.

"What, Lisa!"

"Alex texted him this message: *Levon, Amazing news. Juan Carlos del Castillo was in River Glen! Diego Alvarez was his cousin! Let's meet so I can give you the file. Alex.* Really creepy. Alex thinks that Bakanian's still alive."

"It proves she didn't kill him on that goddamn history walk she took with him!" Will said.

"Diego Alvarez's was the headstone with Bakanian's blood on it," Lisa said.

"Who the hell is Juan Carlos del Castillo?" Jay grumbled.

"He's the pyrate that Bakanian wrote a book about," Lisa replied. "I read that on Bakanian's webpage."

Jay groaned. "Shit, I hate pyrates. Sorry Will, but we still need to talk to Alex to get a definite timeline of when she and Bakanian were in the graveyard, and we still need to talk to Pamela Dodd whom Levon also visited on Sunday."

"Who?" Will asked.

"Pamela Dodd, the woman with the white yacht."

"Dodd?" Will's throat tightened. "D O D D?"

Jay frowned. "Yes. Does that name ring a bell?"

Will briskly shook his head. "Ur, no. Just wondering."

"This is also weird." Lisa stared at the screen. "The time stamp for Alex's text was near three hours ago."

"Why the delay?" Jay wondered.

"According to Norman, the hurricane damaged the local cell towers. Things are just coming back online now."

How could he concentrate on the assignment that Jay had given him at a time like this! Will wiped sweat off his brow ... slowly ... inconspicuously ... as if he was just rubbing his forehead to think. No one could notice his despair, his angst. And no way was he going to have eye contact with Cloris! His head would explode if he had to hear about Sylvester's new cat gym! Jay wanted him to check the older employees at Tolchester for possible criminal records. This would take forever! Everyone employed at Tolchester was prehistoric! Meanwhile Jay had left to do the exciting stuff: return to Tolchester, talk to Zera, and then interview Alex at the marine station. All while he was stuck behind a desk with a broken ankle, suffering from recurring panic attacks over the name Dodd!

When Julia Hale appeared in River Glen during the murder investigation of her ex-husband Randall Allaway, she had told him and Alex about the memoir of Giles Hales. It contained vivid accounts of the sadistic Bartholomew Dodd, who murdered the Irish cabin boy and which incited the mutineers to cast Dodd to the sharks. Pamela Dodd must be a relative of the insane captain of the *Raven*. Insanity could be an inherited trait, couldn't it? Could that insane gene have been passed down over three and a half centuries? Who knew! What Will did know was that there were no coincidences where murder investigations were concerned. Had Bart Dodd survive the shark attack? Or had he produced children before his time on the *Raven*? Pamela Dodd had to be from the same lineage. Why else would she be in River Glen? There was a rival pyrate in their midst and he was stuck running background checks on decrepit professors at Tolchester College! The band of pyrates in the village, the silent protectors of the River Glen treasure, had to be notified. Will slid his phone from his pocket, glanced surreptitiously around the room, and sent a group text to Brad and Byron Smyth, the Wilkins cousins, and their fearless captain James Collins.

Self-important, privileged administrators! Jay stomped out of the Tolchester Administration Building. There was a high probability that a killer was employed at the college and the Weird Sisters told him less than nothing!

Dean Hinkie, located on her putting green with a two hundred dollar PING putter in hand, could barely contain her irritation at the intrusion.

"The continuous police presence on campus is interfering with my recruiting efforts," she had griped. "We have a tuition-based budget model. Without a steady increase in student numbers each year, there's no hope for an annual raise."

Lisa had found from the campus accountant that the faculty and staff had received 0.1% increases last year while the deans and president each received 8% "performance raises." As far Jay could tell, the only performance that was improving was Lana Hinkie's golf game.

"I have no knowledge of an attic in the Riddel Building. I have no idea who changes the buckets of water there, and don't care. Why are you asking me this? This has to do with student recruitment how?" Hinkie shushed him from her office. "Go find Hank Stupens. This is his department."

Only one equation mattered to the dean. Increased students = increased tuition dollars = increased salary for Lana Hinkie.

Dean Wines had been equally unhelpful. She checked her status on Facebook four times during their conversation.

"Any biologists or biochemists with a knowledge of spiders?" he asked.

"How do I know?" she huffed. "My field is Women's Studies."

"You're the head of academics. You must know what your faculty members are doing."

Wines eyed the bonbons on her desk. "No one studies spiders. Our microbiologist and geneticist study yeast. They make beer together. Our ecologist studies eastern screech-owls. We don't see him much. He's nocturnal. And our biochemist hasn't produced a scientific paper in over two decades. During every annual review, he tells me that he's still thinking about it. None of them have lab facilities on campus."

"Are you aware of an attic in the Riddel Building?"

"Like I care about the buildings," Dean Wines said, showing him the door. "Go ask Hank."

Jay had crossed the hallway. The president's gold-trimmed mahogany door had been closed. A chirpy secretary informed him that Mary Blodgen was in Annapolis for the day. She was meeting with State legislators about acquiring state funds for a new academic building.

Hank Stupens was located on the campus green, supervising the groundskeepers. Chainsaws buzzed. They were cutting up branches downed during the hurricane.

"Of course I'm familiar with the attic," Stupens answered tersely. "I check the buckets there after rainstorms."

"When were you there last?"

"During the hurricane. I ran up there to empty the buckets. Why are you asking about the attic?"

Information, like the escapee Brutus and syringe, was best kept to himself. The less the killer knew what the police knew was always the better. "Was Bob Randolph, or anyone else, using the space to store equipment?"

Stupens snapped a stick across his knee and shoved it into a chipper. "Not as far as I know. I've never seen anyone up in the attic. But I don't spend a lot of time up there. I dump the buckets and leave." He shrugged dismissively.

The Security Office was Jay's last stop on campus. Burt was once again under the eaves, smoking. "Burt, anything usual? Anyone coming and going from the building that you wouldn't expect?"

"Nope. Just the faculty, but I'll keep an eye out."

"That evening of Debbie's accident," Jay said apprehensively, "what exactly happened?"

"It's ... it's all my fault! We had an argument. Fortunately Burtie didn't witness it. He was visiting his grandparents and cousins in New Jersey. Debbie and I had a fight over money. As usual. We always fought over money. She spent more than I could earn. Shoes and handbags, a closet full! I stormed out and went to Harlow's Pub to get shit-faced. But she'd thought I'd gone to campus to work the night shift. She came to campus and sent me a text asking me where I was. I read the text but didn't respond." He inhaled deeply. "Something happened while she was here. Maybe she saw something? Something that terrified her and caused her to drive into a tree. The whole thing's my fault ... if I earned more ... didn't nag her about over-spending ... it's my fault my son doesn't have a mother!"

The distraught conversation with Burt Sweeny lingered in Jay's thoughts on his drive to the Office of the Medical Examiner. One never knew with certainty what information in a murder investigation was relevant or irrelevant until the case was concluded and one could review the web of evidence. There were countless bits of information, but what had meaning ... and what was a distraction whose intent was to mislead? He and Will had been called to Debbie Sweeny's accident sometime around one thirty in the morning, that much he recalled. If he had to venture a guess, Debbie saw someone going or coming from the Riddel Building in the wee hours. Maybe someone she recognized? Someone she was not supposed to see – someone carrying plastic tubes of spiders?

At the Medical Examiner's office, Albert pointed Jay to the morgue. Zera was still with Bakanian's body. Jay pushed through the door. The sight of dead bodies, even after so decades of police work, still knotted his intestines.

"Homicide, not suicide," he said to Zera.

"Homicide," Zera said decisively from behind her mask. "Hit multiple times on the back of the head with a blunt instrument. Shattered his right parietal bone. The killer came prepared. One of the blows knocked him forward into the gravestone. His temple hit the stone. He was probably kneeling in front of the gravestone when he was hit. His knees were muddy. Then he was dragged to his car. The tires from his SUV match the tracks in graveyard."

Jay moved reluctantly toward the stainless-steel examination table.

"You might not want to see this. It's bad."

His steps faltered. "Why?"

"The killer opened the windows before the SUV went off the cliff so that it would sink faster."

"But he was dead before the car went into the water?"

"Most definitely. He died in the graveyard. The opened windows allowed the sharks get to him."

Jay's view flitted toward Bakanian's hand. The fingers had been chewed off. "You're right." He backed toward the door. "I don't need to see this one."

Since he was in procrastination mode, he stopped to chat with Zera's secretary about the Orioles dismal record until he had dawdled long enough. He dragged himself toward his car. The most uncomfortable interview had been put off until the end of the afternoon. He pulled onto the highway in the direction of the River Glen Marine Station.

It's not that he didn't like Alex Allaway. He did. She was a light-hearted, if not a bit ditzy, country girl. Though she lacked the polish and wit of her dazzling grandmother, there was no other person that knew the waters and animals of the Chesapeake better than Alex did. Birds, fish, invertebrates ... she knew everything about every species. And crabbing; she was the expert. She knew the right traps, baits, locations, and times to find the biggest crabs, secret knowledge passed down to her from Randy and his crabbing partner Old Ben Hancock. Jay had pinpointed the exact reason for his unease in Alex's presence ... her startling physical resemblance to Julia. Sometimes when making love to Julia, he would suddenly be kissing Alex who would morph back into Julia, then into Alex, and so on. After, he would be laying in blissful befuddlement wondering which woman he had just made love to. When he finally convinced himself that he had actually spent the afternoon in the arms of Julia, a woman closer to his age and life experience, he would pull himself from the bed only to be assaulted by a photo of a smiling Alex and Water Boy on Julia's dresser. The whole muddled Freudian mumbo jumbo made him feel like an old pervert.

Alex was distracting for other reasons. Like her wrestling on the beach with Water Boy, clad only in her bikini. Then there was her fetish for outdoor sex. He and Julia had noticed Alex dragging a euphoric Will toward the forest, or Randy's abandoned grow house, or rowing onto the river in the soon-to-be-rocking rowboat.

"The lass is going to get herself sent to the chokey for public nudity, indecent exposure, or public lewdness," Julia had said to him. "Then I'm going to have to tap into my 401K to hire James Collins to bail her out."

The legal implications of Alex's proclivities had never occurred to him and were in fact the last thing on his mind. His impulse was to fling Julia over his shoulder, rush her to the bedroom, whip up her skirt and down her panties. Except that he would pop a disc in his back, inflame his sciatica, and be out of work for weeks. Instead he prudently poured himself a generous scotch and bummed one of Julia's cigarettes.

The whole thing was unnatural. It was just plain weird having his partner Will date the granddaughter of his girlfriend. Julia should just marry him and move into his house across the river. What the hell – he loved Julia. Maybe she loved him also. They could make it work. They could tango on his back deck and drink scotch in the hot tub. Shit, why not? That way they would have their privacy away from Alex, Will, and Carly. His house was a newer construction with stainless steel appliances, double sinks, and granite counter tops, whereas Julia's house was something hillbillies might inhabit. Nautical flags flapped from her porch railings, and tacky lawn ornaments, a rusty motorcycle-turned bird bath, a VW with a tree growing through the engine, and dog chew toys littered the yard.

"No one will ever think to rob me," Julia had once remarked.

Rob her? What the hell did she have to rob? The house was a dilapidated wreck. Instead of putting on a new roof or installing vinyl siding to increase its value, she had the carpenter Marty Wilkins expand the size of her bedroom to add a walk-in closet. What the hell was it with women and shoes?

The River Glen Marine Station appeared in the marsh. Jay loosened his tie and stopped his car in the parking lot. There were no other cars about because Alex motored the *Vital Spark* to work most days. He climbed from the car into air that smelled of decaying grass and salt water. The last lingering clouds from Hurricane Beau had vanished and the sky was an opaque blue. The place was silent except for fiddling insects and seabirds in the marsh grass.

The marine lab was a gray clapboard building, consisting of one musty room with desks, a lab bench, sink, fridge, and bathroom. He had been here once before to interview Alex during the Randall Allaway murder investigation. He circled behind the building. Alex must be around because the old tugboat was tied to the dock. He pressed his face to the screen of a back window. The lab was empty. Maybe she and Water Boy were somewhere in the marsh, collecting specimens or performing ecological measurements. He walked to the border of the gravel parking lot and squinted across a hazy sea of damp grass.

"Alex! Water Boy!"

He waited and listened. Only insects and birds sounds. He returned to the dock and checked inside the *Vital Spark*; it was unoccupied. He pushed through the back door of the marine station. A mug of hot chocolate sat on Alex's desk. He poked his finger into the brown fluid. It was room temperature. He licked his finger. Alex had a ridiculous sweet tooth. Last Thanksgiving at Julia's house, Alex's plate held three slices of pie – pecan, apple, and pumpkin – next to a heap of turkey and mashed potatoes. As far as Alex was concerned, pie was an entrée. Her seconds were more pie.

He tensed.

It wasn't the absence of her laptop that was necessarily alarming but the presence of something else – Alex's pink water bottle and Water Boy's collapsible water bowl on the planked floor. Alex was fanatical about hydration. Countless times he had seen her fill her water bottle at Julia's sink, stuff it and the collapsible dog bowl into her backpack, and run out the door because she and Water Boy were late to everything. There was absolutely nowhere she went without that water bottle and dog bowl, yet the bottle was on her desk and the bowl was next to the dog bed. Her backpack was on a hook by the front door.

Before he sent his team into a complete panic, he would check Alex's cottage. It was possible that someone, perhaps Nina or Julia, had come by in their car to pick up Alex and Water Boy for some reason. Julia spent most of the day on her porch reading, or strolling around the village with Luna. One of those two might have seen Alex, or at least know something of her whereabouts. He hurried to his car, pulled a fast U-turn in the parking lot. Pebbles shot into the air from his squealing tires.

Spider pondered the data in the laboratory notebook. It would be ideal if the experiments could be conducted on ten live specimens, as that made for an impressive data set and an even number no less, but the best that could be hoped for, as time was ticking away, was an N of six. The writing of the book had been put off for too long. Owen Paco and Henry Herssen represented a population of forty year olds. Shame that they were both males. The data would have been more interesting had one of them been a female, but one has to make due when resources are limited. Fortunately the data from the sixty year olds Sheila Myers and Bob Randolph comprised both a male and a female. Future reviewers who would evaluate this groundbreaking study would want to see if the two genders and at different ages responded differently to the atracotoxin.

Now two twenty-somethings, preferably of different sexes, needed to be acquired. What a shame that Amanda Lamont was not taken alive; she was twenty at least being a college senior.   The car was only meant to wound and disable, but it crushed her instantly. Hmm ... which twenty-something to choose from? The new tier of young faculty provided tantalizing possibilities. Joanne Trent the psychologist? Boris Yulak the mathematician? Levon Bakanian was never under consideration because he was in his mid-thirties. And who knows where he ran off to. Both Joanne and Boris were married and had children so best to go with Nina Vega and Griffin Blake as they were both single and childless. Yes, perfect, those two would be specimen number 5 and 6 in the scientific study.

Alex stirred in a dream.

Diego Alvarez pushed through the underbrush. "I'm glad you stayed here, amada. There's quicksand back there and a deep pool of water. We must hurry!"

"Where did you hide it?" the Condesa asked.

He reached down for his beloved Consuela Diaz del Sevilla, and pulled her to her feet. He kissed her. "In two places. They'll comb the shores, but they'll never find it."

"Now where?" she whispered.

"To the cliff." He pulled her forward. "In my walks, I found a spot. We'll hide there and watch until la Tereza departs. They'll never find us in the thick brush. Then we'll return for the gold and head north."

"Is it well-hidden, my uncle's gold?"

"It's guarded by worms and fish."

Consuela squeezed Diego's hand. "Thank you, querido!"

"Shh ... did you hear that?"

Their muscles tightened like springs. They remained motionless. The orange light of dawn filtered between the black tree trunks. Birds awoke.

"Maybe it was nothing," he said after a minute or two.

"Wait, Diego!" She grabbed his billowing sleeve.

"I don't hear it anymore. It was just an animal. We must hide the skiff, then go to the cliff."

They zigzagged along a narrow Indian trail that ran down the center of the sandy spit and returned to the beach. They tiptoed from the forest and gasped.

Juan Carlos' black eyes smoldered; his cuphilt rapier was drawn. "Thief, you die!"

Diego released her hand. "Run, Consuela!"

She spun, her gown swirling, but pyrates emerged from the underbrush and blocked her path. A circle of daggers contracted on them.

"Draw you, dog!" Juan Carlos said.

Diego fumbled for his sword. He was a courtier and a mapmaker to Rey Carlos de España, not a soldier like his cousin.

Rapiers clanked and flashed as the sun rose between the trees. But the battle was brief. The first slice to Diego's arm caused his weapon to fall in the sand. Another slash of light opened his neck. He wavered. Hot blood cascaded down his shoulder. Juan Carlos lunged at his heart. The impaling sword held Diego on his feet.

"No!" Consuela shrieked.

Diego's knees buckled and he hit the sand with his face. "Hoy me muero."

"Today you die, Alex, unless you help me out."

Alex stirred again. Was it a dream, or something she read?

"Yeah, you heard right. You *will* help me out."

'Where am ...' Alex opened her eyes. Assorted pains screamed out to her. Her head throbbed, the skin on her legs and arms burned, her wrists tied behind her back ached. She was mute! She couldn't move her lips! "Mmm!"

"Don't sweat it. It's just duct tape."

Alex jerked her head toward the twangy southern accent.

Ms. Knot-A-Care sat against a tree with Alex's laptop across her knees.

"Mmm!" She writhed furiously.

"Interesting." Knot-A-Care gazed into the screen. "So there are two treasures in River Glen. Bartholomew Dodd's and Juan Carlos'. And you're going to take me to both of them."

"Mmm!"

"You might as well calm down and save your strength. It's going to be a long day."

"Mmm!"

"Mmm, I'll remove that in second. Mmm, after you agree to my terms. I'm a businesswoman, and you and I are forming a partnership. River Glen Treasure Hunting, Inc., has a nice ring to it." She chuckled. "It's always important to research one's future business partners. Mmm ... so what do I know about Alexandra Allaway? Fisheries biology degree from the University of Maryland. BS and MS. Ooh, Alexandra has interesting blood-lines. Father Colin and mother Carole died in a car fire when Alexandra was an infant. The cause of death was later determined to be arson committed by the Whitbys. Murder – nasty business. The infant Alexandra was raised by her grandfather Randall Allaway, notorious lover boy, crabber, small-time *Cannabis sativa* farmer, and a descendant of the infamous headless Charles Allaway. Decapitation – more nasty business. Alexandra is the granddaughter of Julia Hale, an actress of some notoriety in the UK. Well, look at this ..." Knot-A-Care turned Google images into Alex's line of vision. "Impressive company Julia keeps ... Siân Phillips, Judi Dench, and Peter O'Toole. My, my, Julia was quite cozy with Oliver Reed at that party. And oh, by the way. The reason you won't scream out when I remove the duct tape, not that anyone would hear you out here, or why you won't try to run away, is that I have a gun." Knot-A-Care pulled a Glock from her backpack. "And reason number two, if you don't cooperate wholeheartedly with the formation of Treasure Hunting,

Inc., a misfortunate accident might befall your fencing buddy. Or that little girl who just moved in with you. What's her name again? Right. Carly Wilkins."

Jay's unmarked police sedan skidded to a stop at Julia's house. He bolted up her porch steps, skipping a step at a time. He pushed through her screen door. Soft voices from her bedroom off the living room caused him to lurch. Who ... what? The male voice was vaguely familiar but not one that was heard on a daily basis. That's all he needed – to have fallen for a woman with other lovers. Julia was retired and home all day ... if he could only retire and be home with her ... except that he had stupidly listened to Laura's brother. Troy's brainless investment advice caused him to lose half of his retirement fund in the crash.

Julia's musical lilt prompted a muted laugh from her companion. Shit ... he had come this far. The couple had certainly heard his footsteps. He would look even stupider if he turned tail and slunk out of the house. Shit ... he might as well discover his competition. He stepped over Miranda and Clark and entered Julia's bedroom. He half-expected to see Julia and her boyfriend in a state of rapture under the sheets, but instead she and James Collins were fully clothed and standing by her walk-in closet.

Julia seemed a bit startled. "Oh, hello, love."

"Hello," he said flatly.

"Hi Jay," James said pleasantly. He shut the closet door and placed a screwdriver on the bedside table.

An awkward silence hung in the air. Jay tried not to stare too conspicuously, but neither of them appeared rosy cheeked or hurriedly dressed. James' hair was perfectly cut and meticulously combed as usual.   His dress shirt was neatly tucked into his pants, and his tie neatly clipped to his shirt by a gold seagull tie clip. A barefooted Julia was in her normal attire, a silky blouse and skirt.   Her long hair was neatly clasped by a tortoise shell clip on top of her head. There was nothing hasty or flustered about them, yet James Collins was in Julia's bedroom. For what reason?

"Julia, I do like your new closet." James nodded approvingly. "Maybe I'll put one in my bedroom.   Well, I have a few loose-ends to tie up at the office.   You two take care." He stepped over the dogs and started across her living room.

Closets? James had the biggest, most spectacular house in the village.   Certainly his bedroom already had a walk-in closet. The couple was clearly speaking in code. And what about the screwdriver? Why was James in Julia's bedroom? It was obvious that Julia had a thing for younger men. He was twelve years her junior after all, but James was in his late thirties, forty at the most. Shit! How could he compete with the staying power of a thirty-something?

"Marty Wilkins does excellent carpentry," Julia called after James.

"Great.   Thanks. I'll give him a call."   James' response was followed by the creak and bang of the front door.

Julia knocked a cigarette from her pack, twisted it into her cigarette holder, and flicked at her lighter. She blew smoke through the window screen. "What, love?"

"Don't 'what love' me."

She took a long, pensive drag.

"Well?" he said.

"Well, what?"

He was aghast at his own behavior, yet he persisted. "Well, James Collins was just in your bedroom."

"That did appear to be James, didn't it?" A slight smile twitched at the corners of her mouth.

Now she was toying with him! He was speechless.

"Not that I owe you a bloody explanation, but I'll give you one to assuage your male neuroses." There was a caustic edge to her voice. She opened the door to the walk-in closet. "Have a look."

He stepped obsequiously into her closet, like the pathetic, love-sick dog that he was. The space was in fact just a closet. One wall had racks of shoes. Another wall had hangers with dresses, blouses, skirts, and coats. Against the third wall was a massive wooden wardrobe that had been sent from her family's estate in Aberdeen. It likely held some of her family's jewelry as a lock hung off the two heavy doors.

"James was looking at my closet, then helped me change the light bulb. Marty put the sconce a wee bit higher than I can reach." She pointed to the light fixture high in the wall.

Jay scowled. A visit by James Collins to see her walk-in closet seemed about the lamest excuse one could dream up. Nice touch, the changing of the light bulb, he almost quipped.

She shook her head in disgust. *"O, beware, my lord, of jealously; It is the green-eyed monster which doth mock, The meat it feeds on ..."*

"Fuck the *MacBeth* quotes." Nothing made sense! The years of saturating himself with scotch had done it, rotted away the reasoning centers in his brain. Julia was right – all that was left were his simpering male fears.

"Not *MacBeth*, lad. *Othello*. Iago. Act 3, scene 3."

Best not to respond for she was infinitely smarter than he was. He stepped over Miranda and Clark, and grabbed Clark's leash by the front door.

"Come, Clark."

The black dog struggled from his slumber and made his way across the living room. Clark was Water Boy's pup which instantly reminded him of his purpose for visiting Julia in the first place.

He set his jaw. "Actually, Ms. Hale, I'm here on police business. I went by the marine lab to ask Alex some questions about Levon Bakanian, but she wasn't there. Have you seen her? It's quite urgent that we talk."

Julia appeared disoriented. "No."

"The *Vital Spark*'s still at the lab, but I couldn't find her. I couldn't find Water Boy either."

"What?" Julia's cheeks flushed.

"She was at the graveyard on Sunday with Levon Bakanian who was murdered that same day. We just pulled his body from Guyton Cliffs."

"She wasn't at her lab?"

"No."

Julia gazed into blank space. "Dodd ..." She ran past him, out the front door and down the porch steps. He followed. She jumped onto her bicycle and pedaled madly toward James Collins on the river road. Walking in the opposite direction was Nina Vega with a bottle of wine in her hand.

"James!" Julia cried breathlessly.

James turned. She dropped her bike and gesticulated wildly. They both gazed in the direction of the marina, and then he folded Julia in his arms.

Hank Stupens was delighted. The groundskeepers had finished clearing away the branches by early afternoon which meant an entire hour to himself with the free weights. The administrators had not pestered him with tedious chores, allowing him to sneak off to his favorite fishing hole before five o'clock. He motored his old pickup down the overgrown road through the woods and parked in his usual spot, next to the boulder field. Storms always riled up the fish so this afternoon they would be biting. There was a mysterious quality to the water in the deep hole at the Devil's Spit that caused the largest fish to lurk in the shifting shadows on the bottom. By tonight, with any luck and the right lures, filets would be frying in garlic butter in his pan. Hank wound along the cliff path, anticipating the next moments ... sitting on the fallen tree that formed a sturdy bridge across the hole, sipping a cold beer, and casting his line into the silent water.

Voices from the beach caused Hank to pause. Never, ever had he seen other fishermen back at the Devil's Spit. This was his personal fishing hole! No one else's! He tiptoed forward and ducked behind a tree. It was two women ... two remarkably attractive women. To hell with his original plan. Two lesbians playing a bondage game on the beach was way better than fishing. He nestled himself behind the tree to watch.

"Down!" Pamela Dodd waved the pistol.

Alex dropped onto her knees in the sand.

"Not there!" Pamela directed the gun barrel at a tree. "There!"

"Just shoot me," Alex muttered. "I don't give a shit at this point."

"You're not getting out of this this easy. When you find me treasure, our partnership dissolves but not until then. There. Sit down there, against the tree!"

Alex pulled herself up, limped to the tree, and stumbled to the ground. She was that exhausted. For hours, countless hours, she had zigzagged across the Devil's Spit, swishing a metal detector across the beach, through steam and gnats, while Pamela's gun was aimed at her head. She had been given a water bottle to drink and an apple, and was allowed to pee once, but she was now ravenous.

"Put your hands backwards around the tree. Now! Or Julia and Carly get hurt!"

Alex had no choice but to compile. A tight line of rope formed a figure eight around her wrists. "Ouch! That's too tight. You're cutting off my circulation. I can't treasure hunt if my hands become necrotic and have to be amputated."

"Shut-up."

"I need food and water. I'm starving."

Pamela lifted the metal detector from the sand. "I'm going to soak in my hot tub and get a glass of wine. Then I'll bring you back some food."

"Wait! What? You're leaving me here! It's getting dark. I told you I'd help you! I did! I didn't try to escape."

"But you also didn't find me Juan Carlos' treasure. It's around here somewhere. Brother Guillermo's drawing showed that it was here. We're going to continue until we find it."

"Let me at least go home to eat and sleep. I promise I won't tell anyone about this. Promise! I'll find you that treasure tomorrow."

"Yeah, right," Pamela said sarcastically. She approached with duct tape.

"Don't! I won't call out. Promise. If you leave me here, I'll be eaten by wild animals."

Pamela laughed. "In that case, I'll just have to find the treasure on my own." She shoved a piece of duct tape onto Alex's mouth.

"Mmm!"

"Mmm chill, partner. I'll be back soon." Pamela shoved the *Zodiac* off the beach and rowed down the creek.

"Mmm!" Alex struggled. It was no use. Neither the tape nor the ropes would give. She was doomed; so were Julia and Carly. Before the night was through, she would be devoured by foxes and wild cats, or be carrion to raptors, all while covered with ticks and ants. This was all her stupid doing! If she had not provoked the woman – if she had never mentioned Turtle Island at Levon's lecture – or planted the cheap trinkets in the sand to enrage the psycho ... How was she to know that Pamela, who rushed to the water's edge every few minutes to compulsively scrub her hands, was a complete whacko? She should have heeded Will's warning. This practical joke had gone very, very wrong ... disastrously wrong.

Think, think, stay calm ... despite her diminished IQ due to the inhalation of second-hand weed smoke ... think, think, think ... despite the blinding headache and knot on the side of her head where she had been struck with the gun. If she could just remove the duct tape ... maybe a fisherman or hunter might hear her cry for help. She pushed off one sneaker with her opposite foot, and slipped out of her sock. She rested her bare foot on the opposite knee, bent her leg, moving her foot toward her mouth. She had once read of a woman who could fly an airplane with her feet, so certainly she could remove duct tape with her toes. Her toes brushed her face again and again. After a while, the tape became sandy and dirty, and a corner started to curl. She worked frantically at the curled corner. The muscles in her outstretched neck seized up, forcing her to rest her head against the tree trunk. The cramping gone, she persisted until the tape hung across half of her mouth. She could emit jumbled, half-formed words, but an outright scream for help was still impossible.

A stick snapped in the distance. Alex tightened and listened. Had the relentless growling of her stomach attracted a vicious predator? She was on the Fish and Wildlife Service's e-list; periodically there were sightings of coyotes and mountain lions in these parts, and she was going to be their dinner! Pamela would return to find no more than a shredded carcass tied to a tree. Alex listened once again. Again, there was a crackling of sticks. Do not breathe, do not move ...

Hank Stupens was baffled. It seemed less and less likely that this was the sex game of two bored housewives escaping their husbands for the afternoon. He had assumed that the snooty redhead, playing the role of the dominatrix, who rowed off in the inflatable boat would return at any moment, untie her friend, then have wild sex with her on the beach. But now, over an hour later, the redhead still hadn't returned. The black-haired woman tied up to the tree was anything but aroused. She was furious. Before the redhead's departure, there was a mention of Juan Carlos' treasure.

This had to be same Juan Carlos that Levon Bakanian had discussed in that stultifying lecture last Friday night.

How many frickin' pyrates could there be named Juan Carlos? Worthless academics. Useless lot all together. He was surrounded by them 24-7. Bakanian had never mentioned a treasure associated with Juan Carlos, but some evidence had lured these women to the Spit. They believed that a treasure was close at hand. There was no frickin' treasure on the Spit. He had been coming to this place since he was a boy. How dare these bimbos invade his personal fishing hole! What to do with them?

It suddenly dawned on him ... the perfect remedy to remove the intruders from his private fishing hole at the Spit. He slid his phone from his fishing vest and sent a text: *A woman is here in the woods. Another one is supposed to be coming back some time tonight.*

He received a response almost immediately. *Are they alone?*

Yes.

How old?

Twenty-thirtyish.

Can you capture them both?

I can try.

No try, do! See if everything's still at the field lab. Stay in touch. I'll bring Caligula and Vlad. These women will be my next human subjects!

Pamela Dodd's row to the *Knot-A-Care* only attracted the attention of a doe and fawn at the river's edge. The trip down the twisted creek took some time – possibly an hour – but the paddling was the rough time equivalent to her workout on her rowing machine. That exercise regime explained the great tone in her arms. There was no need for a run on the treadmill before soaking in the hot tub, since she had walked a few miles at least around the Devil's Spit, following that whiny Alex Allaway.

Alex's denial of the *Raven's* treasure was aggravating. She had vehemently maintained that the island on which Giles Hale hid his and Charles Allaway's families had been described on a ghost walk when she was a teenager. That was it; that was all she knew. At the moment that boldfaced lie was a minor point. What was not a minor point was that Brother Guillermo's document in Alex's laptop had referenced a treasury in a store room at the back of the village tavern. That was a stunning revelation! In fact, in all the years of researching the pyrates of River Glen, this was the first documented evidence of a treasury that Pam had ever read.

The treasure had to be of a significant magnitude if it required storage in an entire room and if it enticed Juan Carlos and the pyrates of the *Tereza* all the way from Caribbean waters to the northern Chesapeake. Rumors of the terrible slaughter of the Spaniards from the treasure galleon *El Espíritu de la Virgen* by the pyrates of the *Raven* had floated around the Caribbean for years. Dodd himself had told the Spanish missionaries and soldiers of the massacre on the Florida beach and theft of the treasure.

So ... the Dodd treasure had made it to the Chesapeake after all! That much was fact! Now the treasure was almost within reach. Pam could just feel it. No more slogging along the muddy, bug-infested shorelines of the Glen River after this summer!

But how frustrating not to have found the gold stolen by Diego Alvarez and Consuela Diaz. Guillermo's account said that Diego had buried it "with worms and fishes." This suggested that it had been separated and placed in the ground and water. What bad luck ordering that dreary man and his scrawny boy to the Devil's Spit that day she was with Levon on Turtle Island … but how the hell was she to know? A fishing rod had been clasped in the boy's hand, but was there a metal detector in that old boat? Tomorrow she would have Alex go over the Spit one more time, then have Alex dive in that deep dark well by the swamp. Being a marine biologist Alex would know how to scuba dive. Alex would search the murky bottom while she would stand on that fallen tree crossing the water, the Glock pointed downward should Alex attempt a get-away.

Though Alex intractably refused to reveal the location of the Dodd treasure from the *Raven*, the mention of torturing Julia and Carly while Alex witnessed it, got her instant attention. Eventually Alex would meet a similar fate as Levon, but until the treasures were located, she would be fed and hydrated to keep up her energy for treasure hunting.

Finally. The marsh appeared at the mouth of the creek. The silhouette of the *Knot-A-Care* appeared under a rising moon, and none too soon because Pam's shoulders were aching. White wine, a high-protein low-carb dinner, and the hot tub were almost in reach. A soak with jets of hot water pulsing against her shoulders and lower back would give her time to concoct the specifics of an air-tight alibi for the yokel cops. Boaters at the marina had seen her entertaining Levon over the weekend so an interview with the cops was inevitable. She would charm them, dazzle them, have them eating out of her hand by the end of the conversation.

"Levon stopped by briefly on Sunday to thank me for a wonderful day of picnicking and swimming on Saturday," she would tell the dim-wits. "Before leaving the marina, he mentioned a visit to Alex Allaway, who was going to show him historic gravestones at the River Glen cemetery. I never saw him after that."

This story would place Alex at the graveyard on Sunday afternoon, and explain Alex's sudden disappearance. The simpleton cops would connect the dots. Alex had murdered Levon in the graveyard and taken flight. Yes, a perfect story.

Wait a minute ... Pamela stopped rowing and let the *Zodiac* drift into the tall grass.

A light was on inside her boat.

She had turned all the lights off, of that she was absolutely sure. She silently rummaged through her sea bag for her binoculars, and pressed them to her eyes. Her heart beat timorously. Two jet skis were tethered to the swim platform, and two men in black attire and balaclavas climbed over her boat. Eventually one climbed onto a jet ski and sped off in the direction of the village, but a second black shadow helped himself to a drink at her bar. Her decision to row had been a fortuitous one, as she was unseen and unheard, but the discovery of intruders on her boat was an unforeseen, colossal problem. Worse still, these were not cops. These be River Glen pyrates.

"Hurry here, hurry there," Hank grumbled. "The frickin' story of my life." There was no time to walk through the boulder field and climb the slope to Herssen's property so he backed his pickup out of his hidden parking spot near the Spit and drove up the cliff road. He had to be quick in checking the supplies – the ladder, duct tape, and rope – because the redheaded woman might return at any time and untie her friend. In the off-chance the two women were to act out a bondage fantasy on the beach, he would at least wait until they were through, capture them both, then bring them up to the funnel.

His boss called Herssen's property the Tolchester Field Laboratory. Her first inclination was to call it the Tolchester Center for Arachnid Studies, but she finally decided on the former name.

"With a generic name like Field Laboratory, Hank, we might be able to branch out to other scientific endeavors, after we finish this one."

Finish, yeah right. She had been working on the same experiments for twenty years. What was going to be a series of scientific manuscripts was now going to be a tome. Tome, book – what the hell was the difference?   And she had promised him that he would be the second author on the tome. Not a mere mention in the acknowledgements but second author. Not bad for a farm boy from the outskirts of River Glen, Maryland.

How she knew his adopted parents, the senile farmer Aubrey Stupens and his wife Agatha, was anyone's guess. But his boss-to-be showed up one summer day and said that she needed a laboratory assistant. And a job was opening up at Tolchester College for an assistant groundskeeper. She would put in a good word with the Director of Business and Physical Plant. Hank was about nineteen at the time. He had no interest in intellectual pursuits; he only wanted to fish, so college was never an option. Nor would the Army or Marines take him.   Driving lawn mowers around a college while scoping out co-eds in short shorts beat the hell out of trudging through tobacco fields with a mental degenerate like Old Man Stupens. The envenomation experiments were part of a top-secret government study, she had told him. She could pay him work-study wages – on top of his groundskeeper's pay – as well as throw in new fishing tackle. The Loomis fishing pole clinched the deal.

Because the experiments were funded by a Department of Defense grant, discretion and secrecy were paramount, she had explained upon showing him around the grounds of the Tolchester Field Laboratory. The whole DOD grant sounded like a crock of shit, but sure, he would stay mum about the project and its requirement that they use small mammals in the experiments. If some general at the Pentagon said that the study called for an occasional human subject, then human subjects it was.

The two human subjects, that had been buried under the floorboards of the building many years before his employment, were Enemies of the State and supplied by the general, his boss explained. Then a new bill in Congress had been passed that nullified the use of human subjects in the form of foreign spies and terrorists. His boss had been asked to take initiative. Six years ago, she had decided upon Professors Bob Randolph and Sheila Myers. The pair had just retired, were both single, and had no children. They were logical choices.

During the retirement party in Blodgen's sunroom, Dr. Randolph had mentioned a trip in his RV to the Shenandoah National Park. Hank had readily volunteered for that road trip because the creeks of the park were reputedly hopping with brook trout. He had caught one of record size – it was no fish tale, it really was mammoth – while awaiting nightfall. After nabbing Dr. Randolph, he and his boss had dumped the RV outside of the park and drove the writhing professor back to the Tolchester field lab in a van that they had rented. An unbelievable coincidence ... a fly fisherman was painted on the sides of the rental van. It was such weird karma that he had landed that monster trout on the same trip.

At the same retirement party Professor Myers said that she would be working from home all summer to finish up a book on forensic accounting. The discovery of "the administrators' discretionary fund" earlier that spring by the Finance Committee, headed up by Drs. Randolph and Myers, had really pissed off his boss. A few years later, the Student Government representative on the Finance Committee and economics major Amanda Lamont had discovered other anomalies with the books. Amanda was supposed to be another human subject, but his boss' foot had been too heavy on the gas pedal the morning of the PedCan fundraiser. So back to Professor Myers.

A number of complications had occurred during the Sheila Myers' experiment. For whatever reason, the venom from Nero's bite didn't pack enough punch to kill her. As usual, his boss had refused to budge from behind her camera and lab notebook, and ordered him back to the college to pick up a bigger spider, in this case, Saddam. Hank had felt a pang of remorse that Professor Myers had to suffer so. Despite her being hideously ugly with the warts and wrinkles, she had been very pleasant to him; she always stopped to chat with him about his fishing excursions, which was more than he could say about the other self-important windbags on campus. When he had tossed dirt into Myers' grave and lamented aloud about her short retirement and agonizing death, his boss reminded him that "great science requires great sacrifices."

Staging Myers' disappearance in Philadelphia had involved an impressive level of planning and forethought that required a day trip to the city. He and his boss had surveyed 30th Street Station, the Reading Terminal Market and found a convenient parking lot near Penn's Landing and Route 95 South back to Maryland. At the end of the reconnoiter, his boss had treated them both to Philly cheesesteaks and water ice that they ate on a bench in Love Park. Because there had been no reason to rush back to Tolchester that day – exam week and the semester were over – they had visited the Franklin Institute for a few hours.

Days later, his boss, dressed in clothes from Myers' closet, boarded a bus at the River Glen bus station and headed to 30th Street Station. Her disguise had been remarkably realistic and included a flaming red wig and hunchback made of plastic groceries bags stuffed in a big wad into the back of her raincoat. He meanwhile had headed up Route 95 to wait in the Penn's Landing parking lot. According to his boss, everything had gone exactly as planned. She had pulled the rolling suitcase into the women's room at the Reading Terminal Market and changed into a long blonde wig and white chef's hat and apron like the cooks at the food concessions, leaving the ransacked suitcase and rifled wallet in a bathroom stall. The syringe was left to suggest to the police that Myers had come across a crazed drug addict shooting up. Perhaps a terrible altercation ensued! Of course the syringe only contained an anabolic steroid that he had purchased from Lanny Landry – that was when he was only bench-pressing one fifty-five – but it would certainly confuse the detectives.

Yes, everything had gone exactly to plan. Then a wonderful thing happened. On their drive back to Maryland, his boss told him to pull off of 95 at the Christiana Mall exit. The Cabelas Store! She had handed him a fifty-dollar gift card as a 'thanks for his invaluable assistance.' For a blissful hour he wandered the fishing section of the store while his boss ate a bison burger and checked her email in the restaurant there. They then headed south to Tolchester College. After all, they had a college to run.

What to do about the pyrate on the *Knot-A-Care*? Pamela's original plan was to locate the treasures of Great Granddaddy Dodd and Juan Carlos by promising Alex the certain torture of both Julia and Carly should she not comply, then kill Alex, raise anchor and head south to Florida. If the police wanted to interview her about Levon Bakanian, she would be charming and accommodating and deflect all attention to the conspicuously absent Alex. But how to get rid of the pyrate on her boat?

Approach innocently, then shoot him with her Glock?

Uck. Blood would be all over her white leather sofas and tanning beds, and impossible to remove like that stubborn blood on her hands.

Call 911?

"I've been treasure hunting," she could tell the police dispatcher. "I returned to find a man – maybe an escaped convict on the run, a pervert, rapist, or the Cliff Top Serial Killer – has commandeered my boat. I'm hiding in the marsh, too terrified to return to the *Knot-A-Care*. I'm a single-woman traveling on my own. Please send assistance!"

Ugh. Talking to the police would delay finding the treasure. No 911 call, at least for the moment.

What a fucking fuck-up!

There was no other option but to row silently back up the creek and spend the night on the beach with Alex. There would be no relaxing soak in the hot tub, no white wine, no salmon filet with omega 3 fatty acids for dinner. Instead it would a bland dinner of water bottles and protein bars. If she slept in the *Zodiac* curled up under a beach towel, with any luck the mosquitos would be attracted to the exposed flesh of Alex. That's all she fucking needed … welts from mosquito bites. Like the poison ivy wasn't bad enough.

Alex listened with remarkable concentration. Leaves and sticks crackled again. 'Do not breathe, do not move.' Whatever was approaching, it was not walking on two feet. Its muzzle was snuffling in the leaves; it had picked up her scent. A rogue mountain lion, wolf, or coyote? The duct tape hung off her mouth allowing for garbled words, but it would be impossible to scream with enough force to be heard. The predator might be kept at bay by her kicking legs though the inevitable blood loss from the bites and scratches would eventually weaken her. Her punishment for this practical joke on Pamela Dodd – this madness of her own creation – was to be eaten alive. If there was any consolation to this terrible situation, Pamela Dodd would no longer have a treasure hunting slave to do her bidding and the River Glen treasure would remain intact, safely guarded by the guardian-pyrates of River Glen. The sniffing was now directly behind the tree. She braced for the worse. Hot breath hit her neck and goose bumps popped from her skin.

Now the animal's fangs would rip into her neck, puncturing her jugular veins. Instead, a large warm tongue lashed her cheek. The bad breath was instantly familiar.

"Water Boy!"

The dog was covered with mud, burrs, and ticks. As a puppy, he had been manhandled by the deranged Frank Whitby, and injured by Desmond Whitby's knife on Mutter Island. Since that fateful day, she and her dog were inseparable. They were likeminded basket cases. Never were a human and dog better suited for one another. Water Boy's insecurities manifested themselves in compulsive, nervous chewing of everything. Now, if it could work to her advantage ...

"Water Boy, my hands! Chew, chew!" He licked her face again. "No lick. My hands Water Boy, a chew rope. Chew chew! You chew and you get a treat!" A moist cloud of bad breath was puffed into her face again.

"Treat, Water Boy, chew the rope." She fumbled with her hands to get his attention. He sniffed down her arms and moved behind the tree.

"Good boy! Good boy! Chew, chew! Then you get a treat." He licked her wiggling fingers. "Chew chew!" She heard the grinding of teeth on rope. "Good, good boy! Treat! Treat!"

The figure eight of rope loosened and she could rotate her wrists. The silence was broken by the rhythmic sloshing of oars in the darkness. "Hurry, boy, hurry!" He continued to chew, prodded by her urgent whispers. Finally her hands broke free and she struggled to her feet. She shook the stiffness from her limbs, tore the dangling duct tape from her lips, and looped the frayed rope through Water Boy's collar.

"Stop or I'll shoot!" Pamela screamed from the shallows. She leapt from the *Zodiac* and dragged it up the beach. She jumped back into the boat and dug through her sea bag. "Alex, I *will* shoot!"

Which way, which way? Alex had been to the Devil's Spit many times but always by boat so the walking trails unfamiliar. Which way? If she headed northeast, she would hit impassable swamp and quicksand, that much she knew. Randy and Old Ben had warned her and her friends away from it. If she headed southwest, there were woods, the boulder field at the base of the cliff, and Henry Herssen's isolated property. Herssens! That was a crime scene! With any luck a policeman or detective might be poking around there. If not, she and Water Dog might flag down a car on the cliff road and get a ride back to the village. Yes, that was it! Herssen's creepy property was preferable to snakes and quicksand. A bullet plunked against the tree, spraying her with bark. She pulled Water Boy into the forest as bullets whizzed through the darkness.

Lisa Paco's spade sunk into the hurricane-moistened soil. She heaved dirt from the hole while envisioning the upcoming conversation with Zera Lim.

Zera would glance curiously at the bone in the plastic bag. "Where did you get this?"

"I can't tell!"

Zera would scowl, yet reluctantly take the plastic bag. Lisa would invariably confess because Zera's expression had the effect of truth serum.

"I just need to know if I had a half-brother, even if briefly! The headstone said the boy's name was Henry Paco

Herssen.   The paperwork for an exhumation will take forever. Maybe not be approved at all. Mom and I need to know!"

Zera would disappear into the back room with all of the scientific instrumentation, inwardly enumerating all of the regulations she was about to break.

Lisa flung another clump of heavy soil onto the growing mound. Since the headstone's discovery, Ricarda Sarova and infant son held a macabre fascination for her, Wanda, and Aunt Helen. In addition to Owen Paco's impressive lists of crimes, he might have fathered an illegitimate child, her older brother by a few years. Even Uncle Seymour couldn't help but chime in; it was he who had suggested that they dig up the Sarova grave to obtain a tissue sample. The idea of digging up bodies in the graveyard appealed to their sense of adventure.   Plus, an outdoor activity in the River Glen cemetery on a lovely summer night was just the thing after being cooped up inside during Hurricane Beau.

The family had waited for the cover of darkness, then with flashlights and spades, she, Helen, and Seymour began to dig. Great care had been taken to peel away the overlaying grass in large sheets so that it could be tamped down later. The removal of the wet soil was slow going. They had been digging for an hour at least while Wanda vigilantly watched from her wheelchair. Should a curious dog-walker or mourner approach, Wanda would wheel herself across the pits and bumps of grass and order the person to stay far away, and remain very silent. They were independent filmmakers, filming the climax to *The Pyrate Zombies of River Glen*.   The camera in Wanda's lap would certainly convince the visitor to keep their distance from the three mud-covered actors with spades. After hours of vigorous digging, the spades thudded against wood.

They brushed the soil away from the coffin and peered into the damp hole. Lisa pulled a plastic bag from her pocket. She had witnessed dead bodies at crime scenes and on Zera's examination table during her years on the River Glen Police Force, but never had she touched one. That chore was always left for forensics. She shuddered. This infant skeleton from which she would steal a bone might possibly be a half-brother.

Wanda leaned forward, her camera rolling. "Don't be a bunch of wussies. Get on with it."

She and Uncle Seymour pushed their muddy fingers under the lid and lifted. At first the lid would not budge; then it creaked and moaned. It gave way and dirt slid into the coffin. They gasped in unison.

No plastic bag would be given to Zera that night. Nor would Zera have to head back to the back lab with all of the scientific instrumentation, inwardly enumerating all of the regulations that she was about to break.

#yikesemptycoffin

What a marvelous turn of events! Spider drove anxiously up the cliff road. If Nina and Griffin were to be human subjects 5 and 6, then the two women at the Devil's Spit would make human subjects 7 and 8. Wonderful! Up to this point in the clinical study, the live specimens obtained had been from their forties (Herssen and Paco) and sixties (Randolph and Myers), but the study had taken on thrilling momentum. The employment records of Nina and Griffin indicated that they were both in their late twenties.

Hopefully one of the captured women in the woods would be in her thirties. Now ... if an individual in their fifties could be included in the study, there would be representatives from each decade spanning from twenty to sixty years of age. Two fifty somethings – with grating personalities – came to mind, the grim detective Jay Braden, and that pessimistic Gloria Wines. It wouldn't be too difficult to find out where Braden lived, and Wines and her parakeets lived in a McMansion off the coastal road. When the timing was right, they would be experimented upon to make an even N of 10. Better yet, Braden and Wines represented different genders.

Yes, a number of fortunate events had occurred in her scientific study using human subjects, one being Hank's passion for weight-lifting and his knowledge of anabolic steroids. The peptide growth hormones that had been injected into the venom glands of *Atrax* had only negligible effects, but the steroids caused an astonishing 212% increase in cell number and 44% in cell size. After years of trial and error with countless growth factors, the precise chemical and dosage to induce maximal proliferation of the venom glands had been elucidated.

Decades ago, the news of her pregnancy had been a jarring bump in the road to becoming the world's leading arachnologist. Suddenly things became very complicated. Who knew if the father was Henry or Owen? The prospect of fatherhood had thrilled Henry Herssen and he insisted on marriage, but there was no time for men if she was to get her academic career on track. Plus, things had gotten dicey with those dirtbag meth dealers; it was time to duck and run. What better way to get them off her trail if they thought her dead? She had Owen start the rumor of her death during childbirth. The loser who owned the funeral home had overseen the bogus funeral. Men will do anything in exchange for sex. Owen was a wild fuck and had a cut athletic body but the mortician at the funeral parlor ... yuck, best to repress that afternoon. The infant – that she and Owen had delivered at the Devil's Spit during an excruciatingly long ordeal – had been placed with the dumb but able tobacco farmers Aubrey and Agatha Stupens. Henry had been told by Owen that she had miscarried and fled for parts unknown to 'to heal and find herself' after such a traumatic ordeal.

And find herself had. Mary Thompkins, a young woman of her approximate age, had died in one of the nameless hicksvilles in Alabama where she was hiding out. It wasn't too difficult to acquire Thompkins' identity. Next Mary Thompkins had acquired a biology degree. Her master's degree had been on growth hormones in begonias, all while she burned the midnight oil reading anything and everything about spiders. If she returned to work in some capacity at Tolchester College, she would be able to spy on the activities of the competition, Drs. Randolph and Towers.

But the last thing she had expected was to be recognized. There she was, in the River Glen post office, picking up a book of stamps when Henry Herssen had tapped tentatively on her shoulder and said a bit amazed "Ricki?"

She was equally shocked, as well as hugely disappointed because significant cash had been spent on plastic surgery to alter her nose and chin. She had also dyed her blonde hair to a dark brown and cut it in a short matronly style. Her blue eyes were changed to brown with contact lens. She had put on about thirty pounds to conceal her previously trim body. The days of wild hair, piercings, and black jeans and black t-shirts were long gone. She was now the model of academic respectability and pleasant competence – a bland version of her former edgy self. Plus, she had worked tremendously hard to quell the violent outbursts. Smile ... laugh jovially ... be a team-player ... and all that positive bullshit.

How Henry had recognized her was impossible to know, but she had told him that she had returned. She flung her arms around his shoulders, pressed her lips onto his, and insisted that they go to his isolated cottage on the cliff where she would tell him everything. Her story of frightening threats by the meth thugs was delivered with breathless pauses to heighten the suspense ... drug deals gone bad, blackmail, extortion ... she had run for her life. To protect herself, she had changed her name, appearance, got educated, stopped using meth and cleaned up her act. The news seemed to please Henry as he never had a stomach for the dealing and drug use; he was content to fish for a living, even if it meant living near the poverty line. Well, the poverty line was not for her. No, she had big plans.

In addition to being an acclaimed arachnologist, she was going to be a college administrator and a wealthy one at that. When she was a landscaper, slaving away in the stagnant summer heat, the deans from their cool mahogany offices, had swishing by her like she was an insignificant gnat. And how dare those haughty professors David Towers and Bob Randolph demote her to feeding the spiders and cleaning glassware! At that moment of career reversal, she had vowed that she would be the world's expert entomologist on the mechanisms of atracotoxin secretion. Her researches would eclipse all others.

But how?

Then it dawned on her while she watched Henry sip a beer on his porch swing. Not only would she become an expert on *Atrax* envenomation but also its action on the prey. Her experiments would have *so much more impact* if they were conducted on human subjects rather than small mammals like squirrels, rabbits and the occasional neighborhood cat or dog.

Henry Herssen would be human subject number 1! Other than Owen Paco, Henry had no other pals that she knew about. Nor had there been physical evidence in his cottage that another woman had replaced her. No one in the world would miss the introverted fisherman. While a contented Henry watched the Glen River flow by, she had lifted an oily wrench next to the disassembled outboard and knocked him on the head. She tied him up with boat line and duct tape, then rushed to her car for her experimental supplies: spider, hand-held video camera, and lab notebook. Just as Henry was coming to, she tapped the plastic cylinder and Manson fell into Henry's shirt. She started to film.

After the experiment with human subject 1 had been completed, her predicament became apparent. Rolling Henry's body over the cliff in broad daylight would have been too conspicuous. He was muscular and heavy so dragging him along the trail to the beach and to his boat *Atrax* – he had let her name it years before – to dump him in the bay was not feasible. And digging a grave in the forest would have taken hours. Her time that afternoon had been limited because she had an appointment with the academic dean Milton Blodgen, an anthophile who simpered endlessly about flowers. He had hired her, an expert on begonias, to teach botany labs at Tolchester College. That gawky old bachelor would be her entrée into college administration.

But what to do about Henry?

The short-term solution had been to pry up the warped floorboards in the bedroom and stash his body there until her next moves could be devised. Inevitably Owen would start snooping around, searching for his friend. Maybe he would contact the police to fill out a missing persons' report. It was an age before cell phones so she had spent the better part of an hour on Henry's landline trying to track down Owen. He was located at the Lame Dog Saloon. He was his usual surly self and still complaining about his bitch of a wife and idiot daughter.

"I can take Wanda off your mind," she had purred. "We're partying at Henry's tonight to celebrate my return. Let's get Henry soused so we can fuck."

Owen agreed to the plan. "I'll be there at nine."

Mary Thompkins, soon to be Blodgen, had just found herself human subject 2.

James Collins pulled off his balaclava and unzipped his black windbreaker. It was too hot, even in the air-conditioned salon of the *Knot-A-Care* to be wearing so many layers of clothing. Everything about the *Knot-A-Care* was garishly ugly and white. Horrid ... white leather sofas. More horridness ... white fiberglass bulkheads. Boat interiors were meant to be constructed from wood, preferably teak or mahogany. Salon furniture should be warm brown leather with splashes of blood red and cobalt blue in the pillows and carpeting. And there were too many lights. Lighting was an obvious necessity in the reading areas near bookshelves, but accosting white lights lined every edge and flat surface. Their blinding brightness felt like an interrogation. He checked his cell phone. Still no word from Brad Smyth on the other jet ski.

Pamela Dodd had been on their radar screen for a while. Most treasure hunters appeared in the village for a few days at most, wandered the shoreline with metal detectors, ate at the restaurants, and bought pyrate trinkets in the gift shops on Main Street before heading home. If some insurance salesman and his son from suburbia wanted to pretend that they were Long John Silver and Jim Hawkins hunting for a treasure chest, then go for it; it was all good fun and stimulated the local economy. But the intensity and fanaticism of Pamela Dodd's treasure hunt was troubling. For the past few summers he, from his house on the bluff, and Brad, from the *Banana Republic*, had watched the *Knot-A-Care*. Nothing for years had set off any alarms. He had spotted Dodd at Levon Bakanian's lecture that he attended with Judith Ann. (Brad avoided the college whenever possible since he worked there. Plus, the Orioles-Mets game was on that night).

That afternoon James had received Will's frantic text about a Dodd being in the village. The naivety of the text was stunning. How did Will not know of a Dodd in the village? How did he not know who she was? Clearly one of the RGPs (the River Glen Pyrates had an acronym for everything) had forgotten to tell him. The communication lapse could in part be blamed on Aunt Luna. If her hydroponic system did not produce such a potent marijuana crop, and was John Wilkins not such a stoner, John would have remembered to pass that vital information on to his son. And if Will had better attendance at the clandestine RGP meetings and did not skip them regularly to spend evenings on the *Vital Spark* with Alex, then he would be aware of these things!

James sighed and downed his glass of rum at Dodd's tacky light-trimmed bar. Why him to lead this band of foolhardy pyrates? Why him?

He should be in New York or Paris, drinking bottles of red wine late into the evenings with other wanna-be-poets, painters, and novelists. The Victorian era and steam-powered technologies fascinated him. He had it in him ... one great work of historical fiction or steam punk. Instead he was stuck in River Glen, filling out tedious legal documents. Now the police were searching for Pamela Dodd. Never before had Dodd been involved in any nonsense in River Glen. Besides treasure hunting, her interests seemed to be personal training and threesomes, both forms of healthy exercise. After all, if she had been in trouble, he would know about it because every hangdog client ended up in his office, requesting legal advice.

If he wasn't the only lawyer in this one-lawyer-town, his mind wouldn't be so cluttered with wills, estate taxes, and title searches. This whole mess was his fault, not Luna's or John's. How had he forgotten to tell Will about Pamela Dodd? There was too much minutiae fettering his mind. On top of his mind-numbing job, there was the endless sorting through the voluminous records in the historical society archives with Judith Ann. If the senior citizen volunteers would actually do some work, and not drink tea and chatter about reruns of *Downton Abbey* all day, something might actually get accomplished. If Lady Sybil wanted to marry the chauffer Tom, then please, someone, let her marry the goddamn Irishman!

James exhaled in frustration. He had spread himself too thin. Way, way too thin. It was that simple. Best to commiserate with another glass of Pamela Dodd's excellent rum. Yum, Havana Club Máximo Extra. Perhaps he should take on a partner – maybe a kid right out of law school? But what young person wanted to live in a backwater like River Glen? The only person who would apply for the job would be the class dolt.   And a partner would mean working with someone; worse, supervising them.   Then he wouldn't be able to wander across the village green to the historical society at any whim, or when some tax document got too boring – which was all the time. Alas, he was never meant to be a lawyer. But for his entire youth, his father, grandfather, and great-grandfather had told him ad nauseam "it's the Collinses who are the legal guardians of River Glen." Why him?   He had double majored in English Literature and History at Columbia University.   He was destined to write historical novels and live in a thrillingly exotic locale like Barcelona, Nairobi, or Jakarta. A thousand plotlines jostled in his head. Every time he sifted through the disintegrating boxes at the historical society another story leapt from the yellowing pages and dashed wildly through his thoughts. Who could concentrate on legal work after that? In addition to pyrates, River Glen had produced countless colorful personalities like the treacherous Civil War spies Josiah and Abigail Wedgewood-Smyth, and the fearless World War II submarine captain Lincoln Wilkins.

James suddenly remembered that he was on a secret mission. He climbed off the barstool and wandered by Dodd's entertainment system. Sadly there was no Nintendo or Xbox with which to play a shooter game to pass the time until she returned. He passed through the sliding doors to the deck and scanned the marsh with his binoculars. The water was a silent glassy black. Not a single night breeze rippled the marsh grass.

Grandma Julia's text had afternoon had given him an excuse to stretch his legs, check out the electrical glitch in her closet alarm caused by the hurricane, and a change a light bulb. And she had nagged him about that other family matter. Then she madly peddled after him to relay the news of Alex's disappearance. That had jolted the RGPs from complacency into action. After all the waiting and watching, Dodd had finally acted. That spurred the men to set off on jet skis to comb the shoreline. A pyrate of great importance was missing. The search was not a matter for the overworked police force, chasing the Cliff Top Serial Killer. This was a matter to be settled between a Florida pyrate and the pyrates of the Chesapeake.

The Cuban rum made James feel restless. He pulled the throwing knives from his belt and searched for an appropriate target. Everything was hideous white fiberglass. Oh good ... the hot tub was wood. *Thwack.* The razor-sharp blade embedded dead center in a knot in the wood. He would return Alex Allaway, the pyrate treasurer – and his half sister – to her brethren of the bay.

Thwack. Thwack. Thwack.

Nina Vega checked her cell phone for the umpteenth time that evening. So did Julia. Alex was a no-show for their dinner engagement; Alex was missing. Numerous times unrecognizable men on jet skis pulled along the dock. Each time Julia had gestured for Nina to stay put on the porch while she hurried down the dock, spoke to the men in emphatic whispers before returning to the porch and lighting another cigarette. The jet skis then sped off into the night. Never before had Nina witnessed such a response. The villagers obviously loved Alex to organize so swiftly. But why the secrecy? Why the black attire, shoulder holsters and pistols? And why no collaboration with the police? The locals were clearly acting on their own and under the veil of darkness. Something ... larger than Alex missing ... was in motion. Nina could sense it.

It was more inexplicable River Glen weirdness.

That weirdness – or was it her? – was causing Griffin to leave. So very badly she needed to talk to Alex, to share a meal, a bottle of wine and her confusion. Laugh hysterically or bawl outright, go with any emotion that the wine and conversation coaxed out of her. Too much had happened in too short a period of time. If she could only talk with a trusted friend ... The list of weirdness was now lengthy, the giant wake, the lost finger, Richard dumping her, the spider ... her jumping into bed with a complete stranger! How stupid could one person be? It had been an evening and morning of sexual bliss, and then she had rolled over in bed to see Griffin packing his duffel bag.

"Are you going somewhere?"

"This place is cuckoo, Nina. I'm leaving for my father's in the Keys. Today."

"What?" Could her quick response have sounded more desperate?

"You can come with me, if you want." His tone was less than convincing.

Best to deflect the focus from her. "You can't leave now. You signed a contract with Tolchester. Students are depending on you tomorrow."

"Fuck them. The morons can't be bothered to pry their eyes from their cell phones. Besides, I hate teaching. I hated being a teaching assistant at Michigan. I'm not sure about any of this. And Tolchester can't even give me an office that's rain-proof and has internet. The building's filthy and infested with poisonous spiders. And now we're living in a detective's house. How crazy is this?"

She had to concede that it was crazy. All of it, exceptionally crazy.

"And Dean Wines screwed up my computer order." He circled the room, searching for his belongings. "It's the cheapest piece of shit on the market. It crashes every time I try to open Word. She probably did it intentionally since I'm gay."

"But you're not gay. Why do you have gay pride stuff all over your door?"

"I told President Blodgen and Dean Wines that I was gay during the interview, so I figured I'd better play the part. I told them that I'd be moving down here with my partner. If they asked about the alleged partner, I'd simply say that we broke up. He wanted to stay in Michigan."

She had unconsciously scowled.

"Jeez, Nina, why the face? Every one lies at job interviews."

"No, they don't!" One of Ricardo's insults, that she was 'pathologically honest,' sprang to mind.

"Don't be so naïve," he scoffed. "How's a white male supposed to get a job in this world without lying? All of the jobs are wired for gays and minorities. Why do you think you were hired, *chica*?"

"Don't *chica* me. I was hired because I had a good interview. My research is strong, all of my data statistically significant and very interesting. And I won a teaching award as a graduate student."

He shook his head condescendingly. "You're a latina, honey. The administration doesn't give a shit about your research on impoverished fishermen, just like they don't give a shit about my inane research on gay gyms."

"Which you did just to get yourself an interview," she said coldly.

Griffin had grinned. "Yes, and it worked. That dissertation topic got me five interviews." He stuffed his shaving kit into his duffel bag. "You're sure you don't want to come with me? Tropic breezes, tiki huts, palm trees and it's always five o'clock. My father will employ us at the coffee shop. You could bake your Honduran bread. Just think of it, Nina. No mindless students, no pompous deans, no spiders, no worries. Besides, we click in bed."

"I can't believe you lied ..."

"I can't believe you're so naïve." He zipped up the duffel bag with a gesture of finality. "I'm going to clear my things out of the apartment. I'll leave my key on the kitchen island."

"Guatemalan. Not Honduran. I'm Guatemalan," she had called as he stepped through the door.

Thwack. Thwack. Thwack. Silence.

Enough practice with his throwing knives. James Collins checked his cell phone once again. Marty Wilkins and Byron and Brad Smyth had nothing to report. Nor was there a text from John Wilkins, probably because he had misplaced his phone again, or forgotten it at Aunt Luna's. Alex Allaway and Pamela Dodd were nowhere to be found.

Alex Allaway was his half-sister, a fact that was still difficult to comprehend, especially having grown up as a doted-upon only child.   Should he hyphenate his name? Would it be Collins-Allaway or Allaway-Collins? Or remove Collins entirely? A name change would mean getting new business cards and letterhead, and a new sign for the front lawn of the law office. Such tedious tasks would distract him from sketching out an outline for his novel about Josiah and Abigail Wedgewood-Smyth. Maybe he should go with the hyphenated name, Allaway-Collins, otherwise his novels might get lost amidst the Jackie and Suzanne Collinses in the bookstore, though how cool would it be to have one's book next to Wilkie Collins' *The Moonstone*!

James had learned about his new sibling from his dying mother Elizabeth.   Deathbed revelations were an atypical occurrence in real life; they were a device of kitschy movies and TV serials which allowed the writer to create a tantalizing, teasing scenario that promised viewership into the next season. But then again, if the surreal did occur in real life, it usually happened to the citizens of River Glen. Therefore, he was not entirely surprised to find himself at his mother's beachfront condo in Boca Raton, Florida, listening to the story of a Paris-Dakar rally in the 1970s, in a time before the race had been moved to South America because of terrorism in the Middle East. The participation of his father Theodore in the race seemed ludicrous from the start because he only remembered his father either in his home library or one-man law firm. There was not an adventuring bone in Theo's body. Theo even avoided Giles Blood-hand Days for fear that the pier was going to collapse under the weight of the tipsy dancers. Yet according to his mother, Theo and a crony from Harvard Law School had been tearing across the Sahara when the Jeep flipped, crushing his father underneath. It was certainly the morphine drip that fueled his mother's fantastical story, but James had listened intently, poised for an illustrative point that was forthcoming. At her next words ... damaged scrotum ... low sperm count ... he found himself squirming in the chair at her bedside.

"For years Theo and I tried to conceive but to no avail," Elizabeth had said.

One's parents' sex life was never appealing to contemplate and he suspected that this story would not have a good outcome.

"We finally decided to locate a sperm donor, someone local, a neighbor whose sperm we could rely on. In sperm we trust," Elizabeth laughed.

If he could just slip down to the beachfront tiki bar for a very strong drink ...

"Of all of the pyrate families in River Glen, we're not closely related to the Allaways," she explained. "Randy was dashing and witty and would certainly have helped a neighbor in need, but he'd recently married and his new bride might not have appreciated him visiting my bed at the time of ovulation."

A giant drink at the tiki bar, a double ...

"But Randy's studious son Colin fit the bill. He was highly intelligent, and had been accepted into the University of Pennsylvania's architecture program for the upcoming fall. What the teenager lacked in experience, he made up for in enthusiasm. He was the sweetest thing ...""

James glanced at himself in his cougar mother's dresser mirror. His face was averagely average. This explained everything. He could have had Randy's handsome genes, but his mother had opted for Colin's smart ones.

"After I pass, please contact your Grandmother Julia," his mother insisted. "She knows all about it. She's thrilled about having you as a grandson. But she wants you to tell Alex the wonderful news."

Huh ... the flaky boater babe was his half-sister? Before this startling revelation, he had almost asked her out until he learned that she was dating Will Wilkins.

Not a double ... a triple at the tiki bar was definitely required. Maybe two triples.

James yanked his knives from the wood of the hot tub and slid them back in the holder on his belt. "Chicken," he said to himself, "big chicken." He had had the perfect opportunity to tell Alex about Colin and Elizabeth's insemination parties when she had showed up out-of-the-blue during the hurricane. All he could do was grin stupidly and show-off with one of his favorite knives.

He pulled the binoculars to his eyes once again. Still no movement in the marsh. Dodd had seen his jet ski. It was futile waiting on the *Knot-A-Care*. Alex was in danger. He rushed down to the engine room where he pulled every wire and cable he could find and stuffed them in his windbreaker pocket. This garish white yacht was going nowhere. He pulled the balaclava over his head and climbed onto the jet ski. He jerked down the throttle and raced back to River Glen.

"What the hell was going on?" Jay grumbled to himself. Lisa Paco – #mshashtagalwaysonthejob – was nonresponsive, and Will was in the men's room again. No one had to pee five times in an hour. Even someone in their fifties, and with prostate issues, didn't have to pee that often.

Will was talking to or texting someone in the men's room. Something was afoot with the locals. Will's distraction was understandable because Alex was missing, but he still had to run background checks on the Tolchester employees. It was impossible for Will to search for Alex with a broken foot – besides, a fleet of police cruisers was looking for her – so Will needed to help here. There were too many ancient professors employed at that creepy, spider-ridden college.

Jay stared at the computer screen. "Don't these old geezers ever retire?" He knew the answer to his own question. The professors were getting paid too much to do basically nothing. Nina and Griffin had mentioned a Mon-Wed-Fri schedule. Two days off in the middle of the week – must be nice.

A PhD behind one's name doesn't make one immune to bad behavior so the Tolchester faculty, like the general population, had their share of scumbags. There was a pedophile in the English department, a shoplifter in Economics, and a political scientist had been selling coke to students in the dorm. A math professor-Republican delegate was involved in voter registration fraud and the intimidation of minorities on Election Day. Lana Hinkie had run over her next-door-neighbor's border collie, but she had denied it, despite dog blood and fur on her bumper. A biochemist was cited for public intoxication at the Giles Blood-hand festival, which was an unusual infraction since the whole village was intoxicated. The chemist had the bad luck of grabbing the wrong breast at the wrong time, that of the voluptuous no-nonsense undercover cop Irene McIntyre. The thought of breasts put Jay in an even worse mood as his mind leapt into Julia's blouse. No way was he seeing those beauties ever again.

He'd blown it.   Now he would have to return to own house, sleep in his own lonely bed, and make small talk tomorrow morning with two millennial professors that were living in his house and only working three goddamn days out of the week!

Plonk. Plonk. He turned. The sound came from the window behind his desk. He peered through the venetian blinds. *Plonk.* All that was visible was the dark forest. The picnic table where the state troopers smoked cigarettes was hardly visible. His cell phone vibrated. The text was from Lisa Paco.

"Is the captain in?"

He typed, "Yes."

"Then come out back. Please sir. It's urgent."

What the hell ... why couldn't Lisa come inside? Why the pebbles cast against his window?   Why the mystery, the drama?

"OK."

With a groan, he rose from his chair. This was the time of night that his back seized up. He hated going to the back of the building. It was where he used to sneak a smoke, back by the air-conditioning units in the tall grass. The place reminded him of Laura's decline. And he never knew what he was going to see. One night he had stumbled upon two state troopers humping on the picnic table. According to the office rumor mill, they were both in horrible marriages. Belts with holsters and tasers, uniform pants twisted around their black boots ... it was not an attractive sight.

He rounded the corner of the building and stopped abruptly. He had seen Lisa Paco only once in civilian attire, at his surprise party at Zera's condo. At the time she had been wearing high top leopard sneakers, faded jeans and a long-sleeved Pokémon t-shirt, unremarkable clothes for a female of thirty. Now she was dressed in galoshes, police academy gym shorts, and a tank top, also unremarkable. But two things caused some surprise. Every section of her skin, from wrists to neckline was covered with tattoos; both legs were entirely covered with ink as well. It was impossible to make out the details in the dim light. A second unusual thing was that she was covered with mud – her face, hair, arms, legs and boots. Mud everywhere.

Lisa extended her arm. "Sir, this one's the coolest. Holmes and Watson chasing Jack the Ripper. Check out the detail!"

A mosquito bit him behind the ear. He smacked himself. "Shit."

"That's why I couldn't come in. You know the captain's lame policy about tats." She rolled her eyes. "If you ever want to get one, there's this amazing artist at Sublime Ink."

He knew the joint. Laura had insisted on getting a tattoo on her hip. Her mid-life crisis tattoo, she had called it. The tattoo artist had lightened his wallet of two hundred dollars for a dolphin leaping out of the water. "Lisa, what's so urgent?"

She pulled her cell phone from her pocket and swiped through the photos. "Here."

He gazed at the image and swallowed hard. "You-um- you dug up a grave without a court order?"

"Mom and Aunt Helen said you can blame it on them. We had to know if I had a baby brother. I wanted to take a bone sample to Zera."

He was transfixed by the image. "My god ..."

"Yeah, no shit. Ricarda Sarova and her boy, possibly my brother, could still be alive."

Burt Sweeny pulled a Jack Sparrow blanket over his son Burtie, and closed the bedroom door. He shuffled through the trailer, located his cigarettes and lighter on the kitchen table, and stepped outside. He dropped onto a milk carton and lit a cigarette. Across the dirt road, his bony neighbor in her nightgown and slippers was dumping her cat box into the weeds behind her trailer. The mutt Kit that lived down the road had slipped from his collar again and was sniffing around the dumpster.

Burt inhaled deeply. For days he had been a man on a precipice, his feet poised precariously on the edge of the unknown. His step off it would be irrevocable. The step was an opportunity. Not certain death but a rare opportunity, and opportunities were unheard of for him. Then why was it so hard to take that goddamn step? His life to this point had been devoid of opportunity. Now that one beckoned, flashing like neon, he was beset with paralyzing fear and indecision. His foot was glued – no, cemented – on the cliff's edge. At the moment that Debbie had whispered to him by their high school lockers that she was pregnant, he became a workhorse walking endless circles around the millstone. Endless, endless circles and circles. The belief that there was more to life had long ago vacated his thoughts. It was better not to dream dreams, or hope hopes. His was not a life; his was an anti-life.

The only work he had been able to find without a high school education was as a security guard at Tolchester. He was grateful for the steady work – truly he was – but he could barely support his family on minimum wage. At least he had health benefits. Then his prick of a boss Hank

Stupens said that benefits might be cut. "A cost-saving measure that President Blodgen has decided upon. The cuts will only apply to staff and faculty, starting in the next academic year," Stupens had said. "Health benefits will be retained for the administrators." Yeah, of course they would. The startling news had caused Burt's blood pressure to spike. How to pay for Burtie's asthma medications and doctors' visits? He would certainly have to find a part-time job, or a second job. But when could he squeeze that in? He barely saw his son as it was. Then, when he had asked the other security guards, secretaries, and landscapers about the benefits cuts, not one of them had heard anything about it. He had been played for the fool once again, and all he had done was alarm everyone. It was just another of Stupens' sick mind games. It wasn't the first time. The messed-up bastard seemed to delight in harassing him.

Burt lit a second cigarette off the butt of the first and circled his toe in the dirt. One step off the edge, he thought to himself. Just one step ... An incredible opportunity had been presented to him, but what to do with it? He had so few male friends to confide in. Wrong, he had no male friends to confide in. Who had time for friendships? He worked 24-7. He was sort-of-friends with Jay Braden, and he had a drink with the pleasant attorney James Collins after Debbie's funeral. Maybe one of them could advise him. Yes, it was an incomprehensible turn of events. All because of that obnoxious bitch at Turtle Island ...

He had been sitting on the beach at the Devil's Spit, fuming. Steam, he was sure, was coming off him. What was the word for more furious than furious? ... because that's what he had been. Her driving them off the state game land of Turtle Island was one thing, but threatening Burtie, a boy

... well, that was too much! And Levon Bakanian ... what was the word for more useless than useless?   If he had an education, he would know these vocabulary words. Burtie was also shaken by the encounter, but with youthful resilience he proceeded with the treasure hunt. Bakanian's talk the night before had enthralled his son. Burtie had read every book about pyrates at the town library.   The kind librarian Judith Ann always located new pyrate books for him. "Dad, I'm going to be a pyrate historian," he said three times on the drive home from the lecture.   Jerk though Bakanian was, his talk fueled his son's sense of adventure that Saturday.

Burtie was imagining himself a buccaneer and swishing the metal detector across the sand, concentrating fully on the task, when he wandered too close to the bog.

"W-whoa, buddy," he warned. "There's quicksand back there."

"Okay." Burtie veered back toward the beach.

The metal detector started to *ping*.

"Something Captain Sparrow!" Burtie said.

The last thing Burt had wanted to do was dig rusty trash out of the sand, but it had been such a shitty afternoon, the least he could do was encourage Burtie's fantasy.   He lumbered across the sand with his spade.

"S-stand aside, Will Turner." He looked around with bombast. "We're not being watched by Captain Barbossa, are we matey?"

Burtie giggled. "No, Captain."

"And I hope this gold's not cursed by the Aztec Curse of Cortés."

"I hope it is!"

He had taken the metal detector from his son's hands and swished it over the sand. *Ping, ping, ping* sounded in rapid succession.

"It's probably a buried lawn mower, Dad."

"I'm sure it's Aztec gold."

"Maybe it's an outboard engine."

"Argh, hold my rapier, Will." He handed Burtie the metal detector.

Burtie grinned. "Okay."

Burt began to dig while the humidity glued his t-shirt to his body. He finally hit a solid object and he and Burtie got down on hands and knees to brush away the sand. The sun shone into the hole and they gasped. Some of the leather bags had split open, while others had rotted away. The reflection from the sun on the gold coins blinded them.

"Captain Sparrow," Burtie whispered, "we found Giles' treasure!"

Burt stood from the milk carton and ground his cigarette butt into the dirt. "I guess I can afford to buy myself a lawn chair."

Alex tugged Water Boy up the bluff. If she had half a brain in her head, she would have counted the bullets shot at her! How many bullets does a pistol even hold? If she had half a brain ... and hadn't inhaled all that second-hand weed smoke, or drank so much rum with Julia, she would know this. She was an American; how did she not know everything about guns?

Miraculously she and Water Boy had dashed along the twisty Indian trail through the boulder field without being hit, but she had torn up her feet on the rocky terrain. If she only had sneakers! ... but she had removed them in attempts to pull off the duct tape with her toes. Pamela was wearing sneakers and was gaining on them; the taunts and jeers were approaching fast. If Pamela were to pick them off, it would be here as they clawed their way up the exposed bluff. The moon through the black trees was providing ample light to be seen. Yes, Pamela would certainly hit them here as they scrambled up the bluff.

Where would Julia have her buried? In Philadelphia, with her parents Colin and Carole? She hoped not. River Glen was her home, not Philadelphia. She could only hope that her name Alexandra Allaway would be carved right under Randall Allaway on the obelisk in the River Glen cemetery. She hoped Julia had the wherewithal to bury Water Boy with her, if he too were to be killed by this psycho. For some minutes, the bullets had stopped because it was difficult for Pamela to climb and shoot accurately. Maybe she was saving her bullets for the slaughter by the cliff. That had to be her strategy.

The edge of the bluff finally appeared. Alex and Water Boy heaved themselves over the top. She glanced over her shoulder. Pamela was about halfway up the bluff, barely winded. Her own lungs were heaving. How was she in such horrible shape? Probably because she did no cardio. All she did was tap away at a computer at the marine station, collect specimens in the marsh, and clean glassware. From pulling crab pots, she did have strong arms ... all crabbers and fishermen did ... but if it came down to hand-to-hand combat, did she stand a chance? Would Water Boy help her in the fight? Doubtful – he was friendly wimp. And with her terrible luck, Pamela was probably a black belt in karate or judo. Why did Pamela even need a gun? Pamela would probably snap her neck instantly.   It would be over in seconds without Pamela having broken a sweat.   But that psycho better not harm her precious Water Boy!

Which way to go next?   Which way!   The woods were entirely black. There seemed to be a trail to the left ... yes yes to the left!   The trail was easier on the feet than the rocky bluff, but it was slow going in the sandy soil.   The weedy clearing at Herssen's property couldn't be much further.   Please ... please be a policeman ... or anyone with a cell phone!

"You're a dead Googan!" Pamela yelled.

Alex glanced over her shoulder again.   Pamela was only thirty feet or so behind them. "Hurry, Water Boy, hurry!"

Water Boy barked and strained at the rope, yanking her off the trail.

"No, Boy, this way!" Alex struggled to keep them on the trail.

He barked and pulled her into the underbrush.

"You're fucking dead, Allaway! I'm going to cut off your head and put it on a pike!"

"Water Boy, faster!"

Pamela was now only yards behind them.   Any second Pamela would leap on to her back, and grab her throat.   They would scuffle in the leaves.   It would be a battle to the death.

Water Boy continued to pull Alex toward the edge of the trail. Branches whipped her legs like switches.   Suddenly there was a crackling of branches and a whoosh.

Alex turned over shoulder.

Pamela Dodd had vanished.

Pamela came to. She spit dirt from her mouth and brushed dirt from her arms and hair. "What the fuck?" She had fallen into a deep animal trap. It was definitely man-made and steep-walled. Every time she grasped the soil in an attempt to climb out, the muddy walls collapsed because the hurricane had saturated the soil. Worse, there were no handholds. The roots were too thin and weak. When she tugged on one, it pulled right out of the wall with a big clot of slick soil. She patted down her pockets for her cell phone. "Fuck and double fuck!" Her phone was in her backpack on the *Zodiac*. In her haste, she had grabbed the Glock and took off after Alex without taking her cell phone.

Even if she had her phone, who the hell would she call? What abysmal luck sending the twins away. Call 911? This predicament would be awkward to explain to the police. What excuse would she give them? Um ... maybe not call the police at all. The hunter that dug this frigging pit must check his traps frequently. Fuck! Spending the night in this shit hole was going to be cold. Certainly Alex would go straight to the police and tell them that she had been kidnapped, tied up, and shot at. Maybe the police would come up here to check out Alex's story. Then the cops would remove her from the pit. 'Alex had forced me into the woods with the Glock and pushed me into the pit,' she could say. It would be Alex's word against hers. Who would believe a redneck crabber over a modeling magnate with a PhD in Psychology from Oxford? Of course she would deny all of Alex's allegations. Her lawyer could raise doubt about Alex's mental stability, especially after the murder of her parents and grandfather. Her lawyer would get the case tossed out before it even went to court. Maybe he could even get Alex locked up in a mental hospital for her delusional tendencies.

If the hunter arrived before the police and helped her out of the pit, she would return to her *Zodiac* and remove all evidence that she and Alex were ever on the beach. But how to deal with the pyrates on *Knot-A-Care*?

One thing at a time! First, getting out this pit ...

A flashlight beam illuminated her; her arm jerked up to shield her eyes. "Oh, thank god."

"How'd you get down there?" a man asked.

"I fell obviously. Is this your pit?"

"It's a funnel. Didn't you notice the tapered walls?"

"Of course I noticed. Now, get me out of here. It's cold and wet down here."

"Yeah, sure. I'll need to get my ladder. It's by my work-shed. It's not far."

"Thank you!"

"Yeah, no problem."

"Shine the light in your face so I can see you."

He turned the flashlight toward his face and smiled broadly. Where had she seen him? He looked so familiar. Right ... it was the muscular man standing in the doorway at the lecture Friday night.

"I know you. I saw you at the lecture at Tolchester College," she said.

"Yeah, that was me. I saw you down at the Devil's Spit when I was fishing this afternoon."

"Really?" Pamela's heart lurched. "So ... you saw my friend?"

"She wasn't your friend. I killed her and her dog." He waved the Glock over the opening.

It was a completely unexpected, unnerving response. He was making a joke. That was it. A disturbed joke but a joke nonetheless. "Oh funny. Ha ha."

"No, really. I did."

"Oh. Ah ... why'd you do that?"

"Because you didn't like her. You were angry with her. Right? I saw you trying to shoot her."

Alex and the black dog were dead? If nothing else, this eliminated the problem of Alex going to the police. She had reason to punish Alex for that humiliating practical joke on Turtle Island, but he had no cause, no cause at all. A dreadful apprehension set in. She smiled tautly. "Ah, you're just kidding about the woman and her dog."

"No." He smiled back.

She muted a gasp. She just needed to know the maniac's name. "You are ...?"

"Hank, just call me Hank."

"Well, Hank, will you please get your ladder so I can get out of here?" She forced another smile. "Then we can talk."

"Let's talk about Juan Carlos' treasure first. Then, I promise I'll get my ladder."

She smiled again. "Promise?"

"Absolutely. I promise. You're a treasure hunter. Aren't you?"

"Yes. We can look for treasure *together* if you get me out of this hole," she said seductively.

"But you didn't find treasure at the Devil's Spit."

"No, because someone found it before me."

"Who?"

"That man and his boy at the Friday night lecture. The boy asked about Giles Blood-hand's bloody hands."

"Burt Sweeny and little Burt?"

"You know them?"

"Burt's the most worthless employee I have. A complete sucker."

"Then help me out of here! Let's go find him and get that treasure! What are we waiting for, Hank? That treasure's ours!"

"Yes!" He paused. "Wait. What about Giles' treasure?"

"I have no clue."

He wagged an admonishing finger back and forth. "No, no. I don't let you out until you tell me everything you know about Giles' treasure. That's the big one. Don't you think?"

"Hmm ... possibly," she said to stall. Quick thinking, Pam, quick thinking. Where would Giles' treasure be? Where, where? The treasure from the elusive tavern treasury described by Brother Guillermo. It suddenly came to her. In case this asshole didn't help her up, at least she would lure him into a nest of cops. Alex's strapping boyfriend, Carly's father, was a cop. "The woman you shot, the one with the black dog. Alex Allaway. I'm almost certain that she and her grandmother have Giles' treasure in their basement or attic. It's the house by the Point with the tugboat and lawn ornaments."

"Really?"

"Do you know the place?"

"How can anyone miss it? There's only one tugboat in the village."

"With Alex gone, it will be easy taking the treasure from the old grandmother. Her name's Julia Hale. She's a descendant of Giles Hale. That old lady has got to have the treasure. C'mon, let me out of here. It'll be like taking candy from a baby. C'mon, Hank. Get that ladder. I'll throw in a bonus. I'll have mind-blowing sex with you, when you get me out of here." Fucker, I'll blow your brains out when I get my hands on my Glock. "I'll blow your ..."

"Oh, for god's sake, Hank," a female voice interrupted. "We have work to do. We don't have time for this exasperating banter. I have so many important meetings tomorrow morning."

Hank turned toward his unseen companion. "The police confiscated the chair with the restraints when they searched the property. What do we do about that?"

"There's no time for that tonight," said the irritated voice. "Turn off the flashlight."

The funnel and the forest went black.

"Shit no! What the hell are you doing?" Pamela's eyes adjusted to the darkness and Hank's silhouette became visible against the moonlit canopy. She scratched at the dirt wall and debris rained down on her. "Inbred assholes! Let me out of here!"

All was instantly clear. Alex was not dead. Alex had tricked her once again. That fucking Googan! Alex had led her into the lair of the Cliff Top Killers! Alex was one of them! Alex was watching and muting hysterical laughter.

A hot jab scalded Pamela's shoulder. "Owww!"

A metal lamp, like those used to highlight her models, shone into the funnel and bleached Pamela's skin a sickly white. Her head snapped toward the black spot in her peripheral vision. A mammoth spider impaled her shoulder. She swatted it into the dirt wall, but the black fangs poked from her stinging skin. She squinted upward in terror. Peering over the edge of the funnel was a white-haired woman in a white lab coat, filming her with a smartphone.

Alex staggered from the underbrush, dragging a panting Water Boy behind her. The section of road was familiar. She was near the intersection of the cliff road and the highway, miles outside of River Glen. She and Water Boy were starving and exhausted. At least he was able to stop and drink from puddles. She was so dehydrated that she was almost tempted to do the same.

If they ever made it back to River Glen, the first thing she was going to do was drink a gallon of water and grill Water Boy the biggest steak she could find. He deserved it. He had chewed through her ropes to free her hands.

"You are the best." She scratched him behind the ears. "Absolutely the best."

Dogs have a sixth sense that humans do not. Water Boy had sensed the pit and pulled her to the side of the trail. It must have been the pit that Will had fallen into and broken his ankle. She wasn't about to go back and check on Pamela Dodd's wellbeing. The pit was the perfect holding pen for that lunatic. The police could pick Pamela up later. and charge her with kidnapping and attempted murder.

The road was hard on Alex's torn up feet, far worse than the soft forest floor. Hobbling along the shoulder of the highway was going to take forever. They would be lucky to make it home by sun-up. Eventually a pair of headlights appeared in the distance. A sports car convertible slowed down behind her.

"Oh my god ... no ..."

It was a BMW Z4 Roadster coming from the direction of the cliff road. What was the knife-happy lawyer doing here at this time of night? He must be the Cliff Top Killer! Why else would he be here? This couldn't be happening ... Water Boy barked and pulled her toward the car.

"Water Boy, wait! No!"

The dog continued to yip and pull.

"Wait!"

Maybe Water Boy was right. Maybe James was no threat. He had been helpful when transferring the title of Old Ben's cottage to her name. And he and Julia had become close recently. They had lunch together twice last month.

But still, why was he here?

"Are you okay?" James pushed open the passenger's side door. "Hop in."

He had a line of razor-sharp knives in his belt. Those were for ... what? To carve up bodies? She hesitated. This nightmare had gone from bad to disastrously bad ... she had escaped one psycho in the woods only to be offered a ride by another!

He looked quizzically at her. "Alex, come on. Hop in. Lets' get you home."

"Um, I can walk. It's really no problem."

"You're in shock. And your feet are bleeding. Please get in."

He pulled his phone from the pocket of his black windbreaker and swiped some buttons. "Here. Call Will. He's worried sick. We've all been looking for you."

Will's number glowed on the screen. "Thank you!"

The conversation with Will was a blur. "Yes, yes, I'm on the cliff road. Yes, James will bring me home. Yes, I love you too!" She rang off.

Will and the police knew her whereabouts, and who she was with. This changed everything.

"Climb in, sister."

She smiled reluctantly. That was an overly familiar remark from a man she hardly knew, but she was too exhausted to psychoanalyze its meaning. She dropped with a thud into the bucket seat and pulled Water Boy on to her lap.

"Call Julia to let her know you're okay. Then there's something interesting I need to tell you ..."

CHAPTER NINE
Wednesday

Well past midnight Mary Blodgen sent two emails. The first was to her secretary saying that the meetings with legislators in Annapolis were running into the next day. "Tremendous headway was being made with acquiring funds for the new academic building," the secretary was to inform the First Line Staff on her behalf. Her second email was to her right-hand-woman Lana Hinkie. Forming friendships with females had been rare over the years, but she and Lana had really bonded. Lana competently managed things on campus when she departed 'to Annapolis.' And thanks to Lana, she had really improved her golf game. Lana had a promising future in college administration; a provost or college president position was not entirely out-of-reach. Gloria Wines, on the other hand, had been a disappointing hire; she had never quite fit in ... never become one of the girls. Gloria was a little too self-absorbed and would never amount to anything more than a dean. Before logging off, Mary's eyes lingered on her title – President Blodgen. My goodness, she had come far in this life.

Mary sipped her decaffeinated latte and looked out to the vast Chesapeake. Tankers heading south to Baltimore appeared like jewels on the water. That night had been another in a long string of successful experiments. She had reviewed the footage from her smartphone twice already. The effect of the venom on an unrestrained human subject was fascinating. This was certainly the first psychological response to the venom, in addition to the physiological effect, ever documented. Panic, rage, incredulity ... a whole spectrum of emotions had been recorded. The limbic system and sympathetic nervous system were working in overdrive. All together groundbreaking research. Why hadn't she thought of that sooner? Future experiments would be conducted in the absence of restraints. If nothing else, it would make for an interesting footnote.

It really was time to start writing. She had procrastinated long enough. The completed tome would be put in a safety deposit box to be opened upon her death. Her lawyer would see to that. Funds from her research grant would be earmarked for its publication. The fact that she had awarded herself a research grant from monies skimmed from various campus budgets was irrelevant. It was best to let Hank think that he was part of a top secret government study whose funding came from the Department of Defense.

Hers' would be a controversial piece of research. Great science always is. Think of the trials and tribulations of Galileo and other superstars of scientific inquiry. Some critics might not have a belly for the experiments with human subjects, but other like-minded geniuses would be pouring over her work for decades. A posthumous award might even be bestowed upon her. The College's Board of Trustees might vote to have a statue erected in her honor. Would they place it the quadrangle of Tolchester College, or in front of the Administration Building? Would she be standing or sitting?   Perhaps gazing thoughtfully into a plastic cylinder containing an *Atrax robustus*? She sighed. That, she would never know.

Mary hadn't expected to conduct experiments at the Tolchester Field Laboratory for many months, at least until the police concluded that their Cliff Top Killer had escaped the area.   Their attention had to be focused on the long-absent Henry Herssen.   Then she received that timely text from Hank that two women of the correct age were at the Devil's Spit. That location was not far from the funnel at the field laboratory.

Years before, it had taken her and Hank many weeks to dig the funnel. It had been back-breaking, dirty work, but she insisted that the spider's natural environment be exactly replicated if they were to record an authentic behavioral response from the spiders. That was key to obtaining high-quality data; otherwise a referee might criticize her for that oversight in her experimental design. Hank had complained the whole time that forced her to tap into research funds to buy him a new tackle box; this encouraged him to continue with the dig. It was vexing that Aubrey and Agatha Stupens had not instilled in Hank a better work ethic.

What to do about Hank? He had really dropped the ball yesterday. First, he had snuck off campus once again to fish at the Devil's Spit. She had little issue with him using the weights in the weight room – everyone needed a lunch break after all – but his contract stipulated a Monday to Friday eight am to five pm work schedule. And he had mentioned two women at the Spit but only delivered one. Alas ...

According to Hank, he had gone to check on the supplies at the shed when the two women appeared in the forest. They had apparently climbed up the bluff from the Spit below. At the sight of them, he hid in the shed. One, he explained, had fallen into the funnel so he dashed over to check. The redhead had in fact dropped conveniently into the funnel. That was very good luck, but when he went after the second one, she and her dog had disappeared into the forest. He had no clue where they had run off to. So frustrating not to have an N of 2 for that age category!

By the time Mary had arrived with Vlad and his back-up Caligula – they had learned their lesson with Sheila Myers – and the spotlight and its power-pack, the redhead was just coming to. Time was of the essence in case the woman with the dog had told someone about the redhead's disappearance in the funnel. Hank knew that they were in a rush, yet he continued to chit-chat with the redhead. At the suggestion of sex, she finally had to step in and start the experiment. The redhead's promise of sex had stuck a chord as she had used similar tactics when a young woman. After all, that was why her geezer of a husband Milton accelerated her promotion and assisted her entrée into college administration, despite her lack of publications and a PhD. His premature heart attack was a shame.

Hank's chatter with the redhead about the pyrate treasure had caused Mary's ears to perk up. If she could acquire the River Glen treasure, then it would mean not having to skim from student computer fees, faculty pension plans, or other college accounts. When Bob Randolph, Sheila Myers, and Amanda Lamont had discovered 'discrepancies,' that moved them straight to the top of her human subjects list. What audacity to question her ability to keep the books? Now that the police were poking around the cliff top, it would mean the construction of a new lab and funnel elsewhere. The treasure might fund an expansive facility.   Maybe she could hire post-docs to conduct the experiments while she went on a lecture tour?   Maybe they could set up an *Atrax* breeding program so she could distribute spiders to labs around the world.   Create an anti-venom on her own?   The possibilities with such a vast funding source were unlimited. The redhead had mentioned that the Sweenies had found a portion of treasure at the Devil's Spit, but the bulk of the load was watched over by an old woman.

Mary finished her latte and slipped into bed, supremely confident of her plans for the next day. "Like taking candy from a baby," the redhead had said.

Jay awoke guilt-ridden.   The source of the guilt wasn't the usual, drinking a half a bottle of gin, or sneaking a cigarette from the garage – yeah, he lived alone and hid cigarettes from himself – but for not apologizing to Julia. He had been dog-tired last night. The case was confounding and grinding him down. He had behaved irrationally. Jealousy was a sick, insidious emotion, a cancer gnawing away at his gut.   It had to stop.   He had never felt jealousy before yesterday because he never had reason to distrust Laura, nor she him. He was at Laura's dorm every weekend in college and, once married, home with her every night for over three decades. Even when he had business travel, like to the police conventions in Atlantic City, he had taken Laura with him. They had a ball. He snuck away from the droning lectures to play the slots at the Borgata with Laura. She loved to gamble and something about the hotel bedrooms turned her right on.

Jay's intention was to stop at Julia's on the way home from work last night, but then they got the call that Alex had been located. He sent Will home to tend to her while he set off with the police cruisers to the cliff. God only know where Lisa had run off to ... probably home to wash the mud off her impressive square footage of crime scene tattoos. Her revelation about the Sarova grave was a startling one ... Ricarda Sarova and her son Henry Jr. were alive and possibly in River Glen, living under alias. By rough estimates, Sarova would be in her sixties or seventies and the son in his thirties or forties. Since the grave was bogus, the dates on the gravestone might be also. Ages could only be guesstimated. Hank – Henry Stupens fell into the age range of the son. He would be interviewed first thing that day.

While there had been no sign of Pamela Dodd in the funnel, Alex's story checked out. People had been there because a number of footprints were trampled into the moist soil around the funnel's entrance. The yellow crime scene tape had been pulled away. A giant *Atrax* was flattened into the dirt at the bottom of the pit. Something large, a possibly a body, had been dragged to the cliff's edge and rolled over. Someone had crawled down the steep cliff path and probably weighted down the body with stones. The tide had washed away any footprints on the narrow beach below. The police underwater recovery team would search the river for Pamela Dodd this morning.

When he had returned home late last night, his house was empty. Mrs. Pulaki's note on the kitchen counter informed him that Griffin Blake had packed up and left for Florida and Nina Vega was staying at Julia's house to be with Alex.

There was no time to dwell on yesterday's comings and goings. Jay hurriedly showered and dressed. So much to do that day! Chewing a cold untoasted bagel and swilling a mug of coffee he sped down the coastal road to Tolchester College. He pulled into the parking lot of the maintenance building. The garage doors were opened. He passed snow blowers, lawn mowers and gas canisters en route to the small office of the Business and Physical Plant director. Jay knocked. Nothing. He wiggled the door knob; it was locked. He peered through the opaque glass window. Hank Stupens' office was empty. A landscaper approached him.

Jay flashed his badge. "Hank Stupens, have you seen him?"

"Nope. Hank's usually here by eight."

Jay glanced at his watch. It was 8:15 am. He handed the man his business card. "Call me when he arrives."

He rushed over to the Security Office to talk to Burt Sweeny, but a secretary behind the counter notified him that Burt had not shown up yet. "Sweeny's shift started at 7:30 am. He's almost an hour late."

Both Stupens and Sweeny were no-shows that morning. Jay had a very bad feeling about that. Now what? He stood outside the Security Office, unsure of what to do next. He checked the messages in his cell phone. Nothing from Julia. Big surprise there.

Will's text read: "I'm taking Alex to the hospital to get an MRI for the lump on her head. Hopefully I'll be back at headquarters around noon."

His text from Lisa read: "Shh ... on a top secret mission."

Yeah, okay, whatever. Lisa, as usual, was up to something. He had long ago resigned himself to the fact that she was smarter than the whole unit combined. She was best left off a leash.   He then called Cloris at headquarters, and ordered a squad car to Hank Stupens' apartment. Jay flew to his car and headed to Burt's trailer at the Sea Gull Cove Trailer Park.

Mary Blodgen decided to appeal to Hank's fanatical love of fishing. Clever clever her. At 6 am that morning, she had sent Hank a lengthy text:

After our experiment at the field station the last night, I swung by the Devil's Spit and retrieved the redhead's backpack from her boat. What an amazing discovery in her laptop! A map showing a motherlode of treasure at the Spit! Maybe Burt only found a small portion of it? I'm sure I know where most of it is. Treasure hunting first, then you can have the day off to fish! Meet me there at 7:30 am sharp. We'll get the rest of the treasure from Burt tonight. Burt and Burtie can be additional human subjects. I don't have any children in my study.

At 7:48 Mary heard Hank's pickup wind along the dirt road toward the Spit. 7:48 – eighteen minutes late. Agatha and Aubrey Stupens had failed to teach Hank the importance of punctuality. For the moment she would forego the reprimand because his cooperation was paramount.

He pulled fishing equipment from the bed of his pickup truck. First tardiness ... now misaligned priorities.

"We treasure hunt first, Hank."

"Can I at least eat breakfast?" he grumbled.

"Yes, of course."

He went back to his truck and returned to the beach with a coffee and breakfast sandwich in hand.

"I copied down the redhead's map because I didn't want to get sand in the laptop. The map is definitely of the Devil's Spit. That's why the two women were here." She moved next to her muscular son. "There." She pointed to the hand-drawn map. "Those three dots attached to three strings."

He looked at it and shrugged. "What does it mean?"

How uncouth ... talking with a mouth full of bacon, eggs, and biscuit! Had Agatha Stupens taught him nothing about table manners? Well, no need to harp on his shortcomings now.

"The pyrates must have buried the treasure in three parts in the bog. Look! They probably attached three loads to three ropes or chains and lowered it into the bog."

"That's the area with the quicksand," he said skeptically.

"See that row of trees? They must have tied the lines to the trees. Ingenious pyrates! That's why no one's found it until now. Maybe they covered the lines over with sand. All we need to do is find them and pull them out."

"It's possible." He sipped from his coffee.

She stuffed the map into her pocket and lifted a spade. "Let's go have a look. I'll dig until you finish your breakfast."

"Alright." He followed her to the bog.

She walked around, searching the terrain. "Oh my goodness!"

"What?"

She stared intently out to the murky water.

"What?" he asked again.

"Hank really ..."

"What?"

"Don't you see it?"

"What?"

She pointed. "There!"

"Where?"

Ha! ... so easily he took the bait ... so easily she hooked him. Who was fishing now?

"Open your eyes. There!" She pointed adamantly. "That log sticking out of the muck there! It's got to be a marker! We'll be as rich as pharaohs. You can buy all the fishing equipment you want, and I can open an arachnid research center. *That* tree is in direct alignment with *that* log. You keep your eyes on that log and I'll see if a rope is tied around the base or roots of that tree. The rope must be buried. I'll find it! Do not take your eyes off the log treasure marker."

"Yeah, yeah, okay." He chomped on his sandwich.

Really ... like rope would not have decomposed in three hundred years since pyrates walked the shores of River Glen. Hank's idiocy had been inherited from his father. Was it Henry or Owen? It was probably Owen. They had so much wild sex when Henry was passed out. Henry was such a lightweight; he just couldn't keep up with them.

"Keep your eyes on it, Hank ..."

He gazed obediently at the log marker.

Mary inched behind him and whipped the spade through the morning air. Déjà vu. She was a young woman once again, swinging a butcher knife at that upstart cook who accused her of stealing from the till. Then that swine Landry had the nerve to fire her, despite her being the best barmaid he ever had.

The spade arced and glistened. *Crack!* What an intriguing sound ... a cleaving skull!

Hank teetered and thudded face-first in the sand. She pressed her ear to his back. No heart beat. No heaving of the lungs. The spade's edge had gashed open his lambdoidal suture. Everything was going splendidly.

"Now, to roll this lug of a son into the swamp. He simply had to go."

So many cumulative things had become untenable ... his sneaking from work early .... his cruel baiting of Burt Sweeny. Hank was in a managerial position and a role model to subordinates ... those behaviors were bad for morale. Then came the banter with the redheaded woman and his fibbing about killing her friend and dog. What was that all about? It was more of Hank's mean-spirited jesting. But then their conversation degenerated toward the sexual. Mary was a biologist and understood everything about sex, both asexual and sexual ... bacterial, fungal, plant, and animal. Young people had strong libidos but please ... they were in the middle of conducting an important experiment. That was not the time, nor the place. Then Hank had mentioned second-authorship on her *Atrax* tome when he was rolling the redhead over the cliff. The threat in his voice was alarming.

Well, that was the last straw.

The *Atrax* research project was *her* original idea, *her* experimental design, *her* data, analysis, literature search ... *her* creative accomplishment. He had been no more than a lab flunky. That's when the brilliant idea about the map dawned on her. Unfortunately she had been unable to access the contents in the laptop the night before because it was password protected. Besides, she had been dog-tired and needed sleep. Gabe Issacs from IT Support would open it for her later.

Mary got down on her knees and rolled Hank toward the bog, which was no easy task as she was no longer a spring chicken, though she had kept quite fit by power-walking with Lana during lunch breaks. It was one of life ironies that

Hank had died at the exact location where she had given him life. Long ago she had decided against revealing to him his true maternity. It was wise to watch him grow up from afar. She had her career to think about. Great sacrifices had to be made if she was going to become the world's premier arachnologist and a college administrator. Besides, she had done good by Hank in giving him a job, promoting him far beyond his abilities, buying him a cheesesteak, water ice, and a ticket to the Franklin Institute in Philly, and a gift card to the Cabelas Store for new lures and bobbers. That had been a lovely mother-son bonding day.

She groaned. "Just a few more feet." She pushed with all her might and he slipped into the gooey water. With the handle of the spade, she shoved him beneath the surface. She flung the bloody spade, and Hank's rod and tackle box out toward the middle of the bog.

Now to treasure hunt. "Dead men tell no tales," she chuckled.

Burt and Burtie Sweeny were alive and well but were nowhere to be found at the Sea Gull Cove Trailer Park. A creaky woman with countless cats skulking around her trailer had seen Burt and Burtie climb into their car that morning. The only unusual thing was that Burt was not in his security guard uniform, the old woman told Jay. They had a cooler, towels, and snorkeling gear, and appeared to be going to the beach. He exhaled. Yes, good. A day at the beach would keep them out of harm's way.

Jay returned to headquarters, told Cloris about his conversation with the eighty-year-old Cat Woman, and dropped down at his desk. Tedious hours investigating the backgrounds of sixty to seventy-year-old women and thirty to forty-year-old men at Tolchester College would be his day. Lisa's illicit graveyard activities had helped to narrow the search. But what if it wasn't Sarova and/or her son? What if he was stumbling down the wrong path, following the wrong leads … misleads and miscues … entirely? He clicked open the tape of Bob Randolph's RV leaving the Shenandoah National Park. The face of the person in the black hoodie was shadowed, but for a split second they turned over their shoulder away from the security camera and appeared to be talking to someone in the back of the camper. An accomplice? Or Bob Randolph bound in the back? Somehow Bob Randolph had, dead or alive, made it back to River Glen.

"Damn it … nothing noticeable at all in the footage."

He opened up the tape of Sheila Myers in Philly and observed her walk through 30th Street Station and her purchase of coffee and a bagel. From the angle and position of the security cameras it was impossible to tell if she was being followed. There was a time disconnect in the footage from the moment she had taken a cab and then reappeared at the Reading Terminal Market. He watched Myers weave through the booths and concessions at the marketplace until she disappeared into the ladies room. A blonde chef from a food concession left a minute or two later. Then a mother and toddler entered and departed. Next three African-American teenagers entered, then left a few minutes later.

Yet Sheila Myers entered the bathroom and never reappeared again. According to the Philly police, a window in the bathroom had been forced open and Myers had been forced or carried through it into an alley. From the alleyway into a van? From a van, to anywhere. Myers' suitcase had been ransacked and her wallet emptied of cash and credit cards. A syringe had contained not a street drug but an illegal steroid used by body builders.

Cloris tittered, looked surreptitiously around for their priggish captain and, finding him absent, waved Jay over to her desk. Hell, why not? This case was at an impasse – like everything in his life. He muted a moan, dragged his bad leg with the sciatica over to Cloris, and leaned toward her computer. Cloris' new kitten Felix had been obtained from the SPCA to assist with Sylvester's weight loss program. Sylvester needed an exercise buddy, she said. Reducing the cat's caloric intake had never occurred to her. Her film on You Tube showed Felix climbing frenetically around a carpeted cat gym while a morbidly obese Sylvester – more fur-covered bowling ball than feline – watched with malaise from the window sill. The cat was fat yesterday, he was fat today, and he would be fat tomorrow. That was Sylvester's fate. Jay found himself not so much watching Felix leap from platform to platform, nor Sylvester's ennui, but Cloris' hand sliding the scroll bar back and forth, showing him anything and everything in the brief time she had his attention.

Jay grinned and patted the corner of her desk. "Thanks, Cloris!"

He hurried back to his desk and dragged the scroll bar to ten minutes before Sheila Myers had entered the bathroom at the Reading Terminal Market. Two yuppies in business suits entered and exited together. An African-American cop entered and exited. An Asian woman in running attire entered and exited. A slovenly teenager entered and exited. Enter exit enter exit.

But never did a blonde woman in chef attire enter. She only exited, unless, of course, she had been in the ladies room for a period longer than ten minutes. He scrolled back twenty minutes. Nothing.

Sheila Myers entered, a blonde chef exited.

What exactly did Sheila Myers look like? The professor had not been employed at Tolchester College for over six years. Inept as the administrators seemed to be, they certainly would have taken down Myers' faculty webpage after six years. He checked the Business Department homepage. As expected, there was no Sheila Myers listed as a member of the Business faculty. He typed Sheila Myers Forensic Accountant into Google's search box and clicked on Images. The same photo of Myers appeared a number of times. It appeared to be a photo from one of her accounting textbooks. Just as Brad Smyth had told him on the *Banana Republic*, Myers had wrinkles on wrinkles, warts on warts. Warts on her nose, cheeks and chin.

Jay scrolled through the entire footage again, searching for an angle that revealed Myers' face, but not much could be seen with the floppy hat and large sunglasses. Replay stop replay stop. There! In one frame the textures of her face could be observed. The person was not a young woman, as there were wrinkles around the mouth and creases down her cheeks. But no warts were on the chin, nor on the cheeks and nose.

He scrolled back to the blonde chef leaving the ladies room and zoomed the frame. The blonde was not a young woman either, and was slightly overweight, not bowling-ball-fat like Sylvester, but bulky in appearance ... most likely because Sheila Myers' floppy rain hat, red wig, hunchback – however that was created – and green raincoat were stuffed into baggy white pants and a white shirt, and concealed behind a long white apron. A Sheila Myers impersonator had boarded a bus in River Glen and strolled through the 30th Street Station and the Reading Terminal Market, because the real Sheila Myers, dead or alive, was still in River Glen, Maryland.

So far, so good. A slow drive by the house with the lawn ornaments revealed only one car in the driveway, a mini Cooper painted in the colors of a British flag. Hopefully it was the grandmother's car and she was home alone. Mary Blodgen was familiar with this house. Every local was. It was one of two rundown houses on the river road down by the Point. The tugboat was absent from the dock that morning. Another good sign.

Mary parked her car at the Point amidst the young moms and children whom had set up their towels and coolers for a day at the beach. She walked up the road to the house, prepared to coax information about Giles Hale's treasure from the alleged keeper of the pyrate treasure Julia Hale. With the treasures to be obtained from both Burt and Julia, the Blodgen Arachnid Research Center might also house an insect museum and library for visiting scholars, in addition to the research wing of the operation. Perhaps she might fund a student scholarship called the Blodgen Award for Undergraduate Excellence in Entomology. This would clinch her legacy. In the off-chance Julia had visitors, perhaps a sewing circle of ancient women huddled around the living room, she would mention a search for a lost dog, then depart with a pleasant wave. The flighty old woman routine worked every time. If nothing else, it would give her a chance to scout out the lay of the land and return later that night. She looked around her. The river road was silent. Better yet, no one appeared to be at home in the cottage next door. She crept up Julia's porch steps and peered through the window.

A mature woman was watching a fencing video on TV. Furniture had been pushed to the borders of the living room and her épée flicked through the air of the living room. Was this Julia Hale? She was not a decrepit old woman. Far from it. She was exceptionally fit and was lunging and swatting at an imagined competitor. Yes, it was possible that this woman was related to Giles Hale, depicted on the banners around the village during the pyrate festival. She had the same black hair and striking good looks, in fact, maddening good looks, possibly exceeding her own. No matter. Mary reached into her bag and grasped cool reassuring metal. She shoved through the screen door, ready to convince Julia Hale that an épée was no match for a Glock.

Burt Sweeny felt a lightness of heart that he hadn't felt since ... Jeez, who could remember back that far? He borrowed Cousin Calvin's rowboat with the outboard and his metal detector, just like he had last week, and headed up the narrow creek to the Devil's Spit, but this time he and Burtie came prepared. They were slathered with bug repellent and bottles of Gatorade floated in a cooler of ice.

It was a glorious summer day on the beach with his sweet son and he hadn't a care in the world! He had decided not to give two weeks notice to Hank Stupens. That asshole had harangued and intimidated him from Day One. Why show Stupens an ounce of consideration that he had never been shown? Nope. He just up and quit that very morning.

Never – ever – would he have to work at that freak show called Tolchester College.

Tomorrow he had appointment with the lawyer James Collins. How to liquidate bags and bags of Spanish gold? Mr. Collins would know. Now he could afford to take Burtie to the Pirates of the Caribbean ride at Disney World. But how could a ride surpass this? They were real-life treasure hunters who had found real Spanish gold! The first thing he would have Mr. Collins do would be to set up a college fund for Burtie. And he would finally have the time to get his GED. Then he would go to college ... anywhere but Tolchester. What did he even want to be? He had never hoped to hope, or dreamed to dream. Now he hoped and dreamed all the time! A paramedic, a tax accountant, a computer scientist? He and Burtie both loved colonial and pyrate history. A historian? Hope and dream ... dream and hope. That's all he did now and it was wonderful.

That morning Nina had rushed out of Julia's house to make her eight o'clock SOC 101 class. Her lecture went well, but the air-conditioning unit on top of the Learning Lodge had ceased to function. The thermostat read eighty-eight degrees by the end of the period. Nina's eyes became increasingly dry as the temperature rose, and she realized why. Her travel cosmetic case with her eye drops and contact lens solution had been left in Julia's upstairs bathroom. Nina checked the time. She had just enough time to drive to Julia's to retrieve the cosmetic case, and be back to campus in time for office hours.

Nina turned off the River Glen bridge and accelerated down the river road. Alex's pickup truck was gone; she must still be at the hospital with Will. Phew ... Julia's mini Cooper was in the driveway. Nina pulled into the spot where James Collins' sports car had stopped the night before to drop off a dazed Alex. She climbed from her car.

"Julia?" she called, flying up the porch steps.

"Come in ..." The pleasant voice wasn't Julia's Scottish lilt, yet it was vaguely familiar. It had to be one of the many people Nina had met in her chaotic week in River Glen.

"Rum!"

Did Julia say rum? Perhaps it was a Scottish greeting that she was unfamiliar with. Nina pushed through the screen door. "What?"

"Run, Nina!" Julia shouted.

President Blodgen held a pistol to Julia's head. "Halt, Nina!"

"What?"

"Run!"

"Shut up, Julia! Get in here! Now Nina!" Blodgen waved her inside with a pistol, and returned the muzzle to Julia's temple.

"What's hap..."

Julia's green eyes flashed at Blodgen. "You barmy ..." She slid toward the edge of her chair and eyed the broken épée on the floor.

"Julia, goddamn it! Sit still! You fucking move again and I shoot Nina."

Nina's heart convulsed. Blodgen's pleasant drawl had become vicious. Everything she had seen to this point ... Blodgen was all an act ... a very convincing act. Oh ... my ... god ... the Cliff Top Killer ...

Blodgen exhaled. "Julia is so obstinate, Nina. She refuses to tell me the whereabouts of Giles Blood-hand's treasure. I just had a brilliant idea. You're going to help me persuade her." She waved the pistol once again. "Nina, go to the mantel. Face the mantel. Put your hands it. If you look at Julia, I shoot Julia. Julia, you as much as flinch from that chair, Nina's brains are all over your duck decoys. That," she hissed, "is a promise."

The pistol stabbed the back of Nina's head, jamming her chin into her sternum. Her slippery palms jittered across the mantel.

"Let her go," Julia said. "This has nothing to do with her."

"I mean it, Julia, you move a muscle, or say another word, and Nina's head is splatter. Not one word. You either Nina."

Who ... who could talk? Nina's knees buckled; she grabbed the mantel to keep upright. From a reflection in a painting, she watched Blodgen back toward the kitchen. A muted dog growl and bark was heard from somewhere in the house.

"The gun is still pointed at you, Nina, directly at your head. Julia, if you dare move ..." A kitchen drawer was opened. "Nina's still in my sights." Then came a jingle of silverware. Blodgen's reflection return to the living room. A carving knife flickered in Nina's peripheral vision. "Nina's already lost one finger ..."

"Oh no! Not her ..." Julia broke in.

"Oh yes, Julia. You're going to watch me systemically remove finger after finger from Nina until you tell me where the treasure is."

"Wait! I'll tell you if you promise not to harm Nina, and you let her go. She won't say anything to anyone, will you, lass? This will be our secret, about the treasure."

Treasure? Julia had to be bluffing. It was a stall tactic. Whatever Julia was planning, she would go along with it. "I-I promise."

"See? She won't tell."

Blodgen huffed. "You're in no position to negotiate. I'm the boss here. I'm a college president after all. Where is it?"

"Only I know the passcodes," Julia said. "Only you and I go. We let Nina go."

"Wrong," Blodgen said. "We're all going. Or I shoot her right here, on the spot. Your choice. Now, where are we going?"

"In to my bedroom closet," Julia replied.

Blodgen paused. "How old are you, Julia?"

"Bloody hell ... why does that matter?"

"Tell me!"

"Sixty-eight."

"You, Nina?"

"Tw-twenty-nine."

"Two more human subjects!" Blodgen proclaimed. "Three away from an N of ten!"

Jay stared at the pixels of his computer screen. By enlarging the face of the blonde chef in the Reading Terminal Market and comparing her wrinkles to the elderly female faculty on the Tolchester College's website, Jay had narrowed it down to Professor Jane Marvin from the English Department and Associate Professor Sharon Getty from Chemistry, but the closest resemblance was to President Blodgen.

"Let's check on the cheery President."

Jay opened up Mary Blodgen's curriculum vitae on Tolchester College's website. She had earned a BS and MS in Biology from an obscure university in Alabama. Her publications list consisted one item. Huh ... how does a person with a master's degree in biology and one self-published, non-refereed work – a botany study-guide – become a college president? Weren't college presidents supposed to be preeminent scholars ... world authorities on a minute facet of esoteric bullshit?

One strategy that Mary (maiden name Thompkins) had discovered was to marry her boss, the academic dean Milton Blodgen, who furthered her career whether she had an iota of competency or not. Shortly thereafter she was promoted to the Director of Learning Communities, whatever the hell that was. "Wasn't a college inherently a learning community? They needed a director for it?" Then she became the Director of the Committee on Faculty Committees. "You're kidding me. They formed a committee to talk about committees? Ridiculous!" Jay was sickened. The administrative bloat being funded by eighteen-year-olds crippled by an eternity of student loan debt was obscene. Next she was a dean, provost, and finally the college president. But was Mary Thompkins aka Mary Blodgen, also Ricarda Sarova?

Jay's phone vibrated on his desk. The call was from Zera.

"Pamela Dodd's body has been located in the river by the cliff. It was weighted down with rocks. A welt with two puncture wounds is on her right shoulder. Two fangs are still embedded in the inflamed tissue."

"Okay. I'm on my way to have a look." He rang off.

Jay's gut told him that President Blodgen had never been in Annapolis meeting with still more useless bureaucrats to acquire funds for a long overdue academic building. Forget about renovating the Riddel Building; it was a death trap that should just be leveled. He told Cloris that he would be at the Medical Examiner's office and then Tolchester College, interviewing Professors Getty and Marvin, and Ms. Blodgen who, despite lacking a PhD, had risen suspiciously high in academia.

Jay was ducking into his car when his phone vibrated again. Shit. Just what he didn't need ... an email from The Competition. Blood throbbed against his temples. James Collins was decades younger than himself, could pleasure Julia all night long, and did not complain every second about a bad back and hot zings of pain shooting up his leg. Jay's first impulse was to delete the email. It would be too agonizing to read. The message probably read: 'I'm madly in love with Julia, and she with me. We're marrying, taking a round-the-world-honeymoon and blah, blah, blah' or some variation on that excruciating theme. His second impulse was to reply with "Fuck off, asshole." What to do! He was completely befuddled. Why not read it? True, the message would be worse than torture, but at least there would be closure.

Hi Jay,

I have a favor to ask you. If you have a chance, would you mind swinging by my grandmother's place? My phone app to her alarm system is pinging and she's not picking up. She's probably at Luna's and it's probably nothing, but in light of recent circumstances ... I'm stuck here at the county courthouse until later today. It's not Grandma Edith

Collins' alarm. It's the alarm of Grandma Julia Hale. I'm indebted to you. Best regards, James.

Jay stared at the request.

James, I'm on my way, he typed quickly.

What? How could this be? No one had never mentioned to him that James Collins was Julia's grandson! James had never been to any family gatherings. Neither Julia or Alex ever spoke of him. Why the hell not? That made no sense. He would worry about it later. He turned the key in the ignition, stamped on the gas pedal and flew out of the parking lot. Nor was he aware that Julia had a house alarm system. That too was news. Alex, Will, Carly, Luna and the unruly dogs wandered in and out all day long. Julia's house was a dilapidated ruin. There was nothing at all to rob, except bottles of expensive scotch.

Jay's emotions bounced back and forth between apprehension and elation. He had suspected the worst of Julia when in fact her grandson James, a fact that had not sunk in, had dropped by to visit his grandmother and change a light bulb for her. But why hadn't Julia told him that? She was a rational woman; she must have had a good reason.

He was a neurotic jerk, plain and simple. Still, he must win back his beloved. But how? Maybe he should grovel at Julia's feet, begging forgiveness ... not curse out aloud in the dog park when picking up Clark and Miranda's shit, not grumble when she told him to clean his toothpaste spit from her sink, and not say 'oh-fuck-it' when she told him to pick up his socks from the bedroom floor. Hers were not unreasonable requests, and it was her house, after all. No more cursing, grumbling, and oh-fuck-its.

At the rate he was speeding it took only minutes to get from headquarters to the village of River Glen. His car crept over the bridge where a maintenance crew was repairing its foundation, but he floored it again down the river road. Julia must have just come home because her tiny car was next to the house. Nina Vega's car with Rhode Island license plates was also there.

How best to apologize to Julia? On bended knee? Should he kiss her hand while proclaiming his undying love for her? If he had half a brain, he would have stopped for flowers and scotch. Instead he climbed her porch steps, empty-handed. As usual the door was unlocked. Miranda barked from the kitchen. Strange. He found the dog locked in the kitchen pantry. Never, ever, did Julia lock up her dog. Miranda dashed past him.

"Julia?"

Her épée was in the middle of the living room floor. His blood pressure soared. Julia was tidy. No way she would drop her precious foil on the floor and just leave it there. And how did it break? He hurried toward Julia's bedroom.

"Julia!"

Miranda circled the new walk-in closet, and sniffed at the ornate carved wardrobe from Aberdeen. A sock had been lodged between its doors. He opened the doors and tensed. It wasn't a series of drawers at all. Nor were coats and dresses hanging in it. It was an empty space.

A dim halo of light shone from the perimeter of the back panel. He pushed. The back panel swung aside. He stepped into the wardrobe and poked his head behind the panel. Incredible! This was not a wardrobe at all but a portal to a musty crawl space. A distant lamp provided just enough light to see down the wooden steps. He wiped sweat from his forehead. This was the second dark, creepy place he had found himself in in days, the first being the spider-infested attic of the Riddell Building.

"Miranda, you don't want to go first, do you?" The dog plunked down on the closet floor. "Thanks, sweetheart."

He tiptoed down the stairs. A fluorescent light flipped on; he jumped. He must have triggered a motion-sensor. It was not a crawl space at all but a cluttered room, reminiscent to a store room of a colonial museum. Wooden ships wheels, mermaid figureheads, ancient globes, barrels, and dusty sea-chests filled the space. His blinking eyes adjusted to the glare.

"Oh Jesus!"

He rushed to Nina Vega who was tied up to a rusty anchor. He gingerly removed the duct tape from her mouth.

"Julia!" she choked.

He spun. Julia was collapsed against an old barrel. She had taken the brunt of the assailant's wrath. Her eye was bloodied and swollen shut. He dashed across the room and dropped to his knees. He untied her restraints, removed the duct tape, and pulled her to him.

"Who?"

"The woman's certifiable ... an absolute nutter!" Julia said.

"Who!"

"Nina knows her."

He turned.

Nina shuddered. "M-Mary Blodgen."

Jay whipped his cell phone from his pocket. "Send cruisers to Tolchester College to pick up Blodgen! Seal off all the offices in the Administration Building. I want to know what the hell's going on there!" He rung off and kissed Julia's sore face.

"Julia love, what is this place?"

She struggled to her feet and lifted the lid from a barrel.

He leaned over the rim, wide-eyed. "No-no way. It-it can't be. It's just a silly legend."

"Lad, thar be pyrates in River Glen and unspeakable treasures."

Three wonderful features of the Presidential Estate – Mary's name for her home – were its secluded location, stunning views of the Chesapeake, and a private back road into the property that meant that her comings and goings with the scientific equipment were undetected by the campus community. She pulled the black Tolchester van into her garage, closed the door behind her, and entered her house.

What a morning of staggering revelations! Giles Blood-hand's treasure, missing for more than three centuries, was sitting in the basement of a resident of River Glen. Thank you for the tip, redhead in the funnel! By day's end, the treasure would be hers. The Blodgen Arachnid Research Center was more than just a dream. Better yet, two more human subjects had been obtained. It was rather disappointing to discover that Julia Hale fell into the same age category as Bob Randolph and Sheila Myers, but the good news was that Nina would be the first experimental subject in her twenties. This opened up the possibility of a paragraph or two in the tome on the effects of spider venoms on women in their reproductive prime.

Mary leaned across her granite kitchen island and sipped her latte. Goggle Earth on her tablet showed a trail leading from the Point, through the marsh and the woods, into Julia's back yard. She would sneak back to the house later that day with two jumbo spiders, film the experiments with Julia and Nina, and haul out as much treasure as possible throughout the night. The police would search the premises in a day or two, when a friend reported Julia missing. But that was no concern of hers. She had worn gloves in Julia's house so no fingerprints or physical evidence linked her to that place. According to Lana Hinkie, who was ghoulishly following the Cliff Top Killer story, the police were searching for Henry Herssen.

So much to do in preparation for the next experiments. This was no time to let irrelevancies slow the momentum. She tossed down the rest of her latte and headed to the basement. It had been terribly inconvenient to move the male spiderlings from the Riddel attic into her basement, especially in the rainstorm. The males and females in her breeding program were best segregated until mating sessions, but there was no alternative but to move them. That insane hurricane threatened to blow the roof off the Riddel Building. It meant an annoying evening of rearranging the begonias under the growth lamps, and sliding aside the terraria of the female spiderlings to make room for the boys. Hank had complained the whole time because he was missing Wrestle Mania.

In hindsight, moving the spiders from the Riddel building was a blessing in disguise. With Hank gone, she would be caring for the spiderlings on her own now. She grabbed the bag of crickets from the workbench and started toward the plastic animal containers. How about Adolf for Nina, and a really vicious bastard like Caligula for that arrogant Scot? She had really shown Julia who was boss. Too bad that the redhead, in a fit of rage, had flattened Vlad. He would have been perfect for the experiment with Julia.

Mary bent toward the containers. What a minute ... where were Adolf and Caligula? She always arranged them according to size and ferocity. *Her two meanest boys were missing!* Would Hank have put them somewhere else? No, impossible. It was she who saw them last night, when she had returned the back-up Caligula to the basement after the experiment with human subject number 5, the redhead.

"Are you looking for *these*?" said a voice from the darkness.

Mary's head snapped around.

A woman in black combat gear stepped from behind the furnace. Mary recognized her instantly. It was that mousy detective who had visited the campus with Jay Braden. Lisa Paco. That name had jumped off her name tag. At the time Mary had tried not to stare. Was Lisa Paco related to Owen, or the other Paco family who owned the bakery?

The temerity of that little twit to intrude! How dare she? Paco was wearing Hank's bite-proof gloves. In one of her hands was a plastic animal container housing the two missing spiders. In her other hand was a pistol.

Where was her gun, the Glock stolen from the redhead? No! ... it was upstairs, in her bag on the kitchen island. She was defenseless!

"You're trespassing! Do you have a search warrant?"

Paco blew a bubble and let it pop. "No search warrant. I've gone rogue. Lucky you." She placed the animal container behind a begonia but firmly held the gun. "I wanna to ask you a few questions, then I'll be going."

"You'll be talking to my lawyer!"

"Chill ... there's no need to be so testy. We don't want to involve lawyers. That would mean the world finds out about your snuff films."

"Snuff films? I have no idea what you're talking about! Anyway, who's going to believe you? It will be the word of a college president against a lame-brained cop."

Paco shrugged. "Maybe, Ric."

"W-what did you call me?" She became rigid with indignance.

"Ric." Paco blew another bubble. *Pop.*

"You impertinent ... I'm President Blodgen to you!"

"That's me ... paco@impertinent. And so impertinent that I dug up your grave. Cool ruse. So Ricarda Sarova and Henry, Jr. are alive and well in River Glen ..."

"Grave robbing is illegal! I will see you in court, then in jail!"

Paco shrugged again. "On what grounds? There was nothing to rob."

"Out. Get out!"

"Jeez Ric, don't get your back up. I'm not here to bring you in. I'm just curious to know about my father."

"Who's that? I have no idea what or who you're talking about."

"Yeah, you do. Owen Paco and Henry Herssen were friends."

"I have no idea ... you're mad."

"But not so mad that I couldn't download the snuff films from your computer."

"What snuff films? Are you referring to my experiments? You ... you dared to touch my computer ... with my experiments?"

"Yup, I dared." Paco patted her pants pocket. "Everything's right here on a flashdrive. We don't need to discuss how Owen died because I already saw that. Grisly things, those spiders. I just want to know about Henry, Jr.

Being an only child, I'm kinda curious about that. Was Owen Junior's father? This would make Junior my half-brother."

Mary nodded slyly. "I remember now. You're Owen's idiot daughter."

"Is that what he called me? What a loving dad."

"So … I tell you about Junior's paternity, you leave me the flashdrive, you leave, and we never discuss this again?"

"Yup. Easy peasy."

"That's the deal?"

"That's the deal. Promise."

"I have no clue!" Mary gloated. "It could have been Owen, or could have been Henry. Go find Junior and perform a DNA test, you stooge." She paused. "How can this possibly matter now?"

"You're right. It doesn't."

"The flashdrive … give it!"

"A deal's a deal." Paco patted her pockets again. "Um, I thought it was here."

"You little bitch, if you tricked me …"

"No fear, Ric. There it is." Paco pulled the animal container from behind the begonia. "Hold out your hands."

A flashdrive – her own flashdrive from her office upstairs – was in the container with Adolf and Caligula! "What? No!"

"C'mon, hold out your hands. I'm just curious to see if the spiders will bite their master … oops mistress."

"Of course they'll bite!"

"C'mon, just a little experiment. You love experiments."

"No!"

"You don't get the flashdrive if you don't put out your hands."

"You're mad!"

"Yup. Possibly." Paco blew another bubble. "Have you ever been bitten?"

"Once. A long time ago."

"Why didn't you die?"

"Because I'm impervious to their bite. I'm immortal. They're my children. My spiderlings would never kill their mother."

"Yeah, right. You used an anti-venom. C'mon, put out your hands and you get the flashdrive. I leave right now. We'll never speak again."

"No!"

Paco backed toward the stairs. "No big deal. I'll just take the spiders and flashdrive back to headquarters."

"Wait!" Mary's hands formed a shaky cup. Her face contorted as she braced for the bites.

"I was always horrible in science and math classes, but I can count. This experiment will make an N of six."

"Fucking idiot," she snarled.

"Are you ready?"

"Yes! Give me that flashdrive!"

"You sure?"

"Yes, yes!"

"Well, okay then. A deal's a deal."

Paco spilled the spiders and flashdrive into Mary's cupped hands. The fangs of Adolf and Caligula punctured Mary's fingers and a scalding pain shot across her palms. That infuriating cop was a black streak up the basement stairs, and thankfully gone. Mary shook the spiders from her hands ... "bastards!" ... and stomped them into the cement floor. She raced toward the workbench.

"Where is it? Where? In which test tube or vial?"

She frantically searched for the anti-venom. It had been Hank who injected himself with the anti-venom all these years. She hadn't handled the spiders in decades. Animal care was not her job. Her job was to design brilliant experiments, film the experiments, analyze the data, and write a groundbreaking tome ... do the heavy mental lifting. Animal care was so beneath her; that had been Hank's menial job.

"Where ... where? Where is it? There ... thank god!" She stabbed a syringe into the vial and filled it. She injected the anti-venom into her arm. "Ahhh." The burning sensation would subside ... at any moment ...

How dare Owen's idiot daughter call her Ric! How dare the idiot daughter not address her by her proper title, President Blodgen of Tolchester College!

CHAPTER TEN
Giles Blood-hand Day

"Goddamn spiders!" Alex Allaway slammed her hand down on the dockside table. Her glass of wine spilled. "That's the second one I killed this afternoon. And my leg went right into a web under the table. I'm going to have sticky web on my knee all afternoon."

Jay smiled wryly. Alex was an obsessive insectophobe. If she wasn't fretting about spiders, it was Water Boy's ticks, mosquitoes by the old grow house, or gnats getting through her bedroom screen.

"I still don't understand it," said Nina Vega. "You work in a marsh all day. You, of all people, should be used to creepy crawlies."

"Yeah, I guess." Alex relaxed. "Spiders are defiant and territorial. I swear that they hang out on my boat just to torment me, and today they followed me to the pyrate festival ... ugh! ... to continue the torment."

Will Wilkins untied his pyrate bandana and sopped up the spilt wine. "Alex, let's get you more wine."

Jay inwardly smiled. Will's ulterior motive was probably to get Alex tipsy, then take her to the berth in the *Vital*

Spark. Hmm … Jay lifted the bottle of scotch and refilled Julia's plastic cup.

"I'm starving," Will said. "Let's get lunch."

Carly sprang from her chair. "I want crab fries!"

"Me too," said Burtie. "Daddy, can I go with Carly?"

Burt Sweeny handed his son money. "Yes, of course."

"Does anyone want anything from the food concessions?" Alex asked them.

Nina, Burt, and James Collins shook their heads in the negative.

"Jay?" Alex said.

"No, I'm good." Truer words were never spoken.

Alex and Will departed with the children, leaving him with Nina, Burt, and James. From their respective projects at the historical society, that trio had become inseparable. Nina had found stacks of fishing records and spent her afternoons there when not teaching. James was researching his first novel about the treacherous Civil War spies Josiah and Abigail Wedgewood-Smyth, and Burt was running the archives during Judith Ann's maternity leave. Months before Burt had quit his job at Tolchester. The new president Lana Hinkie was now running the asylum. Cream rises, turds float; Hinkie was case in point of the latter.

Jay's eyes traveled up the bluff to Burt's new house. How Burt could afford to build such a grand house was anyone's guess. Maybe he had inherited zillions from a mysterious uncle in Zurich? Who the hell knew? But Jay now saw Burt and Burtie often, when he and Julia walked the dogs around the village.

Jay's attention returned to the pier. Once again inebriated throngs of suburbanites from Annapolis, Wilmington, and Philadelphia invaded the village of River

Glen. Miraculously the pier was still holding under the pounding feet of the dancers. The music was dismal because the band was playing the Eagles and America; he had hoped for the Stones or the Dead. Another miracle ... no one had fallen off the pier, though it was still early in the day. On the village green, ponies with toddlers on their backs walked circles around a pen, and barefooted children jumped inside the Moon Bounce. Lines of tourists had formed outside of Harlow's Pub, the Dockside Café, and Luna's Palm Reading Shack. There was a limbo contest at the tiki bar behind the Nauticus.

Jay pulled his vibrating phone from his pocket. The text was from Lisa Paco, who was in her happy place – headquarters on a summer afternoon. She had attached a selfie. Her whole face was hidden behind a pink bubble.

Her text read: #worldssickestbubble

He texted her back: Kudos. I'll see you in the Guinness Book of World Records.

He tossed back the rest of his scotch. A spider peeked from between the slats in the table. He swatted at it and missed.

"Goddamn spiders." He had to agree with Alex on that point.

Lisa had figured out the culprit in the Cliff Top Killer case before all of them. Once again. Clever, clever young woman. She had noticed a small scar on Mary Blodgen's right wrist at the cuff-line. Lisa's mother Wanda had an identical scar where she had had a tattoo surgically removed that read *Wanda loves Owen*. On the night that the Paco family dug up the Sarova grave, Lisa and Uncle Seymour dropped by the Lame Dog Saloon. She had asked Lanny Landry two questions.

"Did Ric Sarova have a tattoo?"

"A black-widow spider," Landry had answered.

"Where?"

"On her wrist, her right wrist. The psycho told me that female black widows eat the male after mating. Messed up! How could I forget the fucking tat after that?"

This revelation led Lisa to stake out Blodgen's palatial house. Norman from IT started monitoring the e-traffic between Blodgen and Stupens. When Blodgen drove to the Devil's Spit to dispose of her son, Lisa downloaded from Blodgen's computer the snuff films labeled Human Subject Experiments 1 to 5. The footage documented the deaths of Henry Herssen, Owen Paco, Robert Randolph, Sheila Myers and Pamela Dodd. Their suffering was horrific. Jay wished he could repress it; he couldn't.

Jay and the squad cars had descended upon the president's house with enough manpower to subdue a small army, but instead they found a silent house with a basement full of spiders and begonias. The old woman was dead, spider bites on her hands and empty syringes beside her on the floor. Why she had been handling spiders without protective gloves was anyone's guess. Stranger yet was that she had injected water into her veins instead of an anti-venom. The vial in her basement labeled *Atraxotoxin Anti-venom* was oddly filled with tap water.

Jay stared at the giant pink bubble on his phone for a second longer.

Julia ground her cigarette butt into pier and returned to the table. "That's not work, I hope."

"Ur, no." He stuffed the phone back in his pocket and shifted his gaze to Julia's low-cut wench gown.

"Let's dance." She reached down to him.

"It's the Copacabana," he moaned. "It's just about the worst song ever wri ..."

"All I hear is a tango." She smiled a to-hell-with-the-rest-of-the-world smile and pulled him out of his chair.

"I'm fluid ... I'm hot flowing water ..."

"Aye, lad, you are." She pressed a smoky-scotch kiss onto his mouth and pulled him into the crowd of pyrates.

Jay slipped his hand around Julia's waist. Thar be pyrates in River Glen – real and imagined – and unspeakable treasures.

THE END

ABOUT THE AUTHOR:
Leah Devlin

Leah Devlin is a writer of mystery-thrillers, biologist, and adventurer who grew up in Washington, DC. *Spider* is the second novel in the Chesapeake Tugboat Murders. These stories are set in the fictional village of River Glen on the upper Chesapeake, a site of a 1690s pyrate massacre that lures modern day treasure hunters and unsavory characters to the village in search of the elusive treasure of Giles Blood-hand. *Vital Spark*, which introduced the series, was published in 2016. Leah is presently writing *Chrome Divas* (working title), the third in the series.

Leah's Woods Hole Mysteries (*The Bottom Dwellers, Ægir's Curse,* and *The Bends)* centered on the scientific village of Woods Hole, Massachusetts, where Leah worked as a marine biologist at the Marine Biological Laboratory for over ten summers. At the epicenter of the action is the troubled Nobel laureate Lindsey Nolan, a magnet to men, murder, and mayhem.

Leah enjoys outdoor adventures of all kinds: motorcycle journeys, boating, diving, rock-climbing, skiing, and long-distance trekking. She divides her time between Philadelphia and the Chesapeake Bay.

Visit www.leahdevlin.com, and Leah Devlin's Mystery-Thrillers on Facebook for Leah's short fiction, blog, and essays on her nautical adventures aboard her tugboat named ... what else ... *Vital Spark.*

IF YOU ENJOYED THIS BOOK

Visit

PENMORE PRESS

www.penmorepress.com

All Penmore Press books are available directly through our website, amazon.com, Barnes and Noble and Nook, Sony Reader, Apple iTunes, Kobo books and via leading bookshops across the United States, Canada, the UK, Australia and Europe.

THE BOTTOM DWELLERS

BY

LEAH DEVLIN

Bioengineer and Party Girl...

Lindsey Nolan has it all: inventions paying large dividends, a dream job in the scientific village of Woods Hole, Massachusetts, and a stable of eager playmates. But when Lindsey wakes up in rehab with no memory of how she got there, her world is turned upside down. Her roommate, an HIV-positive teenage prostitute named Maggie, is the most volatile patient on the ward. The facility is plagued by disturbing thefts. And another theft unfolds when her competitor, an engineer named Karen Battersby, discovers and steals Lindsey's astonishing new invention from her Woods Hole lab. Lindsey and Maggie must face the consequences of past transgressions if they hope to deal with present perils and ascend from the desolate world of the Bottom Dwellers.

PENMORE PRESS
www.penmorepress.com

ÆGIR'S CURSE

BY
LEAH DEVLIN

A thousand years ago, the Viking colony of Vinland was ravaged by a swift-moving plague ... a curse inflicted by the sea god Ægir. The last surviving Norseman set the encampment and his longboat ablaze to ensure that the disease would die with him and his brethren.

In present-day Norway, a distinguished professor is found murdered, his priceless map of Vinland missing. The ensuing investigation leads to the reclusive world of Lindsey Nolan, a scientist and recovering alcoholic who has been sober for five years. Lindsey reluctantly agrees to help the detective who's hunting the murderer, but she has a bigger problem on her hands: a mysterious disease that's spreading like wildfire through the population of Woods Hole. As she races against a rising body count to discover the source of the plague, disturbing events threaten her hard-won sobriety—and her life. Will Lindsey be the next victim of Ægir's curse?

Leah Devlin is rapidly establishing herself as a writer of modern day mystery-thrillers. This story is as tight as a piano wire. Life at a seaside town in New England is full of treacherous undercurrents and peril, as residents are threatened by a menace from a thousand years ago. Murder, romance and deceit are a potent mix in this gripping novel, which I didn't want to put down.—James Boschert, author of the Talon Series and *Force 12 in German Bight*

PENMORE PRESS
www.penmorepress.com

THE BENDS
BY
LEAH DEVLIN

Maggie May has only weeks until graduation when Edward Gripp, a wealthy benefactor and the architect of Maggie's art college, goes missing from a campus Halloween party. Bill Bleach, the gawkish young detective assigned to the case, discovers a mysterious labyrinth within the walls of the art college where it appears Gripp spied on the activities of the faculty and students. When Gripp's mutilated body is found and a gorgeous art professor is also slain, panic spreads through art college. No one escapes Bleach's scrutiny, from the party's most distinguished guests to the terrified art students. But his investigation is complicated when he finds himself attracted to Maggie, whose dark and troubled past makes her a prime suspect. Bleach fights to stay focused, determined to untangle the web of lies and stop a devious serial killer from striking again.

Leah Devlin is rapidly establishing herself as a writer of modern day mystery-thrillers. This story is as tight as a piano wire. Life at a seaside town in New England is full of treacherous undercurrents and peril, as residents are threatened by a menace from a thousand years ago. Murder, romance and deceit are a potent mix in this gripping novel, which I didn't want to put down.—James Boschert, author of the Talon Series and *Force 12 in German Bight*

PENMORE PRESS
www.penmorepress.com

VITAL SPARK

BY

LEAH DEVLIN

After eking out a living as an adjunct professor in Washington DC, fisheries ecologist Alex Allaway lands a job running a small marine station back in her hometown. Arriving in River Glen to surprise her grandfather with her the good news, Alex is horrified to discover him dead, a bloody dagger in his heart. His clenched fist grasps a piece of pirate gold and a cryptic map with her name on it.

While the police investigate the murder, Alex begins her own search for answers. Aboard the tugboat Vital Spark she sails the Chesapeake in pursuit of treasure that belonged to a distant relative, the pirate Giles Blood-hand. But descendants of a rival pirate family are also looking for the bounty that's been hidden for over three centuries, and they'll think nothing of dispatching Alex once they discover she's in the way.

The first book in the Chesapeake Tugboat Murders series, Vital Spark draws us into a world where ancient feuds lurk beneath hidden waterways.

Leah Devlin is rapidly establishing herself as a writer of modern day mystery-thrillers. This story is as tight as a piano wire. Life at a seaside town in New England is full of treacherous undercurrents and peril, as residents are threatened by a menace from a thousand years ago. Murder, romance and deceit are a potent mix in this gripping novel, which I didn't want to put down.—James Boschert, author of the Talon Series and *Force 12 in German Bight*

PENMORE PRESS
www.penmorepress.com

Force 12 in German Bight

by
James Boschert

Considering that oil and gas have been flowing from under the North Sea for the best part of half a century, it is perhaps surprising that more writers have not taken the uncompromising conditions that are experienced in this area -- which extends from the north of Scotland to the coasts of Norway and Germany -- for the setting of a novel. James Boschert's latest redresses the balance.

The book takes its title from the name of an area regularly referred to in the legendary BBC Shipping Forecast, one which experiences some of the worst weather conditions around the British Isles. It is a fast-paced story which smacks of authenticity in every line. A world of hard men, hard liquor, hard drugs and cold-blooded murder. The reality of the setting and the characters, ex-military men from both sides of the Atlantic, crooked wheeler-dealers, and Danish detectives, male and female, are all in on the action.

This is not story telling akin to a latter day Bulldog Drummond, nor a James Bond, but simply a snortingly good yarn which will jangle the nerve ends, fill your nose with the smell of salt and diesel oil, your ears with the deafening sound of machinery aboard a monster pipe-dredging ship and, above all, make you remember never to underestimate the power of the sea.

–Roger Paine, former Commander, Royal Navy .

PENMORE PRESS
www.penmorepress.com